"An excellent metaphysical reconstruction in the form of a novel. Reading Ashby's remarkable work has one cooking on all levels."

Jean Houston- The Possible Human and Jump Time

"The central plot is both well conceived and finely executed once the story really gets going. It is also highly informative on an occult level and taken vividly and convincingly to its surprising conclusion. I liked it."

Kenneth Grant - BCM Starfire

"Writing a novel about mysticism and magic, usually means writing a boring novel. Frank Ashby has broken that rule. The Katabasis is full of human emotion, adventure and a deep love and understanding of the world. The average reader may not realize that his book manifests ancient mysteries and simply be enthralled—and there is a great deal more for the average reader."

Don Webb- Essential Saltes and The Seven Faces of Darkness

The Katabasis is a modern day version of the ancient Greek myth of Kore and Demeter in which the maiden Persephone is abducted into the underworld by the dark god Pluto.

THE KATABASIS

A Novel

Frank Ashby

Published by Eidolon Theatre Productions

Order this book online at www.trafford.com
or email orders@trafford.com

Most Trafford titles are also available at major online book retailers.

Note for Librarians: A cataloguing record for this book is available from Library and Archives Canada at www.collectionscanada.ca/amicus/index-e.html

Printed in Victoria, BC, Canada.

ISBN: 978-1-4269-1557-4 (sc)

ISBN: 978-1-4269-1558-1 (dj)

Library of Congress Control Number: 2009936085

Our mission is to efficiently provide the world's finest, most comprehensive book publishing service, enabling every author to experience success. To find out how to publish your book, your way, and have it available worldwide, visit us online at www.trafford.com

Trafford rev. 9/15/2009

www.trafford.com

North America & international
toll-free: 1 888 232 4444 (USA & Canada)
phone: 250 383 6864 • fax: 812 355 4082

Works Cited

1. The Sirius Mystery" by Robert K.G. Temple
2. The Source" by James Michener. Random House-1965.
3. Encyclopedia of Witches and Witchcraft" by Rosemary Guiley. Facts On File-1999.
4. The New Gnosis" by Roberts Avens. Spring Publications-1984.
5. Earth and Gods" by Vincent Vycinas. The Hague, M. Nijhoff-1969.
6. Psychology and Religion" by C.G. Jung. Yale University Press-1938.
7. The Mystical Element In Heidegger's Thought" by John Caputo. Ohio University Press-1978.

This book is dedicated to Kenneth L. Frank

for his support and encouragement...

Special thanks to my son, Chris

for all his support and assistance on this project.

Author's Preface

The mythological Prometheus was a Titan or one of the children of Uranus and Gaia and was responsible for bringing the gift of civilization to mankind. This gift, he stole from the gods in the form of fire and as a result was condemned to be punished. What is this fire? According to the asceticism of Yoga, this fire is known as the Kundalini power, which manifests in the Muladhara Chakra or the genital region. The elaborate esoteric system of the kalas as divisions of time comprises a large portion of the ancient Sanskrit texts. However, in the Western World, the creation of the bindu or the astral body is a forgotten science even though alchemy warranted a serious investigation because of its spiritual aspects.

The soteriological mission of the ancient alchemist was to redeem matter from its 'fallen' state, as they believed there was motion in matter, as did the Pre-Socratic philosophers. What they deemed as necessary mystical incantations were made to the seven planets as a way to overcome the tyranny of the archons because the alchemist was essentially a Gnostic optimist even though he faced the initial dangers of the Royal Art in the nigredo, which was the katabasis or the initiatory journey beginning with Saturn.

In much the same way, the advanced Tantric Adept was aware of the initial dangers in the early phases of Kundalini Yoga for the 'awakening' of the Kundalini caused the Fire Snake to traverse ancient neural pathways long forgotten with the ultimate goal being 'Sahasrara', which is the qabalistic equivalent of Kether, the 'Crown'.

There is a psychic correlation that can be made between the Kundalini power and the archetypal Shadow as Mercurius, who is the chthonic counterpart of Christ. The alchemical myth is full of references to this nature deity as being both the Devil as well as the Holy Ghost. The strange theomorphic symbolism portrayed this ultimate paradox of nature and the alchemist was indeed mystified by the Philosophic Mercury as the goal of the work because he put the Philosopher's Stone on an equal par with Christ as the 'Quintessence of Thought'. Thus, the Hermetic art became the last vestige of the sacred, until the end of the Renaissance.

Millenniums of history cover the animistic core of the unconscious and modern man has no concept of the" internalized fire ritual" of the ancient Vedic priests when the link between the soul and nature became established as a manifestation of Agni, the 'mouth' of the gods. From a psychological standpoint, the Logos principle as the 'Cosmic Order' became our logic and reason, while the Hidden God became the power principle inherent in our sex drive, both of which became perverted and the result is the Wasteland. If our Gnostic forefathers believed in the doctrine of the Anthropos or the Primal Man within as going through a continuous process of evolution then where are we as historical beings?

-Frank Ashby

Austin, Texas

May 27, 2001

Prologue

That night, the new moon was a baleful influence. The stars, in the overarching vault of the sky, were an eternal reminder of man's place in the grandiose scheme of creation. Out of this entire stellar display, no one star contained the ultimate mystery as did the Sirian constellation. On the beach, the waves gently lapped the shore; the ebb and flow was like a game being played between the stationary shore and the sea. A high bluff that had been eroded over millennia overlooked the beach and the sea. A figure made it's way down from the bluff, stumbling. It reached the level of the beach, weaving an erratic course as it approached the sea. With a groan, the figure sank slowly to the sand; the incoming waves approached within inches of the figure. In many ways, the peaceful serenity of the sky and the sea were diametric to the ravaged figure with a mind in a state of chaos.

Like the vanguard of a silent blitzkrieg, a police car drove along Commercial Street approaching the bluff.

"Dispatch to car 128," came the crackling static filled voice over the radio.

The officer driving picked up the microphone on the dashboard.

"Car 128 over," the officer said into the microphone.

"Reports of a naked man staggering towards Commercial Street have been reported. Copy?"

"Ten-four. I'm on Commercial Street right now approaching the beach, over."

"Ten-four. Be on the lookout for this figure. Over."

"Ten-four. Car 128 clear."

"Dispatch clear."

The officer turned to his partner.

"Nuts," the driver said.

He was young, just out of the police academy. He wore his blonde hair in a crew cut. His eyes were blue and he hoped were sufficiently penetrating to scare any felons he happened to run across. He was of medium build, although just a little over six feet tall. His uniform was immaculate. He glanced over at his partner, a middle-aged man with salt and pepper hair. Pellucid blue eyes in a weary face that looked half amused and half disgusted. He sat there scratching his potbelly, the smoke from a cheap cigar filling the enclosed space of the patrol car.

"Always some damn thing," he growled, looking slant-wise at the young officer at the wheel. His tone suggested to his partner that he was taking this personally. He had been, he had told the new officer when they had first been assigned as partners by the Provincetown police department, on the force for almost twenty years and in that twenty years had seen just about everything. The young officer had drunk up all his supposed pearls of wisdom." Better turn on the light and sweep the beach."

The young officer did as he was told as they approached the beach. The searchlight, on the driver's side of the patrol car, swept the beach. The car had slowed down to almost a crawl.

"See anything yet?" the older officer asked.

"No, not yet," the driver replied.

"I'll tell you something, Steve, some nut probably got drunk, shucked his clothes and probably decided to go skinny dipping in the surf."

"We still have to investigate, Earl, " Steve said.

Hell yes, we still got to investigate. All I'm telling you is, it's just some harmless drunk. Some poor guy just trying to have fun. That's all."

Steve didn't say anything. He had heard Earl sound off now for the past six months. The pearls of wisdom that he had been hoping to hear had instead been nothing but the bitching of a twenty-year veteran who was burned out on his job and close to retirement.

The slow pace of the patrol car and the searchlight sweeping the beach seemed interminable to both officers. They were both looking out the driver's window trying to discern the figure that they were searching for.

As the car began to climb the hill, the searchlight caught a figure on the beach.

Steve jammed on the brakes.

"Hey! Watch it, kid!" Earl said angrily." I damn near went through the windshield."

"Sorry," Steve muttered as he put the car into park." Look! Down on the beach!"

Earl followed his pointing finger, spotting the figure sitting on the beach.

"There's the poor bastard. Let's go," he said, opening his door.

He laboriously got out of the car, settling his night stick into it's holder on his left side while making sure the flap of his holster was unsnapped. He got his flashlight. His partner was already out of the car and with the quickness of youth, was already far in the lead; his flashlight beam lighting his way.

"Kids," Earl muttered as he hurried to catch up.

Both men descended to the beach and the figure that just sat there. Slowly, the officers approached. One hand holding the flashlight, the other on the butt of their guns. This was standard police procedure, at least in Provincetown. Far off, they could hear the barking of dogs.

The twin beams of the flashlights hit the figure. They could see that he was a man, totally naked. His brown hair was disarranged, as was his beard. It was his eyes that caught their attention as they shone the light on his face. They were vacant. If the eyes are the windows of the soul, then there was no one home. He sat tensely, leaning slightly back. His hands gripped the sand as if it was an anchor. His legs were outstretched and trembling. In fact, his whole body trembled. The look on his face seemed to be of pure horror.

The two officers looked down at the man then at each other.

"Drugs?" Steve asked.

Earl shrugged expressively.

"Could be," he muttered." Hey, mister!"

The man didn't respond. He just kept staring upward at the sky, watching the stars. His eyes remained blank.

"Sir?" Steve said, gently shaking the man.

Again, there was no response.

"Should we call for back-up?" Steve asked.

"Whyinhell do we need backup for?" Earl asked." Does this guy look dangerous to you? Do you think that he's carrying a concealed weapon?"

"No."

"The war...the war," the naked man mumbled almost incoherently.

"What?" Earl asked, shining his light into the blank, upturned face.

The man didn't repeat his words. He just sat there as if he was totally unaware of their presence." Should we take him in?" Steve asked.

Earl looked down at the man.

"Steve, I think we're going to need an ambulance. Why don't you go call for one? I'll stay here and keep our friend here company."

"But Earl..."

Earl turned angrily on his young partner.

"Look, kid," he said in a grating voice," this guy is catatonic. D'you know what that means? Look at him. What do you want to do, stuff him in the back seat of the car? This guy looks like he's in an advanced state of rigor mortis. Look how stiff he is! Look how rigid his arms are! Look how stiff his fingers are, clutching the sand! Take a real good look at him, Steve."

"Okay, Earl," Steve said placatingly." I'll go call for an ambulance."

Earl nodded, shortly, turning his attention back to the man at their feet.

Steve hurried back to the patrol car. He opened the door and reached in for the microphone.

"Car 128 to dispatch. Car 128 to dispatch."

"Dispatch. Go ahead Car 128."

"We need an ambulance to Commercial Street by the bluff overlooking the beach. We found the suspect. Over."

"Ten-four. What is his condition, over?"

"Earl says that he's in a state of catatonia, over."

"Roger, that. Ambulance will be on it's way, over. Do you need backup, over?"

"Negative. Just the ambulance, over."

"Ten-four. Dispatch clear."

"Car 128 clear."

Steve replaced the microphone and activated the flashing lights on top of the patrol car to guide the ambulance to his location. He debated whether to rejoin Earl on the beach or wait for the ambulance. He stood there, indecisively, fiddling with his flashlight.

Back on the beach, Earl stared down at the rigid, reclining figure. He had been on the police force for twenty years and was fast approaching retirement. In those twenty years, even though Provincetown was a small place, he had seen plenty. But he had never seen someone like this poor bastard at his feet. He had read the symptoms of catatonia. This guy at his feet had those symptoms. His flashlight now hung limply from his hand, his arm down by his side. The light played on the sand. It shouldn't be too long before the ambulance arrived, he thought. He reviewed the small hospital quickly in his mind. They really weren't qualified to handle cases like this. Only Boston had the facilities.

In the distance, he could hear the siren. At first, it was faint then grew louder as it approached the beach.

"The war...the war," the man mumbled again.

Earl snapped his flashlight back on the man's face. Still that withdrawn look.

"Help's on the way, buddy," he said softly, not sure whether the man could hear him.

He looked up at the top of the bluff. He could see the flashing lights from the patrol car and his eyes went down the road. He could see the flashing lights of the ambulance. Looking down at the figure at his feet, he shook his head pityingly. Above, the ambulance came to a stop behind the patrol car. The wailing siren turned off and the lights flashed in time with those of the patrol car. Earl fumbled in his shirt pocket and came up with a cigar. He unwrapped it and put the wrapper in his pocket, the cigar in his mouth. He took a match from his pocket and fired it up on his thumbnail the way he had once seen someone do in a movie. The match flared brightly before he applied it to the cigar. He could hear the sounds from above, but really wasn't paying much attention to it.

"Earl!" Steve called.

"C'mon down," Earl called back.

He looked up to see Steve leading the way with two paramedics carrying a stretcher following him. One carried a bag filled with medical equipment. Standard procedure. They approached quickly.

"Hello, Earl," the paramedic in the lead said.

"Hello, Bobby," Earl said in greeting.

"What do we have here?" the second man asked.

"Got a guy who shows signs of catatonia," Earl said.

"Hmmm," Bobby said." Shine your light on him, Earl. Okay?"

"Sure thing."

Both Earl and Steve shone their flashlights on the figure at their feet. The two paramedics squatted down on either side of the man. Bobby took a flashlight from his bag and put a stethoscope around his neck.

"Tom," he said to his partner." Take his blood pressure."

"Sure," Tom said.

He dug into the bag and came up with the blood pressure apparatus. He wound the band around the man's arm as tight as he could before pumping it up.

"Shine your light on the gauge," he told Steve.

Steve shone his light on the blood pressure gauge. Tom took the reading, making a notation on his chart.

"Blood pressure's okay," he announced.

Bobby nodded. He shone his flashlight into the unseeing eyes, then he used the stethoscope, listening to the man's heart and breathing. When he was finished, he rocked back on his haunches and looked up at the two police officers.

"He's definitely catatonic. Has he said anything?"

"All he's said is 'the war...the war'," Earl said.

"Hmm. 'The war...the war.' How many times did he say that, Earl?" Bobby asked.

"Twice."

"We don't have the facilities here to treat this guy. He needs to be taken to Boston," Bobby said, looking at the catatonic man.

"Long drive," Tom said.

Bobby nodded.

"I think that Boston General has a helicopter. D'you know, Tom?"

Tom scratched his head thoughtfully, his eyes becoming unfocused.

"Yeah, I believe that they do," he said."Why don't we get this guy onto the stretcher and put him in the ambulance. We can call for the helicopter to take him to Boston General," Bobby said.

"All right," Tom said." You guys want to give us a hand here."

"Sure," Steve said.

"Wonder where his clothes are," Bobby said as he prepared the stretcher.

"I wonder who the hell he is and what happened to him," Earl said.

"What do we do here?" Steve asked.

"Just put him on the stretcher. That's all," Tom said.

"Simple," Bobby said, smiling.

Earl snorted.

"Sure," he said." Simple."

It wasn't as simple as Bobby had said. The four men had a hard time trying back his grip on the sand. It should have been a simple thing to do. The man started to put up a fight, becoming violently agitated.

"Maybe we should give him a shot or something," Tom said.

"Yeah, let's do that," Bobby said." This guy sure is strong."

"What are you going to give him?" Earl asked, watching Bobby digging into the bag.

"Sedative," Bobby said, finding a hypodermic needle, which he handed to his partner. He continued rummaging into the bag until he found a vial.

"Shine your light on this so that I can see what it is," he said to Earl.

Earl shone his flashlight on the bottle in Bobby's hand.

"This should do it," he said." Give me that syringe, Tom."

"Here," Tom said, handing him the syringe.

"Hold the light steady, Earl, so that I can see what I'm doing. Wouldn't want to give him an overdose."

"Nope. You sure as hell wouldn't want to do that," Earl said.

They watched as Bobby filled the syringe, holding it up to the light of the flashlight. When he had the syringe filled, he put the empty vial beside him.

"Swab him," he told Tom.

"Right," Tom replied.

He dug the antiseptic cotton out of the medical bag, ripping open the packaging. He swabbed the man's arm.

"Shoot him," he said.

"Hold him steady," Bobby said as he approached the man's arm with the poised syringe.

"Got him," Tom said.

Bobby plunged the syringe into the man's arm and depressed the plunger until it had gone all the way to the plastic housing of the syringe. When he was finished, he pulled the needle out and replaced the syringe into the bag along with the empty vial.

The four men watched, waiting for the sedative to take effect. Time seemed to drag before the man lost his rigidity and with a groan, loosened his death-grip on the sand.

"Let's load him," Bobby said.They had no problem loading the man onto the stretcher. Each man took one side and they lifted the stretcher up. Earl and Steve, on either side of the stretcher, led the way; their flashlights lighting the way. Once they were on top, they placed the stretcher onto a gurney and strapped the man on. They slid the gurney into the ambulance.

"I'm calling for the helicopter," Bobby said as he strode towards the driver's door.

Earl followed him while Tom and Steve stayed at the rear of the ambulance.

Bobby reached in and grasped the microphone.

"Dispatch, this is Unit 5, do you copy?"

"We copy, Unit 5."

"Dispatch, we have a man in a state of catatonia, heavily sedated at this time. We're going to need a helicopter from Boston General to meet us at the hospital. Over."

"Roger. ETA to the hospital?"

"Ten minutes, dispatch. Over."

"I'll call for the helicopter. Should take about half an hour. Over."

"Roger. Half an hour. Unit 5 is clear."

"Dispatch clear."

Bobby and Earl walked to the rear of the ambulance.

"Dispatch is calling for the helicopter. Said it should take a half-hour," Bobby told the others. Tom glanced at his watch.

"If it's available," he said.

"Right," Bobby agreed." If it's available."

He turned to the two officers.

"Do you want to lead the way or follow us?" he asked.

"We'll lead the way," Earl said.

"Fine. Who's driving?"

"I am," Steve said.

"Well, don't lose us, Steve," Bobby said.

"I'll try not to," Steve said solemnly.

Tom closed the back doors of the ambulance.

"Let's head out," he said.

The two officers nodded and the four men separated. Earl and Steve walked back to the patrol car and got in. Steve turned off the flashing lights on top of the car and noticed that the ambulance also turned off their flashing lights. He made a U-turn and began the drive back to town. In the rear-view mirror, he noticed that the ambulance had made the U-turn and was now following behind. He glanced over at his partner, who sat staring out the passenger window.

"Earl?"

"Yeah, kid?"

"You alright?"

Earl turned his head to face him.

"Sure, I'm alright. Why wouldn't I be?"

Steve shrugged.

"I just wonder what drove that poor bastard to become like that. That's all."

Steve just nodded and they drove on in silence.

Doctor Ben Lassoe was among the doctors and nurses who greeted the incoming helicopter. Boston General was a massive high-rise hospital that covered every aspect of health care including mental health. He was a tall man in his mid-thirties. His short brown hair was blown by the descending helicopter blades. He looked as if at one time he had been in a fight and his nose had never been properly re-set. His brown eyes, behind rimless spectacles, were compassionate. His wide mouth, with its sensual lips, were at that moment compressed into a tight line of disapproval.

The helicopter settled down on the pad. The pilot cut the motor. Those waiting for the patient that he had brought in stepped forward as the whirring blades slowed and finally stopped. Doctors and nurses looked inside the helicopter at the man on the stretcher. His eyes were closed, but the babble of voices snapped his eyes open. As face after face peered down at him as if he was an exhibit in a zoo, he seemed to be coming off the sedative that he had been given in Provincetown. His hands began scrabbling on the thermal blanket as if trying to find something solid to hold onto. Yet, the look in his eyes was still as vacant as they had been on the beach.

The driver, a burly man with an eye patch over his left eye, jumped from the helicopter.

"Let's get this guy out of here," one of the doctors said, motioning for an orderly to bring up the gurney.

The gurney was rolled into position by the open door of the helicopter. The stretcher was gently moved forward and placed on the gurney. The man was still beginning to show signs of extreme agitation.

"I think this guy's for you, Ben," the pilot said to Lassoe, who had not joined the crush around the helicopter. He had stood back while his colleagues had looked at the man inside.

"Fill me in, Phil," Lassoe said, looking at the pilot, lights reflecting off the rimless spectacles.

"Seems like the cops in Provincetown found this guy nude on the beach. One of them thought that he might be catatonic and called for an ambulance. One of the ambulance drivers told me that it took four of them to get the guy sedated and on the stretcher."

"What sedative did they use?"

Phil shrugged.

"Well, whatever it is, it sure didn't last that long," Lassoe said, looking at the crowd around the helicopter." Did he say anything?"

"He was out when I picked him up," Phil said.

"No, I meant, before he was sedated."

Again Phil shrugged.

"Beats me, Ben. They didn't mention him saying anything to me."

Lassoe looked thoughtful and annoyed at the same time.

"Well," he said with a sigh," I wish I knew if he said anything and what he said."

"Is that important?" Phil asked.

"Could be very important."

He looked over again as the patient was taken from the helicopter. He looked around him and spotted his head nurse, a petite strawberry blonde with mischievous green eyes set in a perfect oval of a face. Her lush figure stood out in her green smock and matching scrubs.

"Sue," he called.

At the sound of her name, she turned around and saw Lassoe beckoning to her. She fought against the tide of humanity until she reached his side."Yes, Doctor?" she asked, her voice sounding like a caress.

"Phil, here, says that the guy over there is catatonic. Do a work-up on him, will you? I have an appointment. But let me know anything he says. Okay?"

Her green eyes watched him carefully.

"Yes, Doctor," she said neutrally.

"Good," he said briskly.

"I'd better go claim him, then," she said.

"You make him sound like a prize that you just won," Lassoe said.

"Maybe he is," she said softly as she turned away.

Lassoe stared after her, not sure whether he had heard her right. He wondered if this appointment was really all that important. He could break it, pleading an emergency. It wouldn't be the first time that he had done so. Maybe he'd better stay and find out for himself what the patient might say. He stood there battling with his desires. One desire was for an examination of this patient. The other was for physical release with the woman that he had met a week before in a bar. He enjoyed her body and her conversation, but he was a doctor.

A psychiatrist was a doctor and like a medical doctor, was obligated to relieve pain. He dealt with the mental anguish, not the physical pain.

As he stood there trying to make up his mind on what to do, he saw the gurney being wheeled towards the emergency room entrance with his nurse right beside it, talking to the man. He couldn't hear what was being said, but he saw her frown. The man seemed to be talking. What was he saying? Professional curiosity won out as he walked over to the group surrounding the gurney.

At his approach, his nurse looked up. The patient seemed to have stopped talking. He looked quizzically at her.

"Take him to Psychiatrics," she said to the orderly, who was wheeling the gurney.

"Yes, nurse."

They watched as the gurney disappeared inside the building along with everyone else. Even the helicopter pilot had vanished inside. They were the only ones still standing on the roof.

"What was he saying?" Lassoe asked her.

"I've been a psychiatric nurse for a long time, so I think I know what I'm talking about."

He nodded.

"Go on. What's your diagnosis?"

"Paranoid schizophrenia coupled with catatonia."

"What do you base your diagnosis on?"

"He's incoherent when he talks, which isn't much. He believes that he's in a war. He, also, believes he's in Jerusalem."

"Hmmm. Does he have an accent?"

"If you mean does he come from the Mid-East, then the answer is no. Of course, he might have been doing research over there. He is American."

They stood there looking at each other.

"Don't you have an appointment, Doctor?"

"I'll take a look at this patient, nurse."

"Very well."They entered the hospital and took the elevator up to the sixth floor. Neither of them spoke. Lassoe was pondering what his nurse had told him. In his profession, he had heard many strange tales. It constantly amazed him just how complicated the human mind was; what sort of fantasies and psychoses could erupt.

The elevator stopped on the sixth floor and they got off. They went to the examination room where the patient lay, still strapped on the gurney. He looked up at the ceiling. Lassoe approached him and looked down at him. He looked at his eyes, vacant. He was rigid beneath the thermal blanket.

"Hello. I'm Doctor Lassoe. You're in Boston General hospital. Can you tell me what happened to you?"

The man said nothing. He continued staring at the ceiling.

"You said that you were in Jerusalem. Is that right?"

Again, there was no response.

"You said that you were in a war. Did you participate in the Mid-East war?"

Again, there was no response.

Lassoe sighed.

"You're going to be okay. Can you tell me your name?"

Again, there was no response.

"Hopefully, you'll tell me who you are and what this war is all about."

He didn't expect a response and so was not disappointed when he didn't get one. He turned to his nurse.

"Better admit him and put him to bed," he told her.

"And what name should we admit him under, Doctor?"

"Hmm. How about John Doe?"

"Original."

"You can name him anything that you want."

"John Doe is as good as any. I'll get him settled. Are you staying?"

"No, I'm leaving. I'll see him in the morning."

"Yes, Doctor."

He looked down at the man then turned away and left the examination room. He hadn't expected the man to say anything. But he had to try. This man was an interesting puzzle. Who was he? What happened to him that turned him into a catatonic zombie? He didn't know, but he was determined to find out. He knew that sometimes it took a long time for someone to come out of catatonia. He also knew of people who responded right away. He wondered, as he rang for the elevator, which one this John Doe was.When the elevator came, he rode it in silence down to the parking garage. He walked to his car and got in. He'd keep his appointment. There was nothing he could do tonight. He'd have to consult with his colleagues to determine the best course of treatment. That was after determining just how severe the trauma was. He knew that the human mind used a variety of mechanisms to blot out painful or distasteful memories. Amnesia was one mechanism the mind used. Catatonia was another. Catatonia was the severest form of psychosis. Only something so horrific and terrifying could induce this condition. What had happened to induce this state of mind in this man? He shook his head to dislodge these thoughts. He didn't want them to ruin what was left of his evening. Or hers. And so he drove to keep his appointment.

The following morning, freshly shaved, Lassoe stepped off the elevator on the sixth floor. He went immediately to the nurse's station. All was hustle and bustle as he approached. The nurses looked up as he approached.

"Good morning," he said pleasantly.

"Good morning, Doctor Lassoe," his head nurse said.

"And how's our patient this morning?"

"The same," she said, handing him the new patient's chart.

"Except for something really strange."

Lassoe raised his eyebrow.

"What was really strange?" he asked.

"There were claw marks on his arms and there were fang marks on his neck. I looked away for a moment and when I turned back to look at him, they were gone."

She looked at Lassoe expectantly.

For a moment, Lassoe did not say anything. A frown crossed his face.

"Claw marks and fang marks?" He asked incredulously.

"Yes, Doctor."

"My God! " "Lassoe exclaimed." They were there and then they were gone?" The nurse nodded.

"Have you ever heard of a stigmata?" he asked her.

"Wasn't it a movie?"

"Yes, but in the movie as well as Saint Francis of Assisi, the stigmata was on the hands and feet where Christ was nailed to the cross. Much like you described to me, these manifestations are ephemeral in nature.

Evidently, the person so identified himself with Christ's agony that he or she had identical marks on them.

The nurse looked stunned.

"But, Doctor, these marks that I saw last night were not like that."

"Bats!" Lassoe exclaimed excitedly as he began to pace back and forth. "]Those bite marks that you saw on his neck were the fang marks of a bat." he paused dramatically." Maybe a vampire bat!"

At this point, her mouth dropped open.

He took the chart and ran his eye over it.

"Has he said anything during the night?" Lassoe asked.

"Not a word," the nurse said.

"I'll go take a look at him," he said, turning away from the nurses' station.

He walked down the corridor and entered the room that the new patient occupied. He stood there in the doorway looking at the recumbent figure on the bed. There seemed to be no change since last night, Lassoe thought. He walked over to the bed and looked down at the man.

"Good morning," he said cheerfully." Did you have a good night, last night?"

The man lay there, motionless.

Lassoe conducted a physical examination on him, hoping that this might provoke some response from the recumbent, withdrawn figure on the bed. He sighed at the passivity he encountered.

"I sure wish that you'd tell me who you are and what happened to you," he told the man softly, his compassionate brown eyes studying the man." Were you attacked by bats last night? Possibly even vampire bats?"

The man remained silent.

"Any response, Doctor?" the nurse asked as she came into the room.

"Not a peep," he said, feeling a little frustrated.

"Do you want to sedate him?"

"No, not unless he becomes extremely violent. We need to find the right medication program for him so that hopefully he'll be calm enough and talkative enough to answer our questions."

"What do you propose using?"

"We'll start with a mild anti-psychotic."

"Brimos is dead! The House of the Two Crescent Moons! Second time in hell... Wailing Wall... sin!"

With a start, both Lassoe and his nurse turned towards the bed. The man was sitting up, his face a mask of terror, his eyes wild and staring. As they approached the bed, he laid back down as if what he had said had exhausted him. Lassoe leaned over him.

"Who is Brimos? Where is this House of the Two Crescent Moons? What happened at the Wailing Wall?" he asked urgently.

The man lay rigid, not saying a word.

Frustrated, Lassoe straightened up.

"Damn!" he said softly.

"What do you make of all this, Doctor?" the nurse asked.

He looked at her."Right now, I don't know what to make out of it. But I'm going to find out. This case interests me greatly, nurse."

She watched him as he left the room, then turned to the patient.

"I wonder what's locked up in your mind," she said softly.

She stood looking down at the man in the bed then turned and left the room.

Lassoe strode down the hall to his office. He entered the office and snapped on the lights. He walked over to the bookcase and stood looking at the volumes, searching for the one that he wanted. He couldn't find it and wondered if he had lent it out to one of his colleagues. He sat down at his desk and leaned back in his swivel chair. What the man had said had started his mind to thinking. What had happened to this man? Where was the House of the Two Crescent Moons? It definitely sounded mid-eastern. Could it be in Jerusalem? What was this sin by the Wailing Wall? So many questions like who is Brimos and what does his death signify? It was frustrating. He sighed. Why couldn't the patient just tell him? Being a psychiatrist was like being a detective. The patient had given him tantalizing clues, cryptic as hell. He drummed his fingers on the arms of his chair, staring at the walls as if somehow the answers would suddenly become clear. Sometimes being a psychiatrist could be frustrating. Besides, there were the dangers of getting caught up in his patients' fantasies and psychoses. When a patient like this one came in with his infrequent cryptic utterances, he became very frustrated. He wanted to know what the meaning of his words meant.

He swiveled in his chair to face the window. Looking out at the buildings opposite, he ran through possible treatments to use on this patient. He needed to consult with his colleagues on this case. Sometimes, he felt very inadequate. Sighing, he swiveled back to his desk and picked up the phone. He dialed the extension he wanted.

"Hello, Carl? Ben," he said into the receiver.

"Hello, Ben. What's up?"

"Did you hear about the patient who came in last night from Provincetown?"

"No, I didn't. What about him?"

"A man was found naked on the beach in Provincetown last night in a state of catatonia. He was flown in here by helicopter. He's made some cryptic statements."

"Such as?"

"Such as being in a war, being in Jerusalem by the Wailing Wall and someone named Brimos who apparently is dead. What do you think?"

There was a silence on the other end of the line.

"Interesting, Ben," Carl said, after a while." What do you make out of it?"

"To be honest, Carl, I don't know quite what to make out of it. I'd like to come down and see you; talk about it."

"Sure. Come on down."

"Great. I'll be down in a couple of minutes."

"Fine."

Lassoe hung up the phone and got up. He left his office and walked down the hall. He opened the door with the name Dr. Carl Stevenson on it. Behind a large walnut desk, sat a gray-haired man with bright blues eyes set in a lined face. He was immaculately dressed in a two-piece charcoal gray suit with a light blue shirt and a red tie. He looked up as Lassoe entered, smiling."Come in, Ben. Tell me more about this patient," he said, standing up to shake hands.

"Thanks for seeing me, Carl," Lassoe said as he crossed the intervening space and shook Stevenson's hand.

"Sit down. won't you?"

"Thanks."

Both men seated themselves. Stevenson leaned back in his chair, elbows on the arms of the chair, his fingers steepled.

"Coffee?"

"No, thank you."

"So, tell me more."

"There's really not much more to tell you than what I told you over the phone, Carl. What really gets me is that this patient utters these cryptic statements and then lapses back into a catatonic state. It's frustrating as hell."

The older man nodded sympathetically.

"What do you propose to do to treat him?"

"Use anti-psychotic drugs."

"Shock treatment?"

"I don't know. Not at this point."

"I've been practicing psychiatry for almost forty years and I've seen many cases of catatonia in my time. It's not easy to treat, as you well know. Some don't say a word; there seems no way to get through to them. Others, like your patient, may utter some cryptic statement then relapse into catatonia. By all means, try the anti-psychotics. Depending on the severity of the trauma, these drugs can be very beneficial."

"That is what I was thinking, Carl. I wanted to touch base with you because of your experience in cases like this. I was wondering if you could take a look at him and tell me what you think?"

"Sure, I'll see him. Why don't we go together?"

"That'll be fine."

"Maybe we'll get a couple more doctors. Say Jim Henry and Jack Thornton."

"Fine. Let's round them up."

"Let me call them."

Lassoe nodded as the older man picked up his phone. He sat back in his chair while Dr. Stevenson talked quickly into the phone, his mind split between the conversations he was listening to and the prospect facing him.

"Well, they're agreeable. They'll meet us. Shall we go?"

"Sure."

The two men stood up and left Stevenson's office. They walked down to the nurse's station. A couple of minutes later they were joined by the two doctors that Stevenson had rounded up to assist.

Jim Henry was a tall cadaverous man with a mournful expression on his face. What with his brown eyes, he looked like a basset hound. His grizzled hair was thinning and he looked out of place, yet he was considered brilliant.Jack Thornton was short and stocky with a red face that gave him the appearance of belligerency. Yet, nothing was further from the truth. His soft-spoken voice had the effect of calming agitated patients.

"Here you have an interesting case, Ben," Henry said.

"Yes, I believe I do. I hope that you gentlemen concur," Lassoe said." Shall we go visit the patient?"

"Lead the way," Thornton said.

The four men walked down the hall to the room where the patient was. For a moment, they stood in the doorway observing the man in the bed. Then they walked over to the bed. They stood on either side of the bed looking down at the man. They noticed the withdrawn expression on his face and in his open, staring eyes.

"Looks like a classic case of catatonia to me," Stevenson said.

"I concur," Henry said, intently studying the patient.

"And you said that he made some cryptic statements, Ben?" Thornton asked, looking at Lassoe then back at the patient.

"Yes, he did. He seems to believe that he's in Jerusalem by the Wailing Wall where he also believes that he committed some kind of sin. Also something about someone named Brimos who's dead."

He looked at his colleagues.

"Hmm," Thornton said, stroking his chin thoughtfully." Very interesting. And after he said all this, then what happened?"

"He sunk back into the condition that you see him in," Lassoe said.

"Where was he found?" Henry asked.

"Naked on a beach in Provincetown. He was flown in by helicopter," Lassoe said.

"Then we have no idea who he is?" Stevenson said.

"No, sir. We gave him a generic name," Lassoe said.

The three consultants nodded.

Suddenly, from the bed, the patient sat up looking from one man to another. The four doctors waited wondering what would happen.

"Will you hold hands with me?" the man asked.

"Why?" Lassoe asked.

"We need to form a circle of protection to ward off demonic spirits. Eventually, I will awaken from this nightmare. To sleep is to die. Please join hands with me."

He seemed to be agitated.

" Of course, we'll join hands with you," Lassoe said quietly.

The four doctors joined hands with the patient in the bed. The doctors looked at the patient, who once they joined hands with him, began to calm down. A light seemed to come into the vacant eyes and for a brief moment they were almost able to see the man trapped inside the turmoil of his mind.

The patient was the first to loosen his grip. The circle was broken and he sank back into the bed, sweat beading his forehead as if he expended great physical activity.

"Are you alright?" Lassoe asked softly.

The man said nothing.

"I'll be right back," Lassoe told the others." Stay with him.""Where are you going, Ben?" Stevenson asked.

"To get something from my office. I won't be long."

"We'll wait right here," Henry said.

Lassoe left the room and walked quickly down the hall to his office. He knew what he wanted and it didn't take long for him to secure the item and hurry back to the patient's room. It seemed as if no one had moved, the tableau seemed frozen.

Lassoe strode over to the bed and thrust something into the man's hand.

"This is a mandala," he said." What I would like for you to do, is to study these patterns at intervals. Will you do that for me?"

The man looked at the small metal disc that Lassoe had handed him. On the inside of the mandala, there seemed to be a cross enclosed in a circle.

"This is a symbol of psychic wholeness," Lassoe explained.

The man seemed to have difficulty focusing his attention on the object in his hand. His eyes became unfocused then he relapsed into catatonia again as the mandala lay in the palm of his limp hand. He was completely withdrawn.

Lassoe straightened up with a frustrated sigh and looked at his colleagues.

"Well, doctors?" he asked, the frustration obvious in his voice as well as the expression on his face.

"Let's get some coffee and talk about this," Stevenson said.

"Fine with me. Most unusual," Thornton said.

"I concur," Henry said.

The four doctors with a backwards glance at the man in the bed left the room. They walked to the elevator. When the elevator came, they got on and Dr. Stevenson pushed the button for the first floor. They rode down in silence. When the elevator stopped, they got off and walked through twisting corridors until they came to the cafeteria. Entering, they got in line and got their coffee. They looked around for a table and found one in the crowded cafeteria towards the back of the room near the window that overlooked the garden.

"Nice touch, Ben," Dr. Stevenson said as they sat down.

Lassoe looked quizzically at the older man.

"I'm afraid I don't follow you, Carl," Lassoe said, stirring sugar and cream into his coffee.

"The mandala," Stevenson said." The magical circle that promotes psychic healing. Very holistic."

"I thought it might calm him somewhat. He was very agitated."

"Yes, he was," Henry said." Wanting to join hands in a circle to ward off demons."

"It's a good thing that we're psychiatrists and not priests," Thornton said, looking at his colleagues.

"Why's that?" Henry asked Thornton.

"If we were priests, we might have decided that the poor guy needed an exorcist."

The others stared at him for a minute, then laughed.

"Very good, Jack," Stevenson said, his eyes twinkling.

Henry looked a little insulted.

"It is very good for him that we don't perform that mumbo-jumbo," Lassoe said."Most priests, who believe in demonic possession, believe that we 'shrinks' are doing more harm than good and that only an exorcism can cast out these demonic spirits," Stevenson said. He drank off the rest of his coffee and looked at his colleagues.

"Yes, I've heard the arguments. There is still so much that we don't know about the human mind and why it does the things that it does," Lassoe said." The reason that I became a psychiatrist, was because I wanted to explore the unconscious. Jung fascinated me. I'm not, as you know, a Jungian analyst, but I thought that he was right about so many things that we are learning today."

"Yes, old Carl Gustav was a pioneer, no doubt about that," Henry said." I'm going to get more coffee. Anybody else?"

"I want another cup, too," Thornton said, looking at Lassoe." Do you know that Jung believed that in a mental hospital, a strange synchronicity prevailed?"

" Jung's theory on synchronicity was quite a conversation piece among the quantum boys," Lassoe said.

The other two at the table simply nodded their heads.

"Consensus rules," Stevenson said." We all share a hallucination, but who is saved?"

Silence reigned for several moments. The four men got up from their table and refilled their coffee cups then returned to their table. There was another brief moment of silence while they prepared their coffee to their individual tastes.

"Shall we talk about our patient or engage in metaphysics?" asked Stevenson.

At this point, Lassoe bent his head down.

"Tell me, Ben, what treatments do you propose to use on your patient?" Stevenson asked Lassoe as he looked over the rim of his coffee cup.

"I thought of using Thorazine along with various sedatives," Lassoe said.

The other three men looked thoughtfully at him.

"Very strong anti-psychotic," Henry said." Do you think it's wise to use something that strong?"

"Yes, I do. The man is catatonic. He needs something strong to jolt him out of it and get him talking in a rational vein. I want to know what drove him over the edge. I want to know who he is; what happened to him; what this 'war' is all about. Is he a Vietnam veteran?

Is that the war that he's talking about? I want to know the answers to these questions. I want to know his name. We listed him as John Doe."

He looked intently at his colleagues as he spoke.

"John Doe?" Thornton asked, his mouth quirking a little into a smile.

"Best I could come up with," Lassoe said with a shrug.

"Just right," Stevenson said brusquely." I approve of your methods of treatment, Ben. You're a very good psychiatrist. And I'm sure that you'll unlock 'John Doe's' memory and get the answers to all your questions."

"I hope so, Carl," Lassoe said earnestly, leaning forward in his seat.

"Oh, you will. I have great faith in you, Ben. Your record with difficult cases is outstanding."Lassoe felt a warm glow suffuse him at Stevenson's words of praise. He respected the older man not only for his knowledge, but also for his compassion. He was Lassoe's ideal of what a psychiatrist should be. Stevenson was his mentor. He remembered attending his lectures at Harvard when he decided that he wanted to be a psychiatrist. He never regretted his decision.

The men finished their coffee and left the cafeteria. They rode the elevator up to the fourth floor and went their separate ways. Lassoe checked on his patient. His head nurse was in the room when he entered.

"Any change?" he asked softly, looking at the man in the bed.

"No, Doctor. There's been no change. He just keeps staring at the ceiling," she said.

"We'll try Thorazine on him."

"That's very strong."

"It is, but sometimes strong medicine is needed, Sue."

She nodded.

"You're right, Doctor. Sometimes strong medicine is needed."

"I'm glad that you agree. I'll be in my office if you need me."

"Alright, Doctor."

Lassoe, with a last look at his patient, left the room and walked thoughtfully back to his office. He hoped that his treatment would unlock the door to the man's mind and he could get the answers to the questions that he knew were locked inside. With a sigh, he entered his office and took up the cases of his other patients.

For the next several days, Lassoe used alternate therapies on his nameless patient. When the patient was extremely agitated, he used Thorazine to try to unlock the doors to the man's mind. When that proved too extreme, he administered a sedative so that the man could find some rest. After each session, he made notes on the patient's chart.

There were days when he felt that he was getting close. Then there were days that he felt very frustrated. On those days, he had to caution himself to be patient. On this particular day, the patient seemed to be regressing even further; he would just lie in his bed staring at the ceiling and saying nothing. It was days like this that Lassoe felt particularly frustrated.

Sitting in his office, the night was beginning to fall. Outside his window, twilight was giving way to a deeper shade of black. The coming of night matched his mood. With his back to his desk, he stared out of the window at the buildings opposite the hospital. In the gathering darkness, the lights were coming on both in the buildings and in the streets. From his pocket, he took a mandala similar to the one that he had given to his patient and stared at it, trying to concentrate. It was his way of meditating, to bring order out of chaos. Most of the time it worked. He was startled by a knock on his door.

"Come in," he called, swiveling around to face the door.

Carl Stevenson entered the room.

"Come in, Carl," Lassoe said." Have a seat."

"Thanks," Stevenson said as he sat down." How goes it, Ben?"

Lassoe shrugged.

"Today has been one of total frustration. Just when I feel that we're on the point of a major break-through, he relapses."Stevenson took a pipe from his pocket and put it in his mouth. There was no tobacco in it for the no smoking policy ran throughout the hospital. He liked to have it in his mouth. He said, to those curious people who asked, that it helped him to think.

"Don't worry, Ben, things will come together," he said consolingly to the younger man.

"I know, I know. But don't you find it frustrating when you can't help someone who needs help so badly?"

"Frequently."

"What do you do about it?"

"I just remember that one day, everything will become crystal clear and that I must be patient until that day is reached."

He looked shrewdly at Lassoe.

"Be patient, Ben," he said." One day, hopefully very soon, everything will become crystal clear and then you'll have all the answers to your questions."

"I hope so," Lassoe said." Do you know what really puzzles me?"

"What puzzles you, Ben?"

"That nobody has reported this guy as missing. Does he have a family? Friends? An employer who must have wondered where he is? That's what I find puzzling."

Stevenson nodded.

"Have you checked with the police here to see if anybody has reported someone fitting his description as missing?"

"No, I haven't. Maybe I should."

"Of course, he may not be from Boston at all."

"Thanks, Carl, I needed to hear that."

Stevenson just smiled.

"Check with the police anyway. Even if he's not from here, someone might have reported his disappearance."

"I will. Thanks, Carl."

"No problem."

Stevenson looked at his watch.

"Well," he said, standing up," I'd better be running along home or my wife will report me as missing. Patience, Ben, patience."

"Thanks, as always, for your words of encouragement, Carl."

"My pleasure. Have a good night."

"You, too. Drive carefully."

"I always do at my age."

With a wave of his pipe, Stevenson left Lassoe sitting in his office. Lassoe stared at the door for a few minutes before he decided to go home himself. There was nobody waiting for him. One more look at his patients then he'd go home.

Patience, he thought wryly. Easy to say, hard to do. Why was it so easy to give advice, yet not be able to follow that advice yourself? Shaking his head, he left his office turning off the light. He made a final round of the ward talking with the on duty nurses saving John Doe for last. He stood in the doorway looking at the mystery man."I wonder," he said aloud," if you have any friends who might have reported you missing? Maybe they have and I can at least call you by your name instead of the generic John Doe. What do you think?"

The man on the bed said nothing, just stared up at the ceiling with unseeing eyes.

"I guess I really didn't expect you to answer. Just hoped, that this one time, you might."

Again there was the silence.

"I'm going home. Goodnight, John Doe."

Lassoe left the room and walked down the corridor to the elevator and got in when it came to the fourth floor. When it deposited him in the parking garage, he got in his car and drove home. There was nothing more that he could do for John Doe that night. Maybe tomorrow there would be a breakthrough. Maybe he wouldn't have to go to the police and find out if there was a missing person report on the catatonic patient on the fourth floor of his hospital.

He fixed dinner, watched television and then read until bedtime. Then he fell into a deep dreamless sleep.

It was early in the morning. Silence reigned in the wards on the fourth floor of Boston General. Everyone seemed to be asleep except for the nurses and the orderlies as they made their rounds, checking on the patients. In the room of 'John Doe', the man sat up in bed and then swung his legs over the edge of the bed, pulling himself into a sitting position on the edge of the bed. He moved with more purpose than he had since being found on the beach. He searched the drawers of the bedside table and came upon paper and a pencil. Balancing the paper on his lap, he began drawing on the paper. What he drew had strange geometric designs. He filled up sheet after sheet. After completing one sheet, he let it fall to the floor. When he was finished, he lay back down in bed and stared up at the ceiling.

One of the orderlies on his round some time later, found the sheets with the strange drawings and brought it back to the nurses' station.

"I found these in John Doe's room," he said, handing the nurse the drawings.

She took the drawings from him and studied them, frowning.

"What do they mean?" she asked, puzzled by the strange geometric designs.

The orderly shrugged.

"Beats me," he said.

"I'll show these to Doctor Lassoe in the morning. Maybe he can make heads or tails of it. I can't," she said.

She put the drawings in the patients chart so as not to lose them and then returned to her work. Silence, once again, reigned.

The next morning, Lassoe studied the drawings that the nurse had given him.

"He drew these?" he asked her.

"The orderly found them on the floor of his room," she said.

"Did you check him afterwards?"

"Yes, there was no change in his condition. Can you decipher what these drawings mean, Doctor?"

"I'm not sure what they mean. I'm going to see the patient now."

"Do you need me to come along?"He shook his head.

"No, I'll just go see how he is this morning."

"Yes, Doctor."

With the drawings in his hand, Lassoe walked down the corridor to the patient's room. The first thing he noticed was that the patient seemed to be sexually aroused. His erection was very noticeable. Did it have something to do with the drawings that he was holding in his hands? Would he finally get some answers to his numerous questions? He stood in the doorway for a moment longer before finally crossing over to the bed.

"Good morning," he said.

The patient slowly turned his head to the sound of the voice.

"Do you know who I am?" Lassoe asked him.

Slowly, the man shook his head.

"I'm Doctor Ben Lassoe."

He waited for a response.

"Doctor... Ben... Lassoe," the man said, his voice sounding unnatural to Lassoe.

"That's right," he said encouragingly." Can you tell me who you are?"

The man frowned as if in supreme concentration.

"I... don't... know."

He seemed to be getting agitated.

"Don't push it," Lassoe said soothingly.

He placed his hand on the man's shoulder.

"These are very interesting drawings that you did early this morning. Very interesting. Can you tell me about them?"

He showed the man the drawings that he held one by one. The man looked at them.

"I have a great desire to fecundate the earth. It's a type of renovation."

"Why?"

The man shrugged.

"And these drawings? What do they represent?"

The man looked at the drawings once again.

"They are the ellipitical orbit of Digitaria around Sirius."

"What is their significance?"

Again the shrug.

"I..."

"Yes?" Lassoe asked encouragingly.

The patient shook his head, a frown on his face.

"I am the eighth priest!" he exclaimed.

"The eighth?"

The man nodded.

"What happened to the other seven priests?" Lassoe asked.

The man looked at him.

"They were sacrificed."

"Why?"

"To re-nourish the Dog Star. I made the trip. I discovered Digitaria, so I'm the exception. I devised a new calendrical system."

He looked at Lassoe.

"Do you think that I'm crazy?" he asked.

"What would make you think something like that?"

The patient shrugged.

"You know, that God created Digitaria before any other star," the patient said.

"No, I didn't. Why did God do that?" Lassoe asked, his voice gentle.

"Because it is the egg of the world. It gave birth to everything else, everything that exists," he said, looking at Lassoe expectantly.

"Everything?" Lassoe asked, gently probing.

The man nodded.

"Everything," he said.

"Why do you believe this?" Lassoe asked him.

"We're cosmic pariahs. Nature has a way of dealing with such as we. We're in a state of quarantine. We're impure. Humans that is."

"Why are humans impure?" Lassoe asked gently.

"Because of Lucifer's rebellion. Creation has remained unfinished. Not until Oannes returns will mankind be fully redeemed."

Lassoe nodded, not saying anything for a moment.

"Who is Oannes?"

At this point, the patient looked above him at the ceiling.

"He is the incarnation of the Logos, who came up from the depths of Remu."

"According to theological doctrine, isn't Jesus Christ the incarnation of the Logos?" asked Lassoe.

The patient remained silent, staring up at the ceiling. Lassoe prodded further.

"Let's say, for the sake of argument, that you're right. Then the second coming will complete creation and mankind will be fully redeemed?"

"Yes," the man said becoming excited." Only Oannes' return can turn back the powers of Lucifer's rebellion for he has the power."

He struggled to sit up.

Lassoe helped him.

"Would you like to take a little walk?" Lassoe asked.

The man nodded.

Lassoe helped him on with a robe to cover the hospital gown and also the slippers. He helped the man to his feet and led him from the room. He was curious to see how being with other people would affect him.

They walked slowly. It was as if the man was uncertain about where to put his feet. He kept looking down at them. There was a hesitancy about him as if he was unsure of himself in this new environment.

"You're doing fine," Lassoe said encouragingly.

The man looked up, taking in his surroundings: the corridor with the rooms on either side leading to the nurses station, the people, either in uniforms or hospital attire who were also walking in the corridor. The man stopped suddenly. Lassoe stopped with him, looking at him.

"Are you alright?" he asked.

The man nodded.They stood there for a minute within sight of the nurses' station. There was nothing unusual about a patient walking in the corridors even with their doctors. Nobody seemed to be paying any attention to them. Yet, Lassoe could sense the man's growing distress.

"Would you like to go back to your room now?" Lassoe asked.

"Yes. I'm very tired," the man said.

"Very well. Maybe you can walk a little further everyday," Lassoe said.

"Maybe," the man said.

"I really wish I knew your name."

The man said nothing as they continued walking down the hall until they reached his room. Lassoe helped him off with his robe and slippers. The man lay down on the bed. He looked at Lassoe, a little smile twitching at the corners of his mouth.

"Thank you for the walk," he said.

"You're welcome," Lassoe said.

Lassoe turned to leave the room, considering that he made some kind of break-through. He was at the door ready to leave when the man called to him.

"Doctor Lassoe?"

Lassoe turned at the sound of the voice.

"Yes?" he asked.

"We're all the incarnate thoughts of God."

"What do you mean?" he demanded.

There was no answer to his question.

Lassoe looked at the man as he turned his face and looked straight up. He was rocked to his soul by the man's utterance. He crossed quickly over to the bed and looked down into his eyes. The eyes became blank, staring up at the ceiling.

"Answer me," he said almost pleadingly." Why are we the incarnate thoughts of God?"

There was no answer from the man on the bed.

Feeling frustration welling up in him again, he turned away and left the room with that cryptic remark ringing in his ears. As he neared the nurses' station, the nurse on duty looked up.

"I saw you walking with the patient, Doctor," she said." That seems to be a good sign."

"It would be," he said shortly," if he didn't want to go back to bed and be a vegetable."

She looked at him in surprise. She had been working under him for five years and had never heard the bitterness in his voice that was there now. She could see the frustration that seemed to be etched into his face.

"Keep an eye on him, will you? I want to know everything he says and does," Lassoe said." We have him on video, don't we?"

"All the rooms have cameras in them, Doctor," she said quietly." And I'll personally keep an eye on John Doe."

"Thank you, nurse. Would you happen to know where Doctor Stevenson is?"

"Yes, he said that he was going to go to the roof. There was a mischievous glint in his eye when he said it."

Lassoe smiled.

"And Doctors Henry and Thornton?"

"They went up to the roof with Doctor Stevenson."

"Thank you. That's where I'm going then. If you need me page me or call me on my cell phone," he said.

"Yes, Doctor."

Lassoe strode to the elevator and pressed the button. When the elevator came, he got in and pressed the button for the top floor. When the elevator stopped, he got off and found the stairs for access to the roof. He knew why Stevenson had gone up on the roof. He was glad that the others were there, too. He needed to talk to them, tell them what had happened. He hoped that their combined wisdom would lift the fog that he seemed to be in at that moment.

He opened the door to the roof and stepped out. Far below, he could hear the sounds of traffic; a muted roar punctuated by impatient honking as if by enraged geese. He looked around. From the roof, he could see the harbor with ships tied up. Farther out, he could see ships heading out to sea and here and there a sail tacking into the wind. He walked around until he found the three men he was looking for. They were standing back from the edge looking out over the city, smoking. They turned as he approached.

"Ben! Come join us," Stevenson called, blue-gray smoke from the pipe clenched in his teeth curling skyward.

"Yes," Henry said." Come join us, Ben and tell us what's happening with you."

Thornton nodded a greeting as Lassoe joined them.

"I'm glad that I have all of you together," Lassoe said.

"Smoke, Ben?" Thornton asked, producing a pack of cigarettes like a conjurer.

"No, thanks, Jack. You know that I don't smoke," he said, shaking his head.

"You look like you could use something," Henry said, puffing on a cigar.

Stevenson looked keenly at him.

"Nice day, nice view. Don't you think so, Ben?" he asked shrewdly.

"Yes, it is and it is," Lassoe agreed.

In his hand he still had John Doe's drawings.

"What is that in your hand, Ben?" Stevenson asked.

"Drawings that our John Doe made early this morning. An orderly found them and brought them to the nurse who showed them to me," Lassoe replied.

"Let me see them, Ben," Stevenson said, holding out his hand.

Lassoe handed him the drawings. He studied them then passed them one by one to his colleagues. They studied them intently then looked at Lassoe.

"Did he say anything, Ben?" Stevenson asked.

As if a dam broke in him, Lassoe poured out everything that the patient had said. He watched their faces as he told his story. When he was finished, he waited for them to speak.

"Is that all he said, Ben?" Stevenson asked, looking intently at his younger colleague.

"As I was about to leave, he said one more thing," Lassoe said.

They waited for him to continue.

"What did he say?" Henry demanded impatiently.

"He said that we're all the incarnate thoughts of God," Lassoe said.

"We're all the incarnate thoughts of God," Stevenson repeated slowly.

"Did you ask him what he meant by that?" Thornton asked frowning.

Lassoe nodded."I did, but unfortunately he relapsed into his previous state," Lassoe said.

"Mmmm! Very cryptic that last statement," Stevenson said." What do you make of it?"

The others shrugged.

"Hard to say really," Thornton said, looking up at the sky as if seeking the answer to the question, yet not finding it.

"What these poor unfortunates say defies true interpretation," Henry said, crushing his cigar under his heel.

"How about you, Ben?" Stevenson asked.

Lassoe shook his head.

"His statement really rocked me, Carl. We're all the incarnate thoughts of God. Does he mean that all this," Lassoe asked with a wave of his hand around the roof," is not real? That we live in a world that has no meaning? I really don't know what to make out of it."

Stevenson was very careful as he emptied the ashes of his pipe into the can at his feet.

"People like him have great insight, insight that we, who are rational, cannot fathom," Stevenson said slowly." What do you plan to do about this, Ben?"

"I'm having him monitored twenty-four hours a day. I want to know if he moves or speaks. I want to know what he does, if anything," Lassoe replied.

"Wise to take precautions like that," Stevenson said approvingly." Well, gentlemen, shall we descend back into the inferno?"

"Might as well," Thornton said.

The four men left the roof and went back to the fourth floor. They went their separate ways. Lassoe was busy for the rest of the day. Before he left, he visited John Doe. There was no change in either his position on the bed or his expression. He left instructions with the nurse in charge that he be called any time of the night if the patient did anything worth noting, i.e. if he left the room, did more drawings or talked. When the nurse said that she would call him, he left for the day and went home.

The hospital was quiet in the early morning hours. The patient known as John Doe, as if by a pre-arranged internal signal, silently arose from his bed. There was a cunning look on his face; his eyes glowed with a strange light. He put on the robe and slippers and left his room. At the door, he looked up and down the corridor seeing no one in sight. Prompted by some inner compulsion, he silently crept down the corridor making a stop into each room.

"Come with me," he whispered to each of the occupants of the rooms.

When each of the patients awakened to the urgent whisper, there was an unspoken question in each of their eyes.

"Come with me for he comes like a thief in the night."

Making urgent gestures to them, they joined him one by one. Silently, they crept down the silent corridors of the fourth floor. Like the Pied Piper, they followed him not knowing where he was leading them or why, not caring. Some walked like they were not mentally disabled, while others walked in a somnambulistic frame of mind.

He led them to the recreation room.

"Form a circle," he told them.

Silently they formed a circle around him. He stood in the middle of the circle."Join hands," he told them.

Silently they joined hands.

Standing like a priest about to deliver a sermon, he surveyed his" parishioners". What seemed like a long time, he stood there.

"The time has come," he began," for a celebration. The sixty-year period, which is the number of the placenta, has just concluded. Digitaria has completed its orbit around Sirius. Thus, it is time for the renovation of the world. Jupiter stands on the face of his father, Saturn. Now, please be quiet so that you can hear the music of the spheres."

The silent circle obeyed his injunction as they strained to hear the music of the spheres. Their faces were a study in contrast. They concentrated as hard as they could to hear this celestial music. Some had slack faces; mouths hung open with drooling saliva. Others looked up towards the ceiling as if that was where the celestial music would be coming. From the ping pong tables to the television to the chairs scattered around the room, they stood in the middle of the room, each trying to obey the injunction to hear the music of the spheres.

John Doe also listened to the music. There was not a sound in the room.

"We acknowledge the deep resounding bass of the sixty year cycle for that is the ultimate poetic myth," he said.

He walked around the circle.

"I will show you God's last gesture," he said in a hushed voice.

With their eyes on him, he showed them the gesture: he raised one hand and lowered the other. How long he walked around the circle nobody was sure, not even himself.

"Each of you," he said," must prepare yourselves for circumcision. Why do you ask? By this mutilation of Saturn by Jupiter and the various creations which sprang from the resulting blood and seed."

They stared at him, fascinated. They were ready to put themselves totally in his hands. What he was saying made perfect sense to them. So engrossed were they, that they were unaware of the psychiatric orderlies entering the room with the nurses.

"Here they are," one of the nurses said.

They advanced on the silent circle grimly like prison guards ready to quell a riot. In the doorway, Ben Lassoe stood arms folded across his chest. A nurse, upon discovering that John Doe was not in his room, had called him. He had hastily dressed and must have broken every speeding law in Boston before arriving on the fourth floor.

"Gently," he called softly to the advancing nurses and orderlies.

They didn't acknowledge his comment as they began to break up the circle. As the circle was broken up and the patients were led away to their respective rooms, they fell back into apathy. Their shoulders slumped as if the spell that they had been under rendered them incapable of maintaining their interest.

As each patient passed by, Lassoe studied their faces briefly. The last was John Doe. Like the others, he seemed incapable of interest. Where his face had once been animated as he conducted his ceremony, now he moved like a zombie; he walked mechanically, a broken-down figure. The light in his eyes had gone out and now there was no sign of comprehension.

"John?" Lassoe said softly.

There was no response."John? What were you attempting to do?"

John Doe stared straight ahead.

Lassoe shook his head in frustration.

"Take him back to his room," he told the orderly.

"Yes, Doctor Lassoe," the man said.

Lassoe watched them go down the hall. The night head nurse came up to him.

"Doctor Lassoe?" she asked.

He looked at her.

"Yes, nurse?"

"We have all of this on tape."

"Thank you for calling me. I want to see the tape. I just don't understand this man."

She didn't say anything. They were all absent from their posts when John Doe had begun his gathering. When they had returned, they had noticed on the monitors that all the rooms were empty of their occupants. It was then that the head nurse had called Lassoe. By the time he had arrived, they had located the patients in the recreation room. Now, they had broken up this strange ceremony and were herding the patients back to their rooms. They would be sedated so that they could rest. Together, Lassoe and the head nurse walked back to the nurse's station.

"I'll get that tape for you, Doctor," she said.

"Thank you, nurse," he said.

He watched her while she got the tape. She handed him the tape, looking him in the eye.

"You weren't here when all this began," he said to her.

"No, we weren't."

He sighed.

"Maybe it was best that you weren't, but if anything had gone wrong..." he let the sentence trail off.

"I take full responsibility, Doctor," she said calmly.

"I'll be in my office studying this tape," he said.

"Yes, Doctor."

She watched him as he strode towards his office, the tape clutched tightly in his hand.

Lassoe entered his office and turned on the light. He walked to the television-vcr combination and turned them on before inserting the tape. He turned on his desk lamp then turned off the overhead light. With the remote control in his hand, he seated himself at his desk and pushed the play button. Silently, he watched the tape of the bizarre ceremony; stopping it at various parts to either rewind it to play again or to freeze it. His face was an expressionless mask.

After watching the tape for half an hour, Lassoe re-wound it and ejected it from the vcr before he turned off the television set. He sat at his desk trying to make sense of what he had seen. His colleagues would have to see this. He rubbed his hand over his unshaven face, grimacing. Here was another puzzle. He looked at his watch. It was three in the morning. He looked at the couch along one wall. Many a night, he had slept on that couch. Yawning, he went to the closet and took the bedding and carried it to the couch. He took off his jacket and shoes, loosened his tie and lay down. He tried to sleep but sleep wouldn't come. He stared up at the ceiling, images from the tape running through his mind.Light was coming through the blinds in Lassoe's office when he finally arose from the couch, unrested in both body and mind. He went into his private bathroom where he kept toilet articles and shaved and brushed his teeth. His stomach growled.

He was eating in the cafeteria when Stevenson joined him.

"Good morning, Ben," he said, setting his tray down opposite Lassoe.

"Good morning, Carl," Lassoe said looking up.

"You look like the wrath of God," Stevenson commented, sitting down.

"I didn't get much sleep last night. Did you hear what happened?"

"No, I just got in. I haven't been up there yet. What happened?"

Briefly Lassoe told him what had happened. Stevenson listened intently, sipping his coffee. When Lassoe had finished, he sighed.

"What do you make of all of this, Ben?" Stevenson asked.

"I don't know what to make out of this, Carl. I'd like for you and the others to see the tape. Maybe one of you will be able to make some sense out of this. I can't. At least not right now. You said that I looked like the wrath of God? Well, I didn't sleep all night. I just laid on the couch in my office with that tape running through my mind."

"Yes, I'd like to see that tape. Do you think that your patient is about to come out of his state and provide some answers?"

Lassoe shrugged.

"At this point, Carl, I'm not sure. I'm not sure what he'll do. This... this ceremony, his cryptic remark yesterday afternoon."

"Yes, well, I think that you're making some progress with him," Stevenson said.

"You do?" Lassoe asked incredulously.

"Yes, I do," Stevenson said, smiling at the younger man.

"Why do you think that I'm making progress? I feel that I keep running into dead ends."

"First off, the patient is becoming more animated. He's talking. Of course, what he's saying doesn't seem to make any sense. The ceremony early this morning is another example. Of course, I do want to see that tape. Patience, Ben, patience. Even without seeing the tape, I feel that you're on the brink of a major break-through with this patient. Whatever sent him over the edge, I believe that he's ready to come back."

"I hope so."

"Keep hope alive. When can I see that tape?"

"How about now?"

Stevenson looked at his watch.

"Yes, I have time. Finish your breakfast and then we'll go to your office."

"Alright."

Lassoe finished his breakfast and the two men left the cafeteria. They rode the elevator up to the fourth floor. Silently, they walked to Lassoe's office. Lassoe set up the equipment and together they watched the video. From time to time, Lassoe glanced over at the older man to see what his reaction was. Stevenson's face was an impassive mask.

When the tape had ended, Lassoe turned off the vcr.

"What do you think, Carl?" Lassoe asked.

Stevenson took his time before answering."Quite remarkable," he said." Evidently the man is highly intelligent and educated. I think that he might, indeed, be a priest, Ben. Have you come to that conclusion?"

"Yes, it's been seeping into my mind that he might be a priest."

"Of course, what he said is pure gibberish, but the way that he said it is significant. His tone of voice, his gestures, everything suggests to me that this man is of the cloth. We know most of the priests around here and as we don't recognize him, he must be of a different parish. Maybe out of the city itself."

"Once he can tell us his name, then we'll be able to get in touch with his bishop."

"Yes. Of course, his story and what happened to him is vital. You'll get all your answers, Ben. It won't be long now. I think that the others should see this tape."

"Yes, by all means."

Both men got up. Lassoe handed Stevenson the tape.

"The others should be in their offices by now," Stevenson said looking at his watch." Are you coming, Ben or are you burned out on this tape?"

"No, I'll come with you, Carl. I want to know what they think of all this."

"Come along, then."

Together, the two men left Lassoe's office to find the others. Gathering them together in his office, Stevenson explained why they were gathering.

"By now," he began," you all know what happened earlier this morning."

Henry and Thornton nodded.

"There is a tape of the... incident is the best word that I can come up with for what happened. Ben, here, didn't get any sleep last night over this. I've seen the tape and now I want both of you to see it and give me your opinions."

"I'll be very interested in seeing what went on last night," Henry said.

"I would, too. I got a garbled account of what happened," Thornton said.

"Ben, would you please put the tape in and play it?" Stevenson asked.

Lassoe put the tape into the vcr.

"Ready?" he asked the others.

"Ready," Stevenson said.

Lassoe turned out the lights and the four men watched the tape. From time to time, Lassoe looked at the others to gauge reactions to what they were seeing. Henry sat hunched in his chair, eyes intent on the screen. Thornton leaned forward in his chair. Stevenson lcaned back in his chair totally relaxed.

When the tape had ended, Lassoe re-wound it and turned on the lights.

"Well, gentlemen?" Stevenson asked.

"Fascinating," Henry said clearing his throat." He seemed to be conducting some sort of religious ceremony, not a mass, but some sort of ceremony."

Thornton nodded.

"Most extraordinary," he said." I don't believe that I've seen anything like it before."

"I'm of the opinion that this patient of Ben's is a priest," Stevenson said.

"I concur," Henry said.

"Most definitely," Thornton said.

They all looked at Lassoe.

"Have any of you a clue as to what the constellation, Sirius is all about according to myth or legend?"

Everyone shrugged.

"About twenty five years ago, there was some controversy surrounding a book about Sirius, the Dog Star. The author proposed the theory that the Dogon tribe in Mali had, at one time, been visited by extraterrestrials. The way, he supposedly found out was rather interesting... Decades earlier, some anthropologists had studied certain sand drawings and were able to determine the elliptical orbit of Canus

Minor or Sirius 'B' around the Dog Star. Does any of this ring a bell?" asked Lassoe.

"Well to be serious, no pun intended, do you think that Sirius has anything to do with your patient?" asked Stevenson.

"His rather fragmented commentary on the strange geometric drawings interested me. He made the comment that he is the eighth priest and that the seven preceding him had been sacrificed as an act of re-nourishing the Dog Star. I would hazard a guess that his drawings match up to the sand drawings of the Dogon tribe."

Silence reigned supreme. Doctor Lassoe straightened up.

"Well, if he is a priest then I'm going to find out if he did some time in Mali." said Lassoe." Is that okay?"

Everyone nodded their heads in the affirmative. They were interrupted by a knock on the door.

"Come in," Stevenson called.

The door opened and the head nurse stood there.

"Is something wrong, nurse?" Stevenson asked.

"The patients that were involved in the ceremony are not exhibiting any signs of distress," she said, looking from one man to the next.

"Mmmm," Stevenson said." Gentlemen, let's see our patients to see how they are this morning. Shall we?"

"I think that would be the next logical step," Henry said, getting up.

The men got up and followed the nurse out of Stevenson's office. They visited their patients, some who were chronically distressed. What the four psychiatrists found were men and women who were very calm, almost rational. They didn't really understand what had happened. Many of these cases were so severely traumatized that hopes for recovery were very slim. But here they were looking alert, talking rationally as if they had never been doing anything else since they had been there. The doctors and the nurses were nonplussed.

"Have you ever seen anything like this before in all your professional life, Carl?" Lassoe quietly asked Stevenson.

"Never," Stevenson declared emphatically." I don't understand just what is happening. Do any of you?"

Henry and Thornton both shook their heads.

"Whatever happened, I just hope that it lasts a while," Thornton said.

"Sure makes our jobs a lot easier," Henry said.

"If this lasts, it will be a miracle," Stevenson said." And I don't believe in miracles."

Lassoe stood silently, head down, thinking. His strange patient had, somehow, with his ceremony managed to affect a miracle no matter how briefly in these poor, deranged souls. It was like they were psychically whole again as they had probably been when they had been born. But somewhere along the way, they had had fallen prey to various mental disorders that had left them, in some cases, totally unaware of their surroundings. Now, they all seemed to be alert, talkative, and active. Had that ceremony in the recreation room with the strange gibberish for a sermon really worked a miracle and as Stevenson had said, for how long? They had yet to visit the author of this 'miracle'. He was anxious, no, curious to see if John Doe had similarly been affected. Might the ceremony that he had conducted also have a healing effect on him?

"Let's go see John Doe," Lassoe said, raising his head.

"By all means," Stevenson said a trifle grimly." I want to see this 'miracle worker' who can effect such a radical change."

"Yes, I think that we should pay your patient a visit," Henry said.

"Most appropriate," Thornton said.

They four doctors walked down the hall to the room where John Doe lay.

"He is a priest," Lassoe said emphatically.

"What have you to go on, Ben?" Henry asked." I know that we conjectured that watching the video, but what empirical evidence do you have that John Doe is a priest?"

"And why a priest?" Thornton asked." Why not a minister? Practically the same thing."

"Give us your conclusions, Ben, before we see John Doe," Stevenson said.Lassoe stopped ten feet from John Doe's room. The others, also, stopped and waited for Lassoe's explanation.

Lassoe looked at them for a moment, gathering his thoughts.

"One of the first things that he said to me was that he wanted to 'renovate the world'. That implies, to me, an extreme soteriology. I think that his whole psychosis stems from this. Look at the drawings that he made, yet denies. Hell, we all saw the tape of his 'ceremony'. It was almost like he was conducting a mass."

"He didn't cross himself," Thornton pointed out.

"That's true, he didn't, but I believe that he was conducting a mass. Maybe not a high mass, but a mass nonetheless. I think that something drove this man over the edge and that his 'ceremony' last night, or rather, early this morning, was his attempt not only to right himself but his 'parishioners'," Lassoe said.

"Christ, himself, would have preached to the mentally ill," Stevenson said.

"Exactly," Lassoe said." I truly believe that John Doe is a Catholic priest. Maybe from one of the suburbs. I am more and more anxious to cure this man and hear his story. I want to know what drove him over the edge."

"Well, let's see if he is as alert as the others," Stevenson said.

The four doctors walked the remaining ten feet to John Doe's room.

John Doe was sitting up in bed. Upon their entrance, he turned his head towards them.

"Good morning, John," Lassoe said.

Lassoe didn't know whether his patient would answer him. Studying him, he really didn't notice that he was all that alert. His eyes were still vacant. Yet, he seemed to be more aware.

"I'm Doctor Lassoe. Do you remember me?"

"Yes," John Doe said.

"That was quite a ceremony that you conducted in the recreation room earlier," Lassoe said conversationally." Can you tell me more about it?"

John Doe frowned as if he was concentrating. His right hand spasmodically clenched the mandala that Lassoe had given him.

"What... ceremony?" he finally asked.

"You don't remember the sermon you delivered to the patients?" Lassoe asked.

John Doe shook his head.

"No," he said.

"It seemed to have a very healing effect on the patients here."

Silently, John Doe studied Lassoe who studied him.

"I don't remember anything," John Doe finally said.

"These are my colleagues," Lassoe said, indicating the three doctors with him.

John Doe's gaze flickered briefly to each man then returned to Lassoe's face.

There seemed to be an impasse. Lassoe was beginning to feel the frustration that this patient engendered in him, rising. As for the man on the bed, it was hard to tell what he was thinking. His face was unreadable.

"Are you a priest?" Lassoe asked, suddenly.

There was silence from John Doe."I think that you are," Lassoe said, peering into his patient's eyes." The ceremony was like a mass. You delivered a sermon."

John Doe frowned.

"A priest?" he asked as if the word was strange to him.

"Yes, a priest. A Roman Catholic priest," Lassoe said.

The other three men in the room seemed to be forgotten by Lassoe and his patient. They were engaged in a staring contest; a contest of wills. That was the impression that the three silent psychiatrists became aware of. Whose will would win out, the three watching doctors didn't know. The silence in the room became almost palpable.

It was John Doe who broke the eye contact. He turned his head away from Lassoe, looking at the window.

"I... don't know who... or what I am," he said in a voice that was a whisper.

"But you might be a priest?" Lassoe asked insistently. His voice was like that of a police officer conducting an interrogation of a suspect.

"It's... possible," John Doe whispered.

"Okay, John. Someday, soon I hope, you're going to tell me your story. I bet that it's fascinating. You're going to tell me what happened to bring you to the condition that you're in. Rest now," Lassoe said gently.

He placed his hand on his patient's shoulder.

John Doe didn't turn his head from the window.

"I'll see you later," Lassoe said.

With a gesture of his head, Lassoe indicated to his colleagues that they should leave. With a last look at the man in the bed, the four doctors left the room. Each was thoughtful as they walked down the hall.

"Well, that was an interesting confrontation, Ben," Stevenson said.

"In what way, Carl?" Lassoe asked.

"It sounded like you were interrogating him. Were you?" Stevenson asked.

"In a way. Everything about him frustrates me. He's like the Sphinx."

"That's a good description," Thornton said chuckling." The Sphinx. Maybe we should change his name again to that."

"It might confuse him," Henry said, not seeing the humor in Thornton's remark.

"Can he be more confused?" Thornton demanded.

"I'm for coffee," Stevenson said." Any takers?"

"We'll all join you, Carl," Lassoe said," so that you won't be lonely."

"That's kind of you, Ben. All of you," Stevenson said with a smile.

They approached the nurse's station.

"Sue," Stevenson said to the head nurse.

"Yes, Doctor?" she asked.

"If you need us, we'll be in the cafeteria having coffee," he informed her.

"Very well."

They walked to the elevator and took it to the first floor. They walked to the cafeteria and stood in line to get their coffee. They took a table in the rear, carrying their coffee. When they were all seated and sipping coffee, Lassoe looked at his colleagues.

"How should I proceed now?" he asked them."Did you ever call the police to find out if anybody has reported him missing?" Stevenson asked his young colleague.

"No, I haven't," Lassoe said.

"That's what I would do," Stevenson said.

"What if he's not from Boston?" Henry asked.

"If he's from around here, whether it be Boston proper or the suburbs, then someone is bound to report him as missing. And if he is, as Ben surmises, a priest, then someone is bound to report him missing," Stevenson said to his colleagues.

Lassoe nodded his head.

"That makes sense," he said." If someone has reported him missing, then we'll have a name to call him by. Maybe that will trigger an association."

Stevenson leaned back in his chair, arms folded across his chest looking satisfied with himself.

"Exactly, Ben," he said." If we knew his real name, we can call him by that."

"Worth a try," Lassoe said.

"Let's finish our coffee and make that call," Thornton said.

The men finished their coffee and went back to the fourth floor. They all went to Lassoe's office, watching while Lassoe called the Boston Police Department.

"Police," said the voice on the other end of the line.

"Can I have Missing Persons, please," Lassoe said.

"Just a moment," the voice said.

Lassoe heard a ring on the other line before it was picked up.

"Missing Persons," the voice, a rough baritone, on the other end of the line said.

"This is Doctor Ben Lassoe at Boston General."

"What can I do for you, Doctor?"

"I have a patient who has no idea of who he is. He was found naked in Provincetown, no identification. He was catatonic. I wonder if you've received a missing persons report."

"Describe him and we'll see if we can make a match."

"Very well."

Lassoe described his patient to the officer on the other end of the telephone line.

"Hmmm. Let me look on the computer to see if we can make a match."

"Take your time." Lassoe said, trying to curb a rising sense of excitement and retain his calm, professional demeanor.

"We have a person matching your description, Doctor. He seems to be a priest in Marlborough."

"Marlborough," Lassoe said thoughtfully." Who reported him missing?"

"A Bishop John Everly."

"Do you have Bishop Everly's telephone number?"

"Yes. Hold on while I find it."

"Certainly. By the way, what is the name of the missing man?"

"Father Joseph Bennett. Yes, here's the number."

He gave Lassoe Bishop Everly's number.

"Anything else that I can do for you, Doctor Lassoe?""No, thank you. You've been very helpful, officer. Many thanks."

"That's what we're here for."

"Thank goodness for that. Good bye."

"Bye."

Lassoe hung up the phone.

"Father Joseph Bennett is our John Doe," he announced to his colleagues." He's a priest in Marlborough. I'm going to call his bishop, a John Everly right now."

"Excellent," Stevenson said." I knew that calling Missing Persons could facilitate things."

Lassoe dialed Bishop Everly's number. The phone rang four times before it was answered.

"Hello?"

"Hello. Is this Bishop John Everly?" Lassoe asked.

"Yes, I'm Bishop Everly. Whom am I talking to and what is this in reference to?"

"I'm Doctor Ben Lassoe at Boston General Hospital. I'm a psychiatrist. I got your name and number from Missing Persons at the Boston Police Department."

"Yes?"

"A few days ago, a man was brought in to Boston General suffering from catatonia. He had been found naked on the beach in Provincetown. He was unable to tell us his name or indeed anything about himself."

"Father Bennett is in your care?"

"Yes, he is. I just found out who he is and I called you immediately, Bishop Everly."

"Thank God, he's been found. I've been quite worried about him."

"Can you tell me anything about what might have caused him to slip into a catatonic state? Anything at all?"

"Father Bennett was a spiritual counselor for other priests and nuns. He's a Jesuit. There was an incident when one of the nuns that he was counseling disappeared and he found that she had left the convent after a trip to Japan. Not immediately after, but sometime later. He told me that he had received a call from a woman named Diana Clements. He told me that he had to go to see her as she was calling for him. When he returned, he informed me that she had left the hospital but that her infant was there, dying. I warned him about trying to find her."

"Why?"

"I felt that that there was something amiss. There seemed to be some sort of sorcery, some occult workings."

"What do you mean?"

"I'm sorry, I can't elaborate over the phone, Doctor."

"I see."

"How is he? When may I see him? I'm very concerned about him. I warned him not to go to Provincetown because I was afraid that something dire would happen to him."

"Right now, Bishop Everly, he seems to be in a confused state of mind. When he's more stable, then you may visit him. In fact, I'll let you know. At that time, you can bring some clothes for him for as I told you, he had been found naked on the beach."

"Yes, I see. Of course, you're right, Doctor Lassoe. I really would like to meet with him."

"Yes, Father, I will keep you informed. You mentioned a nun who disappeared from the convent after her return from Japan?""Yes, what about her?"

"Is it possible that this missing nun might be Diana Clements?"

There was a pause on the other end of the line.

"To be honest, Doctor Lassoe, I really couldn't say. Why?"

"Just a thought. I'm sure that you're very busy, Bishop Everly. I'll let you go now."

"Cure him, Doctor. He's a fine priest."

"I'll do my best," Lassoe promised.

"Thank you. Goodbye."

"Wait. I have another question." said Lassoe.

"And what is that?"

"Did he do any time as a priest in Mali?"

There was a pause.

"Why, yes… In 1980, he was in Africa… At Mount Elgon and in Mali, if I remember correctly, for six months… Why do you ask?"

Doctor Lassoe remained silent for several moments.

"Doctor? Are you still there?"

"Yes… Yes… As in reference to Mali, just forget it… That's all…" Lassoe responded.

"Okay, if you insist. Goodby, Doctor."

"Goodbye."

Lassoe hung up the phone.

"Well, Ben?" Stevenson asked." What gives?"

At this point, Lassoe recounted his conversation with Bishop Everly.

"What do you think?" he asked his colleagues.

"Very strange," Henry said." Sorcery. Occult workings that he wouldn't go into over the phone. I wonder what it's all about."

"Gentlemen… There is something that I have not told you about the patient."

"What are you hiding, Ben? Stevens asked jocularly.

"When he was brought in, he was examined. During that first night, Sue Patterson, the nurse on duty, saw claw marks on his arms and fang marks on his neck. She turned away for a second and when she looked back at the patient, they were gone."

There was a period of silence and then Thorton said," Why didn't you tell us that first day?"

"I did'nt want to start any rumors."

Stevenson looked thoughtful.

"Very strange, he murmured." Sounds like a stigmata."

"From my conversation with Bishop Everly, could it be possibly a Satanic stigmata?" Lassoe asked.

"Possibly " , Stevenson said," Quite possibly… I wonder…"

"Wonder what?" Lassoe asked.

"I wonder what the hell is going on!" Stevenson said forcibly.

The others nodded like a Greek chorus.

"When Father Bennett can tell his story, then I'll find out," Lassoe said.

"What's your next move, Ben?" Stevenson asked.

"Visit maternity and find out about this Diana Clements and her dying infant and why she wanted to see Father Bennett."

"That's what I would do," Thornton said.

"As a matter of fact, that's what I'm going to do right now," Lassoe said, rising from his chair.

"We need to get back to work," Stevenson said.

The other three men rose from their chairs and they all left Lassoe's office, separating once they were out of the door. Lassoe walked to the elevator and pushed the button. He rode the elevator to Maternity. Once he got off the elevator, he walked to the nurse's station. As he approached, the head nurse looked up. She was a middle-aged woman with graying brown hair worn in a bun on top of her head. Her blue-gray eyes appraised Lassoe as he approached.

"Yes, may I help you?" she asked.

"I hope so. I'm Doctor Ben Lassoe from the fourth floor."

"And what can I do for you, Doctor?"

"I was wondering if you could check your records and tell me about a patient, a woman named Diana Clements who had a baby here. I was told that she left the hospital, but that she left her dying infant here."

"Really? Well, let me check my records. I don't remember any of this, but if she was a patient here, then we'll have her in our records. Won't take but a moment."

"Thank you."

She typed in the patient's name and waited for the information to come up. She frowned.

"I'm sorry, Doctor, but we have no record of a Diana Clements having been here. There certainly haven't been any dying infants, either."

"Thank you for your time and trouble," Lassoe said.

"Oh, no trouble at all."

"Have a nice day."Lassoe walked back to the elevator and rode it to the fourth floor. He was introspective. Did Diana Clements exist? Did, perhaps, Bishop Everly misunderstand Father Bennett? What was the truth here? The only way he was going to find out was by hearing Father Bennett's story.

Getting off the elevator, Lassoe walked down the hall to his patient's room. He stood in the doorway looking at the man in the bed. He was lying in the bed, looking out the window. Lassoe entered the room. As he crossed the threshold, the man's head turned towards him.

"How are you, Father Bennett?" Lassoe asked. He looked closely to see if the use of his name registered.

"What did you call me?" the man asked.

"Your name is Father Joseph Bennett. Bishop John Everly reported you missing after you left for Provincetown and didn't return."

"How do you that that's my name?"

"I called Missing Persons and described you. They came up with your name and the rest was easy. You are Father Joseph Bennett. You're from Marlborough where you're the parish priest. Does anything I've said so far ring a bell?"

Father Bennett frowned in concentration. Then he slowly shook his head.

"I'm afraid not," he said in a low voice.

"You came here at the request of a woman named Diana Clements who had a baby. The baby was dying. I checked with Maternity and they don't have a record of either Diana Clements or her baby. Yet, Bishop Everly told me that you told him about it and that he warned you not to go to Provincetown."

"I... don't remember a Diana Clements. I'm sorry."

"Tell me about the nun who went to Japan? Why did she leave the convent and when did she leave? Is she and Diana Clements the same person?"

At the mention of 'Japan', there seemed to be a flicker of recognition in Father Bennett's eyes. Although he was still frowning in intense concentration, the mention of a nation on the other side of the world elicited some sort of recognition.

Lassoe studied him very closely.

"I..."

Father Bennett looked at Lassoe pleadingly as if asking the psychiatrist silently to understand something. Lassoe had no idea what Father Bennett wanted him to understand. .

Lassoe put his hand on Father Bennett's shoulder trying to calm the priest as he began to get agitated. The strain of trying to remember was beginning to upset the priest.

"It's alright," Lassoe said soothingly." Don't get agitated. We'll talk again. Knowing your real name is better than the name that we gave you. Get some rest. I'll see you tomorrow."

Father Bennett nodded.

Lassoe leaned over and picked up the mandala.

"Here," he said, handing the mandala to Father Bennett." This might help to calm you."

Father Bennett clutched the mandala in his hands as if it were a lifeline that he was being thrown. He looked up at Lassoe, trying to smile to indicate his gratitude but failing.

"Thank you," he whispered.

"You're quite welcome."Lassoe, with another squeeze of Father Bennett's shoulder, left the room. He didn't look back at his patient. Although nothing that he had said to the pathetic figure in the bed seemed to elicit the desired response, he had a feeling of elation that he was very close to breaking down the barriers in the man's mind. Once those barriers had been broken, then like a dam that had burst, Father Bennett's story would come gushing out.

Lassoe stopped by the nurse's station.

"Let me see John Doe's chart," he said to the head nurse.

She found the chart and handed it to him.

"Here's the chart, Doctor," she said.

"Thank you," he said, taking the chart. Taking a pen from his pocket, he crossed out the name John Doe and neatly printed: Father Joseph Bennett. He handed the chart back to the nurse. She looked at the correction before returning the chart to its place. She didn't ask Lassoe any questions. She'd find out eventually how he had learned the patient's name.

"Sue," Lassoe said," I feel that I'm on the verge of finding out what happened to our patient. I feel that he's just about ready to tell his story."

"What makes you think so, Doctor?" she asked.

"Certain things like his name and that of a certain country seemed to trigger something in his subconscious. I think that between now and when I see him tomorrow, his memory will be a lot better and then maybe, just maybe, he'll be able to tell me what happened to him."

"That would be wonderful, Doctor," she said.

Lassoe nodded.

"I'll be in my office should you need me," he said.

"Very well, Doctor."

Sue watched him as he walked down the hall to his office.

Lassoe worked the rest of the day. At five, he left his office and went home. He didn't think of anything relating to Father Bennett or his other patients. He wanted his mind to be free. He didn't want to have any expectations of what the next day might bring. He needed the rest that only a trouble free mind can bring.

It was with great satisfaction that he went to bed that night and to sleep.

The next morning, with a rising sense of anticipation, Lassoe entered Father Bennett's room. He saw that his patient, sitting up in bed was alert; more alert than he had ever been since his arrival.

"Good morning, Father Bennett," Lassoe said almost cheerfully.

"Good morning, Doctor Lassoe," was the reply.

"How do you feel this morning?"

"I'm not sure how I feel."

"Is your mind still foggy?"

Father Bennett considered the question, then smiled.

"That is a very good description of how I felt. Foggy."

"And do you still feel this way?"

"No, the fog seems to be clearing away."

"That's very good. Very good indeed. Have you given any thought to what we discussed yesterday?"Father Bennett looked down at the mandala he was holding.

"What is this?" he asked.

"That's a mandala which promotes psychic wholeness. Did you study it?"

"Yes. It is... interesting."

He looked up at Lassoe.

"I have given thought to what we discussed yesterday, Doctor, but I'm afraid that it eludes me at the moment. I'm sorry for I know that you wanted answers to your numerous questions, but I don't think that I can supply them to you."

Lassoe studied him thoughtfully.

"When I mentioned Japan, that seemed to trigger something in your subconscious. Do you know anything about Japan?"

Father Bennett thought hard for a moment and seemed to be about to shake his head when, as if a light bulb had suddenly gone off in his head, he smiled.

"You do remember," Lassoe said, trying to quell his rising excitement." I know that you remember."

"Vaguely," Father Bennett said.

"I'll be right back. Don't go away."

"And where would I go?" Father Bennett asked, raising one eyebrow.

Lassoe smiled at him and left the room. He hurried down the hall to his office and collected two cups that were very Oriental, two tea bags and a small pot of boiled water from a hot plate. He placed these items on a tray and returned to his patient's room.

When he entered, Father Bennett looked inquiringly at him, but didn't say a word.

"You're probably wondering what all this is about," Lassoe said as he placed the tray down. He put the tea bags into the cups then poured the boiling water over them. Father Bennett watched him intently.

"You're making tea," Father Bennett said.

"We're going to have a tea ceremony," Lassoe announced." This has to steep for a few minutes."

"Why a tea ceremony?" Father Bennett asked, intrigued.

"When I was in Japan, I attended one. They don't let many foreigners attend something that is so personal to them. It's a way to meditate and also mediate. It's a very ancient ceremony."

"I see. And what do you hope to accomplish with this ceremony, Doctor?"

Lassoe looked at him.

"I hope," he said slowly," that this will trigger your memory and that you'll be able to tell me what happened to you. I really can't help you unless I know what happened to you. Do you understand?"

Father Bennett nodded.

"Yes, I think that I do," he said slowly, thoughtfully.

Lassoe smiled at him.

"Yes, I think that you do."

He looked into the cups gauging by the color if the tea had steeped long enough.

"It's ready," Lassoe said quietly.He removed the tea bags from the cups and threw them away. With great care, he handed one of the cups to Father Bennett. Father Bennett took the cup solemnly, cradling it in both hands. He watched Lassoe as he took the other cup and sat down by the bed.

"As I told you, I participated in such a ceremony when I was in Japan. It left a very deep and abiding impression on me."

Over the rim of his cup, he watched Father Bennett, who was watching him in the same way. Smiling, Lassoe raised his cup. Father Bennett responded in the same way. Both men sipped at the tea.

"You know," Lassoe said," I really admire the early Jesuit writer, Saint Francis Xavier."

"Why?" Father Bennett asked curiously.

"He had great insight into zen. In fact, he had great respect for the Japanese culture. The Japanese, instead of having certain astrological motifs, believed and are concerned with the experience of the moment. It's a celebration of oneness and convergence."

"What do you mean by that?" Father Bennett asked.

"It's a conquest of multiplicity and atomization."

Father Bennett looked thoughtful.

"In a way," Lassoe continued," this ceremony is very much like a liturgy, a holy communion on equal par with the early Eucharist or even a primitive Christian agape."

Father Bennett nodded his head.

Lassoe watched him intently, the way that a cat watches a mouse hole waiting for the occupant to come out.

"Yes, I believe that I see what you mean," Father Bennett said slowly.

He looked out the window for a moment then back at Lassoe.

"This ceremony is very soothing," Father Bennett said." Very soothing, indeed."

"You conducted a ceremony the other day in the recreation room," Lassoe said.

"I did?" Father Bennett asked frowning." I don't remember."

"It had a very soothing effect on the patients here. Did you do any time in Mali?"

At this point, Father Bennett showed signs of agitation.

"I do not wish to dream of that dark continent… My dreams are very strange."

Not wishing to elicit a possible psychotic reaction, Doctor Lassoe immediately changed the subject.

" Bishop Everly told me that you were a spiritual counselor to the other priests and nuns."

"Yes, I was. I suppose that I still am. But for the life of me, I can't remember the ceremony that you're talking about. I'm afraid that I really don't know much about Japanese culture. I believe that what you're saying about early Christianity is valid."

The two men looked at each other.

There seemed to be a subtle change in Father Bennett. Lassoe, trying to remain calm, felt the hairs on the back of his neck begin to rise.

"Can you tell me what happened to you?" Lassoe asked, trying to remain calm.

Father Bennett looked at the cup he held in his hands and then at the mandala. Slowly, he raised his eyes to meet Lassoe's.

"To be honest, I don't know where to begin."

"How about at the beginning?" Lassoe suggested.

Father Bennett thought for a long moment and then, with an emphatic nod of his head, he looked Lassoe directly in the eye.

"I believe that it all started with Sister Marcia and the two dreams that she had."

He paused for a moment.

"Yes," he said." That was the beginning."

Chapter One

Sister Marcia's Dilemma

It was high noon and *the scathing rays of the sun beat down on the surface of the pyramid, scorching the flesh of those who dared to ascend for only at the pinnacle did the vector of the sun enter before continuing on its mighty course across the heavens. Slowly, she climbed the steps of the pyramid without the assistance of the Aztec priests and with each step, she sensed a higher vibration. She was losing contact with her body as the divine radiance of the sun beckoned and the gods awaited appeasement. Her pulse was the pulse of the universe as its entire fate hinged upon the voluntary gift of her soul. Her ideal had always been moral perfection and her chastity was held in deep veneration by the priests. At the top of the pyramid, she unfastened her gown and as it dropped to the ground, the priests marveled at her beauty and the perfection of her body. She lay down on the blood-stained altar where there had been many sacrifices before and closed her eyes. A deep masculine voice asked her if she was prepared to die and make the transition. The high priest, with his headdress of red bird plumage and his long cloak that covered his body, approached the altar. In his upraised hand, a knife glittered in the sun. As the vital life force welled up within* *her, she exclaimed out loud:" I am doing this as a true act of celebration of my love for Mother Nature! I am her child and have not forgotten my love! I sing the Body Electric! I chant the Square Deific!" She felt the sudden plunge of the knife deep into her chest and as she opened her eyes for one brief instant, she saw the priest with red plumage lifting her pulsating heart up to the sun in a solemn chant. Now the gods returned their love and her cry of joy reverberated through the heavens and the underworld... The earth was so far away... so remote. Knowing infinity, she felt so playful... but something... someone wanted her back as if she had an obligation to return. Frowning, she felt a strong pull back towards the earth...*

A babble of excited voices, feminine voices, seemed to be calling her back. The young woman awoke to find that the sun was instead an overhead light. The altar which she thought that she lay on was instead a narrow bed with an iron bedstead, the springs were sagging slightly. The bedclothes were disarrayed. She opened her eyes reluctantly. Her long black hair was in disarray; her nightgown was soaked in sweat. Her eyes focused slowly on those crowding around her. Her eyes took in the room. The walls, except for the crucifix opposite her bed, were bare.

There was a commotion at the doorway and a short, gray haired woman wearing a threadbare robe entered the room. Her lined face with the deep-set blue eyes took in the scene. There was an aura of command about her that seemed natural. Her stocky figure was as imposing as her air of command. Those crowding in the doorway, respectfully withdrew into the hall.

"Go back to your beds," the woman commanded." Right now."

With bowed heads and murmurs of consent, the women withdrew and began returning to their various rooms. The woman advanced to the foot of the bed where the young woman began sitting up, clutching the bedclothes to her chin. She looked like a frightened child; her dark eyes reflected this fear.

The woman smiled at the young woman before her.

"My child," the woman began," you were evidently having a bad dream. You woke all of us up."

"I'm sorry, Mother Superior," the young woman said, looking at the woman.

"I'm sure that you are, child. You were quite emotional. I overheard you say some very strange things. I'm quite curious as to what significance those words have. What you said in your sleep was more like a declaration."

The young woman's mood changed from fright back to the previous mood of the dream. She felt exhilarated.

"What did I say?" she asked in a low, husky voice.

"Sister Marcia, I would rather discuss what you had to say in private counsel at a more convenient time," the Mother Superior said." Now, we all must get some sleep. We don't want to sleepwalk through Vespers."

The Mother Superior's smile, which she thought was warm with understanding, seemed to Sister Marcia to be a little strained.

"But, Mother Superior," Sister Marcia said," there's nobody here. You sent them away. I really want to explain. It won't take all that long."

The Mother Superior with a sigh, nodded her head.

"Very well," she said." Tell me what you wish to tell me."

Sister Marcia looked at the older woman.

"The dream that I had was the most beautiful dream that I have ever had in my entire life. I truly believe that I crossed over the threshold. The dream was real... so very real. I feel that it's the culmination of my life, the apex of my career. What happened to me is beyond words."

The Mother Superior looked at the young nun sitting up in her bed. She was shocked. In all her life, in fact, in all her career in the church, she had never heard of anything like this before. Sister Marcia, to her, was a very modest young woman. She rarely called attention to herself and seemed genuinely to be a bride of Christ; radiant and strong in her faith and the sisterhood. The Mother Superior was perplexed. For the first time in her role of Mother Superior, she felt that she didn't know how to help one of her charges. Her hands plucked at the folds of her robe in her agitation.

"Silence, my child. You can discuss your... experience with me later. After breakfast, in my office, when we're alone. It does seem evident to me that whatever happened to you has left a strong imprint on your memory. It is very late and now is not the proper time to discuss... this dream of yours. I know that you're very excited, but please try to get some rest. We have a long day ahead of us."

The eyes of the two women locked. The Mother Superior wondered if this dream of Sister Marcia's was an aberration or something more serious.

"Good night, my child," the Mother Superior said softly." I myself do not put much stock in dreams. When I was eighteen, I had a crush on my theology professor. I was tormented by my desires. Anyway, I had a dream that I married him and had several children by him. You might say that my life is a testimony to the fact that a dream is the heart's work of fiction of a more fulfilling life than that which reality has to offer. I am at the point that I can honestly say that dreams do not matter any more because I have found my peace."

"Good night, Mother Superior," Sister Marcia said, watching the older woman as she walked over to the light switch. The Mother Superior's hand hesitated for a moment over the light switch and she looked back over her shoulder at the young nun still sitting up in bed. Then, as if she had had enough, the Mother Superior turned off the light. She closed the door to Sister Marcia's room behind her, leaving the room in darkness.

Standing outside the door, the Mother Superior crossed herself and heard the creak of the springs as Sister Marcia was evidently lying down.

In her room, Sister Marcia did, indeed, lie down. She lay on her back, staring up at the black ceiling, her hands behind her head. There was nobody to see the smile on her face. She thought about the dream and the feelings that it evoked in her. Her dark eyes glittered in the darkness. She reflected that the dream that she had had did not conflict with her duties as a nun. Feeling that lying in bed was too stifling and that she needed action, she got out of bed and began pacing the small room that was hers at the convent. As she paced in the early morning hours with the dawn approaching, she felt fatigue. Somehow, it seemed that her whole life in the convent for the past ten years was a type of preparation for the dream, for that particular event was a turning point. The coming day's activities seemed, somehow, insignificant in comparison for she now had an inspiration; a light she hoped would never fade. She made an oath of secrecy to herself, promising herself not to reveal the contents of the dream to anyone, no matter what the circumstances. She knew that this might be the initial dream and that other more significant dreams might follow if she kept this pact with herself.

She stood by the window, watching the sky lighting up. As the sun began to brighten the eastern sky, she began dressing for the day. Before leaving her room for Vespers, she crossed herself.

At breakfast, after Vespers, the nuns glanced surreptitiously at Sister Marcia. They had observed her during Vespers to see if there was anything different in her manner. If they were disappointed to notice that she seemed to be the same, they showed no signs of it. The long table where the Mother Superior sat at the head with the light from the sun streaming in through the long windows at her back seemed the same as always. They ate silently. The Mother Superior seemed to the others nuns to be her usual serene self. So did Sister Marcia.

After breakfast, the Mother Superior summoned Sister Marcia to her private study. The young, attractive nun was a type of prima donna in the eyes of the Mother Superior. Sister Marcia was almost always late or totally absent from the various activities of the horaria regarding some personal problem as far as she was concerned. That morning, she had observed the young nun very pre-occupied at the Chapel while she said her Matins and Lauds, followed by a half-hour of mental prayer and twenty minutes of vocal prayer leading up to the Mass. She had been preparing herself for some type of confrontation with Sister Marcia for several months and her strange declaration earlier that morning, in a way, disrupted the continuity of the pious life as far as she was concerned.She studied her hands folded before her on the teakwood desk. She raised her eyes to the portrait of his Holiness Pope John Paul II. She studied the kind face staring back at her. Her eyes wandered from the face of the pope to the crucifix on the wall. She fingered her rosary beads that were wrapped around her waist in agitation. She prayed that she could break through Sister Marcia's demeanor of self-absorption and for once get the young nun to face up to things the way they were, not how she would like them to be. She had the feeling that this was going to be a very difficult interview. Why, she thought to herself, did this have to happen to me? Why, of all the convents, did Sister Marcia have to be at her convent? Why couldn't Sister Marcia behave as the rest of her sisters in Christ behave? Finding no answers to these questions, she sighed heavily and looked at the empty doorway.

"It's just like her to be late," the Mother Superior muttered under her breath.

She didn't know much about Sister Marcia's background. She seemed to be an enigma. In the beginning, she seemed to be like the other novitiates, eager to please, to learn all about her new life. She had, from the first, been very close-mouthed about herself. The other sisters were both fascinated by her and a little turned off by her aloofness. She couldn't quite pinpoint when she had first noticed the change in Sister Marcia's attitude. But the eager young novitiate had suddenly, in her eyes, become the prima donna nun that the Mother Superior considered her to be. Sister Marcia seemed to reject the other sisters. Even though she was attractive and very intelligent, she was not vain about it, nonetheless, the other sisters felt intimidated by her. The Mother Superior had to deal with this problem many times and as far as she was concerned, the prima donna nun had been ostracized when she first entered the convent. And she wondered, not for the first time, why Sister Marcia had chosen this life. Why had she become a nun? Why hadn't she gone on to an academic career instead?

The Mother Superior shook her head; dismayed at the directions her thoughts were taking her. She had to practice Christian charity in thoughts as well as deeds. She tried to compose herself as she waited for Sister Marcia. She considered getting up and looking out in the hall to see if she could see Sister Marcia coming, but instead, sat where she was.

"God give me strength to be charitable and serene with Sister Marcia," she prayed." Let me be able to make her see the folly of her attitude and help her come to a deeper understanding of Your infinite love. Amen."

Raising her head, she noticed Sister Marcia leaning in the doorway. Her attitude seemed to be very nonchalant.

"You wanted to see me, Mother Superior," Sister Marcia said.

"Yes, I did. Please come in and sit down. Close the door."

Sister Marcia closed the door behind her and walked over to the Mother Superior's desk and sat down in a chair.

The Mother Superior looked at the young nun wondering where

to begin. She felt a little flustered by Sister Marcia's attitude, while not disrespectful was at least a little provocative.

"You're in a good mood today," the Mother Superior said, trying to break the ice.

Sister Marcia smiled, recognizing the Mother Superior's opening conversational gambit.

"Yes, I am in an exceptionally good mood today, thank you," Sister Marcia murmured.

The Mother Superior fixed Sister Marcia with an intense look.

"I found out one thing for sure about you last night," she said.

"And what was that?" Sister Marcia asked politely.

"That without doubt, you are a hopeless Romantic."

The eyes of the two women locked onto each other like two duelists about to engage in a duel. They studied each other as if looking for a weakness that could be exploited.

Sister Marcia remained silent, not responding to the Mother Superior's comment. A smile, barely discernible, appeared on her face. For a moment, the older woman stared at the younger woman as if trying to discern for herself the meaning of the enigmatic smile.

"May I ask what your dream last night was about?" the Mother Superior asked.

"I would rather not tell you," Sister Marcia said.The Mother Superior frowned slightly. It was what she had expected from Sister Marcia. Still, she didn't like secrets and to her, Sister Marcia, was being very secretive.

"May I ask why not?" the Mother Superior asked.

"My dream is very personal and not open to interpretation," Sister Marcia replied.

"I see."

The Mother Superior stared at the young nun seated at her desk with the utmost caution. She didn't want to make her questions seem like an interrogation. She understood privacy, but she also understood that the young nun, for all her assumed nonchalance, was sending distress signals that she felt she couldn't ignore.

"Listen, my child, I am not trying to interrogate you or anything like that. Lord knows that those days are over, but I cannot help asking you what you meant by your references to Walt Whitman's poetry by stating out loud apparently while in the midst of your dream, 'I sing the Body Electric and I chant the Square Deific'? I am most curious as to what these two phrases mean to you?"

The Mother Superior felt that her question was not out of line. Indeed, she felt that her request of Sister Marcia was very reasonable. She wondered if Sister Marcia would answer her or would pass it off with the usual air of not wanting to answer any questions that she didn't want to.

Sister Marcia pondered what the Mother Superior had asked her. She frowned slightly as if in concentration before her eyes once again met the Mother Superior's eyes across the teakwood desk.

"Is that what I said?" she asked.

"Yes, my child. That is exactly what you declared."

"Well, then I would not rather say, if it's all the same to you."

The Mother Superior tried to ascertain whether Sister Marcia's refusal to answer her simple question was due to her usual way of deflecting any invasion of her privacy. The silence in the room deepened as the contest of wills fought against the other.

Gently, rising from behind her desk, the Mother Superior walked around the desk and attempted to console the young nun, placing her hand on Sister Marcia's arm. Sister Marcia looked at the hand on her arm then up into the older woman's face as if trying to discern the Mother Superior's motives.

"Sister Marcia, you still seem... very elated to me. It is very apparent to me that you have been through some sort of change. What you share with me in this room will be held in the strictest confidence, I assure you. You can trust me with this burden."

The Mother Superior's face expressed her concern with one of her flock and also to reassure Sister Marcia of her sincerity. She tried to infuse her very being with her desire to help the young nun. She wondered if she would succeed or if Sister Marcia would shut her out as she had in the past.

Sister Marcia stood up to leave. When she reached the door, she turned to confront the older woman with an affirmation.

"All I can say is that I crossed over the threshold to eternity and it was a loving embrace. My entire life was seen in retrospect as a type of preparation for this event. I will never be the same again. This dream is not a burden I carry, but a gift."Before the Mother Superior could say anything, Sister Marcia left the room and she knew somehow in her heart that their relationship would never be the same again. She sighed for the lost opportunity. Was it her or Sister Marcia's attitude that let the opportunity slip away? She didn't know. She didn't want to blame the young nun for what happened; yet in the back of her mind it was Sister's Marcia's fault. Evidently, she viewed the Mother Superior's questioning of her as being too intrusive. Could the child really have crossed the threshold to eternity? She shook her head and looked out the window. The nuns seemed to be going about their chores cheerfully as they usually did. She looked out on the gardens with maternal pride. She was an avid gardener; loving to plunge her hands into the rich soil and watch the fruits of her labor grow. The tomatoes looked especially good this year, as did the asparagus. Her eyes wandered to the flower garden and noted the brightness of the roses and the peonies. The convent, growing it's own vegetables, was practically self-sufficient.

Ten years ago she had a hysterectomy. She felt that her attitude had softened towards her cohorts by trying to be more flexible. Yet, Sister Marcia with her attitude and her attractive appearance seemed to defy the traditional stereotype of how nuns were perceived. As usual, Sister Marcia had pushed her to the limits.

She tore her eyes away from the garden and sat back down at her desk. A mass of paperwork awaited her and she got to it, putting her interview with Sister Marcia out of her mind. While she was doing her paperwork, she thought of Father Bennett.

"Maybe I should consult him?" she said half-aloud to herself.

She was very impressed with the middle-aged Jesuit priest. More than anyone affiliated with the church, in her opinion, her exerted a strong masculine influence on the sisters of the convent. He was well known and respected for his psychological as well as his spiritual counseling.

"Yes," she said," that's what I'll do. I'll consult Father Bennett and maybe he can tell me how to deal with Sister Marcia. She needs to talk with Father Bennett."

Feeling relieved that she had thought of a solution to what was troubling her, the Mother Superior returned to her paperwork.

After leaving the Mother Superior, Sister Marcia wandered out into the garden. She wasn't mad at the Mother Superior for asking her questions; didn't think of her as a meddling busybody because she understood why the Mother Superior questioned her like that. Sister Marcia was still caught up in the euphoria of her dream and everything else seemed superficial: the questions of the Mother Superior, chores and the whole host of things related to her life in the convent. She knew how the other sisters, even the novitiates, felt about her but she didn't care. She was a beautiful young woman. Her face, that peeked out at the world from beneath her wimple, was a perfect oval. She had high cheekbones, a petite nose and, what some would consider, a sensuous mouth. But her most arresting feature was her dark eyes. Her body, if anyone could see beneath her habit, would be considered to be lovely. Her appearance, she took for granted. She was satisfied with her life. Ever since childhood, she had wanted to serve God in some way. She was one of those rare people, both male and female, who attempted to harness her sexual desires. She considered herself to be a woman as did everyone who saw her, but with that minor exception. And because of this one feature about her that no one saw, she had decided that the best way to serve God was to become a bride of Christ--a nun. She didn't know if the rest of the sisters had sexual desires or not. All that was personal and private. She didn't intrude on others and wanted no one to intrude on her. If she gave the impression that she was above everyone else, she didn't mean to. She knew how the Mother Superior viewed her and she didn't care. When she entered the convent, she had broken ties with her previous life and didn't think of it any more. Her faith in God was strong, yet she felt that there was something missing. What it was, she didn't know.

The bells in the church steeple were ringing the hour. It was nine o'clock. She hurried to do her chores. She was on laundry detail that morning.

Dinner that night was the same as it always was, both the food served and the conversation of the sisters. Sister Marcia, from time to time, glanced at the Mother Superior. The older woman seemed not to be paying any attention to her at all, but was listening to the conversations that were going on around her. In fact, nobody was paying any attention to her. She didn't feel ostracized. On the contrary, she observed everything going on around her.

After dinner, she retired to her room for the night. This is what she did every night. Nobody thought that it was strange anymore when she had first done so. They had gotten accustomed to her behavior.

Upon entering her room, she undressed for the night. She brushed her black hair one hundred times as she always did. Sister Marcia was a very disciplined person. Brushing her hair gave her time to think. She was hoping for a repeat of her dream of the night before or one similar to it. She was looking forward with eager anticipation to going to sleep.

She knew that the Mother Superior thought of her as vain, but she didn't consider herself to be that. Like the Mother Superior, she considered vanity to be a sin. She was careless and accepting of her appearance as not vain.

When she had finished brushing her hair, she read for a while from her Bible. Upon finishing her reading, she knelt down and crossed herself and prayed, then she got into bed and turned off the light and went to sleep.

Several days had passed since the Mother Superior had had her talk with Sister Marcia before she consulted Father Bennett. After the morning Mass, she took him aside.

"May I talk to you, Father?" she asked looking up at the tall, austere Jesuit priest.

"Certainly, Mother Superior," Father Bennett said kindly." Is there something troubling you?"

"Yes, there is something troubling me. It's about Sister Marcia."

"What's the problem with her?" Father Bennett asked, frowning slightly.

His kindly blue eyes looked at her troubled face. His brown hair was graying at the temples, as was the full, close-cropped beard that he wore. His face was unlined.

"Shall we go to my office so that we can talk privately?" the Mother Superior asked him.

"Yes, that would be a very good idea," Father Bennett said agreeably.

They left the chapel and walked down the corridor to the Mother Superior's office. Once inside with the door closed, the Mother Superior unburdened herself to the priest."Sister Marcia is somewhat of a problematic individual to me," the Mother Superior began, looking at Father Bennett.

"How is she a problem?" he asked." Does she shirk her chores and other activities of the convent? Is she lax?"

The Mother Superior shook her head.

"No, it's nothing like that, although I feel that her attitude is slightly nonchalant."

"Then how is she a problematic individual?"

"A few nights ago she had a dream--a dream she would not tell me about--that awakened everyone in the convent for she shouted out in her sleep, 'I sing the Body Electric! I chant the Square Deific!' You have studied literature. What do those two phrases from Whitman's poetry mean to you strictly in the spiritual sense?"

Father Bennett's keen blue eyes fell on the Mother Superior for a moment. He was pondering what she had told him. After a minute, he offered his own analysis.

"Really, to be perfectly honest with you, I don't know for sure. It seems to me that these two key phrases represent two modes of Whitman's religious and mystical perception. The former is his absolute hedonism and autoeroticism in which he celebrated the body as something holy and sacred. The second phrase 'I chant the Square Deific' comes much later in his career when more emphasis was put on the soul in nature. You might say that it was his pantheistic phase. The Square Deific personified his conception of the fourfold nature of God, which is not the God of the Christians. Around 1855, he called Him his 'eldest brother', which still implies a certain hierarchy, but, as early as the following year, he boldly proclaimed Him his brother and as an equal. He preferred an immanent God, mingled with the world, and incarnated within creatures. I guess in a way the two phrases might represent a type of spiritual transition in his life. Concerning Sister Marcia, one cannot be held responsible for his or her own dreams. You cannot actually 'sin' in your dream, but if you choose to embrace the supposed heretical nature of such a dream as sacrosanct then as far as I'm concerned, you are on dangerous ground."

There was silence as the Mother Superior considered what Father Bennett had said. She felt that she had to further tell Father Bennett about her observations of Sister Marcia over the last few days.

"All that is very interesting, Father, but I don't consider myself an alarmist, however I have been watching her perform her duties. Not only here but also at the hospital these last few days. She seems very elated--almost manic, I might add. She did state to me the night of the dream and in my office later that very same morning that because of her dream, she had in her words 'crossed over the threshold into eternity'. She also stated to me that the dream was the culmination of her life. There is no doubt in my mind that she was changed by it. Frankly, at this point, I question her allegiance to the church and her true spiritual devotion. In your opinion, do you think what I have to say warrants further investigation?"

Father Bennett scratched his beard absently as he thought about what the Mother Superior had just told him. He looked into her troubled eyes as he considered his reply."First of all, you don't have enough to go on. She seems perfectly normal to me, but then again, I am not observing her in the way that you are. What you consider as a sacrilegious statement might be nothing more than some type of childish nostalgia for an ideal of sorts. Whitman was a Romantic and he was never considered to be a threat to the Establishment. He was confused and his pantheism was not organized into any type of intellectual system. Evidently, Sister Marcia is familiar with his poetry, but as to how deep her understanding of it is remains a mystery. As far as I'm concerned, this is not worth investigating. I would drop the matter if I were you. As long as she performs her duties as required and devotes herself to her job as a nurse, or whatever, as she has done so well in the past, I would not worry. Only she knows what's in her heart and we both hope that her true devotion stems from her love of Christ, our Lord."

"Yes, Father," the Mother Superior said.

She felt, that at this point, that any further attempts on her part to focus attention on Sister Marcia would be futile. As Father Bennett said, she didn't have enough evidence to go on and without enough evidence, there was no case. Evidence, she thought. It sounded like a criminal case for the law courts instead of an, in her opinion, erring nun. Looking at Father Bennett sitting across the desk from her, she had the impression that he would make a wonderful judge. He looked something like the late Supreme Court Justice, Oliver Wendell Holmes. She would return to her study as always with more pressing matters ahead for her responsibilities were never ending. Had one of her flock gone astray or was she simply showing too much concern for just one individual? Sometimes, she felt like a mother hen worrying about her flock. Anyway, time alone would tell in the matter regarding Sister Marcia.

"Thank you very much for listening, Father Bennett," she said, standing up.

"You're quite welcome, Mother Superior," Father Bennett said, smiling at her." Don't worry too much about Sister Marcia. Have faith in our Lord, Jesus Christ, to help Sister Marcia."

"You're right, Father. I'll put my faith in our Lord and pray mightily that Sister Marcia finds peace of mind."

"If anything concerning Sister Marcia comes up, please let me know."

"I most certainly will."

"Well, I must go. I have an audience with Bishop Everly."

"Enjoy your audience with the bishop and give him my warmest regards."

"I will. Goodbye, Mother Superior."

"Goodbye, Father."

She sat down after he had left and began her paperwork.

Several nights had passed. There were days and nights of peace in which even the Mother Superior forgot Sister Marcia's behavior. Things for the sisters of the Magdalene convent in Marlborough some twenty-five miles west of Boston, Massachusetts returned to normal.

One night, a violent thunderstorm descended on the outskirts of the surrounding countryside in the early morning hours. Some of the sisters were restless and the Mother Superior made sure that all the doors were bolted and the windows were sealed shut, taking all the necessary safety precautions. She decided to lead some of the sisters who were awake in prayer to calm them. Outside, the thunder boomed, coming closer to the convent. Lightning streaked the sky with brilliant flashes of light, making everything outside surreal. The wind had picked up and the rain beat incessantly against the windows."My children, try not to be so restless right now and take the abiding consolation in the prayer I am about to offer for our protection. Dear Lord, we ask for your protection on this stormy night and that you please give us Your sweet peace in order that we are safe from this storm. We know that You are with us, Lord and that Your guiding hand will allow us to return to sleep. In Your name, we ask these things, Lord. Amen."

The sisters seemed to be comforted by the Mother Superior's prayer. They returned to their beds and were soon asleep. The Mother Superior, on her way back to her room, noticed the door to Sister Marcia's room open. She watched as Sister Marcia walked in the opposite direction from the bathroom where the Mother Superior had supposed the young nun was going. She followed Sister Marcia. She watched as Sister Marcia unlatched the door to the outside.

"Sister Marcia! Sister Marcia, what are you doing?" the Mother Superior called to the nun. She stood there unable to believe the evidence of her eyes.

Sister Marcia, as if in a zombie-like state, opened the door and walked outside into the ensuing thunderstorm. She walked for several hundred yards then dropped down on her knees.

The Mother Superior was extremely concerned. She called out to her, raising her voice this time.

"Sister Marcia! Sister Marcia, what are you doing?" Please, my child, come back in. You're getting soaked."

The rain continued in a torrential downpour. For a brief moment, lightning illuminated the surroundings. A peal of thunder rumbled in counterpoint to the lightning. In the streak of lightning, Sister Marcia held up her hands and cried out as if pleading with unseen forces.

"Oh, Mother Earth, give me, I pray thee, some of thy breath and I will give thee mine! Let me loose, Oh Mother, that I may carry thy words to the stars and I will return faithfully to thee after a while!"

There was no answer. Sister Marcia sat there drenched by the rain. In a sheer act of desperation, she covered herself with mud and slime.

At this point, the Mother Superior could no longer resist the immediate urge to literally rescue the distraught nun. She quickly left the building, careful how she walked. Her visibility was hampered by the driving rain.

Suddenly, there was another flash of lightning and this time Sister Marcia raised her clenched fists, yelling defiantly.

"I thought I was your child! Now I feel alien to you! I cannot demand an answer! I must await your reply! You give life! You take life! I am at your mercy!"

From her vantage point in the doorway, the Mother Superior watched, horrified by what she was witnessing. Sister Marcia was prostrating herself, debasing herself in the Mother Superior's opinion. A great wave of pity and compassion welled up in her as she watched the drenched figure of the nun. With the intermittent flashes of lightning giving the scene in front of her eyes an aspect of unreality, she knew that she had to go to Sister Marcia. The poor child, she thought, if I don't go to her, she'll catch cold. Whatever is she doing? Who is she calling out to? I have to go to her.

For all her determination, she felt herself unable to move. She looked up imploringly at the sky where, it seemed to her, that all of nature was angry.

"Lord Jesus," she whispered," have mercy on Sister Marcia in her time of trial. Help me to go to her and with your compassion, bring her back inside before she catches cold."

As someone who was about to dive into a pool of cold water, she left the security of the doorway. She walked carefully, the wind buffeting her, the rain in her face almost blinding her.The Mother Superior finally reached the nun and at first, she feared the volatility of the situation, but realized that she must somehow intervene. The moment was extreme. Without further hesitation, she firmly placed her right hand on Sister Marcia's left shoulder. With that touch, Sister Marcia came to her senses.

Sister Marcia looked up into the Mother Superior's compassionate eyes as another streak of lightning illuminated the sky. The wind picked up in intensity as the rain seemed ready to flood everything, drenching both women. Sister Marcia began trembling whether from her exposed condition or for some other reason.

"What am I doing here? My God, what has happened?"

"Try to remain calm, my child. You don't belong out here. Come, let us go back inside the house of the Lord where it is warm and safe. You've been through quite an ordeal," said the Mother Superior soothingly to the trembling nun.

Sister Marcia dropped her eyes. She felt bereft of all feelings. There was an emptiness in her that she quite couldn't fill. She continued trembling violently, her teeth began to chatter.

"Come, child," the Mother Superior said, trying to help Sister Marcia to her feet, " You're going to catch your death of cold."

For what seemed an eternity, the tableau held as if frozen in time: the Mother Superior gently tugging on the young nun's arm and the young nun with her head hanging down, ashamed.

Finally, Sister Marcia got to her feet. The Mother Superior put her arm around her shoulders. Another flash of lightning, another rumble of thunder that affected Sister Marcia violently as if the elements and her mood were one and the same.

It seemed, to the Mother Superior, an endless walk before the welcoming lights of the convent beckoned them. Sister Marcia seemed to need maternal affection. She seemed to be at her nadir to the Mother Superior's concerned eyes.

In the doorway, several nuns were congregated, watching the tableau as if at a play. As the Mother Superior approached with a trembling Sister Marcia, the waiting nuns seemed to come out of their trances and started to come forward to help the Mother Superior.

"Don't get wet," the Mother Superior admonished them.

The nuns hastily stepped back to make room for the two drenched women.

As before, when she had gone out into the storm, Sister Marcia walked like a zombie, hardly paying attention to what was going on. This concerned the Mother Superior even more than her trembling.

"We need to get you out of those wet clothes and into a warm shower," the Mother Superior said." Sister Theresa, will you turn the shower on?"

"Yes, Mother Superior," said an older nun, her wrinkled face showing concern.

The Mother Superior gave orders as she and Sister Marcia walked.

"Should I send for a doctor?" asked another nun, glancing at Sister Marcia's condition.

"Let's see how the warmth of the water works on her," the Mother Superior said.

Another nun, Sister Adrienne, supported Sister Marcia on the other side. Sister Marcia seemed unaware of what was happening.

"Pray for your sister," the Mother Superior told the sisters," that she took no physical harm going out into the storm like that. What emotional harm she might have taken, I cannot say."It seemed like miles before they reached the bathroom where Sister Theresa waited for them. Steam from the shower was beginning to make the bathroom almost like a sauna.

"You need to get out of your wet clothes, Mother Superior," Sister Theresa said.

"Yes, you're right. This poor child can hardly stand. Please get us some dry things to put on after we get out of the shower."

"Certainly," Sister Theresa said.

She gave the crowding sisters a glance and a couple went off to get the Mother Superior and Sister Marcia dry clothes to put on.

"Help me get these wet things off her," the Mother Superior said.

Sister Theresa and Sister Adrienne helped undress Sister Marcia, while the Mother Superior undressed herself. When both women were undressed, the Mother Superior bundled an uncomprehending Sister Marcia into the shower. She vigorously washed the young nun from her mud-streaked hair down the entire length of her body, pausing from time to time to see how the warmth of the water was affecting her.

At first, Sister Marcia still seemed to be listless. But as the water began to penetrate into her body, she seemed to revive a little. The Mother Superior watched her anxiously, examining her motives.

" Did I wait too long before going to her?" she asked herself," Look at her, the poor thing. Did I put my personal feelings for her over my Christian duty to succor her? I just don't know. She baffles me by the things that she does; the thoughts that she espouses. Am I guilty of a sin in not going to her sooner? Did I hope that she would be sick as a result? Do I want her to be sick? Do I want her here in this convent? Why am I afraid of her every time I think about her?"

The Mother Superior felt that Sister Marcia was clean. She herself was cleaned.

She turned off the water and helped Sister Marcia out of the shower.

Sister Marcia still seemed to be unaware of her surroundings and what was happening.

"Let's dry her off and get her into a dry nightgown," the Mother Superior said.

The nuns dried Sister Marcia, while the Mother Superior dried herself off. One of the nuns dried Sister Marcia's hair, toweling it roughly. For a moment, it seemed to the Mother Superior, that action brought a spark of life into Sister Marcia's eyes. When both women were thoroughly dried, they put on warm, dry nightgowns. Sister Adrienne was brushing Sister Marcia's hair.

"Well, she looks better," Sister Theresa said in her dry, disapproving voice.

"Yes, not like a drowned rat," the Mother Superior said." Now, let's get her to bed. Then all of you go to bed. There's been enough excitement for one day."

She fixed the milling nuns with a stern glance and they, like truant children, hurried back to their beds. Sister Marcia seemed to have recovered enough to be able to walk unaided on her own. With the Mother Superior as her only guardian, Sister Marcia walked back to her room. When they entered, the Mother Superior seemed to be gripped with an overwhelming desire to know what this latest escapade of hers was all about.

"I wish you would tell me what is going on with you. You keep me at a distance. I feel powerless to help you. Can you tell me what happened tonight?"

Sister Marcia turned her head, trying to avoid eye contact with the old woman, standing before her.

"I don't know what to say," she said whispering," I just feel that I must keep this all to myself, at least until I feel that the time is right to confess."Her voice trailed off.

The Mother Superior sighed. She really did not have an answer from this enigmatic woman, but she had to try anyway. She pulled back the covers to Sister Marcia's bed.

"I think that this whole thing has gone too far. If I had not brought you in from the storm tonight, you might have caught your death of cold. I wish that you would trust me with your burden just this once, my child. Can we at least pray about it?"

Sister Marcia crawled into her bed like a child seeking the warmth and security that the bed seemed to represent to her. She laid her head on her pillow and closed her eyes. A tear rolled down from her closed eyes.

"I need to be alone," she whispered to the Mother Superior." I will be alright. The best thing for me is to be alone."

She opened her eyes and looked into the concerned eyes of the Mother Superior.

"Please try to understand," she said pleadingly.

The Mother Superior looked down at her. After what Sister Marcia had been through tonight, maybe it was better to honor her request and to leave her alone.

"Very well, my child, if that's what you want. I'll leave you alone. If you need to talk to me, you know where I'll be."

The Mother Superior turned away from Sister Marcia's bed and walked to the door.

"Good night, my child. Your sisters are praying for you as I am. God loves you and has you in His hand. Sleep now. Maybe, tomorrow, you'll be able or even willing to talk to me."

There was no answer from the bed.

With a sigh, the Mother Superior turned off the light and closed the door. Sister Theresa waited for her outside.

"Well? How is she?"

"The same as usual. Never, in all my career, have I ever experienced such a barrier of communication with one of the sisters of the faith. I cannot allow such an impasse to continue. In the morning, I plan to see Father Bennett about this. Hopefully, he'll be able to do something. Good night, Sister Theresa."

"Good night, Mother Superior."

Sister Theresa watched the Mother Superior walk down the hall to her own room. She shook her head and then went to bed.

That next morning after breakfast, the Mother Superior left for the chapel. Her mind was concerned with what she was going to tell Father Bennett about what had happened the night before. When she reached the chapel, she went directly to Father Bennett's study and meditation room. She had seen Sister Marcia's sudden mood fluctuations and the ordeal that she had gone through the previous night had convinced her that the distraught nun needed help. It was with a sense of urgency that she knocked on his door.

"Come in," he called.

The Mother Superior opened the door and entered the study.

Father Bennett rose to his feet when he saw who his visitor was.

Before he could say anything, she volunteered the latest information."I came to you the other morning concerning the matter of Sister Marcia. If you want my personal opinion, I think the whole situation has gotten out of hand. She needs help."

Father Bennett studied her concerned face.

"Sit down, Mother Superior," he said indicating a chair.

The Mother Superior sat down and waited until Father Bennett had seated himself.

"What seems to be the problem now? Is she still having these dreams?"

"Last night, I happened to find her outside covered with mud in the thunderstorm and she was shouting out loud while evidently in her sleep. She must have experienced some type of somnambulistic trance. The intensity of her experience must have compelled her to cover herself with mud. When I got her inside, she again refused to tell me what had happened and simply said that she wanted to be alone. Then today at breakfast, she was almost totally despondent. It's as if she has gone from one extreme to the other. Something like a manic-depressive psychosis. We need to do something. I'm extremely concerned at this point."

While listening to the Mother Superior's story, Father Bennett began frowning. His eyes never left her face while she was relating what had happened the night before. After the Mother Superior finished, he looked at her sharply.

"Did anyone else see her last night?" he asked leaning forward, his eyes never leaving her face. He put his arms on the mahogany desk in front of him.

"Almost all the sisters were awake when I brought her in from the rain, but none of them asked anything. I have not tried to explain anything to them because I really don't know what to say. And Sister Marcia explains nothing. It's very frustrating, Father Bennett. I try to help her but she won't let me."

Father Bennett rose from his chair, stroking his beard thoughtfully.

"Have her come to me at once. She needs some counseling. I don't wish to make this seem like a forced confession. Whatever is tormenting her is getting the upper hand. She is a very strong willed individual and somehow you are going to have to convince her that some spiritual counseling is in her best interest. Most importantly, she must confide in me. That's imperative. She must not be coerced into talking to me about what is troubling her. I believe that I am the best-qualified person in the clergy to handle this matter. Not that you are incapable of handling this, but evidently she seems to be unwilling to confide in you. What we need to do is join forces to pull her out of this predicament before the other sisters are affected by her more than they already have been."

Father Bennett stopped before the Mother Superior, placing his hand on the distraught woman's shoulder in a gesture of sympathy. She looked up into his kindly yet austere face and smiled. She had succeeded in convincing him of the danger signals of Sister Marcia's possible psychosis. She felt that a weight had been lifted from her shoulders. It wouldn't be easy to convince Sister Marcia to talk to the priest.

"I trust that the Lord will give me the right words to say to her and that she will see the light of the truth. As long as she is under our protection, I'm convinced that she will get well and go about her duties with a new sense of vitality. On the other hand, if she does not improve then I feel that it is in her and our best interest to relieve her of her duties and responsibilities as a nurse."

The Mother Superior looked at Father Bennett as she uttered those words to gauge his reactions to her, words."Are you trying to suggest that if she does not improve that she leave the convent?" Father Bennett asked.

"No... not at all," the Mother Superior said a little flustered by his question." I am just trying to say that during this period of her instability that she be relieved of her duties in order to come to terms with her problem. It is a period of readjustment. That's all that I meant."

"Yes, I see what you mean," he said quietly." At this point, everything is in God's hands. What is meant to happen will happen regardless of any human intervention. We both need to pray about this matter."

"I shall pray mightily that I can convince Sister Marcia to see you, Father."

"We shall both pray for that, Mother Superior," he said, smiling at her.

"Thank you for seeing me, Father," she said quietly.

"I am never too busy to see you, Mother Superior. I am concerned for all of my flock and if one member is disturbed, then I will put aside everything to help bring that member back to the path of righteousness. Your concern for your charges is admirable."

The Mother Superior flushed with pleasure at his words.

"I am sincerely concerned with the sisters' welfare, both physical and emotional," she said. She fingered her rosary beads with her blunt, stubby fingers.

"I have taken up too much of your time, Father. Now I must return to the convent and find Sister Marcia," she said as she rose from her chair.

"Yes, please send her to me as soon as possible," he said as he walked her to the door.

"I will try. But it will not be easy."

"Do your best."

"I will try, Father. Goodbye."

"Goodbye."

The Mother Superior left Father Bennett's study and walked back to the convent. When she reached her own study, she fell on her knees and lifted her eyes to the crucifix on the wall.

"Sweet Lord," she began," please help me find the words to convince Sister Marcia to see Father Bennett. She is in need of help. The very plight of her soul is in jeopardy, Sweet Jesus. Help her to see her plight before it is too late for her. Guide my tongue and my actions, Jesus, to make her realize the path that lies before her. With Your Divine guidance, she can be saved. Amen."

The Mother Superior crossed herself before rising. She felt that a great weight had been lifted from her shoulders and that she had the confidence to persuade Sister Marcia to see Father Bennett and tell him what was troubling her.

She walked over to the window and looked out in the garden. She saw Sister Marcia in the garden and left her study to talk to the young nun.

Walking very slowly up the garden path as if she was still in a trance, Sister Marcia suddenly stopped. She could hear someone approaching her from behind. Listening for a moment, she knew from that particular heavy walk that it was the Mother Superior. She was in no mood for conversation and had not acknowledged anyone's presence that morning in an attempt to avoid any type of interaction. Now, her only solace had been interrupted.

She turned to face the Mother Superior."How are you, my child?" the Mother Superior asked as she stopped before Sister Marcia.

Sister Marcia stared straight ahead, not acknowledging the Mother Superior's presence.

The Mother Superior sighed.

"This is not going to be easy," she thought looking at Sister Marcia." Look how tense she is as if she's expecting to do battle with me. Why can't she see that I only want to help her?"

There was a long silence.

"I have been to see Father Bennett about you and we are both in agreement that you need some spiritual guidance at this point... some counseling. I cannot seem to reach you, but I hope that he can."

The Mother Superior looked at Sister Marcia trying to determine whether her words were having any effect on the young nun. She saw the stony look on her face and the faraway look in her eyes. She knew she had to get through to her.

"I prayed about the matter," the Mother Superior continued," and I feel in my heart that you must go to him with your burden. He has helped other sisters in the past and while your problem is somewhat unique, I do feel that dreams or visions, if you wish, are within the field of his expertise. How do you feel about going to him?"

Sister Marcia looked at the Mother Superior as if seeing her for the first time. She noted the concerned expression on her face and the beseeching look in her troubled eyes.

"I... I am confused... very confused," she said in almost a whisper." If you feel that it is right then maybe I should go to see him. What else is there to do?"

"You must feel that it is right to see him. It really doesn't matter what I think. Let your heart speak, child and there you will find the answer."

Sister Marcia lowered her head, looking down at the ground at her feet. She seemed to be considering what the Mother Superior had said. She was listening to her heart speak to her. The Mother Superior gently lifted Sister Marcia's chin, smiling at her.

"There, that's more like it. Listen to your heart for it will not lead you astray, child."

"I... I do feel that the time has come to make a confession. I have deliberated about this since last night. I have prayed for guidance. I had already decided to see Father Bennett before you came out here. But please do not feel that your efforts to get through to me have been in vain. I have been through a lot and I am very confused about all of this," Sister Marcia said.

Now that the ice seemed to have been broken between them, the Mother Superior reached out to embrace Sister Marcia, confiding in her.

"Listen, my child, we have both been through a lot and the time has come to seek an answer to all of this. Trust in the Lord with all your heart and you will find the answer. He is the beacon in the heart of darkness and the true key to your salvation during any time of crisis. I am optimistic that you will find the answer. You should be also."

The two women embraced again. This time the feeling seemed more mutual, yet the Mother Superior still sensed a dark cloud hovering above Sister Marcia as her depression was still apparent to her.

"It is almost time for lunch. Why don't you join me? Sometimes, being alone is not the best idea. Being alone can only make you brood on what is troubling you. You need to be with the others and not be so into yourself, especially at this time.""Yes, you are right. I have been alone too much. I will join you for lunch, Mother Superior," Sister Marcia said, smiling at the older woman.

"That's wonderful, my child. Come, let us go in and give thanks to the Lord," the Mother Superior said, taking Sister Marcia's arm as if she were afraid that the young nun was going to run away and hide from her.

Sister Marcia wasn't very hungry, but she felt that what the Mother

Superior was doing on her behalf obligated her to be as cordial to the older woman as she could. The words that the older woman had spoken to her were beginning to chase away the dark clouds that were in the background of her mind. Growing up, she never had a father whom she could confide in. Her parents died in a car wreck when she was an infant and she and her sister had been raised by her grandmother. Had the time come for her to bare her soul to Father Bennett? After all, she had made this pact with herself not to reveal the contents of her dreams to anyone, yet her dreams in a way cancelled each other out and left her in a state of confusion. The time had come for her to completely humble herself to Father Bennett, however would she be under his jurisdiction from that point on? She still had her doubts, but she would have to make the most difficult decision of her life. She would have to placc hcrsclf in his hands. She was hoping that somehow her confusion would disappear if she turned herself over to him. She felt that she was at a crossroads not knowing which way to turn. For the first time in her life, she was unsure of herself. She was seeking something, some direction. Until her dreams, she had known where she was going. Now, she was unsure of herself. She was beginning to feel like a leaf on water, being carried away with no volition of her own. This feeling frightened her. She felt that she had to regain charge of her life again. She knew that people needed the help of others from time to time and she needed help now. She had prayed but it seemed that her prayers had been useless. The Mother Superior had thrown her a lifeline and like a person drowning, she grasped it with all the desperation in her troubled soul. She felt that she had run out of options and out of time. For that very reason, she hoped that the Father would provide the insight that she seemed to be lacking.

At lunch, Sister Marcia picked at her food. From time to time, the Mother Superior glanced at her, but said nothing. All around Sister Marcia the other nuns were talking. To her, their voices seemed to comprise a babble that was like listening to the sea in a seashell, yet without the soothing effect. She felt on edge and wished to leave the table to be by herself, yet she knew that would worry the Mother Superior. She stayed where she was, listening to the conversations around her without being a part of it.

Lunch was finished and the nuns sat there waiting for the Mother

Superior to give out the afternoon's assignments. After the assignments had been given out and the table cleared, the nuns left the dining room to carry out their assigned tasks.

Sister Marcia rose to leave, but the Mother Superior laid her hand on the young nun's arm.

"I noticed that you didn't eat much, child. Everything will work out for you. Be of good cheer and let God guide your steps as He guides all our steps," the Mother Superior said gently.

Sister Marcia nodded, not trusting herself to speak at that moment.

"Go, my child," the Mother Superior said.

Sister Marcia left the dining room and went to do her assigned chores. The Mother Superior watched her go. She hoped that Father Bennett could help Sister Marcia.

Sunday came. Sister Marcia had decided to wait until that day and to go see Father Bennett after the mass. Now, kneeling in the pews as the choir sang Ave Maria, Sister Marcia crossed herself and waited her turn to partake of Communion. Slowly, Father Bennett came up the aisle of the great church, stopping here and there at each person to offer them Communion. As he approached her, there was a stern look on his face. He offered her Communion and whispered sternly:" Come see me after the service is over!"

She nodded her assent.

She waited with impatience and dread for the service to be over. Finally, after what seemed to be an eternity, the service was over. She saw Father Bennett walk to the confessional and enter.

"That would be as good a place as any to talk to him," she whispered nervously to herself. She watched the throngs as they approached the confessional, hoping to receive absolution for their sins.

Finally, the crowds dispersed and a very nervous Sister Marcia approached the confessional. The confessional stood in the back of the church. It was a wooden box like two dressing rooms side by side. The left door was for the priest to enter while the right was for the penitent to enter.

With slow steps, Sister Marcia reached the confessional and her hands trembled as she grasped the handle of the door on the right side.

She opened it and entered. The dim lighting, the closed panel in the wall that led to the priest on the other side, didn't make her feel any less nervous or distraught. Ever since she had talked to the Mother Superior and had decided to go see Father Bennett, she had wrestled with this feeling that had such a strong grip on her; that feeling that had led her into the storm. While the physical storm was gone, the storm inside raged on. It was time to quiet that storm. And so she went into the confessional that Sunday morning to seek guidance from the one person she hoped could dispel the emotional confusion and show her the path that would lead her back to what she had been before that second dream.

Sister Marcia seated herself on the bench and with a trembling hand, slid the panel open. On the other side was Father Bennett, waiting for her.

It seemed that they had nothing in common. He was an intellectual. She had often heard him discussing some abstract concept or another that she couldn't grasp. The only thing that they had in common was their religion. She hoped, as she sat there in the confessional looking at Father Bennett on the other side of the partition, that he could help her solve her dilemma. She had no place else to turn; there was no one else to turn to except for him."Father... I am Sister Marcia... I... I come... to you... in my hour of need... I am very confused and have turned to you," she said, her voice barely discernible even in her own ears. She looked down at her hands that were twisting the folds of her habit nervously. She had forgotten what every penitent said upon entering the confessional:" Forgive me Father for I have sinned." She had forgotten that in her distress, not noticing Father Bennett's frown at that omission. She was having a hard time talking. Her throat felt constricted as if she couldn't get the words out. Her mind was running in a circle and she couldn't seem to get her thoughts straight in her own mind. Her heart was beating rapidly, the sound of it in her ears sounded like drums beating an erratic rhythm. Her palms felt sweaty and she was beginning to perspire with a cold sweat. She was trying desperately to keep her emotions in check; trying to focus on what she was saying and talk to the priest on the other side of the partition.

Taking a deep breath to calm herself, she continued:" I really don't know what else to do at this point... It's as if I am betraying myself..."

Her voice trailed off into a piteous whisper.

"What do you mean, my child, that you are betraying yourself?" Father Bennett asked, trying to sound calm and gentle to the emotional young nun on the other side of the partition.

There was a pause that seemed to stretch into eternity as Sister Marcia tried to bring her emotions under control. Her fingers continued twisting the folds of her habit and came in contact with her rosary beads. Usually, the rosary beads helped to calm her and give her focus, but the beads which usually did it's work like a charm failed to calm the emotional storm that had swept over her.

"Take a few deep breaths and calm yourself," he commanded her gently.

She took a few deep breaths. One... two... three. She was beginning to feel a little calmer. She was aware that he was waiting for her to answer the question that he had asked her.

Lifting her head, she turned towards the face on the other side of the partition.

"I made an oath to myself that I would not tell anyone about my first dream because I felt that it was special... that this was the culmination of my life in a way.... Now, I have had a second dream and while the first dream was an exaltation to divine honor, the second dream was more temporal... I realized my true limitations... I... I am having a difficult time expressing myself... When I am depressed, it is very hard for me to think in abstract terms..."

From the other side of the partition, Father Bennett saw her head lower. He tried to be calm and gentle to help her in her evident distress. He was careful in the way he chose his words to try to help her gain her composure.

"My child, it seems to me that you are doing quite well despite the circumstances. Please continue. Tell me about your first dream."

Sister Marcia lifted her head and again looked at the priest through the wire screen that separated them.

"Father, this particular dream was proof positive that I had crossed over the threshold to a loving embrace... the whispers of eternity engulfed me in a loving embrace... I was the virgin sacrifice and the voluntary gift of my soul allowed the sun to continue its mighty course... the gods acknowledged this... I was chosen because I was chaste and had lived the perfect moral life..."

Again her voice trailed off. Father Bennett paused for a moment, choosing his words carefully.

"I can understand why such a dream would elicit such strong euphoric emotions from you, but why did you see it as the apex of your life even though the pagan content of your dream is anathema to what you believe as a devout sister of the faith?"

Sister Marcia's stammer seemed to indicate that the question increased her nervousness and her despair seemed to become more evident in the confines of the confessional.

"S-Sometiime... Sometime, when I feel that the time is right, I will shed more light on the sacrificial dream as I have only skimmed the surface of it's true relevance for me. I am still a Christian and always have been. I.. uh.. I feel so empty now... I have only you to turn to... My second dream was kind of a nightmare and more time-oriented than the first..."Father Bennett wanted to pursue an earlier statement that she had made, but decided to leave it for the time being.

"What happened in this second dream to cause you to undergo such a change from extreme elation to a dark depression?"

"I found myself in a forest and came upon an unusually large tree. Upon the tree hung the mask of Dionysus and I somehow knew that it belonged to me. As soon as I retrieved the mask, the storm became more violent and I could sense animals following me. I vividly remember this dream... I came upon a cave beneath an overhanging cliff... Somehow, I climbed down into the cave and came upon four shepherds seated by a fire. They had literally wasted away for the gods as if they had maintained some type of vigil by the fire for years...The oldest and the wisest shepherd noticed that I had the mask and... and he mentioned that each one of them was preparing a place of shelter for a guest over whom they had no authority. The guest was Dionysus and the oldest and wisest shepard said to me that he would come as a thief in the night. I began looking into the fire and could see a child at play. The shepherd made some type of esoteric comment about the child, which I cannot remember and then he finally disappeared... the child disappeared and I never felt so alone... Let's see... I got up to leave, I think and the shepherd told me that I had to return the mask to

Dionysus... that to do so would be like the first day of creation... but, I had to know the secret of the earth in order to find the god... I was perplexed and went back into the storm..."

Again the silence as Father Bennett digested what he had just heard.

"And what, may I ask, is your interpretation of all this?" he asked quietly.

Sister Marcia paused to gather her thoughts and then, speaking very succinctly, offered her own analysis:

"The revelation of being is a gift and that is why I was faced with the burden of returning the mask to Dionysus. It's as if our entire essence is staked on the eventual outcome of the portentous game of being or if you will the inscrutable play of a child. There is no promise of divine consolation as there was in my first dream. They spoke of waiting for the advent of a New Dawn when once again we would look upon all creation in its pristine glory. To totally submit myself to this mystery is a high and dangerous game as the kingdom may, indeed, be in the hands of a child. It's ominous... if there any validity to what I say, but I do take serious stock in this dream and I have nothing more to say..."

It seemed that Sister Marcia had ended her analysis on a note of defiance.

"You have nothing more to say? This is very interesting," Father Bennett said and paused before he continued:" Your analysis could be an ontological proof that there is a dialectic of freedom. Either the soul must become what it is or it cannot become what it is as we are dependent on this 'game of being' as you call it."

Sister Marcia decided to interject one last comment as a problematic to be investigated as to the dream's apparent message.

"What about the possibilities of a New Dawn? What if being shows a new face? Will we all see each other as we really are? Fallen? We will not be able to return to our routines because we will be ashamed. The normal man will have nothing to fall back on because of his inauthenticity. Only the truly spiritual man will stand firm and welcome the New Dawn and look once again upon all creation in it's pristine glory."Father Bennett presented the orthodox Catholic view with extreme optimism as he raised his voice as if sheer volume alone could counter any unorthodox arguments.

"What you consider to be the advent of the New Dawn is the same event as the parousia or the Second Coming of Christ. The resurrection and ascension of Christ and the sending of the Holy Spirit are the beginning of a process already irreversible, in which the history of salvation, mankind's and the individual's, goes on and comes to an end and fulfillment in what Scripture calls the parousia. It will be the final consummation of the world time and will involve individual eschatology and cosmic eschatology. The resurrection of the flesh, in which we will have our glorified bodies once again, will be the consummation of man as a social being in his uniqueness. The consummation of the individual as his own very self is a moment in the history of the cosmos. There is some ambiguity here between what is meant by individual and cosmic eschatology. To me, the day of Christ's judgment will be an act of love and He will fetch home all, who will let themselves be fetched back home. Even though the nature of the parousia has been formulated in abstract terms, it will have a concrete form of being and at present escapes our understanding. The hour of this parousia cannot be reckoned beforehand, as he will come like a thief in the night. While I agree with you that we are living in an age of darkness in which we are almost at the mercy of the technological world that we've created, when Christ comes again, those who believe will have their glorified bodies again and will ascend to Heaven."

Sister Marcia, instead of being comforted and gaining insight from Father Bennett's words, felt more confused than when she had first entered the confessional. She felt that she had to try again to let him know what she was feeling, the growing desperation that washed over her like a dark tide.

"Father... all I can say is that the disparity between these two dreams has left me very confused... I feel that I'm adrift in a hostile sea... I cannot see the farther shore... Please help me to resolve this... dilemma that I find myself in," she pleaded almost piteously.

"My child, what you need is an exit from your own personal labyrinth," he said with as much sympathy as he could muster.

"What do you mean, Father?" Sister Marcia asked even more confused."Soren Kierkegaard was a prisoner of his own personal labyrinth and the victim of a tortured consciousness. He took solace in the Christian faith and he was innovative to the extent that he summarized the basic tenets of Christian thought in what he called 'The Moment' and 'The Paradox'. The Moment is nothing more than the 'second birth' that most believers in the faith have experienced in one way or another. His contention was that the whole of Christianity was based upon the Moment. In other words, if the Moment does not exist, than we remain at the Socratic standpoint. Socrates felt that each moment was important or equally unimportant if you wish. Kierkegaard, on the other hand, envisioned the Moment of the 'second birth' as a historical point of departure from this undifferentiated temporal continuum. More importantly, this had a true significance for the believer. The Paradox is the existence of God in time, which confounds our reason. Only by faith can we access the fact of the Incarnation and this key event proved to be the occasion for all future Moments. In other words, God entered into time in the person of Jesus Christ, but he also enters into time every moment when an individual sets aside his reason in confrontation with the Paradox, which leads to faith. Thus, the 'second birth' is a miracle of sudden transformation. It is a crossing over the threshold into the boundaries of the marvelous. We are never the same again from that point on because our prior life up to the Moment was lived as a lie or what you might mean by inauthenticity."

Sister Marcia, feeling a sudden lapse of mental fatigue as well as even more confusion, decided to ask on last question. She was hoping that Father Bennett's answer would sweep away her confusion and solve her dilemma.

"Is this the same thing as the sudden intervention of divine truth that Saint John of the Cross experienced during the Dark Night of the Soul?"

"Yes, my child, it is. When all hope seems to have vanished and one is on the verge of total despair, Truth comes like a divine radiance and this is the true healing factor for any troubled soul. It seems to me that you may be on the verge of such an experience. You must be patient and wait on the Lord and trust Him with all your heart and soul."

"All I can do, Father, is to totally submit to His will and mercy. My life is in His hands because my confusion and despair has made me blind."

Father Bennett paused for a moment to seriously consider what Sister Marcia had confessed to him.

"I cannot, in all sincerity, agree with you that your confusion and despair has made you blind. There is no doubt that you had two very interesting dreams. It is debatable, depending on whether one has a Freudian or a Jungian orientation, as to the true symbolic significance of the content of your dreams and what it all means from a psychological standpoint. What concerns me is that you seem to approach such phenomena from a spiritual standpoint. I ask you again, the pagan content of your two dreams... should not this be in direct opposition to what you believe as a Christian? You speak of gods. What do you mean by 'gods'?"

Sister Marcia was beginning to feel more withdrawn and her voice was barely audible as she answered Father Bennett's last question.

"To me, the gods are just simply metaphors for the supernatural forces of nature... what you probably consider as demons..."

"Then why call them gods?" Father Bennett demanded." The early history of Christianity was an ongoing struggle with polytheism. The revitalization of the Roman Empire was no easy task. At this point, I am very concerned about your own spiritual evolution. Let me ask you this: Do you believe in your dreams?"

"I... I just don't know," Sister Marcia whispered." All I can say is that I have never had two dreams like these before... I don't *know* what's going on inside of me and that is why I simply want to surrender myself to God and maybe He, in His infinite mercy, will show me the answer to my dilemma... a direction for I feel right now that I have no direction..."

"My child, I am in total agreement with you and if you feel the need, we can pray about this matter. Or if you wish to pray about this alone, I can understand. After all, this is a matter between you and God. I am always available if you need to talk to me further about this matter or for any other thing that troubles you."

"Thank you, Father. I appreciate your concern and I feel that I must pray alone for guidance. This is a personal matter between God and me. May I be excused?"

"Please promise me one thing..."

"Yes, Father?"

"That you will not, under any circumstance, discuss your dreams with any other of the sisters of the faith. I feel that it would be detrimental to their spiritual welfare. Have I your promise on this matter?"

"Yes, Father, I promise that I will not talk about my dreams to the other sisters. May I go now?" Sister Marcia asked, feeling even more bewildered than when she had entered the confessional. It seemed like an eternity since she had begun her confession to Father Bennett. She needed to be alone to sort out all that had been said and to pray.

"Go, my child and may the Lord be with you in your hour of need."

"Thank you, Father."

Sister Marcia got up from the bench in the confessional and left. She walked to the meditation room where she hoped that she could be alone.

What she had hoped to find from talking to Father Bennett had not occurred. Instead of feeling better, she felt worse. She had hoped that he would be able to provide some insight that she was lacking to explain the meanings of these two dreams; that, somehow, he would shine a light to dispel the darkness. But instead of the light, she still felt that she was engulfed in the darkness. He had given her nothing concrete, nothing that she, in her despair, could grab hold of and cling to. All he had to offer was the same Christian platitudes with a more intellectual spin. She had heard of Kierkegaard, but she really didn't understand how his philosophy and his writings had any bearing on her problem. What did it all matter? Where was the hope, the consolation, the direction she was seeking? She couldn't understand anything that he had said directly had any bearing on her problem and its solution.

She entered the meditation room and was thankful that she would be alone to wrestle with her problem.

She fell on her knees and crossed herself.

"Oh, Heavenly Father, show me the way. I feel adrift and need Your Divine guidance to steer me back to where I belong. Sweet Jesus, engulf me in the warmth and light of Your love. Comfort me, Lord, take this pain from me and let me see again, for I am blind. Without You, I am lost forever. Have mercy, I beseech you. Look down on me, Lord and reach down Your hand and lift me from this abyss that I seem to have fallen into. I have tried to live a chaste and moral life, Sweet

Lord. I have tried, with all my might, to be guided by Your words and Your life. I have wanted to be Your bride and to look upon Your sweet beloved face filled with compassion for those who suffer. I am suffering now, my Sweet Lord. Show me Your compassion. Show me Your love. Lift me up, my precious Lord so that I may rededicate myself to Your service. Help me Lord to know you better. Again I beseech you."

Sister Marcia, her eyes raised towards the heavens, was rocking back and forth on her knees unaware of any discomfort. Her whole being was focused on her prayer. She hoped that if she prayed with all her heart and soul, then her prayers would be answered and she would feel the dark curtain in her mind lifted and the pure light would shine through. This was her fervent prayer. In her desperation, she would do anything to gain release from the dilemma that had her in its grasp. She wanted the constricting bands that seemed to be squeezing her tightly to be unloosened. She wanted the release from her despair.Sister Marcia finished her prayer. She felt emotionally drained. Slowly, she lowered her eyes until they rested on the floor that she was kneeling on and a sob escaped her. She prostrated herself on the floor and lay there. She seemed unaware of the passing of time. She was locked into her own psyche and the struggle she was engaged in to escape the dark and walk in the light.

She had hoped to find a surrogate father whose wisdom would banish the darkness that she found herself in; that he would comfort her like a child awakening from a nightmare. But instead, she didn't find what she had been so desperately seeking. All she found was piousness. She didn't need piousness; she needed answers that would shed light on her dilemma. There had been no answers. Instead, there was only more confusion that further fueled her despair.

How long she lay there in the mediation room, she didn't know. She was waiting for the answer to her prayers. Finally, she rose and returned to her room. She didn't feel any better. She hadn't found the answers and the true solace that she needed.

She didn't go down to dinner that night. An anxious Mother Superior tried to get her to come and have something to eat, but she refused. All night, she sat in the darkness, not only the physical darkness but also the metaphorical darkness of her soul.

Sister Marcia was late for breakfast the next morning. She hadn't slept well the night before. There were dark circles under her eyes. She sat down at the only place available next to a nun named Sister Mitchell. There seemed to be an air of excitement as the nuns conversed with each other.

"What are you all talking about this morning?" Sister Marcia asked.

"Are you going to the lecture this afternoon?" Sister Mitchell asked.

There was a murmur of affirmatives from the other nuns. Sister Marcia couldn't help over hearing.

"What lecture?" she asked.

Sister Mitchell turned to her.

"You must be very myopic not to know of the lecture that Father Reynolds is giving this afternoon. It's been on the bulletin board for almost a month now. Don't tell me that you haven't seen it?"

Sister Marcia shook her head. That comment by Sister Mitchell about her being myopic had really stung her. Maybe she had been myopic. Sometimes, it was hard to see yourself as others see you. The truth can hurt sometimes. She didn't care for Sister Mitchell anymore than Sister Mitchell cared for her. Sister Mitchell was an arch feminist, however Sister Marcia respected her for her intelligence. She wanted to know what this lecture was all about.

"I'm sorry. I didn't see it. Can you tell me what the lecture is about?" she asked.

Sister Mitchell gave her a look that said go read it for yourself. Then she relented.

"The lecture is called Zazen and the Art of Meditation. You do know what that is, don't you?" Sister Mitchell asked in a condescending voice.

"No, I am afraid that I don't. Tell me who is giving this lecture," Sister Marcia said trying to elicit an answer from Sister Mitchell.

"Like I just said, Father Reynolds. After returning from his yearlong sabbatical in Japan, he is going to give a lecture this afternoon on zazen and Christian meditation. From what I understand, zazen can be used as a tool to deepen one's understanding of God. " Sister Mitchell said, looking around at her listeners.

Sister Marcia's interest was piqued. What is was, she couldn't say. She was very anxious to hear more about this particular priest and his experiences in the Orient."What exactly happened to Father Reynolds in Japan?" Sister Marcia asked, trying to appear casual; to still the rising excitement she was beginning to feel.

Sister Mitchell turned to her.

"He went through what I would call an epistemological change or a change in his understanding of nature. I feel that he obtained enlightenment that is what we're all searching for. Zazen was the catalyst for this change. He's never been the same since," Sister Mitchell said as she finished her breakfast.

Sister Marcia suddenly felt an uplifting sensation for what Sister Mitchell had just told her was like a sudden breeze that had infiltrated her senses. There was, in the very atmosphere of the room, a sense of increasing excitement. It was catching up with her. She had to attend that lecture that afternoon. She felt that what Father Reynolds had to say might somehow offer her a new direction and the answer to her dilemma. She continued eating mechanically, her mind racing with possibilities.

"Are you going to Father Reynold's lecture this afternoon?" Sister Mitchell asked.

Looking up from her plate, Sister Marcia nodded.

"Good," Sister Mitchell said brusquely." Everyone in this convent should hear him speak. I, myself, have never heard him, but I have talked to those who have and they say that he's a brilliant speaker. He has such a way of explaining things that anyone can catch his meaning."

"Would you consider zazen?" Sister Marcia asked curiously.

Sister Mitchell looked at her in surprise.

"I really don't think it is any of your business," she snapped." What is a valid path for one may not apply to another and culture has a lot to do with this?"

There was an excited buzz around the table as the sisters finished their breakfast. The nuns filed out of the dining hall.

Sister Marcia went to see the bulletin board for herself. There, in the exact center of the board, read the notice:

FATHER MATTHEW REYNOLDS WILL GIVE A LECTURE ON ZAZEN AND THE ART OF MEDITATION YOU ARE

CORDIALLY INVITED TO COME OCTOBER 5TH AT ONE O'CLOCK AT THE AUDITORIUM

Sister Marcia read the notice. She must have really been in the throes of a depression not to have seen this. Here it was in black and white. A direction for her to follow. She felt an excitement begin to grow inside her. She would definitely be at that lecture. It would seem like an eternity before one o'clock came. But she knew she had to wait.

That afternoon, Sister Marcia got to the auditorium at twelve-thirty to be sure that she got a good seat. She found a seat in the front row and composed herself to wait the half-hour until the lecture began. Her mind was still in the throes of depression. She was hoping that this lecture would help her see the light at the end of the tunnel. Hope! That was what she was hoping for. Hope! Hope that she would find her direction. Desperation sometimes made a person grasp at straws to stave off a major depression. She was desperate to get out of the morass of her mind. If what Sister Mitchell had said was correct then what Father Reynolds was going to say would bring her back into the light.

Father Reynolds was young. His brown hair was neatly combed. His brown eyes behind his glasses had a benevolent look. He looked like any other priest wearing a black suit with the white collar, a crucifix hanging around his neck. He carried a portfolio that contained his notes. He entered the auditorium walking slowly down the aisle toward the podium. His smile encompassed the entire room. He nodded to his right and to his left, saying a murmured word here and there. Every eye in the room was fixed on him as he mounted the steps to the podium. He set his portfolio on the lectern and opened it. When he was satisfied that his notes were arranged in the proper order, he looked up, smiling.

"Good afternoon," he said in a light baritone voice." I'm very pleased to see the turnout for this lecture. Very pleased. I hope that I won't bore you into somnolence."

There was a ripple of laughter.

"Before we begin, let us pray together to get us in the proper frame of mind."

Everyone in the auditorium lowered their heads as Father Reynolds led them in prayer." Our Father in Heaven, we have come together for a spiritual purpose in learning the perennial wisdom that the Orient has to offer. We remain steadfast in our faith and only seek Your guidance when it comes to matters concerning the spirit. Throughout history, there have been certain ancient paths towards true spiritual enlightenment. Very few can attain to this experience of Heaven on Earth because we have been conditioned to respond to time in a linear fashion. To those, who experience enlightenment, the contingency of the Moment is what ultimately matters. We as Christians believe that one, who is saved by the Blood of the Lamb, is destined for eternal life. Therefore, we seek the pearls of wisdom that another culture has to offer... A path that leads ultimately to a more intimate relationship with You and more of a fellowship with man for we all seek the Truth of the Divine Light, which is Your infinite Love. What I have to offer may not apply to all Christians... It can only be used as a tool to gain further insight by looking within and discovering Your True Nature as the Divine Source from which we receive communion. Without communion, we wander like lost sheep in need of a Shepherd, who is Christ our Lord. Amen."

When the prayer was finished, the audience looked up expectantly.

Sister Marcia felt her heart beating faster as Father Reynolds started his lecture.

"The cultures of the Orient have been around longer than that of the West. They have developed a method of inner contemplation known as meditation. We, of course, also meditate. But in Asia, they have elevated the art of meditation to a fine art. Christian meditation is what I like to call 'acquired contemplation'. Zen, the ancient meditative techniques of Asia, can be an aid to Christian meditation. Zen focuses your mind, allowing it to transcend the earthly and concentrate solely on the spiritual. Now, in Christian meditation, we focus our mind upon some type of object for spiritual reflection, usually a passage from the Scriptures. Most of my colleagues in the clergy, who approve of this form of meditation, find it to be dualistic. That is because when we, as Christians, meditate, we invariably focus our thoughts on the life of our Savior, Jesus Christ. In Asia, they know of Jesus, but their form of meditation goes back at least a full thousand years before the birth of Christ."Father Reynolds paused, looking out at the audience. He noted that some had shocked expressions on their faces while others wore rapt expressions. It was to this latter group that he was aiming his lecture.

"Unfortunately," he continued," there is very little literature on object-less meditation or acquired contemplation. You have to literally resort to the writings of the various Christian mystics of the Middle Ages such as Hugh of Saint Victor, Meister Eckhart or John Tauler. I believe that the religious devotee cannot reach the deeper layers of the soul as long as he or she is engaged in discursive meditation. The Christian mystics were very sincere in their efforts to reach this ultimate ground of the soul or what they termed the 'naked godhead'. Certain precautions were taken before making the complete transition to object-less meditation. First and foremost, the practitioner had to have a very strong faith and should not attempt to limit the activities of reason and memory until he had meditated on and understood the contents of the Scriptures. What I am trying to say, is this: the basis before proceeding to object-less meditation is the revelation of the truth as contained in the Gospels."

Father Reynolds paused again to gauge the effects of words on his audience. He was very pleased that no one had walked out on him muttering that he was a heretic. He had a well-developed sense of humor. He noted that those who were hanging on his every word seemed to be on the edge of their seats wondering what effect his words were going to have on their lives. There was one nun that he noticed who seemed particularly fascinated by what he was saying.

"The merits of object-less meditation such as zazen, a very ancient meditative technique, are that essentially the person engaged in this form of meditation arrives at a much deeper understanding of the Christian God. I have found from personal experience that using zazen has helped me to occasionally, not all the time, to grasp the meaning of a religious truth or a particular passage of Scripture as I have never grasped it before. I feel that there must be a need to counterbalance the undermining rationalism that has corroded religious thought. Thus, there is the need, an inherent need, I might add, for some type of spiritual alternative. The practice of zazen within the context of the Christian faith is a viable option.

"In conclusion, I strongly believe that the study of theology without meditation on what you studied, poses grave dangers for today's young people. Discursive thought should be complimented by intuition. Only then is one able to grasp the whole truth.

"Thank you for you rapt attention. I hope that I didn't bore you. And I thank you for not falling asleep during this lecture. May God hold you in His hand."

There was applause.

Father Reynolds glanced at the young nun that he had noticed hanging raptly to every word. She looked as if she had been struck by a bolt of lightning.

Sister Marcia had, indeed, been struck in a manner of speaking, by a bolt of lightning. She had hung on every single word that Father Reynolds had spoken as if they were the Gospels. What he had said had struck her and a light bulb had gone off in her mind. She had found the answer she had been so desperately seeking. She had to speak to him. There was more that she had to know, so much more. As everyone began to file out of the auditorium, she approached him, trying not to seem so desperate.

"Father Reynolds, may I speak to you?"

He looked at Sister Marcia, his entire manner kindly and benevolent.

"Of course, my child," he said."

I'm Sister Marcia," she said, introducing herself.

"I'm very pleased to meet you, Sister. What did you think of my little lecture?'

"It was the most inspiring thing that I believe I ever heard. It was very insightful and I agree that anyone studying theology needs to practice some form of meditation to come to a deeper understanding of Scriptural truth. Your lecture has given me a new direction. I believe that I need to try this form of meditation that you spoke of, but my question is this... How many sisters of the faith are now involved in zen in some way or another?"

Father Reynolds smiled at her. His words of encouragement sounded like music to Sister Marcia's ears.

"There have been quite a few sisters of the faith in the past decade, especially from northern California who have benefited from undertaking the practice of zazen. However, no one from your convent has taken the initiative as yet. Why don't you be the first to establish such a precedent?"

Sister Marcia found it hard to contain the growing excitement that she felt at Father Reynolds' words.

"How do I go about this? Whom do I talk to about wanting to go to Japan?" she asked eagerly like a schoolgirl.

"First of all, I would share my interest with your own Mother Superior and Father. If either of them has any questions, tell them to contact me. They know where they can reach me. The next step will be a review of your request by the bishop, as the church will have to sponsor you if you go. Good luck and may the Lord help in you in your decision."

"Thank you, Father."

"You're quiet welcome, my child. Now if you'll excuse me, I really must go."

"Certainly. I'm sorry for taking your time, Father."

"Not at all. I enjoyed talking to you. I hope that you go. I believe that the study of zazen will enrich your spiritual life like it has mine."

"I certainly hope so, too, Father."

"Goodbye."

"Goodbye ", said Father Reynolds in an affirmative tone.

Sister Marcia watched Father Reynolds walk up the aisle of the auditorium. She felt the excitement rising in her until she was unable to contain it. Without a doubt, this young priest had offered her the direction that she needed at this critical juncture in her life. She hurried out of the auditorium. The first person that she saw was the Mother Superior going to the chapel.

"Mother Superior!" Sister Marcia called.

The Mother Superior stopped and turned around, watching Sister Marcia approaching rapidly.

"Yes, my child?"

"I have something that I wish to share with you... something marvelous, wonderful!"

"You seem to be overly excited, child."

"Oh, Mother Superior were you at the lecture? Did you hear Father Reynolds speak?"

The Mother Superior shook her head.

"His lecture was an inspiration, a message that seemed directed solely to me," Sister Marcia said, speaking rapidly.

"Slow down, child. Yes, I can see that you are very excited. Just calm down and tell me just what this message was that has you so excited."

"I think that I have found the solution to my dilemma, one that will help me to achieve the greatest discipline. What I heard this afternoon gave me the impetus to continue with my life and my responsibilities as a sister of the faith. I am going to propose to Father Bennett that I be given permission to take up the practice of zen for at least one year until I am spiritually prepared to return to the convent and resume my duties."

The Mother Superior was a bit taken aback by what Sister Marcia had just proposed to her. She took her time to respond.

"I don't know what to say. To be honest with you, your decision doesn't really surprise me all that much. I know that you have been searching for a direction. I agree that you need to talk to Father Bennett about this matter. I think that you will probably be the first sister of the faith to ever try this form of meditation should the church sanction it."

"I spoke with Father Reynolds after the lecture. He told me that quite a few sisters of the faith have practiced zen in the past decade, especially from northern California."

"Well, all I can say is that there is a much more liberal attitude which prevails in that part of the country. I am sure that you will follow through on this latest quest of yours. Remember, though, whatever Father Bennett decides, you will abide by that decision. If you don't, you must leave the convent and become a woman of the world. May our Lord be with you."

The Mother Superior quickly turned and walked in the opposite direction. Sister Marcia watched her go. She couldn't contain her excitement. The light that she had been searching for had exploded in her brain and the feeling suffused her with a peace and excitement that she had never known before. She could hardly stand still. She felt like running. She felt like singing joyful hosannas to the Lord for sending Father Reynolds to her in her time of extreme need. Now, she knew where she was going. She couldn't see why Father Bennett would be opposed to her going to Japan for a year to study zen if it made her faith stronger and helped her perform her duties better. No, she couldn't see that he would object to her request. When should she see him? Right away or wait? Her every impulse was to see him right away but that might seem too confrontational. She needed to reflect on this. She had to convince Father Bennett that her very soul was in need of this trip; of this chance to study zen."Nobody, not even Father Bennett, is going to deter me from the path that I am determined to go on," she said to herself as she walked along the corridors." I have to think of the right arguments to use to convince Father Bennett. Now is not the time to tell him. I'll wait. I just hope that he can see the benefits to be derived from my going to Japan. I'd be gone a whole year. I have seen the light. Now, I have to make Father Bennett see the same light. It's not going to be easy. But I know that I can do it. I have to do it. If Father Bennett has any doubts, Father Reynolds can dispel them. He might be the most important ally now that I have in my quest to go to Japan. I prayed for deliverance from the darkness in my soul and now it has come in the form of Father Reynolds and his lecture on zen. I know this is what I am meant to do. I know that going through this experience will make me a better person. Father Reynolds was very calm, very focused. I want to be that way. I want that serenity that he has. It's like he can see farther than others. That must be one of the many benefits to studying zen. This serenity, this focus. It is almost like being in total harmony with your surroundings and everyone around you. Maybe it is. I need to discover this for myself. Is that so wrong? I don't think that it is. I believe, truly believe, that I was meant to hear this lecture today and be so inspired by it, that I would go to Japan and learn what it is really all about. My prayers have been answered. Now, I must build my arguments logically, not emotionally to sway Father Bennett. He *must* see that it is for the best. For everyone. For me, for him, for the convent. Yes, everything will be alright. I feel it like it was preordained."

Sister Marcia found herself by the chapel. She went in. There was no one else in there. She approached the altar and crossed herself before sinking to her knees. She clasped her hands in front of her and with a radiant expression on her face, her eyes shining with the light of comprehension, she offered up, thanks to her savior.

"Thank you, dear God for showing me the path that You want me to take. Where once I groped about in the darkness too blind to see, You have shown me the light. Your tender mercy has reached into the very depths of my soul and illuminated it. I will strive in every way possible to be worthy of the gifts that You have bestowed on me this day. I am grateful to You for sending the answer to my most fervent prayers. May You never turn Your face from me. Amen."

Slowly, Sister Marcia lowered her hands and looked up into the compassionate face on the cross. She rose to her feet. She knew that she would be going to Japan. She knew that she would find the right words to convince Father Bennett. She had regained the confidence that she once had and she knew that nothing was going to stand in her way. Her Savior would make sure that she went and would return a much better person; more dedicated than ever before.

It was with a sense of euphoria that she left the chapel. Her feet hardly seemed to touch the ground. It matched the lightness in her heart.

Walking outside, she felt the invisible presence of her Savior. She felt uplifted and comforted. It was with this feeling that she entered the convent as the bell for dinner rang. She was happy and hungry.

After dinner she went to her room and pondered. She wondered if she was somehow a threat to the routine way of life in the convent now that she had decided to embark on a new way of life. Others might seem less tolerant, like the Mother Superior, of her decision. Time would tell. She decided that before seeing Father Bennett that she would read what she could find in the library on zen.

The next night, Sister Marcia went to the library located in downtown Marlborough. After entering the library, she went to the librarian.

"Good evening," she said.

The librarian, a gray-haired woman in her sixties, looked up and smiled.

"Good evening, Sister. Is there something that I can help you with?"

"Yes, I am looking for a book on Zen Buddhism," Sister Marcia said.

"Well, let's see what we have, shall we?"

The librarian came from behind her desk and they walked to a computer terminal. The librarian quickly typed in the words Zen Buddhism and entries appeared. The librarian quickly jotted down a few numbers.

"Come with me, Sister," she said with the piece of paper in her hand.Sister Marcia followed her towards the back of the library. The librarian led Sister Marcia right to the section on eastern religion. She quickly found what she was looking for.

"Here we are, Sister," she said, removing one of the books from the shelf.

She handed the book to Sister Marcia.

"Thank you," Sister Marcia said, taking the book. She looked at it and opened it.

"There are some tables and chairs by the window if you would like to sit down and be comfortable," the librarian said.

"Thank you very much," Sister Marcia said.

Carrying her book, Sister Marcia found the table and chairs that the librarian had told her about and sat down. She opened the book and began reading. Soon, she seemed lost in the pages of the book. She had never really seriously considered any other religions than her own. Now, with a book on a totally different religion before her, she became engrossed in the book.

She found that Zen Buddhism had started in A.D.500 and that it originated in China at that time. It was an amalgamation of Indian Buddhism of the northern provinces and Taoism. Reading further, she discovered what the aims were. That the adherents worked toward abrupt enlightenment striving for nirvana coupled with samsara. Zen masters transmitted to their pupils this enlightened state using a minimum of words. Scriptures and ritual forms are minimized while employing ritual meditation and physical labor. She also learned that this form of mediation crossed from China to Japan. That the Japanese embraced this new form of spirituality to go along with their samurai warrior code and that bushido derived from Zen. She also learned that certain martial arts forms like judo and jujitsu also were derived from Zen and its practices.

The book was very informative and gave her much to consider. The book had stated that anyone who wanted to learn this ancient form of meditation could do so. She very much wanted to learn it, to become enlightened as Father Reynolds had become. There were probably places in Boston where someone could learn about the art of Zen, but she wanted to go to Japan and learn under the auspices of a Zen master or roshi as she had learned that they were called. She closed the book and returned it to the shelf. She now had a pretty clear idea of how to approach Father Bennett, knowing what arguments to use in her behalf.

Sister Marcia left the library after saying good night to the librarian. She walked back to the convent reviewing in her mind what she had just read. When she talked to Father Bennett, she wanted to be well prepared to answer any questions that he might have. What she liked about this form of meditation was that anyone who wanted to practice it could. It wasn't specifically designed for one gender over the other. She was looking forward to going to Japan and learning about a different culture. She felt that the culture and the discipline were almost interchangeable. She felt that she was making the right decision; that there could be no other path for her to follow and stay within the confines of the church. But more importantly, was the chance to become an enlightened being. This ideal was what every person should attain to. This is what she wanted to attain to.

She entered the convent and without talking to anybody, went up to her room. She still was in the grip of the euphoria that she felt after Father Reynolds' lecture. She knew that she would never lose this feeling. Upon entering her room, she crossed herself and said a little prayer before going to bed. She decided that the next day, she was going to see Father Bennett. She turned off the light and went to sleep. The next afternoon, Sister Marcia went to see Father Bennett. She went to the rectory and was admitted to the priest's residence. She was shown to his study by the housekeeper. She knocked on the door.

"Come in," called Father Bennett from the other side of the door.

Sister Marcia opened the door and entered.

"Good afternoon, Father Bennett," she said, trying to dampen down her anticipation.

"Good afternoon, Sister Marcia. What do I owe this visit to?" Father Bennett asked, rising when Sister Marcia entered his study.

"I wanted to talk to you, Father," she said.

"Won't you have a seat?" Father Bennett asked, indicating a chair.

"Thank you, Father," she said as she seated herself in the chair that he had indicated.

After Sister Marcia was seated, Father Bennett seated himself behind his desk.

"I believe that you wanted to talk to me?" he asked.

"Yes, I do," she said." Father, I believe that I found another way which lies within the scope of Christian mysticism. Did you attend Father Reynolds' lecture the other afternoon?"

"No, unfortunately, I was tied up with some personal business that had priority. I heard that his lecture was very interesting. Did he influence you in some way?"

Sister Marcia paused, composing her thoughts.

"Father, what I heard the other day deeply fascinated me and I remember that the meditative way of zen can lead to a more virtuous life untarnished by sin. To pursue this, I would only do it in the context of my Christian faith and hopefully come to a much deeper understanding of my Lord and Savior. It is my wish to achieve this eastern form of discipline and when I feel that I am virtuous then I will return to the convent and continue with my duties as a sister of the faith."

Father Bennett looked at her for a moment.

"What exactly are you proposing?" he asked her.

"I am proposing that I be allowed to visit Japan for at least a year and take up the practice of zazen under the guidance of a roshi or zen master. I want the church to sponsor me."

"What do you mean by virtue?"

"The way of virtue that I propose is not the Confucian way of self-conscious and professional goodness, which is, in fact, a less pure form of virtue. Saint Thomas would have said that it works 'humano modo' rather than with the divine and mysterious spontaneity of the gifts of the Holy Ghost. What I really want is an element of supreme spontaneity, which is virtuous in a transcendent sense because it does not strive. More than anything, I seek a direct communion with reality."

Father Bennett was concerned with Sister Marcia's proposed option.

"I can tell that you have done some research on this topic, but I must express my concern. Have you given up your faith in the Lord, my child? We must wait on the Lord and not be impatient with Him. He works in mysterious ways..."

Sister Marcia interrupted."Listen, Father, I love the Lord with all my heart, but maybe for some reason I am being tested to see if I am worthy of His love. Maybe there will be some kind of atonement. I don't know. What am I waiting for? Was Job's ordeal any worse than mine? I wonder... How do we know that my attending the lecture the other afternoon was not one of His mysterious ways? I made a commitment to Christ before I entered the convent, but now I am choosing a path that has been misunderstood for centuries. Even though some of the great Christian mystics were accused of heresy by the church, they remained committed to the contemplative life, despite the many difficulties and even harassment by their peers. Have times really changed? Are those, who are willing to go against the consensus, still faced with the possibility of being ostracized by the community at large? All I ask of you is that you please do everything in your power to help me realize my quest and believe me when I confide in you about my faith."

Sister Marcia during her last remarks had risen from her chair and had begun pacing the room. She was filled with an energy that she couldn't contain. Father Bennett watched her, noticing her passion, her excitement. At the moment, it seemed almost like she had forgotten that he was in the room. He seemed to be wrestling with what she had said and what he thought was best for her.

Sister Marcia stopped before his desk and looked down at him.

"Father Reynolds can explain this so much better than I can. You can talk to him," Sister Marcia said.

"I don't need to talk to Father Reynolds. My child, if this is your wish then I will see what I can do to help you achieve your goal. I feel that as long as you keep your vows to the Lord in perspective, you are safe wherever you go. Let me talk to Bishop Everly on this matter and I will get back to you. As for the immediate future, keep reading your Bible and pray for strength and the right decision. I will pray also."

"Thank you, Father. I will do what you ask me to do."

"You're quite welcome. I wanted to see how well you thought all of this out, Sister. Sometimes, an idea grabs hold of our imagination and won't let go. Some people don't investigate thoroughly every aspect and become disillusioned as a consequence. You, however, have done a good job of researching all of this. I am aware of the fact that the church is exploring other forms other than the traditional ways that we've followed for centuries. Sometimes, a different perspective can help us to a greater faith as a good Christian. Bishop Everly is a far-seeing man and I believe that he will sanction this trip to Japan for you. But I don't want to get your hopes up. So, again, read your Bible and pray."

Sister Marcia bowed her head.

"Yes, Father," she murmured.

"You may go now, Sister Marcia. It will be a few days before I am able to talk to Bishop Everly. But I will. Go with the grace of God."

"Thank you, Father."

Her interview with Father Bennett over, Sister Marcia left the rectory. She felt the blood singing in her veins; a joyful refrain. She knew that she was going to Japan. There was no doubt in her mind. She had convinced Father Bennett and he would convince the bishop. In a way, she felt that she had already left for her new life. She knew that once she left for Japan, her life would never be the same again. She knew that she would have to compose herself, to contain the riotous excitement and practice patience, until she heard from Father Bennett again. Then she could give free rein to her joy. She knew that when she returned from Japan, she would have embraced the philosophy of zen and still have retained her Christian faith. It would be all the much stronger for her sojourn in Japan.

Upon entering the convent, the first person she saw was the Mother Superior. She had to tell someone of what occurred in her talk with Father Bennett.

"Mother Superior, may I talk with you?" Sister Marcia asked.

"Certainly, my child. What do you want to talk to me about?" the Mother Superior asked.

"I just came back from seeing Father Bennett. I explained to him my desire to go to Japan and he was very helpful. He told me that he is going to talk to Bishop Everly about my desire to go," Sister Marcia said.

The Mother Superior could see how effervescent Sister Marcia was.

It put in her mind of what she had told Father Bennett about the young nun, that she was a manic-depressive. Here, before her eyes, her diagnosis was confirmed.

"And do you think Bishop Everly will sanction this... this trip of yours?"

Sister Marcia looked at her.

"Yes, I do, Mother Superior. Father Bennett told me that he believes that Bishop Everly will sanction my trip to Japan. I believe that the bishop is farseeing enough to know that what I propose to do in no way will detract, but will enhance my faith."

"I see. You are that sure, then?" the Mother Superior asked her.

"Yes, I am. I believe that in a few days, Father Bennett will tell me that Bishop Everly sanctions my trip to Japan and then I will be on my way."

"How long do you suppose that you'll be gone?"

"I don't really know. Maybe six months, maybe a year. I believe that when I return, I will be better able to handle my duties as a sister of the faith; that I will be able to see much clearer how to help people. My faith will be stronger."

The Mother Superior nodded. She wasn't sure that this experiment was for the best. Nonetheless, she would be relieved not to have Sister Marcia in the convent for a while for she was too problematic an individual.

"I wish you well, my child," she said.

"Thank you, Mother Superior."

"Now, if you will excuse me?"

"Of course."

"One other thing, child."

"Yes, Mother Superior?"

"Try to come down a little from your, I don't know exactly how to put it, high."

"Why, Mother Superior?" Sister Marcia asked, puzzled.

"There is many a slip between cup and lip," the Mother Superior said.

"I know that Bishop Everly will give his consent, Mother Superior. I don't believe that I can come down from this 'high' that you're talking about. But I will try to curb my enthusiasm."

"Thank you. That is all that I ask."

The two women parted, each to go about her own duties.

Several days after his conversation with Sister Marcia, Father Bennett finally had the opportunity to see Bishop Everly about Sister Marcia's request. He drove to the residence of his superior. He parked on the tree-lined street in front of the red brick house and turned off his engine. He got out of the car and walked up the path to the front door. He rang the bell and waited. In a few seconds, he could hear footsteps approaching from the other side of the door.

The door was opened and there stood a tall, angular woman dressed in black with her gray hair worn in a bun on top of her head. Her face brightened when she saw who the visitor was. Her dark eyes held pleasure at the sight of Father Bennett standing on the doorstep. Her thin mouth twisted into a smile.

"Hello, Maria," Father Bennett said, smiling at the housekeeper.

"Hello, Father Bennett. Won't you come in?" Maria asked, standing aside.

"Thank you. Is Bishop Everly in?"

"Yes, he is. He's in the garden."

"Thank you."

"You know the way?"

"Yes, I do. Very well. Don't let me keep you any further."

"Very well," she said.

Father Bennett walked down the cool hallway towards the back door that led to the garden. He stood in the doorway for a moment before stepping outside. He saw an elderly man on his knees tugging on something.

As he approached, the man turned his head towards him.

"Joseph," he said in evident delight." It's so good to see you."

"It's very good to see Your Eminence," Father Bennett said.

"Please, you don't have to be so formal," Bishop Everly said as he stood up. In his hand he held a weed." Finally, I got this pest out."

He threw the weed on the ground.

"Weeds," he said, smiling at Father Bennett," are the bane of all gardeners whether they're growing flowers as I am or vegetables. Even for October it is still hot. Come, let's go into the house where Maria will provide refreshments."

"That sounds fine," Father Bennett said, smiling in return.

"Good. Good. Come along, then."

Bishop Everly took Father Bennett's arm. He was a little shorter than the Jesuit, his head just coming up to the priest's shoulder. He had a leonine head with its shock of white hair that was neatly combed. His face was naturally red. His bright blue eyes looked on the world with compassionate humor. His cheeks were a little full as benefited a man who led a good rich life, yet he was not a fat man. He looked like a saintly Santa Claus with only the beard missing. He was a man who enjoyed life and people. He had received his Ph.D. in Theology and the Classics from Harvard Divinity School in 1953 with a minor in Phenomenology. His forte, however, was comparative religion and he welcomed the opportunity to discuss the various aspects of zen Buddhism with any novice. Bishop Everly was a Dominican who seemed to be more concerned with the 'gloria Dei' or the true kingdom of God than with the 'gloria mundi' or the earthly power and the interest of the church. Once, he had confided in the priest that he respected every culture, however primitive as the creative expression of the true spirituality. He was critical of the early Jesuit Fathers 'incursions' into other lands for the purpose of establishing the Christian faith, nonetheless, he had come to accept the fact that the modern Jesuit's objective was to preserve what was morally good in each culture, regardless of the native religion. The two men entered the living room through the door that led from the garden.

"Maria," called Bishop Everly.

"Yes, Your Eminence?" she called back from the recesses of the back of the house.

"Bring some tea and those sugar cakes that you baked this morning, will you. Bring it to my study."

"Yes, Your Eminence."

"Come back to my lair, Joseph," the bishop said, taking his visitor's arm.

The two men walked toward the middle part of the house along the cool, shadowed hallway. They passed the stairway that led to the bedrooms on the second floor. Off the hallway, there was a door, which

Bishop Everly opened. He entered the room with Father Bennett. The window looked out over the garden. In front of the window was a mahogany desk with a large swivel chair behind it. On the wall interspersed with framed diplomas were pictures of various church dignitaries and several religious paintings. Along one wall was a bookcase that took up the entire wall. The bookcase stretched from the floor to the ceiling. As many times as Father Bennett had been in this room, he was always awed by the number of books that he saw. He knew that there were many first editions in their original leather bindings. The books seemed to be the entire history of the church from its beginnings to the present day. There were also books on other cultures' religions. Opposite the bookcase was a sofa that took up almost the entire wall. Next to that was an easy chair and before the sofa was a long low coffee table. There was a reading lamp over the easy chair and a table with another lamp on it. The floor was covered with a tasteful carpet. The room seemed to be an extension of its occupant. There was a vase of cut flowers on the coffee table, sending its perfume out making the room smell like a piece of heaven on earth.

"Sit down, Joseph," Bishop Everly said, indicating the sofa.

"Thank you, Your Eminence," Father Bennett said as he sat down.

"You don't have to be so formal, Joseph," Bishop Everly said reprovingly." Heavens, you make me sound like someone important."

"But, you are," Father Bennett said protestingly.

"Ah, vanity. One of the seven deadly sins as you know," the bishop said, seating himself in the easy chair." My dear boy, let us talk without all this 'Your Eminence' stuff. One really can't be formal in an informal conversation like this, can one?"

He looked inquiringly at Father Bennett.

"No, of course not," Father Bennett said." You're right."

Bishop Everly smiled warmly at his visitor.

There was a knock on the open door.

"Come in, Maria," Bishop Everly said.

Maria came in carrying a tray with two glasses of ice-tea and a plate of sugar cakes. She set them on the coffee table before Father Bennett.

"Will there be anything else, Your Eminence?" she asked deferentially.

"No, nothing more at this time, Maria," Bishop Everly said kindly.

"Will you be staying for dinner, Father Bennett?" she asked.

"No, I'm afraid not," he said.

She nodded as if she had expected his reply. She silently left the room."Excellent woman," Bishop Everly said as he took a sugar cake and bit into it." Have a cake, Joseph. Maria makes excellent sugar cakes. Of course, I shouldn't be eating these things."

"Why not?" Father Bennett asked as he took a sugar cake from the plate in front of him.

"At my age, I'm sixty-two you know, my doctor keeps preaching to me about my weight and the possible dangers of a heart attack due to high cholesterol and all those things that doctors are always talking about. But I do enjoy these things."

There was a twinkle in Bishop Everly's eyes as he told all this to Father Bennett.

"You should take care of your health, sir," Father Bennett said.

"Yes, my dear boy, I know I should, but when God wants me to join Him then I shall."

He picked up his glass of tea and sipped it appreciatively.

"Why don't you stay for dinner, Joseph? Do you have a date or something?"

Father Bennett shook his head, a little taken aback at his superior's jollity.

"No, sir."

"Oh well, I won't press you to stay if you have something else to do. What can I do for you, Joseph?"

"I came to talk to you about something rather important, sir," Father Bennett said.

"And what is it?" Bishop Everly asked, leaning forward a little in his chair.

"There is a young nun in the convent, Sister Marcia, who seems to be troubled. She has had two disturbing dreams and came to me for guidance."

Bishop Everly nodded, his eyes never leaving Father Bennett's face as he talked.

"Go on," he urged when the priest had paused as if to collect his thoughts.

"Due to the nature of the confessional, I cannot tell you about the contents of her dreams," Father Bennett began.

"Quite so, quite so," Bishop Everly said benignly.

"A few days ago, she attended Father Reynolds' lecture on zazen. She was quite ... taken with the prospect of what he had to say."

"To what extent was she 'taken' in your words?" Bishop Everly asked.

"She wants to go to Japan to study zazen with a zen master and wants the church to sponsor her trip. She wants to be gone for a year."

Father Bennett stopped and looked at Bishop Everly.

"Hmm. Very interesting. I didn't attend the lecture. Did you?" Bishop Everly asked.

"No, I had personal business to attend to."

Bishop Everly looked thoughtful. He seemed to be thinking of something.

"There seems to be a trend in the church towards other forms of meditation. First of all, I am a bit bothered by the iconoclastic nature of zen. There are really two paths towards enlightenment for the devotee. One involves discursive meditation on the nature of the godhead or the Trinity, if you like. The other way, which is more characteristic of the oriental mind, is object-less meditation and the deeper the meditation, the less dualistic it becomes. There is an inherent danger here for the westerner not spiritually prepared for this intuitive grasp of ultimate reality. Essentially, it is negative theology because it allows for the abyss of ignorance that separates man from his creator. I approve of the former because it is safer and more in line with the Christian faith. Sister Marcia's quest is nothing more than the desire for experiential knowledge as distinct from knowledge by way of faith."Father Bennett was intrigued, as usual, by Bishop Everly's comments. He wanted to get clarification and so he began asking his questions.

"Bishop, do you feel that the current trend towards the eastern philosophical way of thinking is nothing more than this desire for experiential knowledge that the church cannot somehow give?"

"My son, let me give you a short history lesson, which will help to shed light on this dichotomy we are dealing with here. The basic dichotomy of Christianity or Catholicism is the need for mysticism as a reaction against the rationalism inherent in monotheistic religion. Around the Middle Ages and the time of Meister Eckhart, Christianity was virtually split in two. Eckhart furthered this mysticism by attempting to grasp it in scholastic terms. The opposition among the different denominations soon worsened, until they were carried over into politics and brought about long and bitter years of religious wars. The spiritual battle continued until modern times when finally the bearing of the church in the Second Vatican Council marked a turn to reconciliation. Eckhart's mysticism came to a standstill during these schisms and apologetics was emphasized instead. But now we are witnessing the swing of the pendulum back in the other direction... that of mysticism. The re-dogmatization of ritual is probably the reason for this and time will tell if there will ever be a type of amalgamation of the eastern philosophical ways with our own."

"So I guess that we can conclude that Sister Marcia is part of the vanguard in wanting to try zen Buddhism for its supposed merits?"

Bishop Everly seemed contemplative. He drained his glass of tea and munched another sugar cake. Then he got up and walked to the window. Father Bennett looked at him. For what seemed a long time, the bishop stared out the window then he turned back to his visitor.

"We can conclude that... yes. We must be open-minded about this matter as times have changed and there is more tolerance now than ever before. You must caution her about her true motives and remind her that she can only try this form of meditation in order to come to a deeper understanding of the Christian God. Most importantly, she must be able to make the transition from discursive meditation to object-less or purely contemplative meditation should the situation warrant it."

"What exactly is discursive meditation and what is accomplished in this transition from one to the other?"

Bishop Everly sat down again and looked at Father Bennett. "Discursive meditation or Christian meditation as I call it is usually a kind of mental prayer which reflects on some religious truth... some passage from the Bible or an event in the life of Christ. The meditator ponders the object of reflection and derives a moral from it, developing it into a kind of dialogue with God, Christ or the Saints. Just as I mentioned that there is a danger inherent in object-less meditation as a kind of leap into the unknown, discursive meditation might lead one to set up spiritual idols, as it were, through his all too anthropomorphic imaginings which effectively hinder his striving towards God's being. It could even endanger this faith in the one God. A way to distinguish between the two types of meditation is by following the example of the two types of human cognition put forth by Saint Thomas Aquinas. These are ratiocination and intellection. Typical of the activity of ratiocination is the progression from one known thing to another called discursive or logical thinking. The activity of reason is therefore multiple and progressive. There is a subject/object dualism here. The way of intellection, however is quite the opposite. It is a sudden grasp of the truth in an undifferentiated way. In object-less meditation, the koan is used as a means of opening the student's intuitive mind and as tests to the depth to which it has been opened. To solve the koan, the student, through meditation on it, must reach the same level of intuitive understanding as that from which the master first spoke the words of the koan. With every realization of a koan comes a satori or a sudden awakening to the deeper processes of reality or what the Buddhist refers to as his true home, however momentary."

Father Bennett let Bishop Everly's words sink in.

"So the satori is the goal of object-less meditation?" he asked.

Bishop Everly paused for a moment as if to focus his thoughts on the question.

"I know personally of a Catholic Father, who went to Japan to study and practice zen Buddhism as a way of deepening his intuitive understanding of the Christian faith. Father Lassalle told me, after his satori, that he could reach a much deeper dimension of mind through zazen practice than by traditional Catholic prayer. He said that before zazen practice he could come to a certain depth of mind through Catholic meditation, but to him there was some hindrance he could not break through. When he practiced zazen, he could break through or go beyond that wall. For him, zazen meditation was very helpful to his Catholic meditation. He never would give up the Catholic way because he takes zazen into his spiritual life. This should also be Sister Marcia's approach as she should be very strong in her Christian faith in order to undergo this eventual deepening of her perception. There will be others waiting for her return and she must set a good example for her sisters."

Father Bennett nodded his head in agreement and then offered his own appraisal of the nun's dilemma.

"I have never questioned her faith, but at the same time, I don't know if she is spiritually prepared for the practice of zazen. I think that she feels she can gain a certain amount of spiritual insight from her dreams, instead of regarding them as purely psychological phenomena. This bothers me, nonetheless, I must find out if she is ready."

Bishop Everly smiled.

"The way of zen meditation leads from nothingness to the absolute. The way of Christian meditation proceeds from creation to the Creator. In many ways the two are diametric to each other. Therefore, zen must be used only as a kind of tool in coming to a deeper understanding of the Christian God. Only certain individuals can accomplish this, however and not lose their faith. Go find her, my son, and make sure that she is making the right decision."

Father Bennett stood up.

"Thank you for clearing up certain doubts that I had about Sister Marcia's desire to practice zazen. The church will sponsor her trip to Japan?"

"Yes, the church will. I will speak with the archbishop in Boston about this. The church is trying to broaden itself without chipping away at the infrastructure that holds it all together. The conservatives, of course, don't care much for this, but the Holy Father himself has sanctioned such experiments as the study of zazen. After all, if the Holy Father sanctions it, then the other prelates should move with the times and allow it. I myself don't see that practicing zazen is in of itself a bad thing. Rather, I see it as a tool to strengthen one's Christian faith and nothing else. I am afraid that I have a tendency to pontificate. I get very wound up on my particular subjects. I hope I haven't bored you."

"You never bore me, sir. I find your analyses on these matters to be educational. I am constantly impressed by the depth of your knowledge not only on matters concerning the church and theology but about various cultures of the world."

"You're very kind to say these things to me, Joseph. Are you sure you won't stay for dinner?" Bishop Everly asked, beaming at the younger man.

"No, sir, I really can't."

Bishop Everly sniffed the air.

"Roast chicken if I am not mistaken. Maria makes a marvelous roast chicken."

"I'm sure that she does, sir. But really, I must go."

"Very well. Let me walk you to the door then."

The two men left Bishop Everly's study and walked down the hall to the front door.

"Remember to caution Sister Marcia. While the church allows such experiments, they don't want any renegades. She must be absolutely sure that her desire to study zazen is genuine in order to deepen her Christian faith."

"Yes, sir, I'll make sure that her desire is genuine."

"Well, then my son, have a nice drive back. Thank you for coming to see me. It is always a pleasure to see you and talk to you."

"Thank you, Your Eminence. It is always a pleasure to talk to you."

Bishop Everly watched Father Bennett walk down the path to the street and get into his car. He waved as the priest drove off.

When Father Bennett returned after his talk with Bishop Everly, he decided not to seek out Sister Marcia immediately. He still had his doubts that this was the best thing for her. He deeply respected his superior's knowledge and insight into such problems, but he, himself, felt that Sister Marcia's request was wrong. He had to meditate on this.

He went into the meditation chamber and meditated, sending his thoughts this way and that in trying to divine what was truly best for all concerned. It wasn't an easy decision. Sister Marcia was determined to go. Bishop Everly had given his consent. He had, in fact, said that he was going to speak to the archbishop about it. He decided to wait until the archbishop had rendered his decision. That would be the best thing to do. That way, Sister Marcia would not get her hopes up too much higher than they already were. Satisfied that he had come to the only conclusion that he could, Father Bennett left the meditation chapel and ate a belated dinner.

Sister Marcia was still in a state of euphoria. She knew that patience was necessary to obtain her goal: to study in Japan. She went about her duties in both the hospital and around the convent. She had to keep busy. She prayed several times a day that Father Bennett would bring back a favorable verdict from Bishop Everly. She also studied everything she could find in the library on zen and Japan. She read voraciously, making notes from time to time. She felt that she was retaining what she was reading. She saw Father Bennett several times in church, conducting the mass and at other times, but she did not speak to him about what was dearest to her heart." When he has something to tell me, he will," she said to herself." I don't think that he approves of what I want to do, but if Bishop Everly gives permission, then he has to go along with the bishop's decision. I wonder if he has talked to the bishop yet? Since he has not come to talk to me or sent for me, then I must assume that he has not. But I know that it will be soon. I have already sent off for my passport. Is that being premature? No, I don't believe that it is. I want to be ready. Every night and day I pray for a favorable verdict. I know that the Pope has no objections to what I want to do just as long as I don't lose my Christian faith. But that is exactly the reason that I am going in the first place; I want to strengthen, not weaken my faith. I am very happy being a bride of Christ. I cannot conceive of being anything else. If Father Bennett says that I can't go, then I will, as the Mother Superior said, abide by his decision or leave the convent. I will never leave the convent. I entered the convent to renounce the worldliness, the depravity that I was beginning to see. I wanted to lead a spiritual life free from the demands of the flesh. Should I tell Father Bennett all this to prove to him that my faith is strong and that I only want to strengthen it through the practice of zazen? No, I believe that I already have. If I left the convent, where would I go? What would I be able to do? I have no skills in the work place. How would I live? But I cannot see myself ever leaving the convent for any reason. No, I am sure that I will be going to Japan. I am sure that I will be successful in the art of zen and that my Christian faith will be all that much stronger for my sojourn there. I can already feel a deep change in me. Is that because I am so sure of what is going to happen? Or is it because I will it to happen? I have to be careful of excessive vanity. I cannot presume to know the future. I have put my faith, hope and trust entirely in the hands of my Savior, Jesus Christ and I know that He will show me the way. I believe that all this will happen. I believe with every fiber of my being that Bishop Everly will not reject my desire to go and that everything will be fine. I have never met the bishop, but from what I have heard, he is a man of deep insight and knowledge. Surely, he sees the benefits to be gained from such an experience. I feel in my heart that he does. I also feel that Father Bennett will, also. Sometimes, since I made my decision, I already feel far removed from this place. I can almost see Japan and the convent there. I can almost feel the power that I can gain from the practice of zazen. I am already beginning to study the Japanese language so that I can talk to people there. I am studying their culture, which is more ancient than that of the West. Sometimes, I feel as if I could float over the waters right to Japan. I am learning everything that I can about this place where I shall reside for a year. Yes, I feel that I am already there. I know that the Mother Superior and some of the other sisters have noticed this distancing of mine, but I cannot help that. I cannot be a hypocrite. I cannot pretend for the sake of pretending that I am already, at least in spirit, already someplace else. Is this wrong? I do not believe so. I believe, that in order to prepare myself for my impending journey and experience, which it is necessary to distance oneself from where you are to where you want to be. I believe that this is not a sin; this wanting for something so badly that you can almost feel it. I feel that this is the turning point of my life and that I will never be the same again. That if I am successful, then I will achieved enlightenment and that is something that can never be taken away from you. I feel serene, not anxious. I feel in complete control not being controlled by outside forces. I feel free, not fettered. I feel an inexplicable joy, a lightness of spirit that I have never felt before. As God is my witness, I shall come back stronger in my faith than before I left and that I will set the example for the other sisters who may want to follow in my footsteps. This is not vanity on my part; rather it is a desire to be of help to the other sisters of the faith to help them strengthen their own faith. There is a purpose behind all this and that purpose is to help others gain enlightenment, to strengthen their own faith as mine has been strengthened. Nothing can be nobler than helping others. Nothing can be more sacred."

Sister Marcia's actions were noted by the others in the convent. The Mother Superior wondered what was going to happen but she did not ask Sister Marcia or Father Bennett. They all settled down to a waiting period.

Indian summer was upon the town of Marlborough. The days were warm in anticipation of the winter to come. The people of the town as well as in the church were enjoying the last of the good weather before the onset of winter that the weather forecasters were predicting to be one of the worst winters on record. The foliage was turning from green to red and gold and the leaves were beginning to fall from the branches. The air was redolent with the scent of grass and leaves and the sweet smell of summer. Nature was showing herself in all her splendor for the last time before She covered herself in a mantle of white for the winter.

It was several days after he had spoken to Bishop Everly, that Father Bennett decided to see Sister Marcia. He discovered her walking through the church garden, observing certain plants. When he came upon her, she was studying the Juniper Chinensis for a period of time.

"Good afternoon, Sister Marcia," he said.

"Good afternoon, Father Bennett," she replied, looking at him." So this is Bishop Everly's perennial plant and the oldest I assume?"

Father Bennett noticed a change in her behavior and overall appearance. She seemed more exuberant as she fondled the shrub.

"Yes, I believe that that shrub is sixty-five years old and was originally brought here as a gift from a Japanese Buddhist monk. I gather that you have been doing some reading lately?" he said, looking at her.

"Oh yes, I have been reading everything I can get my hands on about zen. I am growing more fascinated each day. I welcome the opportunity to practice this."

"What exactly do you hope to accomplish?" he asked, studying her closely.

"Basically, I see it as a two-fold endeavor. I want to come to a deeper understanding of God and I also want to discipline my thoughts or somehow harness my libido. I cannot have one without the other. To become truly virtuous entails a certain amount of self control."

"I see. What do you mean by harnessing your libido?"

"Sublimation of one's basic desires leads to the beautiful. Freud, himself, believed that civilization was a result of sublimation. The fruits of one's labors come from the systematic control of the primitive within."

"I see your point, but I still personally feel that only Christ can help you with your problems and that you should not rely on some eastern philosophical way as the answer, but this is strictly my own opinion."

Sister Marcia knew that a decision on her request had been reached. She grew insistent.

"I confessed to you the other day that I would only do this in the context of my Christian faith. I remain and always have been a Christian and more importantly, a bride of Christ. Did you approach Bishop Everly on this matter?" she asked, looking searchingly at his face for any signs of what he was about to say.

"Yes, I did and we do not see any problem with you undertaking such an endeavor as long as you are strong in your faith. You will face many changes and you must be sincere in your beliefs and strong in your convictions. This is very, very important. Bishop Everly wanted me to convey this to you, to warn you," Father Bennett said, trying to gauge her reaction to what he had just said.

At his words, Sister Marcia's face became almost incandescent. A light seemed to radiate from her that was both beautiful and terrible. Father Bennett felt a shiver run down his spine at the sight of her face. She bent down to caress the shrub again, trying to hide the total joy that she felt that she was being able to go; that she was being able to take part in something so wonderful that she could hardly contain herself. She could almost feel herself floating above the garden ready to be blown to her destination.

Father Bennett waited for her to speak, to acknowledge what he had just said. The waiting seemed to take forever and became almost unbearable. Finally, she looked up at him and their eyes met.

"I understand, Father," she said softly." I believe that I have found a way that does not lie outside the Christian faith, but is instead a form of discipline which will enable me in due time to come to a much deeper understanding of my Creator--and when the day comes that I return to the convent, I will hopefully be a strong inspiration to the other sisters who may have encountered some difficulties on the path."

Father Bennett nodded to let her know that he understood what she was saying.

"Have a good journey, Sister Marcia," he said a little awkwardly.

"Thank you, Father," Sister Marcia said.

Father Bennett abruptly left. Sister Marcia watched him leave. The sun was beginning to set. Although nothing had been said, somehow they both knew that their paths would cross again at a later time when they had both been through some changes. They both saw the setting sun and they would later meet again at the sun's zenith.

Chapter Two

The Gulf Which Separates

Six months had passed since Sister Marcia had left the Magdalene convent and Father Bennett approached the Mother Superior one morning to find out if she had heard from her regarding her experiences as a new practitioner of zen.

It was after lunch and Father Bennett had come to the convent purposefully to talk to the Mother Superior. He had reasoned with himself that if Sister Marcia had written to anyone since her departure it would be to the Mother Superior, even though he knew that the two women had never really been that close. He felt tortured by her silence for he had expected her to write at least to announce her arrival in Japan, but there had been no word from her. He had thought of writing to the priest there under whose guidance she was, but quickly decided against it.

And now it was six months later and still no word, unless the Mother Superior had heard from her. It was for this reason that he had sought her out after lunch on a beautiful February afternoon.

Upon entering the convent, he had seen the Mother Superior walking down the hall towards the little chapel.

"Mother Superior," he called out as he hastened down the hall after her.

At the sound of his voice, she turned around surprised. She smiled warmly as he drew nearer to her.

"Father Bennett," she said, extending her hand to him.

"Good afternoon, Mother Superior," he said, taking her hand and giving it a brief squeeze before he let it drop.

The Mother Superior could see that the priest was agitated but trying to hide it. She wondered what was the matter.

"Mother Superior," Father Bennett began," the reason that I came was simply to ask you if you've heard from Sister Marcia? "

"I have not heard from her through the mail or by phone and I was hoping that you had. Personally, I find it strange that neither one of us has been appraised of her current situation," the Mother Superior said, looking into the priest's face.

Father Bennett was apologetic and surmised the lack of communication in personal terms. He still remembered their last meeting in the garden when he had told her that she could go and what her response had been. For the last six months, the sight of her radiant face had haunted him, although he had tried to push it from his mind and get on with his life.

"In a way, I feel personally responsible for what happened. I should have not allowed her to go. Now, I regret my decision. I understood her intricacies, but I did not know how to deal with them. I saw these intricacies more as a peril than as an advantage," Father Bennett said reproachfully.

The Mother Superior nodded her head; her eyes filled with compassion for his words had struck a chord within her.

"I did, too and in the most apparent way. There was a psychological need in her that the church as an institution could not satisfy or should I say ameliorate. But how can one distinguish the psychological from the spiritual? Should not religion be a means to channel all the innate tendencies of the psyche to a much higher goal? Was Freud correct in his analysis of man as infinite libido which can never be satisfied and thus he is existentially distorted?" the Mother Superior asked carefully, watching Father Bennett.

Father Bennett paused for a moment before he spoke.

"According to theological doctrine, man in his essential goodness is not in a state of concupiscence or infinite libido. When one understands and accepts the truth of the Gospel, he has fulfilled libido and is healed from his estrangement in the truest sense of the word," he said.

"But what can we say in all sincerity about the quest of Sister Marcia?" the Mother Superior asked, coming back to the topic of their conversation.

She watched Father Bennett as he began pacing back and forth like the prosecuting attorney in a courtroom drama after having berated himself before the jury. Father Bennett suddenly stopped. He clenched his right hand into a fist and smacked the palm of his left hand to emphasize his remarks.

" If she had performed the Spiritual Exercises of Ignatius under my guidance then she might have been purged of her primitive desires. The purpose of the Exercises is to intimidate, shock and literally blast the soul into the holy ranks. As we know, the person who goes through the Spiritual Exercises has to experience heaven and hell with all the senses, to know burning pain from blessed rapture, so that the distinction between good and evil is forever indelibly imprinted on his soul. With this preparation, the exercitant is brought to the great election, the choice between Satan and Christ. It is to this election that actual life will bring him again and again and it is on this that his good or bad conduct will depend."

"But we no longer live in the Middle Ages when the Spiritual Exercises were so popular among the Catholic clergy and the laity; when various priests from every pulpit preached impressively on eternal damnation; when scientific works gave minute details of the pain of death, and full topographical descriptions of the situation, dimension and the organization of the Satanic kingdom. Can we say that this system of discipline that Ignatius of Loyola devised is still applicable and works in much the same way as originally intended?" the Mother Superior asked.

Father Bennett continued pacing back and forth again as he gesticulated periodically to emphasize his words.

"Even though times have changed in the past four hundred years, the Exercises nonetheless, remain a psychological masterpiece because of the deep psychological knowledge with which understanding, imagination and the will have been made to co-operate. There is a servile fear that the Exercises elicit and much later on, a filial fear of God like a son has for his father and this is natural. The will of the exercitant is merged into the divine will of God; he or she makes a contribution to the greater glory of God and joins the forces in the war against Satan. That was the original idea behind what Ignatius proposed and I fully support that. If I were to think of any one person who needed to go on this spiritual journey full of pitfalls and peaks, Sister Marcia was the perfect candidate, but I do not think that I would have had her complete co-operation because of her priorities."

The Mother Superior nodded her head. She was inclined to agree with Father Bennett's hypothesis."There comes a time in everyone's life when the Spiritual Exercises should be taken up as the road to perfection. We will never attain perfection, but as Christians we should constantly strive for it. I ask you in all sincerity, Father, since you seem to suffer from a burden over the matter of Sister Marcia, have you yourself considered taking up the Exercises in a new light?" she asked, looking closely at him.

Avoiding eye contact, Father Bennett looked down towards the ground as if in an introspective mood. He paused several moments before he spoke.

"I will have to admit that I am subject to a certain amount of apathy since the departure of Sister Marcia... I somehow felt that my efforts to help her were in vain and I could only submit to her will... As a result, the very foundation of my faith was shaken and I felt that my way, which is the orthodox way, was seriously questioned... So many young people are searching for answers and the inevitable result is a cultural transition. Here I am... a Father of the Catholic faith... a spokesman of a major institution, who should act as a type of beacon in the darkness of their despair and I let one of my flock go... I need a reorientation at this point in my career and taking up the Spiritual Exercises would be very appropriate even though I have been in the church for some time now... Please pray for Sister Marcia, but I also ask that you pray for me to have my faith renourished... revitalized so that I will remain first and foremost a soldier for Christ..."

Father Bennett wiped a tear from his eye and the Mother Superior embraced him in a very maternal way and for a period of time, the two of them stood there in the hallway in the shadows. It was a brilliant day outside, although an icy wind could cut through a person's clothes, chilling him to the bone. The priest was oblivious to the weather. His mind was focused inwards, preparing for his severe ordeal.

"I must go now," he announced abruptly.

"Of course, Father," the Mother Superior said, realizing why he was abrupt." Go with God, Father for He will show you the way."

Father Bennett attempted to smile but the smile felt artificial to him instead of natural. He looked into the Mother Superior's eyes, noticing the sympathy that lay within them.

"Thank you," he said.

He walked away, lost in thought. He quickly traversed the hallway and left the convent. The icy wind ruffled his hair and made his eyes water. His breath came out in short puffs. He began walking briskly back to the rectory. He hoped that the walk would be salutary in helping him to calm the chaotic thoughts that were tumbling in his mind. He walked with his hands in his pockets and his head bent. As the wind picked up in intensity, so too, did his pace pick up until it seemed that he was almost running. He turned up the collar of his overcoat and burrowed his head trying to keep his ears warm.

"I should have brought my hat," he thought, although it was a fedora with no earmuffs. His ears and nose were turning red from the cold. Suddenly, the sun disappeared and the sky became a slate gray. He stopped suddenly, looking at the sky and wondered if the sky presaged snow. He had not listened to the weather forecast that day. He sniffed the air, trying to smell if snow was on the way, but could not detect it. He began walking again and finally reached the rectory. He stood in the foyer taking off his coat and hanging it up on the coat rack. There was a mirror next to the coat rack and he looked in it, smoothing his ruffled hair with his fingers. He stood looking into the mirror for what seemed to be a long time, gazing at his reflection without really seeing it. His mind was on his conversation with the Mother Superior. It was strange that Sister Marcia had not contacted her.

Was she so... so offended with both of them that she decided not to write to them?" he asked himself. He couldn't believe that. There should be no reason for her to be offended with either one of them. The only explanation that he could think of to explain her extraordinary behavior was that once she arrived in Japan, she immediately threw herself into the practice of zen and forgot everything else including common courtesy. That was the only thing that made sense to him. She had forgotten. Frowning, he turned away from his reflection and walked down the hall to his study.

He opened the door and entered the room. The room was spartan in its furnishings. There was a desk with a chair with the window behind it. The walls were white-washed with few things on them: a crucifix, a picture of His Holiness Pope John Paul II, a painting of Saint Ignatius of Loyola and his diploma from Loyola University. Along one of the walls was a bookcase that contained his various books on different subjects: theology, psychology and philosophy. On his desk was an open bible, the gift of his professor when he had graduated.

He stood in the middle of the room looking at the couch that served as his bed and besides which stood an easy chair with a reading lamp behind it. His eyes took in every detail of the room and then he crossed to his desk and sat down, reflecting on his life and his career. He swiveled the chair to look out the window at the lowering sky.

"What had made me decide to become a priest?" he asked himself. Never before had he ever doubted his decision to enter the priesthood. He had known that everyone who was called to serve God as either a priest or a nun had felt that they had been called. He, too, had been called. Yet, he could never really put his finger on the precise moment when he had felt this calling.

"When had it been?" he murmured half aloud.

He closed his eyes as he leaned back in his chair; trying to focus his mind back on his past for the moment he had first felt the call to serve God. He had a childhood like most boys even though he attended parochial schools. He had been a choirboy. The choirmaster had told his parents that he had the voice of an angel. He had loved singing in the choir, loved the songs that praised God, the harmonies of the other voices blending in with his. He wondered if during those years that had been the moment when he first felt the call to serve God in some way. He loved the religious paintings and the stain-glass windows depicting the scenes of his Savior's life. There had been something uplifting in Christ's tormented face on the cross, something that spoke to his young heart. What it was, he couldn't remember. All he remembered was how strongly he had felt when he looked into that face. He could still see it in his mind's eye. He could still hear the choir singing Ave Maria and the vestments of the priest as he conducted the mass; the faces of the people gazing rapturously at the priest as he intoned the liturgy. To him, at such a young age, it seemed as if Christ himself were there among the congregation. At times, he could almost recapture those innocent feelings of childhood. He could still see the priest, tall, thin, saintly; his voice a deep baritone that rang out to the far corners of the church so that no one ever slept through one of his services especially the sermons--those marvelous sermons reflecting on the life of Christ and their meaning for all in these times. Those sermons had inspired him to lead a more righteous life; to be worthy of his Savior. He and a group of friends had formed a club: a righteousness club. They had vowed to lead moral lives, to follow Christ's teachings and to never deviate from their path. They would shun girls for girls could distract a boy from the paths of righteousness. They had taken solemn vows that only young boys could make, yet he never ridded himself of his pure desire for the female form. At home, he also led an exemplary life. His father was a hard workingman who always read the Bible out loud to his family after supper. He remembered the discussions that would follow each reading. His father would lead the discussions while his mother knitted and he and his brother and sister would sit spell-bound on the floor. His father had a keen mind although he never used words that were too big, too abstract for his children. There was never any doubt in his mind about how his father felt about his religion. Sundays were special days to him. He lived from Sunday to Sunday. He made sure that they attended Mass regularly and sat in the pews listening to the priest. From his vantage point in the choir, he could see them; their faces would be up-turned towards the altar during the sermons and they would kneel with everyone else, crossing themselves and praying fervently. Yet, they were not fanatics about their religion. They abhorred fanaticism like the plague. After confession, they would all return home and his father would ask his children the meaning of that Sunday's sermon. It was at this time that he had begun training his mind to seek out the nuances of the sermons. His father would smile at him, encouraging him to pursue his train of thought, correcting him when he made an error in his logic. He didn't mind the corrections. He loved his father only slightly less than he loved God. He used his father as an example of what a good Christian should be. He believed that his father was as saintly a man as there was to be found on the earth and wanted to emulate him in every way. He could not remember his father ever being cross or yelling. When he had to discipline one of his children--although never him--it was with a sense of sorrow as if his heart was breaking. His eyes would have tears in them and when the deed had been done, he would leave the room. Whether he cried, he had no way of knowing.

His mother was a good woman, who kept a clean house. She, too, was patient with her children teaching them cleanliness, good manners and respect for their elders. Although she took no part in the nightly Bible discussions, he had never felt that she was inferior to his father but that rather she preferred to let him conduct the discussions. That there was a strong bond between his parents he never doubted. All the children in the house felt the deep love and respect that they had for each other. There were times when other parents were putting their own expectations on their children, pushing them to be something that they didn't want to be. His parents never put their expectations on their children. They both believed that their children would make the right decisions regarding their lives and what careers they wanted to pursue. There was never any pressure put on the children. If one of them didn't do as well in school as he or she might have, then they would quietly talk to that child, telling them how important a good education was. When he was thirteen, he was confirmed in the church. He remembered how proud he had been dressed in a new blue suit with his family in attendance. For a confirmation gift, he had received a book on the life of Saint Ignatius of Loyola. He had read the book and was fascinated with Ignatius' life. He had felt the call then to enter the priesthood. He had told his parents. The priesthood was an honorable profession his father had declared and all during high school he had worked to obtain his goal of attending Loyola University in New Orleans where he had graduated with honors in 1975. It was during the same year that the General Congregation in Rome proved to be a failure in re-uniting the Jesuits. Pope Paul VI intervened, forbidding almost any change in the Constitution and rules. It was in 1974 that he told the Society of Jesus that it must forever cling without wavering to the inspired rules of 'your father and lawgiver Ignatius'. Nonetheless, some members of the Society suggested there could be no answer as long as the Catholic Church remained dominated by a dictatorial Pope and the Roman Curia. Despite the protests, the close Jesuit connection with Rome known as the 'Old Guard' remained virtually unchanged for two more papal conclaves.

It was Father Bennett's intent to eventually join the Old Guard in Rome as he felt that the answer to the modern day Jesuit dilemma was a need for more discipline and a return to ancient norms. At Loyola University, the Jesuit novice-masters took special notice of him as a student because of the sincerity of his vows. He set an example for others with his humble obedience towards his masters. To him, obedience was the highest virtue. The Jesuit must always perceive the Divine Person in his superior and that obedience for him was a kind of 'unio mystica' with the will of God. It was not unusual for the novice-masters to find him on his knees in the novitiate chapel for one, two or three hours at a time with a radiant smile playing over his spiritualized features as he held prayerful converse. Ignatius Loyola, who founded the Society of Jesus, deserved his sainthood as far as he was concerned. Because of his efforts, the Jesuits were the quintessence of Catholicism and had always been in his mind.

Father Bennett understood the Jesuit mission to participate in the social sphere of every culture to further understand its people before introducing the Gospel. He was aware of the social ills which plagued mankind since the Industrial Revolution, but he felt that the answer to Existentialism, especially to a thinker like Kierkegaard was the healing power or what he called the New Reality of the Gospel. Therefore, he understood and accepted the vital role that the church must serve and he feared the increasing secularism in modern society. In many ways, he envisioned himself as the exemplar of the teleological man or what he considered to be the healthy life of a man reborn in Christ. Thus, he felt justified in being invested with a certain amount of ecclesiastical authority by the church as he had grown wise in the faith and felt that it was his obligation to offer his formula for a healthy life nurtured by the Gospel for he was in essence on a redemptive mission.

Now his faith had been put in a totally new perspective because of his experience with Sister Marcia, which he considered to be a spiritual defeat. Somehow, he had allowed this particular individual with a complex personality to go her own way and he felt responsible for what might happen to her in the near future should she embrace the eastern philosophical way of zen. Most importantly, he realized that he must go through the Exercises to re-nourish his faith because he was so fascinated with the Dogon tribe's stories that he lost focus of his original mission. His faith was being put to the test, but somehow he knew that he would persevere and come out of the Spiritual Exercises a much stronger individual and better prepared for Sister Marcia should she return to the convent.The Spiritual Exercises were still used as a type of prerequisite for those entering the priesthood. The Exercitia was composed of four weeks. These four weeks or decades, into which the time of the Exercitia was divided were assigned to the contemplation of sin, of the life of Jesus Christ up to and including Palm Sunday, of His Passion and finally of His resurrection and ascension. Easter Sunday was approximately a month away, so naturally Father Bennett hoped to be finished with the Exercises by then as his performance of the Mass would be a very appropriate event as proof of his renewed faith. However, it was useless and spiritually defeating to have to set goals in mind as he literally had to approach this severe regimen without any anticipations and totally submit his will to what he considered to be the greater will of God. He had decided to perform the Exercises alone without the guidance of a master as he felt he had attained a certain amount of maturity and self -control since his last performance of the Exercises before he left Loyola University. He vividly remembered the ordeal he went through and while it was quite an emotional endeavor, he felt transformed and spiritually rejuvenated in the end. This time around would not be any different as he felt that a certain amount of penance was due during the first week. As far as he was concerned, his allowing Sister Marcia to go her own way was a sin and did not help to promote or to enhance the 'Greater Glory of God'.

He swiveled his chair back to the desk and opened the top drawer of his desk. He pulled out the little black book entitled *The Spiritual Exercises of Saint Ignatius* from the drawer and felt the challenge as he opened the book to the first chapter on the 'Introductory Observations', which would help him to attain the right receptive state of mind for the task ahead. Once again, here was familiar terrain to him, but each time was different and quite an endeavor, which only the most devout and obedient priests could go through in this form of meditation called 'The Application of the Senses'.

It was during the first week of the Exercises that Father Bennett began his contemplation of sin and punishment in hell. Grotesque images of the damned, twisting and convulsing in the flames, appeared to him as he receded further into the dark interiors of his mind. A profound fear of God's judgment and wrath was the ever recurring motif as he read the cryptic passage on the second point which read:" I hear with the ears of the imagination the lamentations, howlings, cries and blasphemies against Christ our Lord and against all His Saints." These were not auditory hallucinations, but the real thing to him. There was no morbid fascination here, but instead the horrifying realization of the eternal ramifications of sin as far as he was concerned.

During the remainder of the first week, Father Bennett had increasing difficulty sleeping as the phantasmagoria summoned up by the Exercises haunted him in various nightmares. At one point, he considered requesting the assistance of Bishop Everly, but he refused to give up his intent of doing the Exercises alone and persevered with the utmost diligence and devotion as he was convinced that this was a journey that he must experience with all his faculties alone.

One particular morning, Father Bennett was actively contemplating what Saint Ignatius meant by the 'Seven Deadly Sins' and he envisioned an image of a partially nude man standing in the center of a circle as seven suspended daggers one by one pierced his skin. Suddenly, a rapid knock on his door sent him reeling to the floor. After regaining his composure, he opened the door and no one was there. At this point, he worried that his mind was playing tricks on him as he realized that one was virtually at the mercy of the Evil One during the first week and it was all the more reason to read the chapter on 'Discernment of Spirits' in order to discipline his thoughts.

The remainder of the first week would be devoted to doing penance, Father Bennett decided. He removed the cords from his closet and then removed his shirt. As he whipped himself, he thought of the last day in the garden; the last time he saw Sister Marcia before her departure. Her excitement and her enthusiasm had been the cause of his sadness as he felt that she had chosen a form of discipline that lay outside the scope of true Christianity. He was thus partially responsible for whatever had happened to her in the past six months. He whipped himself harder and then broke down and cried as the entire ordeal had brought him to the breaking point. He knew that there was no going back... that what had happened had already taken place and was history. He was weak an felt emotionally devastated... enough to kiss the feet of the most despicable beggar as he felt compelled to completely humble himself before God... a total surrender to which God was the potter and he the clay.The next morning, Father Bennett came upon the chapter entitled; 'The Kingdom of Christ' and he envisioned a human king chosen by divine providence. It was the wish of the militant king to conquer the land of the infidels and he once again felt the call to join Him as one of His vassals in the enterprise. To totally submit his will to the 'Greater Glory of God' was assurance that the final victory would put Christ over Satan and his evil hordes of demons. To him, every soul was a potential battleground and everyone had the choice of Christ or Satan and no matter how many diversions one was faced with in a lifetime, the reality of death would either reconcile one with the Lord or he would face damnation. The choice was simple, but the human will insurmountable, it seemed at times. True love was born out of fear... a filial fear, he believed as modern man had lost his sense of awe before the majesty of the 'Eternal King'.

During the second week, Father Bennett was shown the ideal, which he was to imitate as the book admonished him to steep himself in the life and passion of Christ. The entire story of Christ unfolded before him like a three dimensional film and he knew that the spiritual process was underway. He could literally enter into this realm and touch the places where Christ set foot and hear the conversations of the disciples. The Last Supper was pictured very vividly as he found himself sitting at the table, seeing the actions of Christ and hearing the speech of those present. He had tasted the loaves of bread and the fish with which Jesus fed the multitude and he smelled the Magdalene's ointment, and with her anointed the Savior's feet, wiped them and gently kissed them. He knew that all these events were leading up to the Mystery of Golgotha as the true turning point in the history of mankind, he believed.

Father Bennett found himself in the house of the Blessed Virgin and there was an atmosphere of sanctity about it. No one was home. He quietly waited in great expectation and then heard a familiar knock at the door. The person outside kept knocking until he finally came to his senses and realized that he was back in his study. He quickly answered the door and was greeted by the Mother Superior holding a bouquet of flowers with a letter in her hands. She smiled as if she understood what he was going through and the sacred places where he had been.

"I brought you these flowers to assist you in the Exercises at the proper time. I also brought you this interesting letter that I received in the mail today from Sister Marcia. I will let you discern for yourself what she had to say, but please do not let this interfere with your meditations," she said, glancing up into his face.

Father Bennett was surprised and looked down at the flowers and the letter for a moment and then received them into his hands. He did not speak, but simply nodded his head to affirm her gift. As the Mother Superior walked off into the distance, he could see the first indications of spring as he could hear the chorus of birds chirping and feel the slight breeze moving through the leaves of the various oak trees in the courtyard. What he had experienced in the past week stood in stark contrast to the ever-present plethora of natural beauty surrounding him. He knew in his heart that the answer to sin and death was seeking solace in Jesus Christ. He stood there for a moment and allowed everything to permeate his senses and breathed a sigh of relief.Back in his room, Father Bennett inhaled the sweet fragrance of the flowers and imagined the immeasurable fragrance and sweetness of the Godhead. How appropriate these flowers were to him! They symbolized the Godhead and the fruition of the spirit to him and he was grateful. Very carefully, he removed the letter from the envelope and began reading the contents. His smile of agape or true Christian love turned to a look of concern as he realized that Sister Marcia had experienced 'something wonderful beyond words' which she hoped to share with him. It was her desire to return to the convent after a rather brief stay in Japan, but she again emphasized that she had achieved 'something beyond her deepest expectations' and she wanted to return to the convent to share her 'good news'. As to what her experience was seemed very vague to him at this point, but he knew by her stated intent that she was ready to return.

Setting up his typewriter on top of his desk, Father Bennett typed out a brief reply to Sister Marcia, stating that he was presently undergoing the Spiritual Exercises and that Easter Sunday after the Mass would be a very appropriate time to meet again and discuss her experience as far as he was concerned. He indicated that Easter Sunday Mass was a very integral and important event he hoped that she would attend, as it would be the 'culmination point' of the Spiritual Exercises. He also specified that the church would send her the necessary funds for her return trip and most importantly, he stressed that she not share her 'good news' with anyone else in the clergy or laity until he had met her first. He knew in his heart that her arrival and the completion of the Exercises would pretty much coincide as there were two weeks remaining and that Easter Sunday would be a very important event for several reasons. Nonetheless, he could not allow his anticipation of her arrival to interfere with his thoughts devoted to the Exercises for the next two weeks and when the he sealed the letter shut, he put the matter to rest.

Easter week in Marlborough proved to be very eventful. A number of visitors from around the country came to tour the church gardens, as this was the time of year in which numerous plants were in full blossom. Easter lilies were in full abundance and to many symbolized the Passion. Also heralding the arrival of spring were tulips, daffodils, Gerber daisies, button poms and irises, each resplendent with color, besides the array of Fiscus trees and pole ivy. Thus, a walk through the church garden seemed to be a fitting prelude to Easter Sunday Mass as many meditated on the true significance of the crucifixion and resurrection.

The visitors had begun arriving on Good Friday jamming the motels around the area. The natives of Marlborough didn't mind this yearly influx. It was of brief duration and by Easter Sunday afternoon, all the visitors would be gone again and the town would go back to its normal ways. All the churches would be jammed no matter what the denomination.

Father Bennett woke that morning feeling very good. He had

completed the Spiritual Exercises and felt that his faith had been re-nourished and reaffirmed. He dressed and shaved before having breakfast. He stood at the window of his study drinking in the sight of the sunrise as it began touching the eastern sky first with a faint tinge of pink then as the sun seemed to get bolder, spreading it's majestic colors higher, lighting the tree tops and finally bursting out in all its magnificent boldness.

After the four weeks preceding Easter Sunday, Father Bennett felt that this particular sunrise signified a re-birth in him. He wondered, while gazing raptly at the rising sun, whether Sister Marcia had made it back in time for this morning's mass. He had written in his letter that she should not miss mass this particular morning. He looked at his watch noting that he had better get ready to begin the service.He turned from the window looking forward to performing the mass. He left the rectory and walked to the church greeting various people on his way. He entered the rear of the church and went to the room where he would put on his vestments: the white surplice embroidered in gold that almost matched the bishop's, the mitre hat, and the rest of the paraphernalia associated with his dignities as a member of the clergy. He was especially honored that Bishop Everly would be speaking at the mass that morning. Every Easter and Christmas, the bishop would speak before the actual mass began. To Father Bennett, that was for him the highlight of those two particular days.

As he was adjusting his garments to his satisfaction in front of the full-length mirror, Bishop Everly came in, a beatific smile on his face.

"Good morning, Joseph," Bishop Everly said as he closed the door behind him.

"Good morning, Your Eminence," Father Bennett said respectfully.

"Ah, what a glorious morning! What a glorious day for our Lord and Savior! I wonder if it was on such a glorious day as today that He was resurrected. It must have been. Did you see the sunrise this morning, Joseph?"

"Yes, I did, Your Eminence," Father Bennett said, smiling at his superior, not because he was amusing but that his enthusiasm was contagious.

Bishop Everly returned his smile.

"It was glorious, wasn't it?" the bishop asked, his kindly blue eyes twinkling.

"As every sunrise is," Father Bennett replied.

"Yes, you're absolutely right there, Joseph. Since the beginning of Creation, every sunrise has been glorious."

As they were talking, Bishop Everly got ready. If Father Bennett's vestments were magnificent, there was no comparison to those of the bishop's. He seemed transformed from a kindly old man to a stately church dignitary only two notches below the pope.

"Shall we go, Joseph?" the bishop asked, adjusting his hat.

"By all means, Your Eminence."

Father Bennett let Bishop Everly precede him into the church proper. They crossed themselves and genuflected before the altar then mounted the steps. The choir was singing softly, their sweet voices were flute-like in the depths of the church. The organ sounded, that morning, particularly sweet.

Looking out at the growing crowd, Father Bennett looked for Sister Marcia but did not see her. She was not sitting with the others nuns from the convent. He frowned momentarily then decided to forget her absence and to concentrate on the High Mass itself.

"I understand that you did the Spiritual Exercises," Bishop Everly said to Father Bennett.

"Yes, sir, I did. I thought that I should refamilarize myself with the Exercises. I found the experience very beneficial and spiritually uplifting."

Bishop Everly nodded.

"I am glad that you find it so," he said without a trace of mockery in either his words or his tone of voice." When did you last perform the exercises?"

"Before leaving Loyola University," Father Bennett replied.

Bishop Everly nodded.

The last person entered the church, crossed himself and took his place in the last pew.

"Time to start," Bishop Everly said, rising from his chair.He walked to the pulpit, his notes in his hand and looked out benignly at the sea of faces that surrounded him. They were uplifted as if they were the petals of flowers waiting to be touched by the rays of the sun.

"Good morning and Happy Easter to all of you. This is a special time for all Christians for this was the day Our Lord, Jesus Christ, was resurrected. This morning, I am going to speak to you on *The Homecoming of Helios and the Resurrection*. It will be brief," he said, beaming at the congregation.

"In ancient Greece, they viewed Helios or the sun with a mystical adoration for it represented to them the triumph of the soul's descent into the underworld. The shining chariot of Helios was the true embodiment and the supreme symbol that the men of antiquity longed for. This type of solar henotheism or the doctrine that ascribes power to one of several gods for a particular region, was very popular around the time of Julian the Apostate around the fourth century A.D. However, the church's encounter with the sun cult of antiquity was nothing more than the dethronement of Helios. Instead of any type of cultural syncretism, the early Christian's belief in the resurrection of Christ was the spiritual evolution of the Helios principle. The Christians no longer felt the oppression of astral fatalism. Instead, the dethronement of Helios or the homecoming meant for Christian theology that the mysticism and symbolism which had been developed in Hellenistic devotion, were referred back to the concrete, historical and visible person of Jesus Christ and was thus the true incarnation of the Logos, or the Creative Word of God, in whom the whole human race had a portion. This Easter Sunday, as we remember the resurrection of our Lord and Savior, Jesus Christ, we reflect and remember that this is the time for a true celebration of new life over death. We remember His words: 'For whoever so believeth in Me, he will have eternal life.' New life is what we all strive for. The ancient Greeks called it palingenesis but it is a spiritual re-birth that we Christians believe in. As legend has it, King Arthur sent Sir Gawain in search of the Holy Grail and when he found it and brought it back to King Arthur, the king felt as empty as the Grail itself. When the Grail had been filled with wine, King Arthur experienced a re-birth; a new life and felt grateful to Sir Gawain for bringing back this most holy of holies to all of Christendom for it was the Holy Grail that was used at the Last Supper before our Lord went to Calvary and bore the ignominy of bearing the cross on his shoulders all the way along the Via Dolorosa and to his crucifixion. The Holy Grail was used to catch a drop of his blood as he lay dying on the cross.

And so we remember his pain and suffering, but we also remember the miracle of His resurrection and the promise of new life. We believe in his words and are renewed by them for they promise us new life, too. When the Kingdom of Heaven here on earth shall be proclaimed, when our Lord comes to lead us to His Kingdom, then shall we rejoice. A taste of new wine is like the vital sustenance with which we are reborn. When you take Communion this morning, remember the blood of our Lord who died on the cross for all of mankind for when you partake of His body and His blood then you become as one with our Savior. May the Holy Spirit be with each of you this Easter," Bishop Everly said again, beaming down on the congregation. He turned from the pulpit and took his seat again.

After Bishop Everly was seated, Father Bennett approached the altar and performed the mass. The congregation had filled the church to capacity and almost everyone participated in Holy Communion. He could not help but to convey a sense of jubilation to each member of the congregation whom he approached with the wafer and the wine. He felt that he was experiencing the true aftermath of victory as his faith had been reaffirmed and his very actions conveyed this fact, so he believed.After the mass, both Father Bennett and Bishop Everly changed out of their vestments and parted. Father Bennett walked outside of the church and greeted various parishioners who complimented him on the mass. He thanked them cordially, shaking hands with men and women alike.

As he was doing so, a woman approached him. Looking up, he noticed Sister Marcia, the one individual whom he had been waiting for. He also noted a definite change in her overall appearance. She was wearing a small velvet hat with a black illusion veil across her eyes; a high-neck long sleeved black silk dress with a pleated skirt. She gave the impression that she was in a state of mourning. However, her radiant smile seemed to contradict this impression that she had made on him.

"Why, may I ask, are you dressed like that? Have you become a woman of the world?" he asked, frowning at her.

"I am in mourning for my dead husband," she murmured softly, her eyes locking on his.

"Your dead husband? You were never married," he said, growing slightly irritated.

"I am a bride of Christ, am I not?" she asked with just a hint of defiance.

"I don't find that very amusing, Sister Marcia, and am rather shocked that you would say such a thing. Especially today," he said, growing offended not only by her words but also by her attitude.

She stood there looking at him steadily, weighing something in her mind.

"I observed you in there simply going through the motions as always. You did not intuit the sacramental mystery behind the mass and I could see this for the first time," she said, staring straight into his eyes.

He was taken aback by what he considered an insult as well as an accusation. It was with a supreme effort on his part that he answered her as calmly as he could.

"What do you mean, my child?"

"It is in the sphere of sacramental words and gestures that we can see how close to nature the Catholic Church from its earliest beginnings has remained. We honor the Dying God... We make use of natural things... water, oil, bread and by the same token, the sun and the moon."

Her look was candid, yet almost defiant and mocking.

Father Bennett was at a loss for words and tried not to allow his true emotions to show as various parishioners were walking by.

"I fail to understand the hidden meaning of what you just said and I do not care to pursue it here," he said tightly.

She smiled.

"Very well, then, I would like for you to meet me at the Old Village Park outside of town this afternoon at approximately three o'clock. At that time, I will share my good news with you. Please do not be late," she said.

"Why should we meet there? Why not meet in my study?" he asked, frowning.

"Because I am fond of old memories," she said, smiling." Remember, please try and be on time."

Father Bennett watched her walk away, noting with one part of his mind that she seemed to discern everything in her immediate environment to the utmost detail. He was visibly upset by her, by what he considered to be a baseless attack on him and his conduct of the mass. He couldn't make her out.

"It's as if she's a completely different person than when she left," he thought to himself, as he stood still rooted to the spot." Why the park? What does she mean that she's fond of old memories? I cannot make this... this enigma out. This afternoon, I intend to have it out with her."

He walked around for a while deliberating on what she had said and then proceeded in the direction of his study. Suddenly, a voice called out to him.

"Father Bennett!"

He turned in the direction of the voice. The Mother Superior was hastening to catch up with him. She seemed a little out of breath.

"Yes, Mother Superior?" he asked.

She looked at him curiously. Something in his tone of voice made her wonder what was the matter.

"Excuse me, Father, but have you seen Sister Marcia? She was looking for you."

Father Bennett was thunderstruck by the Mother Superior's question.

"I... I just saw her not but a few minutes ago," he said.

The Mother Superior frowned.

"How long ago was it?" she asked.

"Five, six minutes," he said.

"That's strange," she said as if to herself.

"What is strange?" he demanded.

"I left her about two minutes ago. She said that she was looking for you. She told me to tell you that if she didn't find you to meet her in the Old Village Park at precisely three o'clock."

The Mother Superior studied Father Bennett closely as she spoke.

"I met her after mass. She told me herself about meeting her in the park this afternoon at three," he said in a bewildered tone of voice.

"This is very strange," the Mother Superior said, frowning." Are you sure it was her? Of course, you are. I don't understand any of this. She was absolutely bubbling with enthusiasm, but wouldn't share her news with me. She wanted you to be the first one that she told. Can you make any sense out of all this, Father?"

He shook his head perplexed.

"No, it all seems rather mysterious. Will you excuse me, Mother Superior?"

"Of course, Father. Will you tell me what she has to say after you've spoken to her?"

"Yes, yes, I will. Please excuse me," he muttered.

"Happy Easter, Father."

"Same to you, Mother Superior."

Father Bennett, now more confused than before, abruptly left the Mother Superior and hurried to his study. He entered the rectory and quickened his pace down the hall to his study. Upon entering, he locked the door behind him and went to his desk. He was visibly upset. He couldn't understand what was happening. He had seen Sister Marcia and she had insulted him. Yet, the Mother Superior had asked him if he had seen her. He had been on a spiritual high before, during and after the mass. Then for Sister Marcia to question his understanding of the mass had been like having cold water thrown in his face. He had come down from his high and was beginning to reach the depths of desolation. He shook his head again in bewilderment and took from the top drawer of his desk the small book that he had been studying the last four weeks. With shaking hands, he turned to the chapter" On Desolation" and read the seventh rule out loud:

"When one is in desolation, he should be mindful that God has left him to his natural powers to resist the different agitations and temptations of the enemy as a trial. He can resist with the help of God, which always remains, though he may not clearly perceive it. For though God has taken from him the abundance of fervor and overflowing love and the intensity of His favors, nevertheless, he has sufficient grace for eternal salvation."

Father Bennett gently closed the book and placed it on top of the desk then swiveled his chair to face the window and the beautiful Easter day. He tried to gain solace and comfort from the words that he had just read, nonetheless the words of Sister Marcia came back to haunt him and he felt a fresh wave of indignation sweep over him. He knew it had been a mistake for her to go to Japan. Her words proved that. Her criticism of him was unjust and cruel. He began seething. He took a deep breath and then another trying to calm down. It would do no good to retaliate in kind. He felt that he had to be Christ-like and forgive her.

Feeling the pangs of hunger, he decided that it was time for lunch and that he would think clearer on a full stomach. He ate and then returned to his study waiting for the time to pass so that he could keep his expected rendezvous with Sister Marcia in the park.

It was a warm Sunday afternoon when Father Bennett drove up to the outskirts of the Old Village Park that appeared to him to be deserted. He got out of his car and walked into the park. The most prominent feature that he observed was the fountain, long dried up and covered with algae. It was a spill fountain based on the Roman tableau model. It's base was in a wide octagonal basin rising on a single fluted column that went into two tiers. The bottom tier had four clam shaped bowls. The top tier was the same although the bowls on the top tier were smaller. Four dolphins separated the two tiers. On the top tier there were four more dolphins with mouths open. From their mouths the water would have come. He walked over to the fountain and looked into the bottom tier. The bowls were pockmarked, the paint peeling. His initial reaction was that of lost innocence. He could imagine that in it's time, this fascinating fountain was a source of enjoyment for children, who might have played, and lovers, who might have kissed, while tossing their coins into the water. He looked around while still standing by the fountain and noticed the rest of the park. There was a broken down swing set with a slide that stood some eight feet tall. There was also a merry-go-round that was off it's hinges. He walked over to it and tried to give it a twirl. He noticed that one of the swings was still in motion as if someone had just finished swinging as the wind was not blowing. There was a sense of forlorness about the entire park and he wondered where Sister Marcia was. He was still puzzled about why she wanted to meet him here of all places and why she stressed that he be punctual.

Sensing a presence behind him, Father Bennett suddenly turned around and discovered a quiescent Sister Marcia seated in a full lotus position, staring at a rose bush as if she were deeply enthralled. She spoke very succinctly:

"The rose is without why... It blooms because it blooms... It cares not for itself... asks not if it's seen..."

Sister Marcia then looked up at Father Bennett and continued:

"You must not see the rose as you would in a dream, but objectively... the rose, like physis, is a self-sufficient process... It needs no external justification... no rationale for it's being there...The same is true for all nature... As Suzuki said, 'Zen proposes to respect Nature... to love Nature... to live its own life... Zen recognizes that our Nature is one with objective Nature, not in the mathematical sense, but in the sense that Nature lives in us and we in Nature...' In other words, just as we as sentient beings are destined for Buddhahood, so is this rosebush..."

Sister Marcia then returned her gaze back to the rosebush. Father Bennett, feeling somewhat awkward, interjected his own comment.

"When I asked you why you wanted to meet here instead of discussing your experience in my study, you told me that you were 'fond of old memories'. What did you mean?"

Sister Marcia's hair was longer now. She no longer wore the close-cropped hairdo of the typical nun nor was she wearing her habit, but instead a kimono that obviously indicated she felt more comfortable in. She gently swept the hair from her face and again looked at Father Bennett.

"Would you care to sit down beside me?"

"No, I do not think so as I am perfectly alright where I stand. I'm just here to listen to what you have to say."

Sister Marcia returned her gaze to the rosebush and gently caressed various petals as she spoke:

"Very well, I will go back some fifteen years ago and share my secret longings as a young girl. I used to live at the old wooden house up the road with my grandmother and I credit her for introducing me to Walt Whitman's poetry. I was deeply inspired by his 'Leaves of Grass' and shared my unique sexuality with this kindred soul. Late at night, usually on the night of the full moon, I would slip out of my window and walk down the hidden pathway to the park in the nude and masturbate by the fountain. At that time, I responded to nature in terms of my own genitals and virtually transformed everything in my world into a sexual object... whether it was the trees in the forest or the magic fountain. In other words, I was vibrating like a tuning fork to everything I touched or imagined. It was my desire to achieve the ultimate orgasm... the more prolonged, the better... I would see my reflection in the fountain and it really turned me on. I was hoping to cross over the threshold. I thought that the more prolonged and sustained my orgasms were, the greater my chances of achieving this and attaining a type of mystical union with nature. I was wrong and my repeated disappointments turned to shame. When I would finish masturbating, I would walk around the fountain several times just to re-orient myself, as I was kind of deranged for a period of time. There was always the guilty feeling that I had lost something each time and the magic fountain... the type of ritual that I performed after my orgasm would help me to become centered again. In other words, I realized that my sexual experimentation was becoming too dangerous and I felt that my masturbatory adventures were a type of self-pollution, if you will. That is the point where I decided to become a nun because I felt that total sublimation was the only answer to my predicament... to my intense sensuality."

Father Bennett was very quiet, avoiding eye contact. Sister Marcia looked up at him again.

"Well, what do you think of my confession?"

"I am curious as to what particular poem of Whitman so inspired you to commit these sins," he said."You've got to realize that I found a kindred soul in Whitman and his early poetry, especially his poem entitled 'One Hour To Madness and Joy' was exactly my experience also and I was willing to face the consequences. I remember the poem so well... 'One hour to madness and joy! Oh furious! Oh confine me not! What is this that frees me so in storms? What so my shouts amid lightnings and raging winds mean? Oh to drink the mystic deliria deeper than any other man! Oh savage and tender achings! I bequeath them to you my children, I tell them to you, for reasons, Oh bridegroom and bride. Oh to be yielded to you whoever you are, and you yielded to me in defiance of the world! Oh to return to paradise! Oh bashful and feminine! Oh to draw you to me, to plant on you for the first time the lips of a determined woman. Oh the puzzle, the thrice-tied knot, the deep and dark pool all united and illumined! Oh to speed where there is space enough and air enough at last! To be absolved from previous ties and conventions, I from mine and you from yours! To find a new unthought-of-nonchalance with the best of Nature! To have the gag removed from one's mouth! To have the feeling today and any day that I am sufficient as I am. Oh something unproved! Something in a trance! To escape utterly from other's anchors and holds! To drive free! To love free! To dash reckless and dangerous! To court destruction with taunts, with invitations! To ascend, to leap to the heavens of the love indicated to me! To rise thither with my inebriate soul! To be lost if it must be so! To feed the remainder of life with one hour of fullness and freedom! With one brief hour of madness and joy!"

Sister Marcia broke her trance-like stare and looked up at Father Bennett.

"Now, maybe you can better understand the true significance of my first dream, involving myself as the virgin sacrifice and why this particular dream was so important to me."

Father Bennett seemed very concerned and looked down at the complacent nun.

"Yes, I can understand why you would have such a dream and why you entered the convent under false pretenses. Your true devotion did not stem from your love of Christ, but instead from your love of self," he said sternly.

"But all that has changed now," Sister Marcia said.

"What do you mean?" he demanded.

"I had an experience under the guidance of a roshi in Japan that totally shattered my previous conception of myself and now I see everything in a totally new perspective. Where you have embraced the supernatural, I have embraced nature."

Father Bennett put his hands in his pockets and turned as if ready to leave.

"I'm not sure if I want to proceed any further with this conversation as it appears to me that you have used the church to further your own mystical quest or whatever."

At this point, Sister Marcia gracefully rose to her feet and confronted the priest by gently grabbing his arm.

"You must hear me out because you have a stake in my destiny also...Your destiny and my destiny have met up a this point... Our paths have met at a particular juncture and they will meet again later on..."

Father Bennett was puzzled and removed Sister Marcia's grip on him.

"What do you mean?" he demanded."Let me put it to you in another perspective, which I hope that someday you will understand... When the soul and the mind meet in a perpendicular line, so to speak, in that moment complete unity between the universe and the self will be realized. The mind becomes an infinite landscape and one forever appreciates... one is forever grateful for that moment..."

"I'm not sure I understand, but please proceed... about your experience in Japan."

Sister Marcia walked back to the rosebush and picked one of the petals and held it up to the priest.

"What is a rosebush without a petal?" she asked, looking at him.

"I don't follow..." he said, bewildered by her question.

"It's the same kind of perplexing question that the zen koan poses. My particular koan, which I agonized over for almost six months, was 'What was your original face before birth?' At first, I was fascinated by my own personal fantasies or the kleshas... what Jung called the 'Shadow' as a type of threshold I would eventually cross over into pure object-less meditation. Then I was afraid of the nothingness... but once you experience the awe and face the darkness, true creativity is unleashed. Every day in the meditation hall or the zendo, I pondered my koan and tried to understand it from every possible angle. Each time, I thought I had the answer and returned to my master, he would send me away to continue seeking... Gradually, I began to realize that the nature of my koan could not be analyzed or interpreted intellectually... The solution could be known only by being lived... In other words, I experienced my whole self as a riddle without an answer... One day, I stopped trying to understand the koan and I must have experienced that sudden awakening to the multi-dimensional... many-nuanced nature of reality that the Buddhists call satori. This was later confirmed by my roshi. My brief satori was like coming home again... I felt that my love was returned... that there was a reciprocal relationship established with the naked godhead when reality really opened up to me for the first time... It was as if a great flash of livingness surged up... This is the moment when the phoenix escapes from the golden net and when the crane breaks the bars of his cage... I could see the proscenium arches! Nonetheless, I remain a pilgrim..."

Father Bennett listened in fascination to Sister Marcia as she spoke. Her face had lit up from within as she talked about what she had gone through. He looked at her trying to fathom her true self. The enigma of the woman who stood before him, dressed like a Japanese woman with her kimono, the sandals on her feet and the air of someone who had found peace and... enlightenment? All these impressions struck Father Bennett as he tried to find something to say in response.

"Interesting... very interesting," he said almost absent-mindedly." How, may I ask, has this experience of the satori changed your perspective on everything?"

"I am amused at how funny people appear to me now... as if they are out of touch with themselves and with nature; out of sync with time as if they are trying to force time. As Nietzsche said, 'Sometimes we are like false cartoons'."

"And how do you see me?" he asked curiously, watching her face intently.

She paused for a moment before answering as if trying to find the right words to answer his question.

"You were always afraid to experience the myriad possibilities of the moment and this is important because when one ignores the contingency of the moment, he in a way short-circuits consciousness. More than anything, you lacked true spontaneity. You always seemed to be caught up in something and in a hurry. You mentioned Kierkegaard to me and the 'Paradox' is the flux of time for one cannot step into the same river twice, while the Moment is the freedom or true spontaneity. As with most authoritative people, you had your ways of conduct and your own psychological barriers, which prevented you from developing a more personal rapport with the other sisters and cohorts. You virtually screened out the dark underside of life and thus offered no real insight into my dreams... my own dark mysteries as if you refused to really probe..."

Father Bennett was stunned by her analysis of him. He looked at her trying to discern if there were any ulterior motives for her attack on him. Her face was serene and there had been no emphasis on any of her words. She had spoken in an almost detached way as if discussing some abstract concept for which she had no personal belief in one way or the other. He was a little baffled.

"Well," he said, trying to remain calm," I can see that you have probably been harboring these thoughts about me for some time. I am curious at this point... How do you feel about my performance of the Spiritual Exercises of Saint Ignatius and the possibility of you performing these very same exercises under my guidance?"

"As Suzuki aptly described them and I quote, 'The contemplations and prayers of Saint Ignatius are, from the zen point of view, merely so many fabrications of the imagination elaborately woven for the benefit of the piously-minded and in reality, this is like piling tiles upon tiles on one's head and there is no true gaining in the life of the spirit'."

Sister Marcia walked over to the fountain and sat down. She caressed a portion of the fountain under her hand as if there was, indeed, something magical in the very composition of the fountain.

"We are all prisoners of the psyche in our attempt to define the external world. We only experience true freedom during that magic moment when the mind becomes one with nature... when there is no subject/object dualism, but instead an inner realization of the interrelatedness of all things. You remain a prisoner and a believer in the Christian roulette game of everlasting life or death. Your theological image of the self is in opposition to nature," she said, looking directly at him.

Father Bennett kept smiling as if her were impervious to Sister Marcia's criticism of him.

"Unlike you, I have found my 'locus naturalis' or my true spiritual position in the hierarchal scheme of creation. According to Aristotle, the idea of a hierarchal world order has its roots deep in the foundation of human thought. He recognized that the forms of strict logic represented at the same time a kind of picture of the universe. All logical conclusions rest on the subordination of a particular minor proposition to a generally accepted major premise so that every part of the cosmos is subordinate to the more general and is superior to the more particular and maintains thereby its appointed place in the universe... it's 'locus naturalis'. In other words, it is the natural way to humble oneself before God. I am not a pilgrim in any sense of the word."

"The idea of a holistic universe in which everything is interrelated and interconnected is antithetical to your view, which has its basis in Aristotle and later in the theology of Dionysus the Areopagite, but it is what I believe in. Knowing that you're a part of it all is the real beauty... the beauty of the Eros principle if you will. True love... that of Eros is born out of this realization. It is anything but a filial fear, which Saint Ignatius was so adamant about."

"Let me explain something to you, my child. According to the eminent theologian Paul Tillich, there have been two strains of religious thought, which have been at odds with each other for quite a long time. These are the ontological method of Saint Augustine and the cosmological system as developed by Saint Thomas Aquinas. The ontological method is nothing more than the immediate experience of God as an inner psychic fact and the phenomenon of satori or any type of mysticism falls into this category. The argument of the Franciscan school, which based itself on the ontological method, was the supposed fact that people turn away from this thought of the divine substance, which is based on individual defects but not on the essential structure of the mind. In essence, the mind is able to turn away from what is nearest to the ground of its own structure. As Meister Eckhart said, 'God is closer to the soul than the soul is to itself...'. Thus, a modern day exponent of the ontological method might explain that some form of social conditioning is responsible for our inability to intuit the divine within. However, I tend to support the argument of Saint Thomas that the ultimate reality or God can only be ascertained to a limited extent externally by the faculty of reason. Because of our finite limitations, we cannot totally apprehend the ultimate truth of God... We can only infer to a limited extent His divine nature by the overall appearance of external reality. The radical Franciscans argued that 'sapentia' or wisdom is destroyed by reason in this process, but ultimately one must rely on the ecclesiastical authority of the church as to the discernment of truth per se because, again, human cognition is limited and there is an unbridgeable gap between the finite and the infinite. The church guarantees the truth, which can never be fully reached merely by an empirical approach to God. Duns Scotus put forth the idea of ecclesiastical positivism, which simply means that we must accept what is given to us by the church since we cannot reach

God cognitively. William of Occam went a step further and explained that we can only receive the authority of the church if the 'habitus' or the habit of grace is working in us."

"Well that is the main problem with most people nowadays... that they are unwilling to face their own psychic wounds inflicted upon them by the historical process. What's ultimately wounded in us is the divine child... the true self. The church as an institution has certainly not helped to rectify the nightmare of our western heritage and thus the burden of guilt is placed upon the individual. Unfortunately, the majority of Catholics and Protestants today are like children submitting their will to a parental authority, in this case the church."

Very serious, Father Bennett stared directly at the nun.

"What do you mean by the burden of guilt placed upon the individual?"

"I mean the psychological consequences of philosophical and theological dualism."

"Please explain," he said, fixing her with a cold look.

"As far as I'm concerned the desacralization of nature laid the groundwork for monotheism and the birth of modern technology. This dualistic rift is an artificial barrier that civilization has imposed upon man and to return to an active symbiosis with nature is impossible as returning to one's earliest memories of infancy... at least that's what we're programmed to think."

"So you feel that nature is the true focal point... the true ontological foundation that all ritual and myth proceed from?"

"Yes... but no one is really prepared to make the ultimate sacrifice."

"I don't follow your reasoning."

"Emptying the mind of all conscious contents... What Eckhart meant by the detachment from all creatures."

Father Bennett paused for a moment to consider what Sister Marcia had said.

"But this could be dangerous, especially with the social demands placed upon the individual and what not... The energy, which maintains the kinetics of consciousness, cannot be totally abolished without the threat of a psychosis."

"That is why a special training of indefinite duration is needed in order to set up that maximum tension which leads to a final breakthrough," Sister Marcia said earnestly.

"And I suppose that this 'final breakthrough' is the zen equivalent of satori?"

Sister Marcia smiled as she again caressed a rose.

"Jung himself, was baffled by the idea of 'what would happen if an individual consciousness were able to take in at a single glance a simultaneous picture of every possible perception'. In other words, pure objectivity is seeing everything from the perspective of the trees and the rocks as well from your own perspective. As Father Thomas Merton wrote and I quote, 'The pure consciousness of apophatic mystical intuition does not look at things, and does not ignore them, annihilate them or negate them. It accepts them fully, in complete oneness with them. It looks out of them, as though fulfilling the role of consciousness not for itself only but for them also'. What I see as the basic problem here is the fact that the church refuses to accept this type of mystical experience as orthodox. Not only does the church refuse to acknowledge this but it also goes against the cultural canon. In many ways, going against the consensus view is still considered as a form of heresy... as abnormal. I wish there were some way in which I could influence the clergy, but to be realistic against insurmountable odds, I am better off remaining silent and viewing the human predicament with a sense of amusement as well as concern."

"I agree... I agree to the extent that it is a totally futile endeavor on your part to try to influence the clergy because in my mind, you have used the church to somehow further your own mystical quest. What you have done is a sin in my view, but the entire matter is strictly between you and our Lord. I will leave you here with these thoughts as I have other matters to attend to."

"To me, Father, any act of sin is treating people as objects instead of cultivating their essential worth."

"Well, my child, that is your definition of sin, not mine. Any act of sin is a trangression against the Holy Spirit."

Turning his back to Sister Marcia, Father Bennett proceeded in the direction of his car. Suddenly, she called out to him.

"Father!"

As Father Bennett turned around, he was startled to discover Sister

Marcia removing her kimono and standing there completely nude. She threw the garment on top of the rosebush and exclaimed out loud:

"If I were perpetually doing God's will, then I would be a virgin in reality, as exempt from idea handicaps as I was before I was born!"

Shaking his head as if Sister Marcia was a pathetic sight, Father Bennett walked briskly to his car and drove off. Now that he knew her true motives, it was difficult, if not impossible, to allow her back into the convent. Nonetheless, her complete sincerity and her emotional intensity stuck out in his mind and he knew that he was not finished with the matter. His worse expectations about her had come true. Had she really come home? After all, there were no laurels crowning her head.

He drove for a few blocks and then pulled over to the curb. He was shaken by all that had happened that day. He felt that she had been mocking him. That last gesture of hers--taking off her kimono and standing nude before him--had been the last straw. He felt disappointed in her. He felt angry. He also felt betrayed and sick. He felt that she didn't respect him and more importantly, she didn't respect the church, which had succored her; which had paid for her trip to Japan and sent her back a heathen.

He gripped the steering wheel tightly until the knuckles of his hands turned white. The color had drained from his face and he closed his eyes. He felt tired.

"Why?" he asked himself in a whisper." Why did she say and do those things to me? Why would she turn on me? I knew that it was a mistake for her to go, yet I let her. How could I have prevented her from going? She had been very determined. She believes that she has found the answer, which she is enlightened, but to my mind, she's not. How can I bring her back into the fold of the church? First this morning after mass, she criticized me. Then in the park, she mocked me with her final gesture. That is not respect for me or for the church. She has gone astray and I must pray for her immortal soul. I feel so powerless as if she, or something, has drained me like Samson with Delilah. What will I tell Bishop Everly? He's sure to ask about her. I, also, have to tell the Mother Superior. What will she say? Can Sister Marcia stay in the church that she seems to now despise? I don't know what to do. I used to know but today..."

He shook his head despairingly; his face had become a tortured mask. One part of him wanted to denounce Sister Marcia and drive her from the church, excommunicate her for what he considered as heresy. The other part wanted to try to bring her back into the fold with gentleness and patience; to be the loving, an understanding Father who offered compassion. He was in a quandary that was both personal and professional. There were times when he almost sympathized with her, but there were also times when her attitude drove him almost to the brink of despair. Now, it seemed that she had almost pushed him over the brink. He closed his eyes and tried to pray for her, but the words stuck in his throat.

He opened his eyes and looked bleakly out the windshield of his car, not seeing the beauty of the Easter afternoon with the trees in leaf, the flowers beginning to open their petals to the buzzing bees, the grass turning green after the long cold winter.

He straightened up in his seat and started the engine. He drove off.

Driving into the church parking lot, Father Bennett could see the anxious Mother Superior walking towards him. She had a very inquisitive look on her face. He turned off the engine and got out of the car. He had been hoping to avoid seeing her for the time being until his thoughts had clarified themselves and he could think clearly. Now that she was here, there was no way to avoid the questions that he could see in her eyes.

"Well, what did she have to say? Did you see her?" the Mother Superior asked.

Father Bennett shook his head, doubts still plaguing him.

"I really don't know what to say about her at this point. Her approach seemed to be very insightful, but it is the wrong approach. As far as I'm concerned, she has totally embraced the Buddhist philosophy and my ultimate concern is whether she belongs here and if she is allowed to stay, how will she influence the other sisters?" he said, trying to still the storm that was raging inside him.

The Mother Superior began strolling back and forth holding her hands together as if she were trying her best to come up with a solution.

"I need to see her now and find out for myself if I share your view.

My question is whether she is more stable now than before she left?" the Mother Superior asked.

"I don't know... I just don't know... All I do know at this point is that the entire conversation with her was rather frustrating. I would appreciate it if you would convey the fact that I am not feeling well and that I wish to be excused from tonight's activities to Bishop Everly for me. As for me, I am going to my study and retire for the night."

Gently, the Mother Superior caressed the tired priest as he walked by and the mysteries of the night were unfolding...

Father Bennett returned to his study feeling somewhat nauseous and went directly to bed. Was it fatigue or was it the onset of an illness possibly precipitated by his confrontation with Sister Marcia? He simply did not know for sure. She never did explain what she meant by her insinuation of his performance of the mass, but he never asked her. After a period of time in which he played back the conversation in his mind several times, he fell into a deep sleep.

In a dream, Father Bennett found himself standing at the altar in the chapel wearing a black scapular as he prepared the Host. What appeared to be Sister Marcia approached him, dressed in the same black silk dress as if in a state of mourning. She had a bemused look on her face.

"I am the Scarlet Woman... I transmit the vaginal vibrations of Babalon, the Gateway of the Sun... A Eucharist of some sort should most assuredly be consumed daily by every magician and you should regard it as the main sustenance of your magical life. It is of more importance than any other magical ceremony because it is a complete circle. The whole of the force expended is completely re-absorbed, yet the virtue is that vast gain represented by the abyss between man and God. The magician becomes filled with God, fed upon God, intoxicated with God. Little by little your body will become purified by the internal lustration of God... Day by day your mortal frame, shedding its earthly elements, will become the very truth of the Temple of the Holy Ghost. Day by day matter is replaced by Spirit, the human by the divine...Ultimately the change will be complete...You will become the incarnation of the Logos...Thus spake Perdurabo..."

At this point, the Scarlet Woman gently prostrated herself before the altar and lifted her dress revealing very smooth buttocks. She began massaging her vagina and Father Bennett somehow knew what to do as he placed the sacred Host between her thighs and then devoured it. Afterwards, he could feel the intense warmth spreading throughout his entire body... He could hear a mixed chorus of angels and daimons as his invocation summoned the cosmic forces... He held the woman in his arms and expressed his desire for a marriage, but she spoke of her true allegiance...

"You have summoned the Elementals...You must have dominion over them before you can marry me... Outside is the magic fountain... Come with me to the fountain for it is the true source of knowledge... Come with me and we will cross over the threshold into the marvelous..."

Suddenly, the stern voice of Bishop Everly could be heard but he could not be seen...

"The Scarlet Woman is the great Whore of Babylon! She will corrupt you! Her powers of seduction have no limits and this is the real danger. If you choose to follow her, you do so in sin..."

Feeling very intoxicated and grabbing a hold of the altar for support, Father Bennett felt the primordial urge as the Scarlet Woman left the church like a gust of wind. He had to get outside because he had an insatiable hunger for the night. The drama would soon unfold and he had to be there at the right moment by the fountain. He felt that he could possibly levitate as he approached the door. Again, he could hear the stern voice of his bishop, but he could not see him...

"My son, I am your superior and you must surrender you will to sway the intellect. How can you promote the Greater Glory of God if you leave the church? The Logos is in the mind..."

Feeling a spiritual tug-of-war going on within himself, Father Bennett for a moment lamented his leaving the church and experienced some guilt...

"Where are you, Father? My feet no longer touch the floor... Once upon a time, the church was a citadel of light... It contained my spirit and I was your servant... but now... something greater in proportion awaits me... I must cross over... I can no longer see you..." he cried out.

Outside was the magic fountain with a statue of Cupid pouring forth water and the vast array of stars. The forces were everywhere...

Mesmerized, Father Bennett sat down by the fountain and he felt centered again. He could see everything for what it was and the truth of the fountain as a magic circle became revealed to him as the Scarlet Woman confided to him her innermost secrets...

"Sirius is the Hidden God which we all have as sentient beings! Typhon was the first light in the darkness and she is known as the Dragon of the Deep. Her seven stars or souls were manifested by Set, her son in the South, who, as the eighth was the culmination of her light as the brightest star in the galaxy. You will be the eighth priest to survive the trip around the Dog Star. The seven preceding you were sacrificed as an attempt to re-nourish the Dog Star. Each individual is conceived as the center of his own universe... his essential nature determines his relations with similar beings and his proper course of action... Every individual is a star and their particular orbit is intrinsic to their own nature..."

At this point, Father Bennett looked directly above him at Sirius as the Dog Star became more illuminated and offered his own insight...

"One must understand the way of Dionysus to become a Prometheus... One must have chaos within oneself to give birth to a dancing star..."

Extremely startled, Father Bennett awoke from his dream and quickly sat down at his desk. He asked himself why he had such a dream... such an abomination. He acknowledged to himself that he was not a god. He pulled the little black book from his drawer and began reading out loud:

"The enemy, who redoubles his creaturely nothingness by the worst malice, behaves like a weak and feckless woman, whose strength lies in the obstinacy of her negative will. As a matter of fact, freedom is not attained except by passing through a period during which the enemy never stops opposing freedom's progress and the enemy can get the upper hand through the steadfastness of his opposition. If human freedom, after having shown the fearless face of reason, begins to be mastered by the senses, it will experience the unleashing of a wild animal whose rage and malice surge up and knows no bounds."

Father Bennett sat there for a moment at his desk and stared point blank into space. Was Sister Marcia the suspected sorceress who weaved the tapestry of his dream?

The shadows played over his spiritualized features...

Chapter Three

Meditations At The Fountain

The next day brought overcast skies to Marlborough and Father Bennett knew that it would be a perfect opportunity for him to return to the Old Village Park, as it was not the type of weather conducive to family outings. He had one thing in mind only and that was to see the fountain again because that one single prominent feature is what stood out in his dream of the night before. Never had he had a dream so profound... so hauntingly familiar to Sister Marcia's two visions, which she had taken as sacrosanct. Not that he was so inclined, but nonetheless, the dream was a type of revelation and visiting the fountain might help to facilitate his memory of it. It had been several years since his experience with the Dogon tribe, however the Sirian mystery seemed to be unfolding again.

When he arrived at the park, Father Bennett slowly got out of his car as his attention was immediately directed to this marvelous catalyst for thought... the magic fountain. As he walked up to it, he remembered his student years in Rome at the Via Appia where the ancient Fountain de la Basilica stood. He had always remembered the legend surrounding this ancient fountain when in A.D. 36, the emperor Tiberius slit his right wrist and allowed his blood to pour into the basin at precisely midnight. He had supposedly committed this sacrificial act in order to appease the Olympian pantheon as a famine had brought about the deaths of untold numbers of the Roman populace. According to legend, the emperor's sacrifice worked as it rained for over several weeks afterwards and thus the crops were harvested that spring. Even in those days, the priest knew that there was something symbolic about fountains in general. They were a constant source of rejuvenation and very possibly a gateway as well...

As he walked around the outer periphery of the fountain, Father Bennett remembered his dream. The fountain was a source of wisdom, but the insight derived was at odds with what he was taught to believe. He remembered that even some of the early Church Fathers such as Clement of Alexandria believed that a spark of divinity was latent within everyone's soul and that this primal mystery was diametrical to the Nicene Creed, which formulated the idea of the Holy Trinity around A.D. 325. He knew that the problem of this mystery was ethical and to awaken to this mystery could be quite dangerous because of the social demands placed upon the individual. This primal mystery... Was this power his or did it belong to God?

Looking closely at the fountain, he ruminated:"If the polarity principle is inherent to our own nature does the hidden god exist as the negative aspect of this polarity principle? If we ignore the contingency of the moment, is there a building up of the Shadow as the inferior function? If I, as the eighth priest, am integral to the Sirian Mystery or the Dog Star then what is my true role? Why am I the eighth priest? If this realm is that of illumination, will I derive some insight? There are two spiritual aspects of nature just as there is day and night. I have come to a spiritual realization of the Logos principle and I admire Saint Francis of Assisi who was mystical about this aspect of nature in her pristine state as the telos or the culmination of evolution, however Goethe honored the Walpurgis Night in 'Faust'. Walpurgis night is the sexual celebration of the Elementals, who represent the very beginning of nature at night under the moon. Was Walpurgis Night the night of Pan, who as the ultimate satyr, announced the hidden god as our cosmic link to the stars? The Gnostics were aware of the Abraxas as the coincidence of opposites as taught by Nicholas Cusanus, who was one of the Rhineland Mystics. They were considered heretics...There was some validity to what the Gnostics believed even though they were suppressed by the Church Fathers. Gnosis is the awakening to this divine mystery. I now know why they believed that Christ was a non-corporeal entity. If He is a non-corporeal entity then he is an inner psychic fact. Isn't it heresy to think such things?"

He had questions that had no answers. He shook his head ready to dismiss such thoughts and leave when much to his surprise; he noticed an Indian family entering the park. The whole family was dressed typically in their native apparel and as the father approached him, he made a gesture of folding his hands together over his heart. The priest was curious as to what this gesture meant.

"Excuse me," Father Bennett said to the man," but I cannot help but ask you as to what significance, if any, your greeting has?"

The Indian man smiled, lighting up his olive-complected face.

"This greeting is a gesture of peace and is called the Namaste. Essentially, I am acknowledging the deity within you. I am a Brahman priest from east Bengal and you might say that I am a priest greeting another priest," he said in a heavily accented English.

"Thank you," Father Bennett said, looking up at the sky.

The Indian man nodded and walked off with his family.

At this point, Father Bennett looked back at the fountain and made the connection. Meanwhile, a storm was approaching...

Thunder rumbled ominously and closer while lightning streaked the night sky. A few drops of rain began falling then it seemed to Father Bennett that a great deluge suddenly erupted from the sky. He turned on the windshield wipers and tried to see through the downpour. He was on his way to Boston to attend an ecumenical conference the next day, but the downpour was going to make him change his plans. He couldn't drive to Boston in this type of weather. The tires of his car were going bald not offering much traction. He had to find a motel.

Coming slowly around a curve, he saw through the rain-splattered windshield a neon sign that told him that a motel was just up ahead. Slowing even further, he turned to his right when he reached the sign and pulled up to the motel office. There was a portico where he parked his car. He turned off the engine and got out quickly almost running to the door of the motel office. As he entered, a bell over the door rang.

The office was rather small. There was a desk in front of him. He stood on worn carpet just inside the door. On both walls to his right and left, there were posters of various scenic sights in and around the state. In a corner by the left wall near to the registration desk there was a rack filled with postcards. A similar rack off to his right offered paperback books some with lurid covers. Behind the desk there was a pigeonhole rack with keys protruding from above the room numbers. There was a door leading into another room that was partially open. From it, he could hear the sounds of a television playing. On the counter there was a bell.

He walked to the counter and struck the bell sharply several times. An old man, who badly needed a shave with thinning gray hair that was beginning to fall into his rheumy blue eyes, poked his head through the partially opened door. An unlit cigar drooped from one side of his mouth. He studied Father Bennett for what seemed to be a long time but in reality was only a couple of seconds before he came into the room. He wore a plaid shirt over which a stained sweater opened all the way down to his pants, which showed signs of unraveling.

"What can I do you for?" the old man asked in a wheezy whisky-soaked voice. His breath reeked of both whiskey and stale cigars.

"I need a room for tonight," Father Bennett said, trying not to show the disgust that he was feeling in either his face or his voice.

"It's a real belly-whopper out there, ain't it?" the old man said, leaning one elbow on the counter and leaning forward over the counter towards Father Bennett.

"Yes, it is," he agreed.

"Was you going somewheres?"

"Boston."

The old man nodded.

"Not a nice night to be out driving," he said.

"No, it's not. That is why I need a room," Father Bennett said patiently as if to a retarded child.

The old man nodded again and slowly swiveled towards the

pigeonhole rack behind him. He studied the rack as if trying to find something. Half the rack was filled with keys.

"You're in luck," the old man said, turning back to Father Bennett.

Now it was Father Bennett's turn to nod.

"Fix you right up after you sign the registration card," the old man said, shoving a card towards Father Bennett.

"Thank you," Father Bennett said.

He looked around for a pen but didn't find one.

"Do you have a pen so that I can fill out this card?" he asked the old man.

"Sure. I got everything here," the old man said, rummaging in a drawer. He came up with a pen, which he handed to Father Bennett.

"Here you go," he said." Like I said, I got everything here. Aspirin if you got a headache."

"No, thank you," Father Bennett said, bending over the registration card.

He began filling it out.

The old man watched him. The television in the next room was still going. Both men could hear laughter from some television show.

When he was finished filling out the card, Father Bennett put down the pen. The old man slid the card towards him and turned it around.

"Father Joseph Bennett from Marlborough. That's right up the road. You a priest?" he asked, looking up from the card.

"Yes, I am," Father Bennett acknowledged.

"I'm old enough to be your father, Father," the old man said." Hee, hee."

His laugh was a grating sound to the priest's ears. He turned again to the pigeonhole rack behind him and studied it carefully as if the decision was of vital importance. Finally, he took a key out."Room thirteen. Hope you're not superstitious," he said, handing the key to Father Bennett.

"No, I am not superstitious," Father Bennett said, taking the key." Where is room thirteen?"

"Just drive straight down and it'll be the fifth door on your left."

"Thank you," Father Bennett said as he turned to go.

"D'you need something to read? Got plenty of books over in that rack there. Or send someone a postcard?"

Father Bennett shook his head.

"No, thank you."

The old man shrugged.

"There's a bible in each room," he said.

"That's comforting to know," Father Bennett said." Good night."

"Good night. Are you going to pay in the morning? It's thirty-five dollars."

"Yes, I'll pay you in the morning," Father Bennett said over his shoulder as he walked to the door. Outside, the rain was still beating down in a steady sharp drumming sound. He could hear it beating down on the roof.

"Check out time is eleven," the old man called after him.

Father Bennett nodded again and opened the door, stepping back into the rain-soaked night. He got in his car and turned on the engine and slowly drove down the row of rooms looking for number thirteen. He found it and turned into the parking space in front of it. He turned off the engine and quickly got out with his car keys and the room key in his hand. He walked back to the rear of the car and opened the trunk. He grabbed his over-night bag and slammed the trunk lid down then walked quickly to the door of his room. He fumbled for a minute with the lock of the door before finally getting it open. He entered the room. He found a light switch on the inside of the doorframe to his left and snapped it on. The light, dim and dingy, showed him a bed with a faded bedspread on it, a table with a lamp by the bed with a book lying next to the lamp that he assumed was the bible. There was an alcove off to his right, which he assumed led to the bathroom. He closed the door behind him and locked it, placing the chain in its spot and set his suitcase down. He walked over to the bed and turned the lamp on then he returned to the door and turned off the overhead light. The lamp's light wasn't any better than that of the overhead light.

Sighing, he looked into the bathroom and then unpacked his toiletry articles placing them on the counter in the little alcove. He looked at himself in the mirror. He smiled ruefully at his reflection then went back into the bedroom. He sat down on the bed and picked up the bible and idly flipped through it before replacing it on the nightstand. There was no television in the room nor was there a radio. The drapes were as worn and faded as the carpet and as cheap. If this were Boston, this motel would be a fleabag place; as it was, it certainly qualified in his opinion.

With the rain violently coming down, he didn't want to try to find a better place to spend the night. He got up and opened his suitcase and pulled out his pajamas. He undressed and put them on. He was very tired. He turned down the bed and got into it.

Yawning, he reached over to turn off the light and lay down, his head falling on the pillow and closing his eyes. His mind slowed down and his breathing became even.

Sleeping, he dreamed.

The rain was steadily coming down and he couldn't remember if he had rolled up his windows. He didn't want his car to be soaked in the morning. He got out of bed and went to the window and drawing the drapes aside, looked out the window. He saw a figure across the parking lot. At first, he thought that it was the old man but as it came closer, he saw that it was Sister Marcia wearing the same black dress that she wore Easter Sunday after mass. He frowned. How could she have gotten here? She seemed to be an apparition the way she suddenly appeared. A flash of lightning showed her gliding towards his room as if her feet didn't even touch the ground. He decided to go back to bed, although his curiosity was piqued. He got in bed and lay down, closing his eyes when there was a knock on his door. He knew who it was. Reluctantly, he got out of bed and was surprised when he saw her standing by the closed and locked door.

"How did you get in here?" he demanded.

She smiled, saying nothing.

He studied her closely. She should be soaked, but she was dry; her clothes, her hat. They stood looking at each other.

"Again, I ask you, how did you get in here? The door is locked."

She ignored his question.

"On the night of the next new moon, you must return to the magic fountain," she said.

"Why? Why must I go back?"

He was getting frustrated.

"On that night there will be a meteor shower which is a manifestation of the Fire Snake or the Kundalini power, which has attained the crown of Kether."

He looked blankly at her.

"I don't understand what you're saying."

"You will and you will also come to understand the true gift of Prometheus as revealed through the voice of Agni, the sacred fire."

"You're talking nonsense," he snapped at her.

She continued smiling, a smile that infuriated him.

"Remember," she said," the night of the next new moon and the meteor shower. There, things will be revealed to you."

He stood there staring at her. She turned to go and then, to his astonished eyes, simply walked through the closed door and disappeared. He stood there dumbfounded by what he had just seen and then...

Father Bennett sat up suddenly in bed. He was in a cold sweat. He was breathing heavily as he realized that it had all been a dream. He got out of bed and walked to the window, drawing the drapes aside and peering out. There was no one in the parking lot. The rain still beat down in all its fury.

"God, she was so real! This is the second time that she appeared to me in a dream," he said to himself as he stood there by the window." Why is she dressed like that every time I see her? What does this meteor shower on the night of the next new moon mean? What is the Fire Snake or the Kundalini power? And why should I be there? Who is Agni? This dream is very enigmatic. I don't understand any of it. It seems like she spoke in riddles. What is this 'Crown of Kether'? Who or what is Kether? I've heard of Prometheus. But what is the 'true gift' of Prometheus?"He angrily shook his head feeling frustrated. And then, as he stood at the window watching the rain try to beat the pavement into submission, he shivered as if someone had walked over his grave. He felt as if his legs would not hold him as he walked back to the bed and sank down on it. He leaned forward, placing his head in his hands. He rocked back and forth, his mind in turmoil.

Sitting there, he underwent an inner struggle with himself. One part of him rejected his dream. The other accepted it. One part of him wanted never to see that fountain again while the other looked eagerly forward to returning to it.

"What is it about that fountain that keeps drawing me to it like a magnet? In the park, I thought that I had found the answer, but did I? How do I know that there will be a meteor shower on the night of the next new moon? And why the new moon? Is that significant?"

He shook his head and got up from the bed. He began pacing the room, his mind whirling with thoughts that he really didn't want to acknowledge about Sister Marcia. He had the same feeling after that first dream where she had appeared dressed the same way as on Easter Sunday after the mass and now in this second dream. He was confused and a little scared. The thought that Sister Marcia might be a sorceress once again crossed his mind. There was something very odd going on, something that unsettled him. He tried to reject the idea of sorcery, especially as it concerned Sister Marcia. Was he trying to make her into something that she wasn't and had never been? How could a sorceress become a nun anyway? The whole thought was ridiculous. Why, in his dream, did she dress like that, all in black? Was it because that was what she had been wearing when she had insulted him after the mass? Was attributing sorceress' powers to her an unconscious mechanism on his part to discredit her and what she had told him? Was that why he was doing this in his dreams? What she had said had hurt. His first dream of performing the mass with her there, was that his answer to her criticism? And this new dream, what did it signify? He couldn't make heads or tails out of it. In that first dream, she had been the Scarlet Woman, the Great Whore of Babylon. Who was she in this second dream? And why was she in his dreams? Why not Bishop Everly or the Mother Superior? Why not his late parents?

He felt like leaving right there and then; getting into his car and driving on to Boston regardless of the weather. But he knew that he wouldn't do that. He wouldn't run away. Then he realized that he couldn't run away. He almost wished that he smoked or drank. He still felt unsettled by the nature of his dream.

He looked back over his shoulder towards the bed with its rumpled bedclothes. He wondered if he could sleep without a new dream disturbing him. He was almost afraid to get back into bed and try. He turned back to the window. He wondered when this rain would end. He hoped that it would end by morning.

This was a night that he would never forget as long as he lived.

How long he stood there, he didn't know. But he saw the light growing lighter in the east and the rain, as if it had tired itself out in its fury, begin to decrease and then finally stop.

He turned from the window and went into the bathroom. He undressed and took a shower and then shaved and brushed his teeth. He got dressed and repacked his suitcase. He was glad to be getting out of there.

He made sure that he had the key to the room and opened the door. The rising sun greeted him like an old friend promising to drive away the nightmare of the night before. He opened the trunk of his car and placed his suitcase in the trunk and slammed it shut. He walked to the motel office. The old man was behind the counter as he walked in.

"I've come to check out," Father Bennett said as he approached the counter.

"Be thirty-five dollars," the old man said.

In the daylight, he didn't look any better than last night.

Father Bennett placed the key on the desk and drew out his wallet. He counted out thirty-five dollars into the old man's horny palm. He kept his eyes averted from the look of avarice that he had glimpsed in the old man's eyes.

"Is there a restaurant close by where I can get breakfast?" Father Bennett asked.

The old man scratched his head and pondered as if trying to recall where such a place might be.

"About half a mile on the way to Boston there's a place that serves breakfast. On the left," the old man said.

"Thank you," Father Bennett said.

"Don't mention it," the old man said smiling, showing missing teeth.

Father Bennett turned from the counter and left the motel office. He breathed in the clean, fresh air as he walked to his car. He unlocked the door and got in. He turned the engine on and let it warm up for a minute then he backed out and left the motel parking lot, turning left heading for breakfast and Boston.

Chapter Four

The Night Of The Falling Stars

A week after the conference in Boston, Father Bennett was at breakfast reading the newspaper. He read each item carefully. On page ten, he saw something that caught his eye. The headline read:

METEOR SHOWER TO BEEN SEEN OVER MARLBOROUGH

He felt the hair on the back of his neck rise as he read the article which stated that a meteor shower would be in the skies over Marlborough on the night of the next new moon which was in a few days time. Reading further, the article stated that scientists would be studying the display to check for gravitational anomalies as well as hoping that they could retrieve samples that would further help them study the composition of the universe and help to further determine the age of the universe.

Father Bennett folded the newspaper up, stunned.

"What she said in my dream was true!" he said half aloud to himself.

He was stunned and apprehensive. For the last week after his dream in the seedy motel on the way to Boston, he had tried to put it out of his mind. He had wrestled with himself that night over going or not going to the Old Village Park should a meteor shower actually happen. And now here was the announcement in the newspaper. He got up quickly from the table. His housekeeper came back in.

"Are you finished, Father?" she asked.

She was short and dumpy with graying hair that hung down to her shoulders. Her shapeless dress was covered by an apron. Her brown eyes looked at the priest in puzzlement.

"Yes," he said." I am finished, Betty."

The woman moved towards the table.

"You didn't eat much," she said accusingly.

"I'm just not very hungry this morning," he said.

"You're not getting sick, are you?" she asked, peering into his face." You look a little pale."

"No, I'm fine. I'm just not very hungry," he said, trying to reassure her.

The look on her face said that she didn't believe him. They stood staring at each other for a minute and then he abruptly left the room. She stood there staring after him before collecting the dishes and carrying them back to the kitchen.

Father Bennett walked to his study. He had a calendar on the wall, which he wanted to check to find out the exact date of the new moon's next appearance in the night sky. He entered his study and checked the calendar. It would be on the twenty-third. He sat down at his desk and looked out the window.

"What had she said?" he asked himself." That everything would be revealed to me on the night of the next new moon during the meteor shower. Or something like that. I have to go to the Old Village Park on the twenty-third. I don't feel that I really have any choice."

How long he sat there staring out of the window with his mind whirling around, he didn't know. All he knew was that he had to be at the Old Village Park in a few days and that the answer to his strange and cryptic dream would be revealed to him. At least he hoped that it would. All he knew was that he had to be there. Any doubts that he had before had vanished and he knew that he would be impatiently counting the hours until that night.

It was getting dark when Father Bennett drove up to the Old Village Park. He could see a fire after he had gotten out of his car and began walking to the fountain. As he drew nearer, he could see men congregating around the fire. He had never been here so late before. He could see that they were homeless. He had seen many at the soup kitchen that the church ran to feed them and even counsel them.

They looked up as he approached them.

They were, in his opinion, a sorry looking lot. They hadn't shaved or taken a bath in God knows how long. Their clothes were filthy and their hair and beards were matted. A bottle being passed around also told them him that they were well on their way to being drunk. He wondered if they knew about the meteor shower.

"Hello, Father," one of the men said.

"Hello," Father Bennett said, trying not to show the repugnance that he felt when he saw them." Are you here to see the meteor shower?"

They looked at him blankly.

"What meteor shower?" asked the man who had addressed him.

Father Bennett looked up as the cosmic display began.

"That meteor shower," he said, pointing towards the sky.

The men looked up.

"Far out! Groovy!" came a voice on the outer periphery. The voice was mocking and bitter.

"That's Tim," one of the men said.

"Over there," said another, pointing in the direction of the voice.

Father Bennett could see a man on crutches looking up at the sky. His hair was long and matted as it hung to his shoulders. Father Bennett walked to where the man was standing and looked at him. He had a long matted beard with the same brown color in his hair. There were lines of pain deeply etched into his face. He wore a green jacket that looked to be of army issue as well as camouflage pants and one boot on his left foot. The other foot as well as the leg below the knee was missing.

Feeling Father Bennett's scrutiny on him, the man looked him straight in the eyes.

"Haven't you ever seen a wounded soldier before, Father?" he asked mockingly.

"How did you become wounded, my son?" Father Bennett asked.

"My name is Tim and I'm not your son," he snapped." Vietnam. That's where I got wounded."

Father Bennett could only nod his head.

"Have you ever been in a war, Father?" Tim asked.

"No, I have never been in a war," he said softly.

"I have and I can tell you that it's hell... pure hell! I was eighteen and ready to do my patriotic duty to fight for my country. I served there in 'Nam for two years... two long and bloody years. I saw my buddies die right before my eyes. I saw officers being fragged by their own men because they were such incompetent bastards that you wouldn't believe it. They say that a man who survives a war is forever changed by what he goes through. That's right. I'm forever changed. The government does nothing for guys like me who have given a piece of themselves for their country. The VA hospitals are overcrowded and understaffed. The doctors seemed to have gotten their diplomas out of a crackerjack box. Do you know, Father, that we Vietnam vets were never given a fucking parade when we got home like they did for the World War II and Korean War vets? We were treated like dog meat, Father. We were spat upon and reviled. We gave our all for our country and our country seems to have forgotten about us. Now they have this Vietnam War Memorial down in Washington D.C. on the Mall. It has all the names of those killed. It doesn't help, Father. Do you know what helps me make it through the long days and nights?"

Father Bennett shook his head.

"Drugs, Father, drugs! I'm a waste case. I do pot and speed and did LSD. It helps. War is hell, Father. War is pure, flaming hell!"

He glared at Father Bennett for a moment as if daring the priest to dispute everything that he had just said and then he moved away under the overarching display of falling stars. Father Bennett watched him go, wishing that he knew the words that would help that disturbed soul. He doubted that the man would want to hear about Jesus' mercy to those who suffered as he had.

He became aware of a presence by his elbow and turned. Next to him stood an old man wearing a long coat, black in the light of the fire with a fur collar. A black flat-crowned hat covered his long gray hair with side curls by his ears. He had brown eyes that seemed to hold the wisdom of the ages in their depths. His face was wrinkled and his hands looked gnarled with arthritis. There was a shadow of a smile around his mouth.

"Do not mind, Timothy, Father," he said gently. His voice seemed to come from the very depths of his being.

Father Bennett looked at the strange, old man who looked to him like a Biblical prophet.

"Are you Jewish?" Father Bennett asked.

"Yes, I am Jewish, Father." the old man said.

"Are you a rabbi?"

"No, I am not a rabbi. I, like the others that you see here tonight, am homeless. You might say that I am the stereotype of the Wandering Jew. I dress like I am still in the ghetto of Eastern Europe or on the lower East side of Manhattan."

Father Bennett could only nod his head. He waited for the old man to continue speaking for he felt that the old man had something to tell him that was of great importance.

"Do you know anything about Judaism, Father?"

"No, not really," Father Bennett said.

"Judaism is very ancient, almost six thousand years old. There are the Five Books of Moses that we called the Torah and it is in those Five Books that God handed down his laws that all of mankind could live in peace and harmony. Moses, when he came down from Mount Sinai, also brought down God's oral laws and they have been codified in a form that we called the Talmud. It has helped us during the great Diaspora when we were scattered to the four corners of the world. By following the laws of the Talmud, we internalized our religion. There is a third part of Judaism, Father that is very esoteric. Have you ever heard of the Kabbala?"

"No, I haven't. What is the Kabbala?" Father Bennett asked intrigued.

"Jewish mysticism. There is a myth about the Breaking of the Vessels. Have you ever heard of this myth?" the old man asked, looking straight into Father Bennett's eyes.

"No, I haven't. Will you tell me about this myth?"

The old man smiled.

"The Breaking of the Vessels," the old man said almost dreamily."

God needs our help, Father for sin is upon us and it is our responsibility to bring about the tikkun or the restoration of integrity to the universe..."

Father Bennett frowned. The old man had started to tell him the myth of the Breaking of the Vessels but instead seemed to have taken a detour.

"What do you mean by the tikkun? I am not familiar with that word," Father Bennett said.

"Prior to Creation, God must have been immanent in all things. Before God created the world, He voluntarily withdrew to make space for the physical world. To remind us of his presence, He left behind the ten vessels. Into these ten vessels, He poured His Divine Light so that His presence might be amongst us. Unfortunately, there occurred a cosmic catastrophe for after the first three vessels caught the Light and saved it for us, the lower seven were struck with such a flood of splendor that they could not contain it and the vessels were shattered. As a result, chaos and confusion came into the world. Therefore the tikkun, or the restoration, is our responsibility to reconstruct these vessels so that God can radiate the Light of His Love again. Only we, as the Custodians of the Light, can rectify this inherent flaw in creation or the darkness of evil will spread like a malignant cancer."

Father Bennett was struck by the old man's words and he felt something grip him, something outside himself. He stared into the fire, forgetting the old Jew at his elbow.

"Agni speaks to me! I will give the oracle if the fire is extinguished!"

He seemed to be in a hypnotic trance. The men stared at him in their drunken stupor.

"Put out the fire!" Father Bennett again commanded.

The men looked at each other and with a shrug, put out the fire in the trashcan. They wondered if the priest had taken leave of his senses.

When the fire had been extinguished, the spectacular cosmic display resembled fireworks going off. Father Bennett felt himself gripped by a primordial power that held him firmly in its grasp. He had no will of his own. He was at the mercy of whatever forces were taking possession of him.

Father Bennett looked up into the sky as the meteors made an arching descent towards the earth. He raised his arms towards the sky. Still with his arms raised, he walked to the fountain. The men stepped aside as he passed amongst them.

"This magic fountain is the sidereal nature of truth!"

The men looked blankly at him wondering what he was talking about.

"The falling stars are the 'Mercuries' descending from heaven, who break the Law of Love, which is a general philanthropy ordained by God! The original Initiates of Atlantis have returned in order to prevent these 'Mercuries' from causing extreme secular strife! Because of this, the Fire Snake is now Leviathan or the monster of the Abyss because mankind will always remain ignorant of the fact that their destiny is determined by the stars in these last stages of the Kali Yuga!" Father Bennett's voice boomed out over the entire park.

There was complete silence after Father Bennett had completed his oracle. The homeless men stared at him and they were getting frightened. Slowly, Father Bennett lowered his arms to his sides and looked at the men. He seemed to be coming out of a deep trance. He felt a little weak.

"What did I just say?" he demanded of the men.

"I dunno, Father," one man said, his words slurred due to being drunk. His eyes didn't seem to want to focus.

Father Bennett turned to the others, who looked back at him blankly.

"Where's the old Jew?" he asked.

If anyone would remember what he had just said, the old Jew would.

"He left," one man said.

"Left to go where?" Father Bennett demanded.

"He said he was going home. Back to Jerusalem," the man said.

Without a word to the men, Father Bennett left the park and headed to his car. He got in and drove back to the rectory, his mind whirling with what had happened.

When he arrived, he parked his car and turned off the engine. He sat there for a moment and then got out and went into the rectory. He walked down the hall to his study and turned on the light. Once seated behind his desk, he began to think about what had happened that night.

"The moment that I arrived in the park, the meteor shower began. That was a strange synchronicity. Why should it begin exactly at that moment? When the Jew began talking about the Breaking of the Vessels, what was that power that gripped me? I have never felt anything like that before. It was strange and a little frightening. And what was the oracle that I gave? Those homeless men were so drunk that they could not remember what I said. I wish that I could. I felt that it is somehow important. It is too bad that the old Jew left. He wasn't drunk and would have been able to tell me what I had said. One of the homeless said that he left to return to Jerusalem. Was that metaphorical or does he actually live in Jerusalem? Why did I meet him tonight? All that was said in my dream came true, but I feel that the oracle that I gave was the revelation which, unfortunately, I cannot remember. I wish I could remember it. Maybe Tim, the war vet, could have told me. He was very bitter about what had happened to him. That war has been over for many years, yet he still feels the pain and the bitterness. I'll pray for him," Father Bennett thought as he sat there.

How long he sat there, he didn't know. Finally he got up and went to bed feeling frustrated over not being able to remember what he had said when he was in a trance. There was no doubt in his mind that he had been in a trance.

"Tomorrow, I need to go to the library and do some research. I am beginning to remember bits and pieces but not all of it," he said as he turned off the light.

He settled down and soon was asleep.

The next morning, after breakfast, Father Bennett went downtown to the library. Upon entering, he checked the computer for what he was looking for and wrote down the numbers on a slip of paper. He began wandering through the stacks looking for the numbers that he had written down. Finally, in the section on religion, he found what he was looking for. He pulled the book that he was searching for from the shelf and carried it to a table to read it. He put his notebook down beside it and opened the book. The book was *The Encyclopedia of Religion*. It had been a while since he had looked into this book. The encyclopedia covered all the religions of the world. He went to the index and found what he was looking for. He turned to that page and began reading Ellison Findley's article on Agni.

He read that fire worship in its liturgical context was probably the oldest ritual known to man. It was primarily the source of vision and was held in deep veneration as the revealer of the cosmic mysteries as well as fear for the Vedic priests were aware of its demonic qualities as the destroyer of life, also. This entire process of fire worship reached its highest manifestation several thousand years ago with the Vedic concept of Agni; the 'mouth' of the gods. The" personality" of Agni, as developed early in Vedic thought, delineated both the specific functions of the ritual and the divine models for the behavior of man.

He continued reading that indeed, the single most significant element in Agni's personality was his priesthood. He liked what Findley had to say and he wrote it in his notebook:" As fire, he (Agni) must officiate at every sacrifice; thus he is not only the divine counterpart of the human priest but also the prototype for and most eminent exemplar of all priestly activities, especially that of the hotr priest, the reciter of the liturgy."

"Hmm," Father Bennett said to himself," is that what I was, a hotr priest? Am I supposed to be the ultimate priest? A hotr priest gives the oracle and that's what I did last night! I gave the oracle! I just wish that I could remember the oracle from last night so that I could be sure. I have to talk to Bishop Everly about this."

Like a light bulb going off in his head, he felt a rising excitement wondering if this is what it was all about. If he was the hotr priest, then what did that signify? He needed to know more, so much more. He felt that he could hardly contain his excitement. He continued reading to find out more.

He read that Findley went on to explain that Agni was the official mediator between man and the gods and this was seen in the tripartite understanding of the universe, which the priest had. This system of homologies gave birth to the caste system of ancient India. First was the heavenly or offering fire represented by the priest (brahmana), the atmospheric or protecting fire for the warrior (kastriya) and the earthly or producing fire for the merchant (vaisya). However, with the period of the Brahmanas, the elaborate fire ritual (agnihortra) becomes in the ascetic tradition the" internalized fire ritual" and thus the vital link was established between the soul and nature.

He wrote down another quote by Findley:" As man himself is identified with the sacrificial process and with the cosmos, an elaborate system of correspondences is set up homologizing the microcosmic fires of man's body with the macrocosmic fires of the universe, the whole system manipulable through the asceticism of yoga."

He closed the book and leaned back in his chair thinking on what he had read. He had to talk to Bishop Everly about this. Bishop Everly was a man who could help him to further understand what he had just read. He got up and returned the book to its place on the shelf and left the library on his way to speak with Bishop Everly.

He found a pay phone and dialed Bishop Everly's number.

"Hello?" came the voice of Bishop Everly when the receiver was picked up.

"Bishop Everly, this is Father Bennett."

"Hello, Joseph. What can I do for you?" Bishop Everly asked his voice warm with pleasure upon hearing Father Bennett's voice.

"I was wondering if I could come over and talk to you about something important?"

"Of course you can. You know that."

"I'll be right over."

"Fine, I'll be looking for you. Goodbye."

"Goodbye."

Father Bennett hung up the phone and walked to where his car was parked and got in. He started the engine and drove to Bishop Everly's house. Upon arriving, he parked in front of the house and got out of the car. He walked up the front walk and rang the bell.

The door opened and Martha, Bishop Everly's housekeeper, stood there.

"Hello, Father Bennett," she said, smiling warmly." Won't you come in?"

"Thank you, Martha. Bishop Everly is expecting me."

"Yes, he told me. He's in his study."

"Thank you. I know the way."

Father Bennett entered the house and walked down the hall to Bishop Everly's study. He knocked on the door.

"Come in," called Bishop Everly's voice.

Father Bennett opened the door and entered the study. Bishop Everly rose from behind his desk as Father Bennett entered the room.

"Joseph, it's wonderful to see you, as usual," Bishop Everly said, coming from behind his desk with his hand outstretched.

"It's always a pleasure to see you, Your Eminence," Father Bennett said as he crossed to the elderly prelate.

They shook hands.

"Would you like some coffee and some sweet rolls?" Bishop Everly asked.

"No, thank you. As I said over the phone there is something important that I would like to talk to you about."

"Have a seat, Joseph," Bishop Everly said, indicating the sofa.

"Thank you," Father Bennett said.

The two men sat down and Bishop Everly looked inquiringly at the priest.

"Well, Joseph, to what or to whom do we owe this occasion?" Bishop Everly asked kindly.

"Well, your Eminence, I am not here to discuss Sister Marcia, if that is who you expect to be the topic of our conversation. I will be honest with you in admitting that I am still in a quandary about her," Father Bennett said.

Bishop Everly looked at the priest with a frown for that was whom he was expecting the priest to talk about.

"Very well... We shall put the matter concerning her on the back burner for now. So tell me, what's on your mind?"

Father Bennett paused for several minutes trying to find the best way to bring up the topic that he wanted to discuss with the bishop. Finally he said:" Do you remember the meteor shower last night?"

"Yes... Now that you mention it, I do. I was going to observe it very closely but unfortunately I couldn't find my high-powered binoculars. You know that I am interested in such phenomena. I bet that was a very interesting sight. Did you see it?"

"Yes, I did. I had a rather interesting experience at the Old Village Park that night and it initiated my doing some research at the library on the ancient Vedic concept of Agni, the sacred fire."

Bishop Everly looked at him closely.

"What, may I ask, brought all this about?" he asked, bemused.

"I had a dream and the dream came true..."

Bishop Everly looked bewildered at Father Bennett's cryptic statement.

"And what was your dream about, Joseph?" he asked, intrigued.

Father Bennett shook his head.

"It's not really all that important. Listen, Your Eminence, if I am wasting your time then maybe I should leave."

"For heaven's sake, Joseph, I have always been here for you whatever the situation called for. You know that you can confide in me. What happened last night to prompt your research on such an ancient concept as Agni?" Bishop Everly asked, smiling.

Father Bennett smiled back in return.

"On the night of the meteor shower, I believe that I gave an oracle, however I do not remember the content of the oracle. I read that the Vedic priests considered Agni to be the 'mouth' of the gods and more importantly, the hotr priest was the reciter of the liturgy or the oracle as the original prototype of the priestly function. Are you familiar with any of this?"

Bishop Everly leaned back in his chair, considering what Father Bennett had just said.

"As to whether there is any validity to your oracle, I cannot say for I was not there to witness this event. As you know, I have quite an extensive background in the Classics among other areas and early in my career, I read that according to legend, the ancient Greek philosopher, Pythagoras was known as the Hyperborian Apollo and was the first hotr priest to appear in the Western World around 530 B.C. He understood Theta or the Greek symbol for the Golden Spiral, which might have been a metaphor for time. He found this archetypal pattern everywhere in nature: in a ram's horns, seashells and fingerprints. He wrote the Acusmata as a mystical litany to what he called 'cosmos' or complete order in the limited. The unlimited or aperion versus the cosmos or the peras to make the limited or peperasmenon was the true goal of his school, however the notion of the unlimited became known as the Eternal Feminine, which was an integral factor in the Mysteries. It is what certain psychologists believe to be the collective unconscious as the greater self. Even though Pythagoras believed the psyche to be a square instead of a triangle, the trinitarian concept of the psyche preceded early Greek thought going back to Egyptian antiquity with the Osiris-Isis-Horus triad," Bishop Everly said seriously.

Father Bennett considered for a moment what the bishop had just said.

"So the Nicene Creed was not necessarily indicative of the retrograde movement of the spirit towards the intellect as Jung postulated?" he asked, frowning slightly. "Jung was not a theologian, however he realized the problem of the 'missing fourth' or the Shadow as early as Plato's *Timaeus*. The Nicene Creed adhered to the doctrine of the Father, the Son and the Holy Ghost, however the doctrine of the Homoousia, which maintained that Christ was identical with that of the Father was dismissed as heresy. Nonetheless, the belief in the Holy Ghost remained the ultimate ambiguity in relationship to mortal man because to take it to its ultimate realization could lead to a 'Babylonian Confusion of Tongues'. You do see my point, don't you?"

Father Bennett leaned forward on the couch looking at Bishop Everly.

"In other words, if an individual realizes that he has the gift of the Holy Ghost then his or her new found ontogeny could affect all forms of social cohesion and I guess an accurate analogy would be the Tower of Babel," Father Bennett said thoughtfully.

Bishop Everly nodded.

"And it is the purpose of Christianity to provide, or should I say insure, this social cohesion for civilization has a rather thin veneer. In other words, what we don't know won't hurt us. Thus, the church as an institution is a social safeguard against such things as mysticism and the occult, etcetera," Bishop Everly said intently.

"But there are exceptions and I'm afraid that I may be one..." Father Bennett said, his voice trailing off and his eyes becoming unfocused.

Bishop Everly looked at him concerned.

"What do you mean, Joseph?" he asked softly.

Father Bennett looked into the kindly blue eyes of the bishop as his eyes regained their focus.

"In ancient times, was it possible from the astrological standpoint, that certain pagan cultures believed in Sirius as the hidden god as it was the second sun behind the Copernican sun?" Father Bennett asked slowly.

"I am a bit taken aback by your question, Joseph. What have you been reading lately?" Bishop Everly asked, studying the priest with a suddenly sharp look.

"This is strictly an academic question," Father Bennett said, meeting his gaze unflinchingly.

"As far as I am concerned, the very notion of God cannot be discerned from an astronomical or an astrological standpoint because He is an 'infinite circle, whose circumference is nowhere, whose center is everywhere', but this does not necessarily imply pantheism or God as an Immanent Being. Joseph, when you returned from your mission in Africa several years ago, I was very concerned about your faith as you seemed to have confused mythology with history. To be honest with you, I have no doubt about your faith, but if you do then you should pray with all your heart and soul or we can pray right now at this very moment," Bishop Everly said, leaning forward and touching Father Bennett's hand. There was deep concern in his eyes.

Father Bennett shook his head.

"No, I don't think that is necessary even though I appreciate your offer. Good day, Your Eminence," Father Bennett said reluctantly.

He got up and shook hands with the bishop.

"May you have a pleasant afternoon, Joseph. Remember what we have on the back burner that has yet to be discussed."

"I will, Your Eminence," Father Bennett said.

Bishop Everly watched him leave the room.

"Hmm... the hotr priest... the ultimate priest, but times have changed and so has that most ancient of institutions... the ritual," Bishop Everly said to himself.

Chapter Five

Brimos

Back in the room on the sixth floor of Boston General Hospital, Father Bennett nervously set his cup down; his hands were shaking and there was a haunted look in his eyes. Doctor Ben Lassoe half rose from his seat.

"Are you okay?" he asked, his voice tinged with concern.

For a moment, Father Bennett didn't answer him. He was reliving the past and the past was about to take on a horrifying aspect for he remembered what had happened in the House of the Two Crescent Moons. A shudder wracked his body and a look of horror and despair crossed his face.

Lassoe got up from his chair and crossed the room where his distraught patient sat with his shoulders hunched as if expecting a blow. Lassoe placed his hand on Father Bennett's shoulder. The priest looked up at him.

"Are you okay?" Lassoe asked him again." Do you want to continue?"

For a moment, Father Bennett looked into the anxious face that was close to his. He read the concern in Lassoe's eyes, heard it in his voice.

"Yes," he said, his voice barely above a whisper." I have to tell you what transpired."

"We can take a break. You're becoming very agitated. I don't want you to relapse into a catatonic state again."

"I won't. It's important that I continue, Doctor," Father Bennett said, struggling to regain control of himself.

"Maybe some chamomile tea will soothe you. I don't want to sedate you. Would you like some chamomile tea?"

Father Bennett nodded.

"Yes, I believe that some chamomile tea would be just what the doctor ordered," he said with a tint of irony in his voice as a small smile played around the corners of his mouth.

"Always do what your doctor orders," Lassoe said lightly." After all, your doctor knows what's best for you."

"Yes, so doctors keep telling their patients."

"If you really want to continue, do you mind if I record the rest of your story?"

Lassoe watched Father Bennett closely to gauge his reaction to his question.

"Alright," he said slowly." You can record the rest of my story if you want."

"That's fine. I'll get the tea and my recorder."

Father Bennett nodded.

Lassoe walked to the door and opened it. Outside in the corridor was the hustle and bustle of a busy hospital. He looked back over his shoulder gazing at Father Bennett who still sat hunched over.

"Don't go away," Lassoe said.

Father Bennett looked up at him, puzzled.

"And where would I go, Doctor?" he asked.

"You might want to wander around," Lassoe said.

"No, I'll stay right here until you return."

"I won't be but a minute," Lassoe promised.

Father Bennett nodded. He watched Lassoe leave the room.

"How," he asked himself," can I tell Doctor Lassoe that Sister

Marcia and Diana Clements are one and the same person? Why does he want to record this?"

Perplexed, he shook his head and rose from his chair and walked over to the window. He looked out to the street below trying to collect not only his thoughts but also his courage to continue. Another shudder wracked his body and the haunted look in his eyes deepened.

Ben Lassoe hurried from the room, stopping only to give a brief order to an orderly passing by.

"Jack, get me two cups of chamomile tea and bring them to that room," he said, pointing at the room that he had just left.

"Sure, Doctor," the orderly, a thin youth with pimples and unruly red hair, said." Right away."

"Thanks," Lassoe said.

He watched the orderly hurry away to the recreation room where there were a variety of teas and coffee not only for the patients but also for the staff. He continued on to his office. When he entered, he began searching for his tape recorder.

"Wouldn't you know it," he said ruefully," it's always in the last drawer that you look in."

He studied it closely, checking to make sure that there were batteries in there. The microphone was built in and the range was a hundred feet. Anything else and the voices would be indistinct. He checked the tape, taking it out of the machine.

"Better put in an unused one. I don't remember what's on this one," he said to himself.

He rummaged in another drawer and came up with a package of unused cassette tapes. He broke the seal and removed one from the package. He wrote the date and whom he was recording then he put the tape into the machine and left his office.

He arrived back at Father Bennett's room at the same time as the orderly did.

"Bring the tea in, Jack," Lassoe said.

"Sure thing, Doctor," Jack said as he entered the room carrying two styrofoam containers in his hands." Where will I put them?"

He looked around.

"On the table," Lassoe said.

The orderly placed the two cups on the table.

"Anything else, Doctor?" he asked, his eyes cutting to Father Bennett who still stood by the window, his back to the room.

"No, that will be all. Thanks, Jack," Lassoe said.

"Hey, no problem," Jack said.

Lassoe walked him to the door, closing it behind him. He walked to the table where the tea was and poured them into the cups that he and Father Bennett had been using before. He cleared his throat.

Father Bennett turned from the window.

"Are you sure that you want to continue?" Lassoe asked him, studying him intently.

"Yes," Father Bennett said.

"Better drink this tea before it gets cold. Chamomile has a soothing effect on people," Lassoe said.

"Alright," Father Bennett said almost in a whisper.

He turned from the window and walked stiffly back to his chair. He sat down and picked up the cup, holding it in both hands as if the warmth could invade his soul and still the quaking fear that he was feeling.

"This is the tape recorder," Lassoe said, showing him the cassette recorder in his hand." The microphone is very sensitive so that all you need to do is speak in your normal voice and it will pick it up. But I don't want you to feel awkward because this is being recorded. I want you to be natural. Alright?"

Father Bennett nodded as if speaking would be too difficult.

"Anytime that you're ready to begin, just begin speaking," Lassoe said.

Father Bennett raised the cup to his mouth and swallowed some tea. Lassoe watched him. After a few minutes, he could tell that the chamomile tea was having an effect on his patient. He could see Father Bennett visibly relaxed and looked up at him. Their eyes met and once again the priest nodded. He cleared his throat.

"I'm ready to begin," he said.

Lassoe turned on the tape recorder and waited for Father Bennett to continue his story.

"Eighteen months had passed since I last saw Sister Marcia in the park. I received a phone call that would change my life forever..."

Father Bennett was reading in his study one morning when the phone rang. Startled, he looked up from the book that he had been engrossed in. It took another ring of the phone to bring him back to a realization of where he was. He picked up the phone on the third ring.

"Hello?" he said.

"May I speak with Father Bennett?" said the voice on the other end of the line. To him it sounded like an old woman.

"This is Father Bennett," he said." And who is this?"

"I'm Nurse Caldwell, the head nurse of Maternity at Boston General Hospital, Father," she said; a disembodied voice from sixty miles to the east.

"What may I do for you, Nurse Caldwell?" Father Bennett asked politely. He was a little puzzled about why a nurse from a hospital in Boston would be calling him. As far as he knew, no one in his parish was having a baby in Boston.

"Father, it's a matter of life and death that you come to Boston General," Nurse Caldwell said, her voice urgent.

"Please explain, Nurse Caldwell," he said.

"A woman named Diana Clements delivered a baby boy three days ago. She was calling for you the entire time that she was in labor."

Father Bennett frowned trying to recall the name of Diana Clements.

"I am afraid that I don't know anybody by that name, nurse," he said." Are you sure that she was calling my name?"

"Yes, Father and she gave your phone number."

"That's odd," he said softly.

"How is she?"

"She's gone, Father."

"Gone! Gone where? Did she take her baby with her?"

"Please, Father, come to Boston General. The baby is here, but he's dying. We need to talk, Father and not over the phone."

Father Bennett paused to consider what to do. It took him five seconds to make up his mind.

"Very well, nurse, I'm on my way. Where is Boston General?"

"I'll give you directions. Thank you, Father," she said.

He wrote down the instructions that she gave him.

"It will take me an hour to get there," he said.

"Come as quickly as possible," she urged.

"Yes, yes I will," he said." Goodbye."

"Goodbye."

There was a click on the other end of the line and it went dead. Father Bennett looked thoughtfully at the receiver in his hand then put it down. He checked to make sure that he had his keys and his wallet and left his study purposefully walking down the hall. As he was leaving the rectory, the Mother Superior was on the doorstep.

"Oh, Father Bennett, you're just the person that I want to see," she said.

"I'm sorry, Mother Superior, but I don't have time right now. There's an emergency that I really must attend to. When I get back, we'll talk," he said, brushing past her.

"Of course, Father," she said to his retreating back.

She wondered what the emergency could be that made him almost rude to her. It wasn't like him at all to be so preoccupied almost to the point of incivility.

Father Bennett got into his car and started the engine. He pulled out of the church parking lot and headed for Boston. On the way, his mind whirled with questions.

"Who is this Diana Clements and how does she know me? Why would she be calling my name when she was in labor? Why did she leave when she had just given birth? Why leave her baby behind? The nurse said that the baby was dying. Was that the reason? And where did she go? There are too many questions. I certainly hope that Nurse Caldwell has the answers to these questions. I hope that the Mother Superior understands. When I get back, I'll explain everything to her and find out what she wanted."

Father Bennett soon reached the outskirts of Boston and following Nurse Caldwell's directions soon pulled into the parking lot of Boston General Hospital. He parked his car and got out locking the door. He made sure he knew where he parked and hurried into the hospital. At the front desk, he asked an elderly woman with blue tinted hair where he could find the maternity ward.

She blinked at him and put on her glasses that were hanging by a cord from around her neck. Her blue eyes looked magnified from behind the glasses and her wrinkled face seemed to have soaked too long in water making it look like a prune.

"Maternity is on the second floor, Father," she said.

"Thank you," he said, smiling at her.

"Not at all, Father. The elevators are over there," she said, pointing to her left.

"Thank you again," he said, turning away from the desk and walking towards the elevators. He was about to push the button to summon the elevator when the door opened and he stepped in. There was nobody else in the elevator with him. He pressed the button for the second floor. The door closed and the elevator ascended smoothly. The door opened and he stepped out.

He walked to the nurses' station. As he approached, a woman looked up. She was an elderly woman with gray hair and brown eyes that appraised him as he drew closer to her. Her mouth was a thin line that showed disapproval.

"Yes, Father?" she said as he stopped by the desk.

"I'm Father Bennett. Are you Nurse Caldwell?" he asked her.

A smile briefly lit her face then faded as if the seriousness of the situation didn't call for any lightness.

"Yes, I am. Thank you for coming, Father," she said.

"Could you tell me more than what you told me on the phone?" he asked.

"Come with me," she said, coming out from behind the desk." We'll go down the hall to the nursery. I want you to see the baby."

"That's one of the reasons that I'm here," he said.

She nodded abruptly and they walked down the hall to the nursery.

"The infant has been in the nursery room for three days and I believe by the symptoms that he is showing that his life is in jeopardy. His mother, by the registered name of Diana Clements claimed that her boy by the name of Brimos was her 'gift to the world' and subsequently left the hospital without permission. She had a very difficult delivery and there were several times during her ordeal when she called out your name either out of fear of dying or maybe the possibility that you are the father."

She looked sideways at him as they continued down the hall. Father Bennett surmised the situation, seriously.

"As I told you over the phone, I do not know anyone by the name of Diana Clements and furthermore, my vow of celibacy rules out the possibility that I would be the father to any child."

"I understand. But I'm sure that you share my concern about the infant and I am requesting that you somehow locate the mother and bring her back because I feel that a close intimate bond might somehow revivify him."

"I will see what I can do. I can't make any promises, though. You do understand that?"

"Yes, I do, Father."

"Did she leave an address?"

"All I know is that she lives somewhere in Provincetown in an artist's colony."

"Well, that's not much help, but it is a rather small community from what I know. She really called out my name, did she?"

"Yes, she did. It was as if she really knew you. I just wish that you had been here for her."

Father Bennett frowned and paused to consider what the nurse had said.

"That's really strange," he said slowly." I just don't know what to say at this point."

Now it was Nurse Caldwell's turn to frown. They continued walking down the hall.

"Brimos is somewhat of a miracle baby mainly because he survived a very difficult birth. At one point, Doctor Reubens considered a Caesarean, but she had already lost too much blood to risk the operation. There is no doubt in my mind that he is a very special baby. I think that it's time for you to see him."

"Yes, I think so too," Father Bennett agreed.

They came to the nursery window and approached it. There were many newborns in their little cribs. One was in an incubator. Just from looking at the infant in the incubator, Father Bennett could tell that it was dying. There was a grain wreath hanging on the head of the incubator.

"Why the grain wreath?" he asked." Is there some significance?"

Nurse Caldwell was silent for several moments and then her transfixion became apparent as she lowered her voice.

"Man must bite off the head of the serpent which has crawled into his mouth..."

Father Bennett was taken aback by the nurse's cryptic statement and tried his best to appear calm.

"What was that you said? I don't follow..."

As if suddenly coming out of a trance, Nurse Caldwell smiled and handed the priest a piece of paper.

"Here is a crude map which will hopefully provide you with directions to her house. She drew it herself."

Father Bennett studied the crude drawing for several moments.

"Like I said, I will do what I can. Provincetown is outside our parish, but I'm sure that my bishop will make an exception in this case."

"Thank you, Father. Would you mind saying a prayer of protection for Brimos?"

"Why naturally. I most certainly will."

Immediately, Father Bennett put the piece of paper in his pocket. He crossed himself and bowed his head.

"Our Father in Heaven, we come to you in an hour of need. I ask that You surround Brimos with a circle of light, which will help protect him from any harm or pestilence in order for his condition to remain stable, while I go and search for his mother. We know that You have the power to restore life and also to take life. If Brimos should die, I pray that You will bring him home again for he is without sin. We feel that he is a special child and You may have a special purpose for his life because he and his mother have suffered a great deal. It is in Your name Father that I make this special request. Amen."

"Amen," Nurse Caldwell said softly.

Again, Father Bennett crossed himself.

Nurse Caldwell looked over at the priest and smiled again, extending her hand.

"Thank you, Father," she said." That was sweet of you. Can I show you out?"

"No, thank you. I'm sure that I can find the elevator."

Father Bennett turned to leave. The nurse seemed to scrutinize him for a moment.

"Remember, Father, time is of the utmost importance. It is imperative that you find her."

"I'll try to find her. Goodbye."

Father Bennett walked down the hall to the elevator and pressed the button. He waited until it arrived, not looking to his left or his right. When the elevator came, he stepped inside and rode down by himself to the first floor. When the elevator stopped and the doors opened, he walked out without a look at the receptionist at the front desk. He walked to his car and got in. He started the engine and began the drive back to Marlborough.

On his drive back to the church, his thoughts began whirling.

"Was Nurse Caldwell demonically possessed? Her comment was strange: man must bite off the head of the serpent, which has crawled, into his mouth. What does that mean? What is the significance of that grain wreath on the incubator? Who is Diana Clements and why, in her ordeal, should she call out my name? I still don't remember her name. I should have asked Nurse Caldwell to describe her. When I get back, I need to talk to Bishop Everly and tell him what just happened. Maybe he has insight into this. I also have to go to Provincetown to try to find this Diana Clements and try to bring her back. What was it that she told the nurse about her baby, that he was her gift to the world? All this is so strange that I can hardly fathom it. As a matter of fact, it seems that since that Easter Sunday when Sister Marcia returned from Japan, everything has become strange. And speaking of Sister Marcia, why did she leave the convent? She could have stayed. Together, I believe, the Mother Superior and I could have brought her back to the true faith. Her leaving still haunts me. I don't even know anything about her, not even the name she had before she entered the convent. I must remember to pray for her tonight. It has been too long since I have prayed for her immortal soul."

He continued with this line of thinking all the way home. On the outskirts of Marlborough, he decided to go directly to Bishop Everly's house. In a few minutes, he drove up in front of the bishop's residence. He turned off the engine and sat there for a minute or two trying to collect his thoughts. He put his hand in his pocket and felt the piece of paper that the nurse had given him. He took it out of his pocket and unfolded it. He studied the crude map that would lead him to the mysterious Diana Clements. He folded the paper and put it back in his pocket and got out of his car. He walked up the front walk and rang the bell.

A few minutes later, the door was opened by the housekeeper.

"Good morning, Martha. Is the bishop in?" Father Bennett asked, smiling at the housekeeper.

"Good morning, Father and yes, he is. Won't you come in?" she asked.

She stood back to let him enter. He crossed the threshold and she shut the door behind him.

"He's in his study," Martha said.

"I hope that I'm not disturbing anything important."

She smiled at him.

"I don't think that he'll mind, Father. He's always glad to see you."

"Thank you, Martha," Father Bennett said, returning her smile.

"Just go right back, Father. Would you like some refreshments?"

"No, thank you, Martha."

Father Bennett walked down the hall to Bishop Everly's study. The door was closed and he knocked on it.

"Come in, Martha," called the bishop.

Father Bennett opened the door.

"I hope that you won't be disappointed with me instead of Martha, Your Eminence," Father Bennett said as he entered the study.

Bishop Everly looked up from what he was doing and saw his visitor. A smile spread across his face. Seated behind his desk, he seemed to be studying various catalogues on plants and flowers. Now, he rose to his feet and came from behind his desk, his hand extended.

"Joseph, how wonderful to see you again. Come in, come in and have a seat," Bishop Everly said heartily.

Looking over at the bishop's desk, Father Bennett shook hands with the bishop.

"I hope that I'm not disturbing you, Your Eminence," Father Bennett said.

"No, no, don't concern yourself about that, Joseph. I was just looking at some catalogues. You know how I love gardening. I was just looking at some flowers that I think would look good in my garden. Martha's no help in such matters. She always agrees with me. Speaking of Martha, would you care for some refreshments?"

"She asked me and I refused."

"Please, sit down and tell me what brought you here."

Father Bennett waited for his superior to sit then he followed suit sitting on the couch. He told the bishop about the phone call that he had received that morning and his trip to Boston. Bishop Everly listened attentively. Then Father Bennett related what exactly transpired at the hospital.

"The head nurse was a very strange woman... In fact, the entire affair was rather strange. She immediately informed me about the very serious condition of the infant by the name of Brimos and then we proceeded to observe him lying in an incubator. Well, around the head of the incubator hung a grain wreath and when I asked her about any significance it might have, her whole expression changed to a look of horror and she said that 'Man must bite off the head of the serpent which has crawled into his mouth'. I was perplexed and I might add, a bit taken aback. Her voice lowered when she said that and I wondered if she might be demonically possessed. I asked her to repeat what she had said and she simply smiled and handed me a crude map indicating the directions to the mother's house. Then, strangely enough, she asked me to say a prayer of protection for Brimos and I obliged. What do you make out of this?"

Bishop Everly pondered about the entire affair for several moments and then did his best to form a complete analysis based on his background in the Classics and phenomenology.

"Her enigmatic statement is actually a quotation from the German philosopher, Friedrich Nietzsche, who was explaining metaphorically the necessity of facing the transiency of time. Have you ever heard of the hermeneutic circle?"

Father Bennett thought for a moment before answering the bishop's question.

"I know that hermeneutics is the study of scriptural truth, but I don't understand what you mean by the 'circle'."

Bishop Everly looked at him before continuing.

"Hermeneutics is the science or the art of interpretation, especially in regards to scripture, but understanding is always a circular or a referential operation. There is an interdependence, if you will, of the knower and the known. In other words, what is studied is preconceptually known. As logic cannot fully account for the workings of this circle, a kind of 'leap' into the hermeneutical circle becomes necessary, but the knowledge contained within it is radically finite. In my view, only the superior man finds his way out of this circle by a clearer understanding of the metaphor, which the pre-Socratic philosophers had," Bishop Every explained.

Very confused, the priest scratched his head, probing further.

"This idea of yours must be leading up to something interesting. What is the abstract equation?"

"The abstract equation is the uroboric circle, represented by the serpent crawling into one's mouth. In other words, the uroboric circle is the unconscious and the neophyte must follow a Hermes figure or psycho pomp. Without such a guide, left up to his own volition, the journey is perilous and dangerous. The only way out is either rebirth or madness for one can never possess the 'center'."

"What do you mean?" Father Bennett asked, intrigued.

"Because there is no 'telos' or ultimate aim as the journey is the goal, however circular for the center is ubiquitous or omnipresent. No one really knows why Nietzsche eventually went insane, but he must have had some tremendous insight into the perils of such a katabasis."

"What is a katabasis?"

"The word itself means the march back to the sea of the Greek mercenaries who followed Cyrus against Artaxerxes. The word has a Greek origin which means 'a going down' or in psychological terms, the interior journey into the very depths of the soul."

Father Bennett got up from the couch and began pacing back and forth, deliberating over what the bishop had said.

"What about the significance of the grain wreath?" he asked, looking at his superior.

"Primarily, I feel that the name of the child being Brimos and the significance of the grain wreath have definite allusions to the myth of Kore and Demeter. In my view, never was there a stronger bond between mother and daughter in Greek mythology as that intimate relationship between Persephone and her mother Demeter," Bishop Everly replied.

Father Bennett stopped his pacing and looked down at his superior.

"I'm not very familiar with that myth. Could you shed some light on the story?"

"According to the myth, Demeter was the daughter of Cronos and Rhea, and the sister of Zeus and Poseidon. In an incestuous union with Zeus, she bore a daughter, Kore... known as the 'maiden' or Persephone. Pluto, the god of the underworld, lusted after Kore and Zeus promised the maiden to him without telling Demeter. Anyway, he raped Persephone and abducted her into his underworldly kingdom. When Demeter learned of this, she went into profound mourning, donning black clothing and searching nine days for her daughter. On the tenth day, she encountered Hecate, the patron goddess of witchcraft, who had heard Kore cry out. The two went to Helios, who had witnessed the abduction. Upon hearing the story from Helios, Demeter went into a rage. She resigned from the company of the gods and neglected her duties. Now, bear in mind that she was the fertility goddess and when she neglected her duties, crops failed and famine spread throughout the land. The situation grew worse and worse but Demeter could not be persuaded to act. Finally, Hermes succeeded in convincing Pluto to let Persephone go. However, she had eaten part of a pomegranate before she left and this partaking of food in the underworld doomed her to spend at least part of the time with Pluto forever. Thus, the coming and going of Kore was signaled by the equinoxes. Anyway, Demeter was so grateful to have her daughter back at least part of the year that she initiated mankind into her mysteries and taught him agriculture, symbolized by the corn. Many of the secret rites of her cults were practiced by women because of their power to bring forth life."

At this point, Father Bennett shook his head as if he did not understand what the bishop was trying to allude to.

"I will be honest with you... I'm just simply confused about all this talk about myth and symbolism. All this is beyond my level of comprehension."

Bishop Everly rose from his seat and paused several moments and then with a very serious expression on his face took the priest by the arm.

"Come with me. I have something to show you which will further validate my analysis," he said, beginning to walk to the door of his study.

Silently, Father Bennett accompanied him. They walked into the garden. Father Bennett was appalled by what he saw before him.

"My God! What is happening here? All the plants have died!" he exclaimed, looking at what once had been one of the most beautiful and restful places in all of Marlborough. Row upon row of the beautiful flowers that Bishop Everly had cultivated through the years now lay on the ground, withered and shriveled. Father Bennett looked at his superior.

Bishop Everly gently folded his hands under his chin as if saying a prayer in silence and then opened his eyes to survey the devastation at his feet.

"I discovered my dead Juniper Chinensis this morning, which is the oldest plant in the garden by some sixty-five years... Then I discovered that all the other plants and flowers had died or were in the process of dying... Naturally, I found this to be very strange as I had cared for them on a daily basis for years...They were like my children..." his voice trailed off.

There was a look of profound sorrow on his face and there was pain in his usually sparkling blue eyes.

Father Bennett was very nervous and he grabbed hold of Bishop Everly.

"I ask you again... What in God's name does all this add up to?" he asked, his voice harsh with emotion.

Smiling, the old man gently patted the priest's hands and removed Father Bennett's grip on him.

"It is my conclusion that there is an element of sorcery or witchcraft at work. I base my judgment on the incident of the dying plants and from what you told me about the nurse at the hospital, which in her case the 'magic' was proving to be ineffective as she asked you to say a prayer of protection for the dying infant after ignoring the significance of the grain wreath. I might add that the legendary Demeter was also a nurse and was discovered immersing a dying infant in the fire in order to rejuvenate him. Frankly, I am very curious as to how you fit into this so-called plot."

Bishop Everly observed Father Bennett closely. The priest looked again at the destruction at his feet then back at his superior.

"I don't have any idea," he said." The nurse told me that the mother, by the name of Diana Clements, called out my name several times during her ordeal in giving birth."

"Well let me make a request... an urgent request," Bishop Everly said, gripping the priest's arm and staring into his eyes.

"Yes, I'm listening," Father Bennett said.

"I want you to leave the entire matter alone in order to avoid severer consequences."

The priest was too nervous to stand in any one position. As Bishop Everly's hand dropped from his arm, he began pacing back and forth again.

"I am intent upon solving this most perplexing mystery even though the exact location of Diana Clement's house is somewhere in Provincetown, which is outside our parish. I will never rest until I have solved this whole thing, no matter what the consequences might be," Father Bennett said with dogged determination.

Very serious, the bishop raised his voice.

"You know that I am not the superstitious type, but because your destination lies outside our parish, it might also be outside of the church's influence or protection. In other words, I am afraid that you might put yourself in a vulnerable position and become at the mercy of occult forces."

Father Bennett stopped and seemed perturbed by what the bishop was insinuating.

"Your Eminence," he began," I am not the type of fool who invites danger into his life. I received a phone call earlier this morning, which may prove to be the turning point of my life... I don't know... This is serious business and I believe that it warrants an investigation... I remember that for some reason, the mother abandoned her child after declaring to the nurse that Brimos was her 'gift to the world'."

Bishop Everly stared thoughtfully at him.

"Hmm... interesting... Brimos was the mythical divine child born at the highlight of the Eleusinian Mysteries in ancient Greece. The entire initiatory drama centered around the story of Kore and Demeter and was a major social institution for over a thousand years until it was later absorbed by the Athenian state religion," Bishop Everly said slowly and thoughtfully.

"This is getting pretty deep. Tell me more about this ancient Greek mystery drama," Father Bennett said, his curiosity aroused.

The bishop's eyes widened as he ran his right hand through his hair and his pensive stare gave the priest the impression that he was deep in thought.

"The matriarchal nature of the Eleusinian Mysteries offered a direct contradistinction to the Olympian pantheon in emphasizing the chthonic or underworldly triad of the goddesses Demeter, Persephone, and Hecate. The katabasis was an integral part of the Higher Mysteries when men and women alike re-familiarized themselves with the terrifying darkness... the nocturnal realm of the Great Mother as the point of origin. I believe that the significance of the grain wreath represented the plight of the soul as indissolubly linked to the process of organic life. Indeed, the 'miracle' of the grain seed transforming into an ear of grain and harvested in complete stillness was a sacramental mystery, which probably became more of a numinous event to the pagan than the Consecration of the High Mass does to the modern day Christian, who lost touch long ago with his archetypal foundations. Synchronous with this climax or 'epopteia' was the apocatastasis or the return of one's ancestors in which the moment of the Epiphany or the birth of the divine child merged with the past and the future of one's essential being. This is where the 'underworldly' aspect of the Eleusinian Mystery Drama was as much a vital and necessary stage in the process of psychic evolution than as now in a modern day society where the reality of ontological change is not so apparent."

"I'm curious... Why was there all this emphasis on the underworld?" Father Bennett asked intrigued by what he had just heard.

"The Mystery Schools were alike in the fact that the basic teaching was that a 'spark' of divinity was somehow latent within the neophyte and could only be 'rekindled' by a descent to the underworld. Of course the Christian 'Mysteria' consciously passed beyond this whole realm of roots and sources with a deep and not unfounded distrust towards the phantasmagoria of the unconscious. We believe that Christ's mission to the underworld paved the way for our salvation by His conquering the realm of death forever. Lazarus became the example for all mankind. We will arise, but nonetheless, the eternal struggle between Eros and Thanatos goes on within our souls."

At this point, Father Bennett seemed very restless and stuck his hands in his pockets.

"I need to go for a walk and think about everything you've said. All your rhetoric about myth and mystery cults has me deeply fascinated, but I am still agonizing about the whole affair," Father Bennett said.

Bishop Everly smiled and took the priest by the hand.

"I do understand your dilemma and I hope you understand my concern. From all that I've seen and heard, I just don't think that you are fully aware of what you are about to get involved in. I just ask that you please pray about this," Bishop Everly urged.

Father Bennett noticed the concern in the bishop's eyes.

"I will, Your Eminence. I really must go now to wrestle with my decision in light of what you have said here. Good afternoon," Father Bennett, said, shaking the bishop's hand.

"Go with God, my son," Bishop Everly said softly and with compassion.

Father Bennett nodded and left the bishop's house. He drove off and found a wooded park where he could walk. He walked for several hours and then returned to the church rectory. He went to his study that evening and struggled with the true motive behind his intent. Was it a personal quest or a divinely inspired mission to find the mother, who abandoned her child and claimed some sort of connection to the priest? There was a missing link somewhere, but he did not know for sure. He had mixed feelings about the entire affair. In a strange way, he felt that he was seductively being drawn into a giant web of a black widow spider intent on devouring her prey. Then again, he felt some remorse for the child and for the mother. Maybe it was God's will that he bring them together again. At this point, he prayed...

Chapter Six

The House Of The Two Crescent Moons

The next morning, Father Bennett awakened. He had not slept well the night before. A feeling of anticipation and dread had interrupted his sleep; strange dreams with dying infants had stalked through them interspersed with strange, faceless women. The result had been a restless night. He got out of bed and showered and shaved. He had breakfast.

In his study, he found a map and plotted out his route. The phone rang and he answered it.

"Hello?"

"Good morning, Joseph," came Bishop Everly's voice at the other end of the line.

"Good morning, Your Eminence," Father Bennett said.

"Are you still determined to go on this... quest of yours?"

"Yes, I am, sir," Father Bennett answered.

"Before you leave, please drop by and see me."

"I'll be over in a few minutes."

"Then I will see you in a few minutes. Goodbye."

"Goodbye."

Father Bennett hung up the phone and gathered up his map. He looked around his study for a moment as if to memorize each object in it, then he left.

His housekeeper was dusting in the living room as he walked to the front door.

"Going out, Father?' she inquired, looking up from her dusting.

"Yes. I'll probably be gone overnight," he replied.

"Shouldn't you pack a bag?" she asked, noticing the map in his hand.

"I have a bag in the trunk of my car," he said.

"Have a good trip, Father."

"Thank you."

He walked out the front door of the rectory and walked to his car. There was no bag in his car and he really had no idea whether he'd be gone overnight or not. He unlocked the driver's side door and got in, tossing the map on the seat next to him. He started the engine and waited for it to warm up. He had a pretty good idea what the bishop wanted to say to him. It was pretty much going to be like the conversation that they had yesterday afternoon.

When the car was sufficiently warmed up, he backed out of his parking space and drove to the bishop's residence. He parked in front of the house and turned off the engine. He got up and walked up the path to the front door. He rang the bell and waited for a moment before he heard footsteps approaching. The door opened, but instead of Martha, it was Bishop Everly himself.

"Good morning, Your Eminence," Father Bennett said.

"Good morning, Joseph. Please come in," Bishop Everly said.

He stood aside to let Father Bennett enter then closed the door behind them.

"Have you had breakfast yet?" Bishop Everly asked.

"Yes, sir. Am I interrupting your breakfast?" Father Bennett asked.

"No, I just finished. Let's go back to my study."

Father Bennett nodded and the two men walked down the hall to Bishop Everly's study.

They entered and the bishop waved towards the sofa."Sit down, Joseph."

"Thank you."

The two men seated themselves.

They looked at each other silently.

"I didn't sleep well last night," Bishop Everly said.

"I didn't either," Father Bennett confessed.

The bishop nodded

"Are you still determined to go seeking phantoms?"

He looked at Father Bennett searchingly. Father Bennett looked down at his clasped hands then back into Bishop Everly's face.

"Yes, I still feel that it's my duty to try to find this woman and bring her back to the hospital to be with her dying infant," Father Bennett said slowly.

"I see," Bishop Everly said.

A silence descended upon the room.

"Is there nothing that I can say short of ordering you not to go that would change your mind on this matter, Joseph?" he asked.

"I'm afraid not, Your Eminence," Father Bennett said.

Bishop Everly sighed.

"I was afraid of that. Well, Joseph, I am not ordering you not to go. I suppose that you feel that you have to do this thing."

"Yes, I do, Your Eminence."

"You're leaving now?"

"Yes."

"I'll walk you to your car."

The two men stood up and left Bishop Everly's study. They left the house and walked down the path to Father Bennett's car. They stood on the sidewalk. Bishop Everly embraced him.

"I want you to know that our Lord loves you and that I love you. I ask that you please reconsider this mission of yours for the last time," Bishop Everly said.

"Your Eminence, last night I prayed about this matter and reached a decision. I know in my heart that what I am about to do is right and that if I choose to neglect my duties then I could no longer consider myself a man of the faith. I guess that there are times when our Lord allows evil into one's life, but being strong in the faith, I know that I will surmount any obstacles in my path. I have and always will be a soldier for Christ and no matter how dangerous the situation might be, where I go, the Lord will be with me."

Father Bennett looked into the bishop's troubled blue eyes and broke the embrace. He got into his car and started the engine. The bishop folded his arms and smiled. He came around to the driver's side and tapped on the window. Father Bennett rolled the window down. Bishop Everly leaned forward until he could look inside.

"May our Lord be with you, my son, should you be confronted with the powers of Satan. The wiles of the Prince of Darkness are more complex than any human mind can conceive. I also ask that you please use a little common sense if the situation warrants it."

Their eyes met briefly.

"I understand, Your Eminence. Try not to worry about me. I should be back by tomorrow." Father Bennett said, putting his hand on the bishop's in what he hoped was a comforting manner.

Bishop Everly nodded and went back to stand on the curb.

Father Bennett drove off. Even though he knew that the entire affair had not been sanctioned by Bishop Everly, he was determined. The weather was perfect as there was not a cloud in the sky. He tilted his head back slightly to enjoy the three-hour drive to Provincetown.

"I hope that I'm doing the right thing by chasing off to Provincetown," he thought as the miles flashed by." I know that Bishop Everly is very concerned about this, but I feel that it is something that I must do. I have never been to Provincetown before. I know that it is an artist's colony and that is about all that I know about the town. I wonder what I'll say to this Diana Clements to bring her to her senses and make her care about her own child. I cannot fathom a mother leaving her newborn infant and just going off. What kind of a mother is she anyway? Does she even have any maternal feelings for the child that she bore? That sort of thing baffles me completely. Should I swing by the hospital and see if the child is still alive or just go on to Provincetown? I'll just go on. Whether the child lives or not is in God's hands now. Man can do no more for him. Why would Diana Clements call out my name during her ordeal? I do not know her. Maybe when I find her, then my question will be answered. I hope so. So many questions that need answers. I hope that this house where she lives isn't too hard to find."

At the extreme tip of Cape Cod and one of the oldest towns in Massachusetts, Provincetown was the first landing site for the pilgrims in 1620 before going on to Plymouth. The famous Mayflower Compact was signed there and this affirmation of law and self-government was still considered to be the very root of democratic government in America and was the ancestor of the Constitution. During the 1600's and early 1700's, Provincetown and the Outer Cape were settled by men pursuing mackerel and cod. Enough English settlers had arrived by 1727 to incorporate the area as a town. The early settlers built their homes close to the bay, near the water, with the beach as their main highway. Side streets ran inland and the homes were simple, practical, but comfortable. Even Henry David Thoreau was deceived by the famous Cape Cod house and realized that the rich interior was in direct contrast to the outer facade. By 1800, a population of almost one thousand was living on the riches of the sea and Provincetown had a reputation as one of the greatest and busiest seaports in the country. During the 1800's, there was a large influx of men from Cape Breton and other coastal towns in eastern Nova Scotia who joined the Yankees and Portuguese in manning the fishing fleets. Their descendants still carried on the old tradition to some extent. With the arrival of the twentieth century, the fishing industry concentrated on supplying the fresh fish needs of Boston and New York. The catch was initially shipped from the Old Colony Railroad wharf by train, but by mid-century; trailer trucks had taken over the task. Now a home to a fleet of more than thirty-five boats that sailed out in the early morning hours and returned in the late afternoon, Provincetown was still active as a seaport.Most importantly was Provincetown's celebrated reputation as the nation's oldest continuous art colony which began with the charismatic Charles Hawthorne, who placed his easel there in 1899. For thirty summers, Hawthorne taught painting to hundreds of spellbound students, urging them to work rapidly in the open air as the light changed from moment to moment. By 1910, it was no longer necessary for a young artist to study in France. The secluded art colonies of Pont-Aven and Barbizon soon found American counterparts in East Hampton, Woodstock,

Taos, Carmel and other rural communities. In size and importance, however, none rivaled Provincetown. By 1916, other artists including William Zorach, set up their own schools challenging the dominant impressionistic techniques of Hawthorne. Despite the allurement of New York, most artists were still in agreement about the natural environmental endowments of this seaside community as a true source of inspiration.

Early that afternoon, Father Bennett arrived in Provincetown and pulled up to a service station. When the service station attendant arrived, Father Bennett told him to fill up the car. He got out and stretched. He watched as the attendant put the gas nozzle in then went to check the oil and the other fluids. The attendant washed the windows and checked the tire pressure.

"It's very quiet here," Father Bennett said.

"Oh, aye 'tis," the attendant said.

He was a lean, wiry man with a weathered face burned by wind and sun. His hair was graying; his blue eyes squinted as if seeing into the far distance. He had a New England twang in his voice. He topped the tank off and replaced the nozzle.

"Five dollars and seventy-five cents," he announced.

Father Bennett took out his wallet and handed the man a ten-dollar bill. The man went inside and Father Bennett followed him. Inside the building was a long counter with a cash register on it. There was a long cooler with sliding glass doors filled with beer, wine and soft drinks. There were shelves that carried food items such as bread, peanut butter, jams and jellies and other assorted foodstuffs. There were racks containing sunglasses, maps, and other small items.

"Anything else for you?" the attendant asked as he rang up the sale.

"Just some information," Father Bennett said.

"Been here a long time, all my life, so I reckon I know everything there is to know about Provincetown. What might you be needing to know?" he asked as he handed Father Bennett his change.

Father Bennett took out the crudely drawn map and handed it to the man.

"This is supposed to be a map to a woman's house. Her name is

Diana Clements. I can't quite make out the name of the street here," Father Bennett said.

The attendant scrutinized the map for several minutes and then he smiled as he handed it back to the priest.

"She lives off Commercial Street on Atwood, two blocks away from the oldest house in town called the Seth Nickerson House, which has been a major historical site as long as I can remember."

"How do I get there?"

"Just continue on down Route 6 along the coast until it winds around the Pilgrim Plaque into Commercial Street. Go two blocks and make an immediate left onto Atwood. You could walk from here in less than an hour."

"Do you have a better map than this?"

The old man scratched his head and looked for a map.

"Sorry," he said," Seems like we're out of maps for the time being. So many tourists come through here year round, you know."

"Yes, I imagine that you do get a lot of tourists here."

"Sure helps the economy."

"Well, thank you for your time anyway."

"You're welcome. It won't be all that hard to find."

Father Bennett nodded and walked back to his car. He got in and drove off, periodically looking at the crude drawing next to him to make sure that he was going in the right direction. There was no doubt that he was taking the scenic route for he was surrounded by the crashing surf and sand. He was impressed by the quaint little town and looked up at the Pilgrim Plaque as he drove by. The atmosphere seemed so tranquil as the weather was perfect. He followed Commercial Street going slowly so as not to miss the street that he was looking for.

He found Atwood Street and made the turn. The wind was gently blowing in from the sea carrying to his nostrils the smell of salt water. He stopped his car and got out. He had reached a dead-end. Again, he looked at the drawing but could not discern for himself exactly where she lived. He noticed a house and took the liberty of walking over to it. It was a small one-story house. He mounted the steps to the porch and knocked on the door. He waited and was about to knock again when he heard footsteps approaching. The door opened to reveal an elderly man with a graying beard. His hands shook.

"Yes?" he asked in a high quavery voice, taking in the apparition of a Catholic priest standing on his doorstep." Is it my time yet? Ha! Ha! I'm just kidding, Father. What can I help you with?"

"I'm looking for a certain woman named Diana Clements. It's very important that I find her. According to this map that she drew, she lives on this street," Father Bennett said.

"I ain't never heard of her. She could live on the other side of the street, ya know," the old man said, frowning.

"Why are your hands trembling?"

"Ah, it's just the delirium tremens... I just haven't had my morning drink yet," the old man mumbled, shuffling his feet.

"I am sorry to hear that. My heart goes out to you."

"Listen, Father, I don't need your prayers or anything. I'm a God-fearing man and I'm content with the way that I live. If you're on some sort of mission, I suggest that you walk around the other side of the block in the southwesterly direction of the ocean and you might find this woman you are searching for. Good luck to you."

"May God be with you," Father Bennett said.

The old man shut his door. Father Bennett could hear his retreating footsteps. Feeling frustrated, he walked down the steps and returned to the street. He walked past several houses and walked up to a cottage. He took a deep breath and once again tried his luck by knocking on the door. What sounded like a black woman called out from inside.

"Yeah? Who is it?"

Raising his voice, Father Bennett leaned his head against the door.

"I am Father Joseph Bennett from Marlborough and I am looking for a woman named Diana Clements who lives on Atwood. Do you know where she lives?"

Refusing to answer the door, the woman called out to him again, more irritated this time as Father Bennett could hear a child crying in the background."Ain't never heard of her!

Now you best be on your way!"

Father Bennett walked back in the direction of his car. He was on the verge of giving up hope of ever finding the mysterious Diana Clements. As he approached within fifty yards of his car, he was startled to discover four young black men in the process of stealing his hubcaps. He felt the hard knot of fear in his stomach. The leader of the four toughs looked at him contemptuously. With a sneer on his face, he seemed totally unconcerned about being discovered. For a second, Father Bennett's eyes locked with the young tough's. He quickly turned and began walking in the other direction. He hoped that he could get out of there without any trouble but they followed him. The leader of the group began taunting him with obscenities.

"Hey, mutherfucker! Where the hell you goin'? I'm gonna kick yo' ass, mutherfucker! Hey! Yo' hear what I'm sayin'? I'm personally goin' to kick yo' mutherfuckin' ass and what's left over, my brothers can have of yo' ass!"

Father Bennett began walking faster, trying to escape from his would-be attackers. He crossed himself and began reciting the Lord's Prayer.

"Our Father, Who art in heaven, hallowed be Thy name. Thy kingdom come, Thy will be done on earth as it is in heaven. Give us this day our daily bread and forgive us our trespasses as we forgive those who trespass against us. Lead us not into temptation, but deliver us from evil. For Thine is the kingdom and the power and the glory forever. Amen."

Father Bennett glanced back over his shoulder. The four hoodlums were ambling along behind him, insolently grinning at him. A cold sweat broke out on his face and body. He turned his face ahead.

Suddenly, in the distance standing near the entrance to the street, appeared the ghost-like figure of a woman wearing a white gown. She raised her right hand as if making a gesture to the black men and they backed off from Father Bennett returning one by one to their neighborhood. The mysterious woman then walked around to the other side of the block. Immediately, the priest followed her and as he turned the corner to the other street without a name, he saw the wisp of her gown as she evidently entered a dilapidated mansion. Father Bennett halted before the mansion. There was an aura about the house that he couldn't quite put his finger on. He stood on the sidewalk, staring at the house. The mansion seemed to be a Victorian Gothic style that appeared to be over a hundred years old. His initial impression was of the profound state of anxiety it seemed to exude. The house seemed to be asymmetrical with the smaller left side covered with seaweed and a more pronounced right side that had higher arches. He looked at the masculine crumbling arches that gave way to the feminine curvature of the latticework around the windows. The roof was peaked, looking like the roof of a church without the spire. There was a balcony near the eaves where a door and a window could be discerned. In times past, the balcony was probably used to scan the sea for the approaching fleet, especially if it was overdue. The mansion had turrets as in old-fashioned medieval castles. The shingles on the roof seemed to be falling into the drainpipe that ran around the building. Further down the windows, looked like eyes without any light. There was a porch that seemed to be as dilapidated as the rest of the house. Four steps led up to the front door. The steps sagged in the middle as the weight of centuries had driven it to the ground. The railing of the porch was broken in places and near one of the corners; a swing chair on a rusted chain completed the impression of forlornness. The front door was divided into two sections with frosted glass that made it hard to look in.

Father Bennett attempted to look beyond the outer facade of the house itself; beyond the irreconcilable opposites into the darkness of the labyrinthine interior and he shuddered. At one time, he had been influenced by the famous architectural theorist, John Ruskin, who had a devoutly religious attitude to dilapidated buildings. For him, they were love objects and suffering creatures in need of redemption. Indeed, a building or a house was more beautiful in decay than in its ideal state because it had been victimized by evil forces.

Father Bennett decided to enter the house. He was careful as he walked up the sagging steps to the porch. As he approached the door, he discovered a drawing of two crescent moons above the door. He was baffled by what it meant and without further hesitation proceeded to knock on the door several times. There was no answer. He decided on his own initiative to enter the house and was surprised to find the door unlocked. He was also surprised to find that it was devoid of furniture in the two rooms that he looked into. He cupped his hands to his mouth and yelled several times in each direction of the four hallways that led to God knew where.

"Diana Clements! Diana Clements! Diana are you here? I am Father Joseph Bennett from the Church of the Holy Rosary in Marlborough. Can you hear me?"

There was no answer. His shouting echoed through the mansion, causing the cobwebs that he discerned in the light of the growing dusk to vibrate. A spider in one of the webs hung there malevolently.

Calling out Diana's name proved to be in vain. He wandered aimlessly from room to room. Dust lay heavy on the floors. As he walked through it, the dust rose as if it hadn't been disturbed in a hundred years. He sneezed. He covered the entire ground floor before coming back to the hall. A wide staircase stood before him stretching up into the gathering blackness. He didn't think to bring a flashlight.

With his right hand on the banister, Father Bennett ascended the stairs. The musty odor of stench and decay almost overwhelmed him. At the top of the stairs, he stood still, listening for any sounds. He walked slowly and cautiously down the hall until he noticed a light coming from beneath one of the doors. Arriving at the door, he put his hand on the doorknob and slowly opened it. The hinges had not been oiled in God knows how long. A loud screech seemed to protest his opening the door. He seemed to be in the master bedroom. He stepped cautiously inside, his heart beginning to pound in his chest. He looked around as he went deeper on into the room.

Upon the walls hung various paintings and again, as he studied each one carefully, he was baffled by the bizarre symbolism. He noticed a bed. Advancing towards the bed, he was suddenly overcome with fatigue. He lay down on the bed and attempted to compose his thoughts. Eventually, he fell on off to sleep and in his dream, what appeared to be a shimmering golden fetus appeared as if in mid-air, moving through the darkness of space. It moved slowly over towards the window and illuminated by the light of the moon, appeared an old witch caressing the fetus in the palms of her hands. She began howling at the blood red full moon and an eerie refrain could be heard from a pack of wolves down in the street below. She held up the writhing fetus.

"I offer you this sacrifice in the name of Hecate!"At this point, in the dream, the priest tried to stop the evil witch from her act, but as he reached out to grab the fetus, it disappeared and she literally flew out the window as the wolves continued howling below.

Sitting bolt upright in the bed, his heart raced like a trip hammer. The blood roared in his ears like the crashing surf. A cold sweat broke out on his body and he stared wildly about the room. He jumped off the bed on the left side closest to the window. Suddenly, he felt a cold gust of wind.

"Where did that come from? I'm getting out of here..." his voice trailed off.

At that moment as the priest was getting ready to leave, the mysterious woman walked into the room over towards the window. She opened the blind and stared out at the new moon, gently running her fingers through her long black hair. Her extremely pale complexion gave him the impression that she was nocturnal and the blood stains on her white night gown gave mute evidence that at one time she went through a very violent ordeal.

Not sure if he was seeing an apparition or the real thing, Father Bennett addressed the mysterious woman.

"Are you Diana Clements?"

The mysterious woman did not answer, continuing her vigil by the window. The priest tried another approach, hoping to elicit a response.

"Are these your paintings? They are very impressive."

The mysterious woman smiled but continued gazing out the window. There was something tantalizingly familiar about her but he couldn't put his finger on what it was. There was also something haunting about the way she looked out the window as if expecting her lover. He studied her profile, hoping to find some clue as to who she was.

"Are you aware that there is a new moon tonight?" she asked, her voice was low and husky.

Father Bennett was perplexed. He walked over to the window and verified the woman's observation.

"I believe you're right," he said, gazing out the window." Is there some significance?"

The mysterious woman walked from the window over to one of the paintings. He watched her. Her movements were graceful, sinuous like a cat or a snake. She seemed to pay no attention to him. Except for her question about the moon, she seemed to be totally unaware of his presence.

She turned to face him, seeing him as if for the first time. A shadow of a smile played around the corners of her mouth.

"It is a very appropriate occasion for you to be here tonight and a fitting prelude to what I am about to show you. Would you care to take a look at one of my more esoteric works?"

Father Bennett was flustered.

"Why sure... I would be honored..." he said.

Father Bennett walked over to the particular painting and was astounded by what he saw before him. In the painting were the figures of a nude queen embracing a dragon, which had wrapped its tail around her as they both lay in an open grave. Closer inspection revealed that the dragon's head was wounded and both figures had facial expressions of absolute horror at their predicament.

"What, may I ask, is the title of this particular work?" Father Bennett asked.

He was uneasy by the painting.

"I call it 'The Armenian Bitch', which refers to Luna as the new moon in conjunction with the sun that most of the ancient alchemists envisioned as a most gruesome hierosgamos or mystical wedding. Luna's specialty was love magic and the solar hero, who fell victim to it usually, became mad. Take for instance the story of Diana, who was also another Greek variation of the moon goddess motif and the hunter, Actaeon. Are you at all familiar with the myth?"

"No, I cannot say that I am. I never really had an interest in mythology."

"Actaeon was a perfect example of the heroic lover mesmerized by the sight of Diana bathing in a river one day. She discovered him and subsequently turned him into a stag whereupon his hunting dogs attacked him. You might say that he experienced the tremendum of becoming divine, however horrible it is in the beginning. For in alchemical terms, the Sol Niger or the lunar eclipse of the sun is also a wounding. In other words, the Cartesian ego when first confronted by the matrix of the unconscious, is faced with the hidden dangers of a psychosis because nature must somehow compensate in the instinctual sphere abandoned by the spirit. Thus, orthodox Christianity for centuries ignored the 'dark side' of the feminine and instead exalted her as the Virgin Mary who personified the church."

Father Bennett was silent for several moments as he studied the painting.

"Well, what do you think?" she asked, staring at him, her arms folded across her breasts.

He looked from the painting to her.

"I… I really don't know what to say about it… It's unlike anything I've ever seen before… Would you call this an example of surrealism?"

She smiled almost contemptuously, yet there seemed to be an amused glint in her dark eyes.

"Andre Breton felt that the surrealist image would bring about a 'flight of the senses', but Freud considered surrealist art as a form of spiritual bankruptcy. However, my mentor was the famous abstract expressionist, Hans Hofman, who taught here several decades ago. He considered surrealism closely akin to mysticism."

Father Bennett slowly walked around the gallery and observed the other paintings.

"I can't say that I'm familiar with his theories. Would you care to enlighten me?" he asked her.

"He believed that nature was the process of dynamic life itself. He wrote and I quote, 'Life does not exist without movement and movement does not exist without life. Space is filled with movement, with forces and counter forces, with tension and functions, with colors and light, with life and rhythm and the dispositions of sublime divinity'. Along with Alfred North Whitehead, he stands out by continuing the ancient quest for metaphysical truth. He believed that only the artists have given the most convincing arguments for spiritual reality. He firmly believed, as I do, that it is the mysterious transubstantiated spiritual substance that gives great art its permanence."

Father Bennett stopped at the last painting in the gallery and crossed his arms over his chest, staring at the painting as he had all the others.

"Are you the artist solely responsible for all these paintings?"

"Yes, I am. Why do you ask?" she said almost defiantly.

"I can see with each successive work how you have graduated from one style to the next and this last piece entitled 'The Bacchanalia' is totally abstract. I simply cannot make heads or tails out of it."

With a smile that was hard for him to fathom, she walked back over to the window and gazed outside again. She was silent as she began stroking her hair. The priest watched her for several moments then broke the silence that had descended on the room like an ominous cloud.

"I'm sorry," he said almost apologetically." I'm just not a connoisseur of art."

Suddenly, the mysterious woman turned from the window and confronted the priest. There was a look of contempt in her dark eyes.

"You! You raped me on the night of the Winter Solstice when the moon was the source of life and the sun was in the underworld! I was a virgin until you came to me on December twenty-first like a mad dog and now my menstrual blood is synonymous with the light of the moon! Because you violated my virginity, you deserved the wrath of my grandmother!" she exclaimed, her eyes like the twin muzzles of a shotgun aimed directly at the stunned priest.

Father Bennett was totally perplexed by the accusation and did his best to control his nervousness.

"Listen," he said placatingly." Please lower your voice. I am on a mission and simply came here to inform you about the serious condition of your son, Brimos. I assume that you are his mother and if you are, then you need to return with me to the hospital."

For a moment, their eyes met: hers furious; his bewildered. Then he looked away. Almost, as if in a trance-like state, the mysterious woman lowered her voice, staring directly at the priest.

"The significance of the dying Brimos is the fact that you are losing your ability to see with the 'third eye' and eventually the infant will no longer serve as a psychopomp or guide into the mysteries. Do you understand me?"

The confused priest did not know if he should interpret what the woman said literally or metaphorically. He had seen Brimos in the hospital and knew that she had a very difficult delivery. Why were there bloodstains on her nightgown? Was the infant an entity deeply interfused with his own being? He knew who she was but he was afraid to ask because there was a missing link somewhere. How could he have raped such a beautiful and innocent young virgin, unless he had a dark, sinister side he was totally unaware of?

"You know who I really am, don't you?" she demanded.

The priest remained silent for several moments as he could literally feel the sudden rush of adrenalin spreading up his back and along the nape of his neck.

"I... I know now why you changed your name to Diana..."

His words sounded lame and inane in his ears. He imagined how it must sound to her. He looked at her as she smiled again, running her hands along the drapes that framed the window.

"It's truly amazing how relevant a myth can become," she said softly.

Feeling very nervous as well as awkward, the priest began rubbing his hands together and then folded them under his arms.

"Sister Marcia... What has happened? I'm suffering from a lapse of memory. Did you report the supposed incident to anyone before you left?"

She turned and looked out the window then turned slowly back to face him, noting how drawn his face had become. A look of pity showed in her eyes.

"I respected you at one time... I really did... I even confided some of my deepest secrets to you... After that horrible night, I went to the emergency room to find out how extensive the damage was as you had tried to insert some broken shards of glass into my vagina. The doctor asked me what had happened, but I told him that I was knocked unconscious and could not identify my attacker. Several months later, I found out that I was pregnant and that's when I decided to leave the convent... I moved to Provincetown to get away from it all... to live the life of an artist because I was having some incredible visions... I joined the Fine Arts Work Center and met some truly incredible individuals, who helped me to really express myself... I became addicted to painting... It's in my life's blood and if I were to quit painting... Oh God, if I were to quit painting, I would go insane because I will never totally recover from my trauma..." her voice trailed off and she lowered her head as if ashamed. There was a quality of pathos about her. She seemed to personify lost innocence.

Father Bennett could feel his heartbeat accelerating and he began to take longer breaths in order to slow it down. For a moment, he skirted the issue.

"Why do you wear that gown? Surely, you don't wear it all the time."

Diana continued to run her hands through her long black hair.

"I only wear this particular gown on the night of the new moon and I believe I was clear as to the significance when I showed you my painting."

Father Bennett shook his head as if he did not understand the consequences of what had happened.

"All I can say is that I am totally confused and totally baffled by what I've seen and heard this evening. Why don't you tell me what really happened that night?"

At this point, Diana showed Father Bennett the blood stains on her nightgown as she held it up to him."Here," she said, coming closer to him." Take a close look...Your difficulty in remembering the experience was primarily the horrifying aftermath of the rape when we both experienced the torments of hell. The night you came to me, your manic-depressive behavior gave me the distinct impression that you might be under the influence of a drug. Why you took the drug, I'll never know... Anyway, you had confused the Holy Ghost with the Hidden God and declared to me that you had been outside observing the constellation; Sirius and that you felt you were a part of the force intrinsic to Digitaria or the white dwarf star in its orbit around the Dog Star as if it were the 'seed of creation'. Much as Joachim of Flora, you announced that the era of the Holy Ghost was at hand and that all sacramentalism would be abolished along with the ecclesiastical hierarchy. The fact of the matter is that we both experienced a baptism of fire through the Hidden God instead of the Holy Ghost because your Kundalini was not in balance. Anyway, I went with you to the chapel that night and asked you to perform the mass for the last time because I felt that you lacked a certain amount of insight as to its true significance. What stands out very clear in my mind was the moment of the Transubstantiation when you held up a glass of water and declared that you were the 'original fish of the sea'. You experienced what I would call a 'participation mystique' as you felt your entire being was deeply intrinsic to the glass of water... Suddenly, an unknown force moved through the chapel and literally knocked the glass from your hand. What followed was the satanic counterpart as you were not at all prepared to incarnate the dark side of God. Instead, you ordered me to clean up the mess and when I failed to do so, you commenced to rape me among the broken shards of glass all over the floor. In actuality, what lay scattered upon the floor was the Primordial Man and your severe schizophrenia lasted for the better part of ten hours. Eventually, the parapsychic activity engulfed the entire room and I shared in your hallucinations of hell. In other words, you sacrificed yourself on the night of the Winter Solstice and became the Dying God. You experienced more light than any mere mortal could bear when you were literally hurled into the Abyss. Thus, the night of December twenty-first marked your transition from a servant of Christ to an avatar of the nether world, but your forced entrance into the mysteries was premature and therefore catastrophic."

There was a deep silence after she had finished speaking. He stared at her in shock, his mind unable to comprehend what she had just told him. He shook his head as if to dislodge her words and the ugly images that they conjured up. The silence lengthened and became almost unbearable.

Father Bennett forced himself to turn towards the door, as he was ready to leave.

"This whole thing is totally absurd... I refuse to believe any of it... What I do believe is that your wild imagination has gotten the upper hand here," he said.

Diana returned her gaze to the window. She stood like a statue carved out of alabaster marble. She began stroking her hair again.

"Humpty Dumpty sat on a wall... Humpty Dumpty had a great fall... All the king's horses and all the king's men couldn't put Humpty back together again," she chanted in a monotonic voice.

The priest shook his head as he left the room considering Diana to be psychotic. As he walked down the hallway, he suddenly noticed a small boy cowering in the corner. He was concerned as to why the boy was there and as he approached him, he began to see how dirty he was, wearing rags for clothes.

He crouched down.

"Who are you, son?" he asked the boy gently.

The small boy looked up at the priest, revealing some open sores on his face.

"I am from Bythos... I am from the deep..."

Suddenly, the boy disappeared and the priest remembered a very vivid dream in which the same boy appeared. His excitement increased after seeing the apparent apparition and he re-entered the room and found Diana still staring out the window with a smile on her face. With much emotion in his voice, he related his vision to her.

"I... I saw the Bythos boy sitting in the hallway outside your door! I remember the Bythos boy sitting at the foot of the cross in the church! The child, as a guide, led me on a journey through the underground labyrinths beneath the church and I discovered lepers wearing bandages... Eventually, I was led to the very base of the cross at which I found Adam's skull partially buried... The child gave it to me and it was like transparent glass or pure crystal. I looked into the eye sockets of the glass skull and beheld the sun on the cross bleeding huge gouts of blood, which rained down on the lepers, healing them...The boy disappeared and the dreams subsequently tapered off..."

Diana turned form the window and stared at Father Bennett again, speaking very slowly and succinctly.

"You vision is proof that an element of self-sacrifice is necessary to return to the Adamic state. Professor Jung put it so aptly when he wrote, 'The dichotomy of God into divinity and humanity and his return to himself in the sacrificial act hold out the comforting doctrine that in man's own darkness there is hidden a light that shall once again return to its source... and that this light actually wanted to descend into the darkness in order to deliver the Enchained One who languishes there and lead him to light everlasting.' This, of course, implies Basilides doctrine of the Anthropos for when the Gnostic Nous fell into the embrace of Physis, he took the dark chthonic form of the serpent. The alchemists equated Mercurius to the Anthropos as the entire opus had a soteriological emphasis in redeeming matter. Any form of initiation implies a torture and a certain amount of suffering in the beginning in order for the neophyte to realize his spiritual progress. What you went through was more like the most severe form of shamanistic initiation as I implied earlier with the dismemberment motif, but unfortunately it was imcomplete. Why else would you suffer from amnesia?"

Father Bennett looked down at the floor.

"I don't know... I somehow felt that there was a missing link somewhere, but I did not know for sure."

"Well, now you know and because you know, there is no turning back," she said sternly.

Father Bennett looked up at Diana.

"What do you mean?" he demanded.

"The only way you can 'save' the life of Brimos and 'nourish' him back to health is to make love to me the natural way. In other words, the time that we spend making love is also the vital time for Brimos to enjoy peaceful heavenly sleep. It is imperative that you free your mind of all thoughts and allow your consciousness to merge with the elements. To me, the mind is an infinite landscape and your consciousness should encompass more by responding to the sands of the beach as well as the ocean tide as if it were intrinsic to your own body. It is essential that you free yourself from all attachments to the ego and your habitual way of seeing the world," she told him.

The anxious priest began pacing back and forth. She watched him, her face unreadable.

"I don't really see how this is possible for me under the present circumstances and whatnot... I cannot even conceive of this ideal state--this self-surrender that you are describing. My habitual way of seeing the world is what keeps me sane."

"I can see that language does not suffice here. We must move beyond the conceptual realm of semantics and into the sphere of soft caresses... hushed whispers and the breath of true life. I simply ask that you follow me outside for we will take a walk and then I will dance... and then we will make love for we will know when the time is right," she informed him, slightly impatient.

After some reluctance, Father Bennett gave in to Diana's magnetism and followed her down the stairs and outside into the dark night. A streetlamp gave off a feeble light as if it were about to go out. A gentle breeze permeated his senses as he followed her across the street. They picked their way cautiously down a narrow path to the shore. He felt more relaxed now that he was away from the house because he felt that it contained some kind of deep dark mystery as if it had no real foundation. As he looked back at the dilapidated mansion, he wondered what the symbol of the two crescent moons really meant, but he was afraid to ask her. He remembered Bishop Everly's warning that morning and he chose to ignore it. Was he at her mercy? Could he simply get in his car and leave? At this point, he feared the consequences if he did make the mistake of leaving because she was like a guide leading him on some type of journey into the unknown.Diana seemed to be in a joyous mood as she whirled herself around several times, her gown unfurling, displaying shapely legs.

"I live for the night because I am truly authentic during the night for the dayworld stands in opposition to my playing... to my freedom," she told him." Sublimation is a thing of the past. Now, I give free rein to my every impulse. For my entire being revolves around the different phases of the moon and on this particular night, I will celebrate my womanhood by dancing like the maenads in a new moon ritual. I feel that you must balance your solar masculine nature by participation also so you must urinate in a bowl of my menstrual blood. I must consecrate this area as sacred ground before I perform my dance."

Diana held up the bowl that seemed to have materialized from out of thin air. Father Bennett suddenly felt very awkward.

"Are you sure that we're safe out here? Are you sure that we're not visible to someone, who might be offended by our actions?" he asked nervously as he glanced around. Down the coast, he could see the lights of a marina with the boats bobbing to the gentle waves that lapped their hulls. Up the coast, the lights of the town seemed distant. There didn't seem to be any cars above them on Commercial Street. The waves were gently caressing the shore like a lover in the timeless game that water and sand had played for aeons.

Diana smiled at his nervousness almost as if she was relishing his discomfiture.

"It doesn't really matter because we are like two stone leaves agitated by an alien wind... We are beyond out linear years... We must proceed with the moment unfolding like the quiet undulation of the tide advancing upon the shore... We are two sentient beings soaring..."

Her words seemed to him to be very poetic as the smile on her face was radiant.

"I guess what you are saying is that there is no use worrying about anything at all because it is the reality of the moment that really matters. I think you told me that before, but I really didn't understand at the time what you meant."

Diana smiled as she held up the bowl turning to each of the four directions. The priest unzipped his pants and shared his appreciation by participating. Somehow, he felt drawn to the whole affair and after he had finished urinating, he removed his clothes and sat down on the beach in a receptive state. She began to dance her ritual of the new moon first slowly to the left, celebrating the act of her lunar nature as a moon goddess with a libation as she poured the contents of the bowl into the ocean. All the while, the quiet mesmerized priest carefully watched her erotic movements and became sexually aroused. As if in a frenzy of excitement, she whirled around several times to the right and then suddenly froze like a statue. No sooner did she pause for recompense then she reversed her dance movements back to the left and then suddenly stopped again as if she were trying to communicate something to the moon. She leaped through the air several times like a ballerina and landed gently on the sand perfectly poised. Then her movements seemed to resemble a Tai Chi exercise as she slowly moved her arms in a rhythmic circular fashion to the right and stepped precisely forward. Now, she reversed her movement and walked backward, moving her arms in a circular movement to the left. She then bowed and looked up as if she were in a state of total serenity. Removing her gown, she laid down in a receptive position next to the observing priest. He stretched out on his side next to her, caressing the full length of her body. Feeling totally aroused, the priest mounted her. She gently placed his right hand on her left thigh as they began to have intercourse.

"We must achieve a rhythm together in harmony with the ocean tide... Our climax must be mutual for our souls will merge for one brief instant which will seem like eternity," she gently informed him.

During their lovemaking session, Diana's groans and screams blended in with the sounds of the onrushing waves lapping the shore. She was totally submissive and her whole body moved with each electrifying sensation. Suddenly, the priest found himself on the verge of ecstasy and in the midst of his orgasm; he visualized himself performing the Consecration of the High Mass and looked down at the golden snake coiling itself around the sacred bread.

Father Bennett was overcome with fatigue and rolled over on his back. Much to his surprise, he discovered a blood red full moon.

"My God! What has happened to the moon?"

Diana suddenly stood up and regained her composure by covering herself with her gown. Deeply concerned, she looked down at the priest.

"What did you see during your orgasm?" she asked urgently.

"I was performing the Consecration of the High Mass and as I looked down at the consecrated wafer and the wine, I could see a snake wrapping its body around the bread." Father Bennet told her.

Diana seemed agitated and prepared to leave. She acted as if he had suddenly become a stranger.

"Something went wrong...The snake is the anti-logos and will attack the Logos or the crown of Kether." she muttered almost to herself and then exclaimed," Your soul does not belong to Helios, the sun but to Hecate!"

"What does the color of the moon mean?" he asked her urgently.

She stared at him for a long moment and then said in a voice that chilled him to the marrow of his bones:

"It means," she said slowly," that the canines--the hounds of hell--will be coming!"

Her face lost any color it might have had.

Suddenly, in the distance, could be heard the sounds of barking dogs. Their barking soon rose to full-throated howls that sent shivers of dread down his spine. He felt the hair on the nape of his neck begin to stand up.

" You are in danger! Do not follow me!" exclaimed Diana.

"But... What's going on? "

Like a wraith, she was gone, hurrying across the sand to the steep path that they had descended. He sat there for a moment watching her go. The howling dogs sounded closer. Diana reached the top of the bluff and was soon gone from view heading back to the mansion.

Terrified by the increasing violent sounds of the approaching dogs, the priest quickly scooped up his clothes and tried to catch up with her. He ran across the sand and started climbing the path. He stumbled once and gave a cry of terror as he felt himself beginning to slip back towards the beach. Another prolonged howling lent wings to his feet and he managed to scramble up the path to the top of the bluff. He was beginning to tremble. From his left, he caught the vague, indistinct shapes of the pursuing dogs. He imagined that he could hear their claws scrabbling on the packed surface of the street. He ran, clutching his clothes to him like a talisman."If I can only make it to the house in time, I'll be safe," he said, panting as he began to run.

Sweat began dripping into his eyes and he felt the burning of the salt. He didn't even wipe it away for he felt that would take precious seconds that he needed to run with. It seemed like a long distance to the mansion. Behind him, he could hear the dogs as they pursued him. He looked back over his shoulder and saw them for the first time, clearly and distinctly. They were six black dogs the size of mastifs. To him, their eyes shone with a feral light and their red tongues hung out as if with anticipation of the meal that they would make of him.

"God!" he exclaimed between clenched teeth.

He ran faster than he ever thought he could run. His breath came in tearing gasps from his chest and he felt that if he didn't find shelter soon, his lungs would explode. He passed under a streetlight and again looked back over his shoulder. It seemed to him that they were getting closer, gaining on him. Looking forward again, he could see the shape of the mansion ten yards ahead. With a final burst of speed, he covered that ten yards like a world-class sprinter. He bounded up the rickety steps to the front door almost stumbling but righting himself.

He grasped the door handle and turned it. The door was locked. He looked back over his shoulder and saw the dogs beginning to draw nearer. With sheer desperation, he pounded on the door but for the second time there was no response. Fearing for his life, he broke the door open and closed it behind him as the dogs gained the porch. He could hear their paws scraping against the door. He leaned with his back against the door, listening to the howling from the other side. He felt that his legs were growing weak with the sheer terror that he felt.

Suddenly, the barking ceased as if the dogs had gone away.

"That's what they might want me to think," he said softly to himself, staring wildly around the darkened foyer." If I go out there, they will rip me apart. I have to find Diana."

Another sound caught his ear. It seemed to be the muffled cacophonous laughter of an old woman somewhere in the house. Very stealthily, he crossed the foyer to the stairs and ascended slowly with one hand on the banister, the other clutching his clothes. His fear mounted with each step that he took. He was extremely attentive to each sound like the creaking of the stairs beneath his feet. On his silent ascent up the darkened stairs, he paused to listen. He could hear the strange laughter that came periodically. Finally, he reached the top of the stairs and paused as if to catch his breath. The laughter drew him down the darkened hall to the master bedroom. The door was partially opened and a faint light spilled out into the hall. He stopped outside the door.

"Why don't you come on in? I have something to show you," said a voice from within the room.

Peering around the corner, Father Bennett was startled to discover an old woman totally nude sitting up in bed with what appeared to be a dead infant in her arms. The sight of the lifeless infant and her wicked laughter was a scene that summoned up a primal fear that precipitated a slight spasm in his gut. Her long gray hair hung to her shoulders. Her piercing eyes held his and there was a sardonic smile on her ancient face. Before he could speak, she announced the death of Brimos.

"Now that Brimos is dead, you are on your own in the underworld. You no longer have the gift of the Third Eye or the Ajna Chakra so you will have some difficulty acclimating to the infernal regions. You must not be afraid to die to everything you have known in order to be reborn to the world before the Logos became ratio," she said, her voice high pitched and slightly quavering.

Father Bennett's heart was racing. He tried to control his breathing so that he could speak.

"Where is Diana?" he demanded.

The old woman smiled as she began rocking the dead infant in her arms.

"I am Diana's grandmother and I'm sure you've heard of me. One might say there is a very intimate bond between us that knows no bounds. I first appeared as Demeter at the hospital maternity ward and now Hecate speaks through me... As the goddess of the crossroads and the graveyard, she rules the air, and the earth and the regions under the earth. The dogs belong to me just as the black hoodlums belonged to Diana. Their mission was to bring you to your true destination... the House of the Two Crescent Moons. The two crescent moons are nothing more than the 'Vagina Dentata' or the maw of the underworld. However, its purpose is not to instill dread within the spectator, as did the ancient caves of Greece, but instead to invoke a sense of reverence.

You have violated a supernatural law and the penalty was not my vengeance for what you did to my granddaughter, but instead the wrath of the Great Mother, which is much worse for it is the chaos of the inferno. Are you familiar with the story of Prometheus?"

Suddenly, the priest felt a slight pain in the center of his chest and he again tried to regulate his breathing.

"All I know is that he was responsible for bringing the gift of civilization to mankind as the gift of fire from the gods... I'm not that knowledgeable about mythology," he said, trying to remain as calm as possible under her intense scrutiny.

"Well, there is a lot more to the myth and its ramifications than what you just related to me," the old woman said.

The events of the night were catching up to him and he felt an extreme weariness begin to overtake him. He realized the phenomenon of time dilatation as every minute, which passed seemed like hours crawling by. He leaned his head against the wall for a moment and closed his eyes. Suddenly, he found himself on Mount Caucasus and chained himself to a rock. As he looked up at the dark and stormy sky, he cried out:

"I need my pain! I need my vulture!"

Swooping down from the sky flew a large vulture that landed on the priest and ate at his exposed liver. He cried out again:

"My God! How long must I endure this?"

After his horrifying hallucination, the priest found himself in the master bedroom again with the old witch. Her wicked laugh rang in his ears.

"There," she said." Do you remember now?"

Father Bennett began sweating profusely.

"Remember what?" he asked hoarsely.

"The reason you have amnesia is because you rebelled against your guilt. You rejected your pain. You missed the whole point of self-realization by becoming mad... by going insane... The true god is aligned with the seasonal changes of nature such as the solstices and the equinoxes. This god is the sun, which goes through the seasonal changes of death and rebirth. When you participated in certain initiation ceremonies of the Dogon tribe, you realized that their belief system was somewhat compatible with your own, however we intended to take you to the next level of the Sirian Mystery, but you were evidently not prepared. Had you not dropped the glass on the night of the Winter Solstice, you would have spiraled on up the Cosmic Tree, however you unleashed the Beast within yourself and when the violent storm was over, your entire being was distributed throughout the whole of nature. In other words, by becoming your own god, you could only do so by being punished. Because Prometheus stole the fire, he achieved an ecstasy of punishment by which the theft was justified and explained. However, the fire never needs to be stolen... It was yours all along. Prometheus brought down fire from heaven in the narthex or hollow tube, which is Malkuth-Muladhara. The gift is the fact that the Fire Snake has manifested in the genital region, yet the Hidden God is the origin of the libido. I am willing to make you a wager that if you can maintain an erection while you listen to Persephone tell her story then you will become the true solar vector in Hades and the Hidden God will reveal himself. However, if you should fail to maintain your erection then you will be subjected to surgery again. In your previous initiation, we made you into a new creature... a new man by complex surgical methods...Your body was dismembered...The demons drank your blood...Your bones were counted and you were covered with a new flesh, which became the enpowerment of your astral body."

There was a silence in the room. She looked at him with her ageless eyes as if measuring him.

"Do you except my wager?" she asked.

Father Bennett stood there with every limb trembling as if he had a fever. He looked into her eyes trying to discern her true intentions.

"Yes...Yes, I accept your wager," he said, his voice sounding to his ears as if it came from a long distance.

"Then you must be willing to take the Oath of the Abyss before your katabasis or be faced with madness or suicide."

At this point, Father Bennett summoned up his courage." I understand."

"Then repeat after me. I swear to interpret every phenomenon as a particular dealing of God with my soul."

"I swear to interpret every phenomenon as a particular dealing of God with my soul."

"Then you must enter the underworld with the purpose of putting on a Mystery Play for the benefit of the Dead. However, your true modus operandi is to hear the story of Persephone," she said, fixing him with a baleful look from her eyes." Do you understand?"

"Yes, I understand," Father Bennett said faintly.

The priest wiped his sweaty forehead as he was becoming more weary. The old witch gently placed the dead infant on the side of the bed.

"Why don't you really look at me? I'm not just an old bag of bones sitting here... See me for what I really am... a true entity."

The old woman smiled as she fondled her breasts.

"What are you afraid of? Just release yourself. There must be a willing renunciation of willing..." her voice trailed off as she uttered this cryptic statement.

"What do you mean?" Father Bennett asked, his nerves on edge, yet feeling the growing lassitude descend on him like a curtain being lowered.

"Forget who you are for a moment and let it be..."

The old woman leaned forward on the bed.

The priest was growing more nervous as he stood there clutching his clothes to his chest.

"What's wrong, dear child?" the old woman crooned.

"This may sound trite to you, but I feel that I am between a rock and a hard place, if you know what I mean."

The old woman chuckled.

"Believe me, I know what you mean. You mustn't be scared because I do love you and trust me for I have your best interests at heart. Here... Why don't you lie down beside me? In my arms, you will be safe from the malefic moon and the hounds of hell. You must return to me as the origin of your birth. Come now, child... Let grandmother take care of you because we're in for a long night."

The uroboric hold of the old witch proved to be stronger than the willpower of the priest. He walked over to the bed and dropped the clothes he had been holding on the floor. He lay down in her lap and she pressed his head firmly against her wrinkled breasts.

"I'm afraid to fall asleep," he said with the sound of her beating heart in his ears." I... I remember some artist who wrote that the sleep of reason produces monsters... I don't want to see these monsters... I just want peace... the peace of a tranquil lake... After the storm... After the storm, the lake looks so beautiful..."

"You must return to me as the origin of your birth... as the origin of your birth before you knew mama and papa...You must enter the House of the Hidden God in deep reverence."

Gently, the old witch ran her hands through the priest's hair and lulled him into a deep sleep. The katabasis began as the deepest of dreams...

Father Bennett entered the underworld as the sun king wearing a golden crown with a purple robe and a golden erect phallus. At the entrance to the main chamber stood two stone-faced sentries with their spears crossed. The two guards were massively built. Their arms bulged with muscle upon muscle. Their helmets with the nose guard that bisected their faces gave them a fierce-looking effect. They stared straight ahead looking into the distance as if seeing something that no mortal eye could discern.

He approached them.

"I have come to put on a Mystery Play for the benefit of the Dead," he announced.

At his words, they pulled back their spears and allowed him to enter through a black satin curtain. As he entered, there seemed to be a party going on. A black queen, sitting on an ornate gilded throne, made a toast to her demonic entourage.

"Hail Samael, the Prince of Yetzirah! Who is the dark shadow of the Great Androgyne of Good! Who carries the alien seed, which impregnated Eve, who begat Cain!"

Her voice rang in the chamber, a triumphant toast. Her entourage murmured in agreement. The black queen lowered the golden and gem encrusted goblet and drank deeply of the ruby red wine. Draining the goblet, she noticed the approaching sun king.

"My, don't we have a lot to be proud of?" she said in a sarcastic voice.

"I know you as the Eternal Feminine," he said portentously.

"I am the Elder Lilith! You are very lucky that my husband, Samael and His vampire bats are gone or you would be in deep shit!"She sat there in all her regal splendor looking at him with a smirk of contempt around the corners of her ruby red sensuous mouth. Her dark eyes were like lasers boring into him as if trying to see to the very depths of his soul. Her aquiline

nose gave her face the appearance of a bird of prey. Her long, dark lustrous hair cascaded down her back under the crown that she wore. Her purple robes with the wide sleeves flared at the wrist. In one hand, she held the goblet. In the other, the left, she held a scepter--a long staff with a coiled snake about to strike as the finial. The chamber that they were in was richly decorated looking like something out of the Arabian Nights. Rich tapestries hung from the ceilings depicting scenes that no human could look at without experiencing a feeling of dread. The tapestries depicted demons with hideous faces disporting with human females while huge bats swooped like black winged rodents over their heads. The bat's claws dripped with blood and their fangs dripped with a greenish ooze that could make a person's stomach turn over in revulsion. The floors were bare stone. At each corner of the chamber, tall candles stood in their holders, their lights flickering; casting weird shadows on the wall. Around the queen was her entourage--gross caricatures that resembled anything human. Their grotesque heads with bulging eyes, pointed ears, warty noses and sharp fang-like teeth in drooling mouths gave off an unpleasant odor that the incense was not wholly able to mask. There was the smell of putrefaction in the air and he had a hard time breathing.

"Why are you here?" she demanded of him, fixing him with a disconcerting stare.

"I have come to put on a Mystery Play for the benefit of the Dead," he announced a little pompously.

"A Mystery Play for the benefit of the Dead," she repeated sardonically." My, my, my... Won't they be thrilled?"

Her demonic entourage howled with mirth.

He stood there with his knees shaking.

Suddenly, as if remembering her duties as a hostess, she offered him a chalice of wine.

"Then I offer you the ambrosia of the Gods for you will become the Holy Fool, who is no longer subject to the law of gravity until you experience your final initiation. The Dead are mutually indifferent to what happens here so your Mystery Play will have no effect on them because true occult secrets are whispered between the planets and tonight the sun enters Libra, which is the Balance of the Scales:

Keep watch and ward,
Thyself regard;

Unless with diligence thou bathe,
The Wedding can't thee harmless save;
You'll damage have that here delays;
You must beware, too light that weighs..."

He took the chalice from her and drank the wine. There was a distant rumble that shook the ground beneath him. He looked startled.

"That's old Pluto," Lilith said, amused by his look of consternation." He gets a bad case of the shits every time a sun king enters these halls and you'll never find him because I hold the keys to the Labyrinth."

Still disconcerted by the continued rumbling, he asked:" Where might I find your theatre?"

"At the entrance to the Vagina Dentata where you can address the Dead," she replied, still amused not only by his reaction to Pluto's rumblings but by the fact that he had come to put on a Mystery Play for the Dead.

She pointed in the direction that he was to go in.

"Go!" she commanded imperiously.

Disoriented, the sun king traveled, until he came upon a platform with a facsimile of the Vagina Dentata. The Dead stood sentinel with their ashen faces and stoic expressions. He mounted the platform and addressed the Dead.

"I wear this crown as proof that I am the true meridian of the sun," he said, and then he belched out loud." My solar power has given Pluto stomach cramps which will manifest in his bowels and he hides from me, yet I know that he will reveal himself. Behold this Mystery Play as your Queen's ultimate secret." Again he belched." Please excuse me... I'm a bit intoxicated on this ambrosia... Anyway, the Vagina Dentata beckons me as does her yoni because I long to know how her lotus-flower unfolds as her latent divinity."

Turning, the sun king entered Persephone's bedchamber.

The chamber was richly appointed as the fitting abode for the queen of the underworld. The walls were hung with rich tapestries woven with intricate patterns that depicted scenes of horror though not as strange as in Lilith's chambers. Tortured souls crying out with their eyes raised as fire licked at them; strange reptilian-avian hybrids that either flew or crawled over and around the tortured souls. He turned to see what each tapestry depicted. In each corner, there were tall candlesticks with lighted candles and in the center of the chamber was the bed. It was a round bed with a canopy of purple velvet embossed with gold threads that intertwined like snakes. Under the canopy a woman lay. She raised herself into a sitting position. Her face was a dead white. Her black obsidian eyes were like the eyes of a jaguar hesitant to attack him. Her mouth was a bright ruby red. Her long hair was black with streaks of white. She wore a diaphanous gown cinched in at the waist and scooped low in the bodice showing the tops of her creamy breasts. He could see her nipples, hard and erect. She stared at him as if her eyes had never beheld such a sight before.

"Who are you?" she demanded.

"I am the sun king and I have come to illuminate the darkness," he replied.

She stared at his erection.

"I see that you honor my cave with your Lingam. You must awaken the Fire Snake within me. The Fire Snake is coiled three and a half times around the base of my spine. The only way out of this darkness is a return to Babalon, the Gateway of the Sun."

"I have come to hear your story."

He walked across the chamber to the bed and stood looking down at her.

"If I tell my story then some of the Dead may not return to the Treasure House..." her voice trailed off.

"If Pluto is so wise, then he would not hide from me." he said.

She studied him with amusement. Suddenly, the sound of an infant girl crying could be heard coming from the closet.

"Is that a little girl crying?" he asked, beginning to walk in the direction of the closet.

"No, it is the voice of a very powerful demon... an arch demon, I might add and I warn you not to open that door."

He looked at the door for several minutes and then walked back to the bed.

"I am only here to hear your story," he said.

She patted the bed beside where she was sitting and made an imperious motion for him to sit beside her on the bed. He complied, seating himself beside her and looking into her obsidian eyes. She smiled at him.

"My story is a lament because I once was an innocent maiden in my mother's green fields and one day, I came upon a cave and when I entered,

the vampire bats landed on me like gentle moths... The darkness enveloped me as every orifice of my body was invaded..."

He leaned forward struck by the imagery of her story.

"Did anyone witness your abduction?" he asked probingly.

"Hecate did and I became a bringer of destruction."

"Your story is the fear of every young maiden until she becomes aware of her cycles."

"You have no idea of what it's like to be raped," she said with a hint of challenge in her voice.

"No, I must say that I have never known such a trauma," he said, shaking his head.

"My cry was like the bleating of a sheep before being led to slaughter because that last ray of light had disappeared. After I was taken advantage of by Pluto, I was taught to respect the Great Sow even though I envied her for her shakti or magical powers. She sees clairvoyantly with her womb and she became known as the Evil Eye and brought about Sudden Infant Death Syndrome. I know that the Elder Lilith is the original Scarlet Woman and the Queen of the Night rules on her throne. I desire to sit on that very throne and fuck the Sons of God."

He was startled by her declaration.

"Am I a son of God?" he asked her.

She smiled and lay down on her side, opening her arms. He embraced her.

"You are drunk on the ambrosia of the Gods and I marvel at your brazen body. However, my lotus-flower withers under your embrace because I succumb to the blue mist, which surrounds my cave..."

"In me, you will find new life for I am the true vector of the sun," he assured her tenderly.

"These secrets we share between us go on forever... They infiltrate the blue mist, which envelopes us as the Backward Way unto Death... These denizens of the deep gnaw at my spine... Such a constant reminder that I belong to the stygian darkness even though I hunger for thymos... for the blood vapor of sacrificed pigs," she said, caressing his face.

"As the sun king, I can redeem any soul trapped in this darkness and you are no exception."

Smiling tenderly, she felt for his penis.

"Let's face it," she suddenly cried," You've lost it for me. Don't you

remember me as a fair young maiden, who attracted the most distinguished men of nobility and some even asked for my hand in marriage?"

He looked confused.

"I... I'm trying to remember, but I am having some difficulty," he confessed.

"I was in touch with my menstrual cycles and emitted a certain kind of odor, which had the effect of an aphrodisiac even though I was still a virgin... As a maiden, I would have married you."

"I cannot fathom us being married. We are opposites."

"Yet, opposites attract. It is imperative that we become married or you will become the Dying God again and die for the sins of humanity!" she exclaimed.

"I... I can resuscitate my Lingam..." he said hopefully.

He tried to regain his erection but failed. He looked at her noticing the displeasure on her face, the way her eyes seemed to shoot darts at him figuratively.

"Do you have a love for putrefaction?" she asked, her voice purring like a cat.

"What do you mean?" he asked, startled by her question.

"Why don't you run your hands down my spine to the very bottom where the Fire Snake resides?"

Suddenly, the crying of an infant girl could be heard again coming from the closet.

"I... I must save that poor child!" he cried as he jumped up from the bed.

"I am warning you not to go anywhere near that closet," Persephone said with a hint of steel in her voice.

Ignoring her, he crossed the room and opened the closet. A very beautiful nude woman walked out and greeted him. Her long blonde hair cascaded down her shoulders reaching all the way to her waist. Her youthful breasts beckoned him. Her waist was narrow, tapering down to long shapely legs. Her blue eyes looked at him frankly and the tip of her tongue flickered like a snake's as it caressed her full upper lip.

"I am the Northern Gate of Eden or the eleventh power zone as the next threshold you will cross," she said, her voice sending pleasurable chills up his spine.

Suddenly, it became extremely cold.

"Jesus, it's getting to be very cold in here!" he exclaimed.

She walked over to him in a mesmerizing and undulating way.

"If you can warm me with your royal robe then I can honor you with a kiss," she whispered.

"Then come to me," he commanded.

She came closer to him and he whipped off his robe, covering her. He took her in his arms and kissed her and as they kissed, his crown fell off. Smiling, she picked it up off the ground and laughed at him as she returned to the closet and descended.

"Hey! Give me back my crown! You have no right to that crown! Come back, you whore!" he yelled to her retreating backside.

Persephone rose from her bed and yelled out:

"The Dead are returning to the Treasure House!"

Paying Persephone no heed, he followed the demon to regain his crown. As he entered the closet, he discovered a staircase leading downward. Slowly, he began to descend the stairs. As he descended lower, he began to hear all types of moaning and crying. As he reached the final step, he discovered that he was in a basement. The walls were made of stone that dripped with some type of fluid that was not water. Stalactites and stalagmites were trying to reach each other; one from the cavernous ceiling and the other from the bare dirt of the basement's floor. It was more like a cave or a cavern than a proper basement. He stood on the last step staring incredulously. He took the last step onto the dirt floor and noticed in the exact center of the cavern was a throne. It was set on a high platform. The back of the throne rose and seated on the throne was a colorful transvestite wearing the golden crown. He/she sat with legs crossed wearing a colorful robe with shoulder-length hair that seemed to be burnished with gold among the red tresses. Sardonic green eyes like agate marbles studied his progress as he walked slowly across the floor to the throne. He/she was in the process of putting on make-up. A faint ironic smile touched the painted lips. Around the throne, human rodent-like creatures were slowly erupting out of the ground, waving their hands about in the air.

"Come to me, you little piggies because Choronzon will feed you," the transvestite crooned.

Choronzon leaned forward and it was then that the sun king became aware of the source of the light. He stared hard at the crown that was wobbling erratically on the transvestite's head. The light was coming from there and with every movement that the transvestite made, the light shone on some other part of the basement. There was something else that he noticed. The human rodent-like creatures seemed to be feeding off the light. He stared open-mouthed at the spectacle.

"Do you like my lumen naturae, little ones? Do you like the Light of Nature?" she continued crooning.

The feeding frenzy continued until the hideous creatures seemed to be sated. Looking fondly down at them, Choronzon leaned back on the throne and the light seemed to shine squarely in his eye, although it seemed that Choronzon was either unaware of his presence or just didn't care.

At this point, the sun king tried to get a grip on himself, revulsed by the creatures that began swarming around his ankles.

"What have you done to them?" he demanded." I only know you as the Shadow..."

"Well, I wear this crown because I also sit on this throne and at this moment I am the Light, which illuminates the dream," Choronzon said in a bored voice.

She continued applying her make-up.

"But you have no right to that crown because I serve the Light and you are the anti-logos!" he said angrily.

She laughed, a spine-chilling laugh with a strong demonic quality and lit a cigarette. She inhaled deeply and blew out the smoke into his face. There was a total disregard for his words.

"You need to remember that you no longer have your inbuilt gyroscope, which is necessary to acclimate to these more infernal regions," Choronzon told him sardonically.

"But you don't understand," he protested, outraged by her attitude," that crown belongs to me!"

Choronzon laughed again and looked at him for a moment.

"The only way that you will ever regain this crown is if you are willing to sacrifice yourself," Choronzon said slowly.

"What do you mean?" he asked, alarmed.

Suddenly, as if by a magical summons, two black-masked executioners entered the antechamber carrying a block of wood and an axe. The executioner carrying the block of wood placed the block in front of the throne and stood back. The other executioner carrying the axe stood beside him. They stared impassively at Choronzon, waiting her command.

"You must be decapitated because you have become a black Osiris. You were the solar hero, however we must separate your understanding from the trammels of nature because you understood the Logos before accepting the law of karma!" Choronzon said almost languidly.

"I don't understand..."

He was taken aback not only by her words but by her delivery. To him they were delivered in an almost casual fashion that made them all the more chilling.

"You can forget about being any kind of vector down here because you have lost it, buddy... Your fucking Lingam will not be revivified!" Choronzon said, leaning forward and fixing him with a baleful stare.

"But, I was supposed to be subjected to surgery again if I failed to maintain my erection," he protested.

"Well, if you ask me, this is a lot quicker and there is hardly any pain... Your head will still be alive and you may even go into an oracular mode, but these creatures will feed on your body as the sparagamos."

He reflected as he absorbed what Choronzon had just said.

"Who are these creatures?" he asked.

"They are the Resurrected Mummies of Amenta, who still have vestiges of the solar-phallic energy, yet they honor Set as the Hidden God, not Pluto... The Dead have returned to the Treasure House and Hades will always remain the domain of Pluto, however Set as the Dog Star is the heaven in Hades..."

"So, they can find peace in hades?" he asked hopefully.

Choronzon suddenly jumped up, her whole body vibrating with rage.

"Executioners! Go fetch that fool!" she said, pointing at him." Because you no longer suffer from the law of gravity, you must suffer this death because of the law of karma!"

He decided that this was as good a time as any to get out of there. He retreated to the stairs and began to ascend. The two masked executioners caught him on the second step and their grip on his arms felt like vises. He became panic-stricken.

"God!" he cried out in utter despair." Oh, my God! I long for the Light of the Logos! I love the Light with all my heart and mind!"

"Wimp!" Choronzon said disgustedly, flicking her cigarette in his direction.

The tragic hero awakened in his dream to the loving embrace of Diana, appearing as the heavenly Sophia in her divine radiance. He no longer heard the crying of the undead but instead the total silence of the cave. He breathed a sigh of relief for he was no longer surrounded by the suffocating stillness of the cave of Persephone. The angel looked upon him with absolute love and understanding.

"You must leave the cave and come with me outside where everything essentiates out of its own ground. I call you back to the things themselves," she said tenderly.

They arose and walked hand in hand to the mouth of the cave. They stood there for a moment. They watched the sunrise, awed by the lighting of the sky with its pastel colors. There was a peace and harmony; a sense of well-being that permeated into the tragic hero.

As Sophia and the tragic hero emerged from the cave, she illustrated the resiliency of nature with her hands.

"The mighty river, Eridanus and your blood are the same... You must realize that the eternal struggle between underworldly and the Olympian realms will never be decided upon by the gods... The struggle creates an openness in which a nation can dwell. Whenever this struggle was discontinued, the Greek world fell into disintegration and ceased to be true... For a man to ignore the struggle of such realities and to act as if he were his own lord, is to fall into the act of hubris or self-pride. Modern man treats reality in such a lordly manner without permitting any superior reality to interfere with his will to power..." she said as they walked.

The tragic hero walked with Sophia and was mesmerized by the plethora of natural beauty surrounding him. She spoke in a poetic, incantatory language.

"Nature seems to be sleeping, but this is not known to the man in the street, it is only known to poets... Therefore, a poet names the holiness in the time of the World-Night or the time of the lack of the gods. This vacuum when properly understood, is a firm support or a determining standard for bringing the groundless modern man to a stand. However, to a sober positivistic attitude, whatever is silent or lacking cannot be real... It is nothing... Thus, the mechanical laws holding society together or the moral fabric of social cohesion would collapse once modern man awoke to this vacuum because his status is based on a false concept of being..."

Diana, as the Sophia figure, took the tragic hero on a walk down a country road, which seemed to wind on forever.

"Not man, but the road assembles everything and lets everything stand in relation to everything else. When everything, even man, stands in the assemblage of the road and not of man then everything stands in complete serenity... and when serenity thus is experienced or known it leads to eternity..." Her voice was like the gentle murmur of a brook flowing peacefully and serenely.

The pure golden sunlight filtered through the trees and an eddy of butterflies flew by in a brilliant display of color. Suddenly, the tragic hero was surrounded by a vibrant wall of sound as birds chirped, the river flowed and the wind blew through the trees all in unison. He felt as if he had connected with nature.

"What just happened to me? It was incredible! It was as if everything was making love to my mind!" he exclaimed in wonderment, a beatific smile on his face.

She smiled her joy, which seemed to him to be like the rising of the sun.

"You have experienced the ringing of the Logos," she declared." Somewhere in time, being and ground were somehow separated in the mind of man and instead of openly responding to the Logos of nature, man dictated to it his logical logos and forced it to answer his subjective questions... and he made nature subservient and controlled her... Thus, the true logos-ties have fallen into forgotteness..."

Diana's image had begun to fade and the tragic hero expressed his concern for the plight of modern man.

"Man must remember... He must somehow remember that he is not the center of the stage... We are headed for a serious crisis, which unabated threatens to destroy all the ideas we hold true about ourselves... Where does this road lead to?"

The invisible presence with a haunting voice said:

"To Jerusalem... to Jerusalem... You will arrive too late for the gods and too early for Being for you have lost the Crown of Kether..."

After a brief hiatus, the tragic hero found himself at the Wailing Wall and repeated the ominous portent:

"I have arrived too late for the gods and too early for Being..."

Feeling that now he was in a type of vacuum in direct contrast to the plenitude of vibrant life when he was with Sophia, the tragic hero could see the indentations on the wall where people for centuries had clawed with their hands and beat with their heads, while wailing and praying. At first, he thought that it was a reproduction, but when he touched and smelled the wall, he realized that it was authentic, but for some strange reason a miniature. After a short time, he became very erotic as he attempted to perform the religious rite and disrobed. He noticed that he had an erection and pulled a blanket over him to conceal his nudity. Looking behind him, he saw what might have been a Jewish rabbi or a policeman walking across a balcony very slowly, watching his every move and at this point, he felt he had to prove his sincerity so he reached out to kiss the wall, but he could not do so because of a repelling force. He again felt extremely erotic over the wall and ignored his sacrilegious feelings, kissing it this time. He felt the immediate sensation of being feminine and at this point, the rabbi came down the aisle and painted the wall with plaster of Paris. To his amazement, the rabbi turned out to be Bishop Everly. The plaster seal quickly hardened and he felt the gnawing pain of isolation from the holy wall. Suddenly, a woman veiled in black came down the aisle and began to wail in front of the wall. He felt somewhat ashamed and out of place, realizing the fact that she was aware of the plaster seal and looked over in his direction as if he were the guilty party. She then rose and left. Bishop Everly, as the rabbi, came back down the aisle and put another coat of plaster of Paris on the wall. The tragic hero was very conscientious about his nudity and was careful not to expose himself to the rabbi. Then he noticed at least fifty people, who formed a fairly diverse group of businessmen, college students and army personnel, coming down the different aisles all around him. He desperately tried to put his pants on, but this was to no avail and instead pulled the blanket back over him. To his further amazement, a film projectionist set up his equipment. Suddenly, it was nighttime and he showed a pornographic film on the wall. The people around him were reacting out loud, especially during the scene where the actress spread her vagina, enticing her male lover. The couple began their act of intercourse and the soldiers in the audience began shooting their guns in the air the moment the man finished ejaculating all over the woman's stomach. The film ended and everyone filed out of the amphitheatre. The tragic hero was able to put on his clothes and noticed Bishop Everly, as the rabbi, making his exit to the church cemetery. Eventually, he caught up with him.

"Bishop Everly... Why did you convert to Judaism?" he asked confused.

At this point, the rabbi looked down, refusing to establish eye contact.

"I have become the curator of the holy wall because it has become the last vestige of the sacred... All the churches have become museums for the reason that the majority of parishioners sought a diversion from the truth of their own mortality... The perpetual sense of youthful vitality or the 'They' is forever... True authentic being is ephemeral and is impossible to remain in for a lifetime... Some are dying to the modern world and have discovered their true status as you can see for yourself several men and women standing near a cyprus grove ready to dig their hands into the earth for some old bones... some type of clue as to who they are... for you are one of them..."

Suddenly, the tragic hero heard a woman wailing aloud in the cemetery and looked into the murky distance. Bishop Everly then led him to the woman veiled in black.

"This is Rachael... Because of your sin, Rachael or what I call the 'Soul of Israel'... the shekinah, can no longer return to the sacred shrine," Bishop Everly said.

The tragic hero looked compassionately at her.

"I'm sorry... I am truly sorry for having given into my eroticism... I now realize the actual consequences of my act," he said haltingly.

After wailing for a period of time, the woman looked up and her face was dark and her eyes were sealed shut with tears flowing. It was Diana again and she exclaimed out loud:

"Nature abhors a vacuum! The gods have become our diseases! The moon has disappeared from the night sky! I feel the powers of the other side for I am in a state of exile!"

At this point, the tragic hero dreaded a return to the underworld and a horrible decapitation at the hands of the demons. Instead, Rachael grabbed at both of his legs and pleaded with him:

"You must descend further into the war on the outskirts of Jerusalem for it will eventually spread throughout the entire city and all will become homeless... I weep for my lost children, but nonetheless the war to end all wars has finally come and it is the supreme penalty for a violation of nature on the part of man... It is imperative that you remember the child... For he alone possesses the royal power..."

The tragic hero looked at her.

"I will," he promised.

He looked toward Bishop Everly, but he had disappeared. When he looked back towards Rachael, he saw her walking slowly out of the cemetery with her head bowed in sorrow. He stood there indecisively, then left the cemetery. As he approached the Wailing Wall, he stopped to listen for the sounds of the 'war'. He could hear guns firing and he headed in the direction of the sounds.

As he drew nearer, the sound of gunfire grew more intense. He walked as if nothing could harm him. All around, he saw the effects of war and decided to enter the maelstrom. He saw a child standing in the very center of the maelstrom. He approached the wonderchild standing with the ear of grain between the angels of light and darkness. He suddenly felt the hair on the back of his neck stand up in terror as the child looked at him. And he knew, with certainty, that Samael and his vampire bats were approaching...

Chapter Seven

The Return

There was a silence in the room like the aftermath of a storm broken only by harsh breathing. Ben Lassoe looked at the man seated opposite him who had his head down. It was from him that the harsh breathing came. Lassoe turned off the tape recorder. As if it were a signal, Father Bennett raised his head and looked straight into Lassoe's eyes. Neither man spoke for what seemed to be a very long time. Outside the room, the sounds of a busy hospital could be heard. Father Bennett clasped his hands as if in prayer; a haunted look in his eyes. Lassoe cleared his throat and wiped his sweaty palms.

"Well, Doctor, what do you think?" Father Bennett asked his voice almost a croak from having talked so much.

Lassoe paused to consider his words.

"So that's where the bats came in ?" he asked softly.

"If that's what you want to believe," Father Bennett said," But you didn't answer my question" .

"My initial impression to your story is much like the first time that I observed the *Triptych* by Hieronymus Bosch. There was such a wealth of symbolism that I was virtually lost, in so many words. I am deeply moved by your story and your psychosis might have an apocalyptic significance for everyone. Very few of my patients have plumbed the depths like you have and been able to discuss their experience in such an intelligent way. I have to admit, you are quiet a remarkable individual," Lassoe said.

"Thank you," Father Bennett said humbly." I appreciate your compliments. I am still perplexed about the end of my story, however."

"Do you mean the 'war zone'?" Lassoe asked curiously.

Father Bennett shook his head.

"No, what concerns me is the child with the 'royal power'. What do you make out of it?" Father Bennett asked seriously.

"I can't really say," Lassoe said slowly." I think this particular symbol is the most cryptic to your story."

"So do I," Father Bennett said.

He got up from his chair and walked over to the window, looking out on the world below. Lassoe looked at his back, wondering what he was thinking.

"There has to be some hidden meaning to it," Father Bennett said almost to himself.

"I'm sure that there is," Lassoe said, rising to his feet.

He studied the man whose strange and bizarre appearance in his life had piqued his curiosity; first about who he was and what had happened to him and now secondly about whether what he had just heard and recorded had any validity. In his years of practicing psychiatry, he had heard many strange and bizarre stories--though none as strange and bizarre as this--which had proved to be the demented figments of over-active imaginations. He wondered if this was another case like the hundreds that he had heard in the past. Looking at the priest's back as he stood at the window looking out, Lassoe wasn't sure. That the man had undergone an extremely traumatic experience that had brought on catatonia was obvious. But was his story true? Sometimes the mind, in order to shield itself from something that it can't deal with, invented something as bizarre as a supernatural element. He wondered if this was the case with his patient.Lassoe walked over to the window and stood beside Father Bennett. They both looked out at the street below them with its frenetic traffic.

The silence in the room deepened and threatened to become oppressive.

Lassoe cleared his throat.

"You must be tired after telling your story," he said, studying Father Bennett's haggard face.

Father Bennett turned his eyes from the scene below and looked at his doctor.

"A little," he admitted as if ashamed of being weak.

"Why don't you get some rest or go for a walk? This whole thing has been quite intense for both of us. To be honest, I still do not know quiet what to make of it, especially the enigmatic end of your story," Lassoe said.

Father Bennett gazed at him steadily.

"Do you think that I'm crazy, Doctor?" he asked calmly.

Lassoe was taken aback by the question.

"I don't believe that you are," he said, gazing steadily at Father Bennett.

"I'm not so sure," Father Bennett said.

He turned his head to look back out the window.

"Do you have doubts about your sanity?" Lassoe asked, gently probing.

"Doesn't everyone?" Father Bennett replied.

"Yes, I suppose that they do. Why do you doubt your sanity?"

"Is it possible to blank out something that is so... so heinous that you can't remember it and even after being told about it, still deny that it happened?"

"The rape?"

Father Bennett nodded.

"Yes, the rape."

"It is possible. Amnesia is the mind's mechanism to forget things that it can't quite deal with. You might call it a defense mechanism," Lassoe said.

"I still don't know if what Diana told me about the night of the Winter Solstice is true," Father Bennett said.

"And because of that, you're questioning your sanity?" Lassoe asked, studying his profile.

"Yes."

"Let's suppose, for a moment, that it is true, alright?"

"Alright. Proceed, Doctor," Father Bennett said.

"The fact that you as a priest broke your vow of celibacy and committed an unnatural act, i.e. you assaulted physically and sexually a woman, your mind could not deal with the implications so you suppressed it--forgot it. Then this very same woman tells you what happened. Your mind is telling you that she is lying, trying for some reason of her own to hurt you. Yet, deep down inside you know that you really did commit this heinous crime of rape on a woman who trusted you. According to your story, you had sex with her on the beach."

Father Bennett pondered what Lassoe had said.

"So, according to you, I'm still in a state of denial?"

"Yes. If you're questioning her story about what happened that night."

"Isn't that reason to doubt my sanity?"

There seemed to be a challenge in the priest's voice.

"Yes, I suppose to you, that it is," Lassoe said slowly." But do you really think that you are, in your words, crazy?"

"I... I don't know. They say that confession is good for the soul. I have confessed to you although you are not a priest. I don't know if my soul feels better for it or not."

Lassoe studied the priest's profile in the afternoon light coming from the window.

"I may not be a priest, but you don't have to confess to a priest to feel better," Lassoe said.

"I'm not sure that I do feel better and that's the problem, Doctor," Father Bennett said, looking at Lassoe.

"I don't feel that you're insane, Father Bennett. I feel that you underwent an experience that few, if any, ever go through. Dealing with the supernatural, and I believe that is what you dealt with, can be very, very scary. To be honest, I don't know how I would handle what you went through. Like you, I might have gone into a catatonic state. Each person's mind is different. Nobody can say how he or she will react to something like what you went through. Do you see my point?"

"Yes, I see your point. Still, I do have doubts," Father Bennett said slowly.

"Everyone has doubts. That's only being human. It's when we don't have doubts that we could approach some form of true mental illness. I'm not really talking about a healthy ego. But take that one step further. Suppose that the ego becomes super inflated--it's happened in the past--then what?"

"You have someone like a Hitler or a Napoleon," Father Bennett said.

"Exactly. Those are extreme cases of megalomania. That's what can happen when the ego becomes super inflated. You believe that you are like a god and that you know what is best for all of mankind. Neither Hitler or Napoleon had any doubts about what they were doing or what the effects of their actions on others would be. The megalomaniac doesn't consider others, he's so obsessed with himself, his agenda, that he completely tramples on the rights of others."

"Getting back to the rape, didn't I trample on Diana Clements rights?" Father Bennett asked, looking at Lassoe as if trying to read his mind.

"That was an isolated incident, Father. You are not the type of person who would normally do something like that. It's not because you're a priest, but because you're a caring human being and caring human beings don't trample on the rights of others. What happened that night was a temporary aberration. It sounds, from what you told me, that you were high on something. I believe that was the reason that you raped Sister Marcia and turned her into Diana Clements. Does that make sense?"

Father Bennett sighed and turned from the window.

"Yes," he said," it does make sense."

"Are you trying to punish yourself?" Lassoe asked.

"I think that it is natural for Catholic priests to punish themselves, to ask forgiveness, when they don't measure up to the standards of our Lord, Jesus Christ."

"Yes, I suppose that is true," Lassoe agreed." However, I believe that you were under some supernatural influence."

"And what do you think of that?"

"Unlike many who would deny the existence of the supernatural, I believe that these forces are real, although we can't see them with our eyes. After all, isn't God a supernatural entity? Or did I just commit blasphemy?"

"No, God could be considered a supernatural entity. So for that matter so is Satan," Father Bennett said.

"Exactly," Lassoe said emphatically." God and the devil! One a force for good, the other a force for evil. Both are considered not of this world. It is obvious that this dichotomy is very simplistic. But I believe that you were under the influence of malignant forces, forces that literally drove you to the brink of insanity."

Father Bennett began pacing the room, hands behind his back.

"Why me?" he asked and there was an edge of desperation in his voice.

"Maybe because of what you represent," Lassoe said, watching him.

"God?"

Lassoe nodded.

"And am I to be visited by Satan again and again?" Father Bennett asked.

"I hope not. I believe that you were a victim of circumstances beyond your control. I don't think that these satanic forces will bother you anymore. You made it back from the abyss virtually unscathed," Lassoe said intensely.

Father Bennett looked at him.

"Have I?" he asked.

"I believe that you have. You've gone through quite an ordeal. I can understand why you would doubt whether or not you'll be revisited by these supernatural entities. It's my considered opinion, that they have had their way with you and now they'll leave you alone. You can pick up your life again where you left off."

"Am I fit to be a priest and a spiritual guide?"

"That's not for me to say," Lassoe said gently.

"No, it isn't. It's for Bishop Everly to say."

"Do you feel that you're fit to resume your duties?"

"That's the whole problem--I just don't know."

"Rest. Let your mind relax. Think of something else."

"Like what?"

Lassoe shrugged.

"Do you have any hobbies?" he asked.

"No, I don't."

"That's too bad. Do you like sports?"

Father Bennett shook his head.

"There is a library in the recreation room. You can go down there and pick out a book to read, something that has no religious significance. You need to take your mind off of what happened to you. To dwell on this is not healthy. You need to focus your thoughts elsewhere."

"That sounds like a prescription, Doctor," Father Bennett said, a faint smile tugging at the corners of his mouth.

"It is," Lassoe said lightly." Always follow your doctor's orders."

"I'll try to follow your orders, Doctor."

"Good. Bishop Everly is anxious to see you. Do you feel up to having company?"

"Yes."

"I'll call him and have him come to see you tomorrow."

"That will be fine."

"I want you to get a good night's rest. I want you to focus your mind on other things."

"Is it that easy?"

"No, but try anyway. Okay?"

Father Bennett nodded.

"Okay. I'll give it a try."

The two men stood facing each other. Lassoe put his hand on Father Bennett's shoulder.

"I believe that you will be fine," he said earnestly, looking into the priest's eyes." I believe that you can put all this behind you and resume your normal life."

"Thank you, Doctor Lassoe," Father Bennett said softly.

"You're welcome. Now, if you'll excuse me, I have other patients to see," Lassoe said briskly.

"Of course," Father Bennett said.

Lassoe walked over to where he had placed his tape recorder and picked it up. He walked to the door and opened it. The sounds of the hospital were now louder.

"Relax," he said, looking back over his shoulder at the priest.

"I will," the priest promised.

"Good. I'll try to look in on you before I go home."

"Alright."

Lassoe walked out of the room without closing the door behind him.

He walked down the hall to his office, lost in thought. He didn't stop at the nurse's station as he usually did. He entered his office and went to his desk and sat down. He placed the tape recorder on his desk and stared at it for a moment, and then he picked up the phone. He dialed Bishop Everly's number in Marlborough and heard it ring a couple of times before it was finally answered.

"Hello?" a female voice on the other end asked.

"This is Doctor Ben Lassoe. May I speak with Bishop Everly, please?"

"Just a moment, please."

Lassoe waited for the bishop to come on the phone.

"Hello? Doctor Lassoe?"

"Yes, Bishop, this is Lassoe."

"How is Joseph?" the bishop asked anxiously." Is he alright?"

"I believe that he will be."

"Good. When can I see him?"

"How about tomorrow morning?"

"Unfortunately, I have to meet with the archbishop in your city. But I can come in the afternoon."

"Good. Before you see Father Bennett, we need to talk."

"Very well. Can you tell me what about?"

"Not over the phone, Bishop. I'd rather talk to you face to face."

"I understand. But he will be fine?"

"Yes, he will be fine. He went through something that drove him over the edge. I'll tell you about it tomorrow."

"You have piqued my curiosity, doctor."

"I hope to satisfy it tomorrow, Bishop."

"Very well. I will see you tomorrow afternoon. Will I be able to take him home tomorrow?"

"Maybe the day after. I want to observe him a little bit more closely in light of what he told me."

"Very well. I'm sure that the archbishop will put me up for the night. I will see you tomorrow then, doctor."

"I'll be looking forward to it, Bishop Everly."

"So will I. Goodbye."

"Goodbye."

Lassoe heard the click at the other end of the line and hung up the phone in his hand. He wondered how much he could tell Bishop Everly without breaking the doctor-patient relationship of confidentiality. He should have asked Father Bennett about what he could tell the bishop, but hadn't thought about it.

He looked at the tape recorder sitting on his desk and on impulse, replayed Father Bennett's story. Listening to it in the privacy of his office was quite different than watching the tortured priest relate his story. Slowly, almost insidiously, the idea grew in him to drive to Provincetown and try to find this house of mystery and evil for himself. Should he tell anyone of his decision or should he just go? He had to think about that.

When the tape had finished, he shut it off and rewound it. He turned off the machine and turned towards the window, staring thoughtfully out at the waning light of late afternoon. One by one, the street lights were coming on as they did in the late fall of the year.

"It will be dark when I get there," he said to himself." I wonder if I have a flashlight in the car? I better bring one for he didn't mention that there was any electricity in the house. I'll need some type of light. Let's see if I have one in my desk?"

Lassoe rummaged in his desk and found a flashlight. He turned it on to make sure that it worked. It did. He played the tape one more time to make sure he knew approximately where he was going when he reached Provincetown.

He left his office and decided to ask Father Bennett how much he could tell Bishop Everly. He walked down the hall to Father Bennett's room and found the priest lying on his bed. He entered the room.

Father Bennett turned his head as Lassoe entered.

"How are you feeling?" Lassoe asked.

"Fine," Father Bennett said.

"I talked with Bishop Everly. He'll be here tomorrow afternoon."

"It will be nice to see him again."

"How much can I tell him about what you went through?"

"You can tell him everything. You can even play the tape for him."

"Are you sure that you want me to go that far?"Father Bennett shrugged.

"Bishop Everly is my spiritual counselor, my confessor. He's entitled to know everything about what happened to me. After all, he'll have to make some determination about my fitness to return to my duties as a spiritual counselor as well as my priestly duties."

"I suppose that you're right about that. Have you left the room since I last saw you?"

"No, I really haven't felt like it."

"You should. Brooding isn't good for you. Or for anyone for that matter."

"Yes, I suppose that you're right about that. Maybe I should take a walk. Didn't you mention the recreation room?"

"Yes, I did."

"I don't know where that is. Could you show me?"

"Of course I can."

Father Bennett got off the bed. He looked down at his bare feet and the hospital gown he was wearing.

"I don't suppose that there's a robe and slippers," he said hopefully.

Lassoe walked to the closet and took down a robe and handed it to Father Bennett who put it on. Under the bed were slippers. Father Bennett put the slippers on.

"I'm ready," he announced.

"Then let's go," Lassoe said.

The two men left the room and walked down the corridor. As they walked, Father Bennett looked all around him. Lassoe quietly observed him.

"All this," Father Bennett said, waving his hand around the corridor that they were walking down," is so strange."

"In what way?" Lassoe asked curiously.

"I have a vague impression that I've walked down this corridor before."

"You have. Twice."

Father Bennett looked at him in surprise.

"Twice?" he asked." I really don't remember."

"The night that you gathered the patients and 'preached' to them in the recreation room."

Father Bennett frowned.

"I don't remember. But you said twice. When was the other time?"

"You and I took a walk but you wanted to return to your room."

"Hmm. Again, I don't remember. I'm sure that you are correct about that, Doctor Lassoe."

"It's not surprising that you don't remember. You were... how shall I say it..."

"Not in my right mind?" Father Bennett asked.

Lassoe nodded.

"Something like that."

They continued walking down the corridor in silence.

Father Bennett continued his observations.

"When do you think I'll be able to leave?" he asked.

"Maybe the day after tomorrow."

"No offense, Doctor Lassoe, but I will be glad to get out of here."

"None taken. That's understandable. Here we are."

They stopped on the threshold of the recreation room. From the doorway, Father Bennett observed the other patients. Some were sitting on chairs staring vacantly into space, seeing what only God knew. Others were reading or watching television. Orderlies roamed the room like guards keeping their eyes open in case of some incident. Rarely were the patients left unsupervised in this room. The two men looked at each other.

"Are you ready?" Lassoe asked.

Father Bennett nodded and they entered the room. Lassoe led him over to the bookshelf.

"Why don't you pick out a book to read?" he said." It really will help you take your mind off of things."

"Perhaps you're right," Father Bennett said.

He studied the books and leafed through several before finding one.

"I usually read more substantial fare," he said, exhibiting the book he had chosen.

"There's nothing wrong with coming down a few notches," Lassoe said.

"No, there isn't."

"Do you want to stay here or go back to your room?"

Father Bennett looked around at the vacuous faces.

"Back to my room," he said.

"Alright. Let's go."

The two men retraced their steps to Father Bennett's room.

"I'll leave you here," Lassoe said." Have a good night and I'll see you in the morning," Lassoe said.

"Okay," Father Bennett said.

"Enjoy the book."

"I'll try."

"Good night."

"Good night, Doctor."

Lassoe watched Father Bennett walk into his room and sit down in a chair and begin reading. Satisfied that his patient was ready for the night, Lassoe went back to his office. After all, he had his own plans.

He finished what he had to do then took his leave. He carried the flashlight concealed. He felt like he was a freshman in college again going on a forbidden foray--a panty raid or a secret drinking binge. There was an aura of excitement bound up in the nature of the enterprise; a sense that he was undertaking a fascinating journey almost into the unknown. He had always been somewhat of a skeptic, however he in a way wanted the full impact of this haunted house in Provincetown. He had seen all the films of Alfred Hitchcock when he was a kid, but this time, he was ready for the real thing, if there was any validity to Father Bennett's story.

"Good night, nurse," he said, stopping at the nurse's station.

The night nurse looked up.

"Good night, doctor," she said.

"I don't think that my new patient will be giving you any trouble tonight. All the same keep an eye on him, will you?"

"Certainly, doctor. We always do, you know."

"Yes, I do. See you tomorrow."

"Drive carefully, doctor."

"Thank you."

He walked to the elevator and pressed the down button and waited for the elevator to come.

"It never fails," he thought as he waited." When you're in a hurry the damn thing is stuck on the highest floor of the building and it seems to take all of eternity to arrive."

He smiled at his thoughts as the elevator arrived. He got on and punched the down button that would take him to the parking garage where he had his car. The elevator let him off at the parking garage and he walked to his car. He unlocked the door and got in. He put the flashlight on the seat beside and looked in the glove box. There was another flashlight in there.

"Doesn't hurt to be safe," he said to himself as he closed the glove compartment and started the car. He backed out of his space and drove off wondering what he would find there.

Cape Cod!

He had the summers of his youth on the Cape not far from Hyanis Port where the Kennedy's had lived and still did. He had been just a baby when John Kennedy had died in 1963 and five when Bobby Kennedy had died in 1968. He had not understood his parents' grief then. Now, of the children of the late president and his late wife, only their daughter, Caroline remained. He remembered when the young scion of that family, John F. Kennedy, Junior had died with his young wife and her sister. With those deaths, he could understand how his parents had felt when John and Bobby had been murdered.

Spending summers on the Cape, frolicking in the surf with his brothers, sisters and cousins had been a good time. At night, they would watch the Red Sox games on television. He was a passionate Red Sox fan. He was also passionate about the Patriots, Celtics and Bruins. He was, he admitted to himself, a passionate sports fan. He rose and fell with their fortunes on the field of play whether it was a baseball field, a football field, a basketball court or a hockey rink. He enjoyed watching the games either in person or on television. He always wondered if the Red Sox could unseat the Yankees or the Patriots could win their division and make it back to the Super Bowl this time winning it all. Or whether the Celtics would regain their glory years, the latest being when Larry Bird still played. He hoped the Bruins would win the Stanley Cup.

At the juncture where the right way led to Hyanis Port and the left to Provincetown, he turned left. Headlights cut swaths through the dark night. The radio was softly playing as he drove along. It wasn't long before he reached his destination.

He saw the gas station that Father Bennett had stopped at to ask directions. He passed it and proceeded along Commercial Street until he reached Atwood. He turned onto Atwood and drove slowly along the street. At the end of the street, he parked his car and turned it off. He made sure that he turned off the lights and sat there, listening. From the tape, he had a pretty good idea where this haunted house was. He sat there smoking a cigarette. The night was still. From his open window, he could hear the surf pounding the shore in the distance. He finished the cigarette and snubbed it out in the ashtray.

"Well," he said to himself," there's no time like the present."

He got out of the car and grasping the flashlight, stopped under a street lamp to orient himself. Looking all around, he decided on his direction and proceeded. He walked slowly. There was still enough light from the street lamp to show him the way. The moon was hidden by clouds. He found the house that he was looking for and stopped on the sidewalk looking at it.

To him, the mansion looked like something from a Gothic horror movie. How long he stood there just looking, he didn't know. It seemed to him as if his feet were stuck to the pavement.

"I'm not going to find out anything just standing out here," he said out loud.

Gripping the flashlight tighter, he crossed the sidewalk. With some trepidation, he mounted the steps to the front porch. He stood there listening. He turned on the flashlight and played the beam over the door and found the depiction of the two crescent moons over the door lintel. He looked closer. He grasped the door handle and turned it. At first, it seemed to resist then turned almost reluctantly under his hand.

He pushed the door open slowly. The hinges creaked protestingly. Suddenly, came the sound of something slapping against something.

"God!" he exclaimed, his heart beginning to race.

As a kid, he had gone to all the horror films in the neighborhood and had been scared nearly out of his mind. He had also read all of Edgar Allen Poe's stories, which suggested supernatural happenings instead of actually showing them. Those fears were beginning to well up within him again. He took several deep breaths steeling himself for the ordeal ahead.

Now he stood on the threshold hesitating. His flashlight shone into the interior. He could leave and no one would be the wiser. He had told no one where he was going. On the drive up, his pager hadn't gone off. He took a deep breath and stepped across the threshold and into the house. He debated whether to leave the door open or close it. He closed it.

There seemed to be an aura about the house both inside and out. He couldn't quite put his finger on it, but there was something--something that was beginning to make the hair on the back of his neck try to stand up. Was it his imagination or did there seem to be a chill that had nothing to do with the weather outside. Was this chill supernatural?

He stood by the door, shining his flashlight along the floor then the walls and finally the ceiling. He listened intently. The only sound that he could hear was the pounding of his own heart in his ears.

"Sounds like Poe's *The Telltale Heart* ," he muttered to himself." Boy, did that story scare the shit out of me when I was a kid. C'mon, Bennie, let's *do* this thing!"

Giving himself a pep talk, Lassoe slowly moved across the foyer. He investigated the rooms on his right and left and walked back to the kitchen. His flashlight showed what seemed to be the dust of the ages on the floor and everything else that collected dust. He noticed a door that he assumed led to the basement. He opened it and stood on the threshold, shining his flashlight down into the darkness.

A scrabbling sound and a flash of something caught in the flashlight's beam almost made him drop the light as he jumped back. He felt his heart beating even faster.

"Calm down, Bennie," he said." It's nothing but a rat. Surely you've seen those before."

He crept back to the threshold again and shone his light down the stairs again. The rat--or whatever it was--was no longer visible. He debated with himself whether to go down the steps and investigate or to forget it.

"Father Bennett never saw *this* basement. Or maybe he did. Maybe this was the basement with the throne and the transvestite. To go down or not to go down, that is the question."

He stood there indecisively which was rare for him. He usually knew what he wanted to do and did it. But now he wasn't sure. He put one foot on the top step as if he was testing the temperature of a body of water that did not exist. The step creaked when he put his weight on it. With his heart, figuratively, in his mouth, he began descending the steps slowly. He stopped at every step, flashing his light down to his feet to make sure that all the steps were there. He didn't want to take a step and find nothing under his feet. With one hand, he held on to the banister. He felt almost like an explorer in an unfamiliar land. Finally, he reached the bottom step and stood there. Slowly he shone his light all around the walls, the floor and the ceiling. There was no throne there, no strange creatures, no colorful transvestite. He didn't know whether to be disappointed or glad.

Slowly, he ascended the steps and found himself back in the kitchen. He closed the door to the basement and went back to the front of the house. Arriving at the staircase that led to the second floor, he stopped shining the light upwards. He listened as if expecting--maybe even hoping--to hear the laughter of the old woman; but he heard nothing.

"Might as well go all the way," he said." After all, I came for the grand tour. So onward and upward, Bennie."

It was with some trepidation that he began the slow ascent to the second floor. He stopped every few seconds to listen again hearing nothing except the creaking of the stairs under his feet. Finally, he stood on the top step then placed his foot on the floor and stood in the hallway. He shone the light down the hall. To his imagination it seemed to stretch on forever. He took a deep breath and slowly began walking down the hall. He tried every door both to his right and to his left, but they were either locked or stuck shut. Out of the corner of his eye, he saw what might have been an apparition. He wheeled towards his right, shining his flashlight towards what he had seen or thought that he had seen. A piece of wallpaper--faded from what it had been long ago--hung down by one corner exposing something whitish. It began fluttering as if blown by an unseen wind. He breathed a sigh of relief. He had been ready to get the hell out of there as quick as his feet could take him. He turned back to continue his investigation.

Suddenly, there was a noise like someone trying to dig out of a tomb that had been bricked up; someone alive. It was a scraping sound that sent a chill of fear shooting through him. Again, he was ready to get out of there. He saw a window and walked to it. Outside, a branch from a tree seemed to be making the scraping sound that he had heard. He wiped the cold sweat from his face with his sleeve.

"God, this sure is spooky. It beats any haunted house that we went to on Halloween. But it was just a branch making that noise. It sounded very real. Maybe, it's because it's night and all these sounds are giving me suggestions. I came here to find a haunted house and it looks like I found it."

Finally, he stood in front of the last door and tried the knob. It turned and he pushed it open. Like the others, the hinges creaked protestingly. Slowly, as if it did not want to yield its secrets, the door opened and gently kissed the wall. He looked in.

"This must be the place," he muttered, stepping across the threshold.

Suddenly, there was a moaning sound that almost made his heart stop.

"Jesus!" he cried, almost dropping the flashlight in fright.

The moaning increased sounding like a soul in agony. Again, there was a slapping sound that seemed to be coming from the outside.

"Calm down," he told himself sternly." It's probably only the wind and another branch that's making that sound."

He steadied himself with another pep talk and slowly entered the room. The beam of the flashlight played on the walls. He saw the paintings that Father Bennett had described. He stood in front of the one called" The Armenian Bitch" and studied it then penetrated further into the room. The paintings gave him an uneasy feeling in the pit of his stomach.

His light flashed on the bed and he stopped short. On the bed were clothing arranged side by side. He came closer to the bed and shone the light directly on the clothes. There was a bloodstained nightgown on the left side of the bed and on the right were Father Bennett's clothes. It looked like a bride and her bridegroom except there was no one inhabiting the clothing. On top of Father Bennett's clothes was his wallet.

"Is this supposed to represent a marriage? This is totally bizarre."

He looked around the room almost expecting to see someone--any one. The clothes on the bed deepened the uneasy feeling in the pit of his stomach. There seemed to be no logical explanation for their arrangement. He knew where Father Bennett was but where was Diana Clements and where was the old woman?

To further intensify the haunting feeling, the wind began moaning in a different pitch that seemed almost like a voice talking to him." *Would you like to come and play with me*?" whispered the wind in an eerie refrain. Again, the hairs on the back of his neck were trying to stand up on their own accord because it was like a haunting voice beckoning him.

He kept turning around shining the light, trying to discover if there was anyone there. Out of the corner of his eye, he caught a reflection and immediately thought it might be Diana Clements. He quickly shone the light in that direction, but nothing was there. His hands began to shake as the wind intensified its moaning and the scraping increased also. He knew, in the logical, rational part of his mind, that there was nothing here to harm him; but in the primal part of his mind, he felt the deep fear and knew that it wouldn't take much more to send him running out of there.

A sudden sharp slap startled him. That did it! The impetus of whatever that last slap was caused by something overwhelmed the rational part of him, making him quake with a primordial fear. He grabbed up Father Bennett's clothes and wallet and left the room as fast as he could. He rushed down the hall as if all the demons of hell were at his heels. His feet pounded down the stairs as he practically ran down them. The wind seemed to be intensifying into a gale force. At the bottom of the steps, he raced across the floor to the door, ripping it open in his haste to get out of the house.

He ran down the steps of the porch and out of the gate and into the street and didn't stop running until he had reached his car. He opened the door and slid behind the wheel out of breath and sweating profusely. His hands were shaking as he fumbled for the keys to the car. With some false starts, he was able to insert the key into the ignition. He opened the windows and let the cool air calm him.He took deep breaths until finally he stopped shaking and his heart seemed to be beating normally. He put the clothes and the wallet he still held on the seat next to him with the flashlight.

"Do you believe now, Bennie?" he asked himself out loud." God, I was never so scared in my entire life. Well, I wanted the full impact and I got it. I don't think that I could have taken much more in there. I'm sure glad nobody but myself was in there."

He looked over at the clothes on the seat next to him.

"Who arranged the clothes like that? Father Bennett? Diana Clements? The old woman? How bizarre it all was. The clothes looked like a bride and her bridegroom. Well, the bloodstained nightgown was a fact for I saw it. The paintings are a fact for I saw them, also. Except for there being no people or supernatural entities in there, everything he told me is a fact."

He stared out the windshield, lost in thought.

"God, I need a cigarette," he said.

With still shaking hands, he finally extracted a cigarette from the pack in the console beside him. He had to use both hands to light it for they still trembled. He inhaled deeply, holding the smoke in until he thought that his lungs would burst, and then slowly let it out. He felt himself beginning to relax. He inhaled again, repeating the process. He finished the cigarette and lit another finally feeling calmer.

"I really should give this stuff up, but it sure helps to calm me down."

He finished the second cigarette and snubbed it out in the ashtray. He was about to start his car and drive back to Boston when a thought suddenly occurred to him, arresting his hand halfway to the ignition key.

"I wonder where Father Bennett's car is. It must be around here somewhere."

He started the engine and drove slowly around but there didn't seem to be any cars parked in the street.

"Hmm, that's odd. No car. I know that he didn't drive it because he was brought to the hospital in a helicopter. So where is his car? He drove here from Marlborough so there must be a car around here that belongs to him."

He widened his search area without finding the priest's car.

"If anyone would know about the whereabouts of his car, it would be the police. Better go there before going home."

He drove towards the police station, which he found on the corner of Brown and Shank Painter Road. He parked in front of the police station and sat there for a moment before getting out. He walked into the station. Everything seemed to be quiet.

An officer, sitting behind a desk, looked up as he approached. He was a middle-aged man with thinning brown hair going gray at the temples. His hazel eyes were set close together under bushy eyebrows. His nose had been broken and was skewed sideways. His mouth was set in a thin line of disapproval. He stood up revealing a brawny torso with a well-developed spare tire. He studied Lassoe as he approached the desk.

"Can I help you?" he asked.

"Yes, I hope that you can. I'm Doctor Ben Lassoe from Boston and I was wondering if you had a car here that was parked on Atwood."

"A car?" the officer asked amazed.

"Yes, a car. Maybe with the hubcaps off."

"What kind of a car?"

"I don't know."

"If you don't know then how can I help you? Is it your car?"

"No, it belongs to a patient of mine. A Father Joseph Bennett."

The officer scratched his head.

"Is this guy a priest?"

"Yes, he is."

"And you don't know what kind of a car he drives?"

"No, I don't."

"Hmmm. Let me check the computer."

"Fine."

The officer checked the computer.

"Don't find anything."

"Nothing?"

"Not a thing. Is he sure that he left it here? In Provincetown?"

"He was brought to Boston General from here in a helicopter. He was found on the beach in a catatonic state."

The officer looked interested.

"I remember that," he said.

"Were you one of the officers who found him?"

"No, but I was on duty that night."

"About the car...?"

"Don't remember any car being brought in. Too bad that you don't know what type it is."

"A car can't disappear."

"Can if it's stolen."

"No report of any stolen cars?"

"Nope. We have a quiet town here."

"That's nice. Is there a place where you keep impounded cars?"

"Sure, out back."

"Can I look out back?"

"Don't see why not. Don't think that there's anything there, though."

"Still..."

"Go ahead. Need someone to take you back there?"

"Yes."

"Let's go."

He stood up and led the way down the hall to the rear of the building.

"I hardly come out here," he said.

"Why not?"

"No reason."

Lassoe nodded as if that made perfect sense to him.

The officer opened the door and they stepped out. Under a streetlight, a lone car sat up on cement blocks. The two men walked towards it.

"That's strange," the officer said.

"What is?" Lassoe asked."This car."

"Why is it strange?"

"Shouldn't be here. And look, there's no wheels on it."

"You didn't know that the car was here?" Lassoe asked amazed.

The officer shook his head.

"We don't impound many cars. Nobody told me that it was here."

"Are there any hoodlums in this town?"

The officer looked shocked and indignant.

"Hoodlums? Here? No such thing. This is a quiet town."

Lassoe looked at the car. That it was vandalized was obvious.

"How do you explain this car, then?" he asked.

"I... I can't."

Lassoe walked around the car and opened the door. The light came on and he rummaged in the glove compartment. He took out the registration that showed that the car was registered to Father Joseph Bennett of Marlborough. He showed the officer the registration.

"I can't make any sense of this," he said." I'm totally baffled."

Lassoe replaced the registration in the glove compartment and closed the door. The mystery of Father Bennett's car was cleared up. If there were no hoodlums as the officer maintained, then who took the wheels off the car? He didn't believe that supernatural entities did such things so it had to be humans who had done this. It was a mystery that he didn't want to deal with.

The officer began examining the car from every angle. He looked up under the chassis, at the missing wheels, under the hood, the trunk as if trying to deduce how the car had gotten here and where the wheels were. He was totally baffled. The car must have been towed in. Why hadn't he been told? He almost felt a sense of outrage that he hadn't. Finding the car here in that condition when he told this guy that it wasn't here made him look foolish. He didn't like looking foolish. He straightened up from looking under the car, brushing off the knees of his trousers. He looked at the doctor.

"Is this priest coming back for his car?" the officer asked.

"It can hardly be driven, can it?" Lassoe said.

"No, it can't."

"He lives in Marlborough. I don't know if he wants it towed back there or not. I'll tell him about it tomorrow."

"Yeah. We'll have to charge him for storing it."

"I'll tell him."

The two men walked back into the police station.

"This is very strange," the officer said.

"I agree."

"What do you make out of it?"

"I'm not a detective. I'll leave that for you."

"Could your patient have driven it here and then gone back to the beach where we found him?"

"I don't believe so. If he did, what did he do with the wheels and why take them off in the first place?"

The officer scratched his head perplexed.

"You have a point there."

Lassoe nodded.

"Besides, my patient wasn't in any condition to drive when he was found. He was catatonic."

"Yeah. Makes it hard to drive, don't it?"

"Very. Do you know anything about a house off Atwood?"

"What type of a house?"

Lassoe described it in detail.

"Never saw it," the officer declared." Why?"

"I believe that my patient was in that house before being discovered on the beach by your patrol."

"Could be, I suppose. Do you want me to investigate it?"

"No, it's not important anymore."

"I will if you want me to," the officer protested.

Lassoe shook his head. He was tired and this had been a tiring evening, especially to his nervous system. He wanted to go home and get some rest. He had to talk with Bishop Everly tomorrow and he wanted to be rested for that. He had had enough of Provincetown for one night.

"Good night and thanks for your help," he said to the officer.

"You're leaving?"

"Yes, it's a long drive back to Boston."

"You look a little tired. Would you like a cup of coffee? "

"No thanks, officer. I'm awake enough to make the drive back."

"Well, drive safe, buddy. Let us know what he wants to do about the car."

'Sure thing, officer."

Lassoe walked out of the police station and went back to his car. He got in and drove back to the highway that would lead him back to Boston and to bed.

"This has been the strangest night of my life," he reflected." That house was totally chilling. And the police officer who didn't know that Father Bennett's car was there and was surprised when he saw it. A quiet town. No hoodlums. If there were no hoodlums then who took the wheels off his car and why? I wonder what he'll do with the car? Have it towed to Marlborough? It certainly can't be driven in the condition that it's in right now. I came here to verify Father Bennett's story and I did, at least as far as the house was concerned. That he obviously took some sort of interior journey is also evident. The clothes arranged on the bed. Is there some significance to that? If there is, I don't see it. I think that it's evident that supernatural forces were at work. There may have been random noises in the house, but there was no mistaking the wind. It spoke to me. I will never go back there again. I'll be glad to get home. I think that I'll have a stiff drink when I get there. I certainly need it. It's just what the doctor ordered. I wonder what my colleagues would make out of this? Should I tell them? Not what Father Bennett told me, but about my experiences tonight? No, I won't tell them. Maybe Bishop Everly. I wonder if I'm making sense right now."

He turned on the radio and let the music soothe his still jangling nerves.At the junction, he turned towards Boston and was soon back in familiar environs. He drove to his apartment and parked his car. He carried Father Bennett's clothes and wallet up to his apartment putting them on the table. He mixed himself a stiff drink and drank one gulp, letting the soothing effect of the alcohol burn its way down into his stomach. It radiated from there throughout his entire body, calming and soothing him as he finished it. He fixed another one and sat at the table sipping it slowly, examining Father Bennett's clothes and wallet.

He went through each item of clothing carefully. The pockets yielded the keys to the vandalized car. There was a handkerchief neatly folded, some change and nothing else. He looked in the wallet and counted the money making a note of it. He looked at the driver's license. There seemed to be no pictures. There were a couple of credit cards. That seemed to be all.

"Not much for a man's life," he said, taking another drink." Not much at all."

He leaned back in his chair with the drink in his hand and stared at the items on the table. He was beginning to get sleepy. He didn't know how much was due to the long day that he had and how much to the aftermath of his trip to Provincetown and the alcohol he was consuming. He looked at his watch. It was almost midnight. Time for bed.

He drained the glass and carried it to the kitchen where he rinsed it out. He placed it on the edge of the sink to dry and turned off the light. He stopped by the items on the table and then turned out the light and headed for the bedroom. He was too tired to think any more. What he needed was sleep and a clear head for tomorrow.

In the bathroom, he looked at his reflection while brushing his teeth.

"Well, scared out of my wits as I was, my hair didn't turn white. I wonder how I would have explained that?" he thought.

Finished in the bathroom, he went into the bedroom and got into bed. He turned off the light and lay there staring up at the ceiling and then nature took over and he fell asleep.

Chapter Eight

Ruminations

Bishop Everly got off the elevator on the third floor of Boston General Hospital and looked around. Upon seeing the nurse's station, he walked down the hall in that direction. The head nurse looked up as he approached.

"May I help you?" she asked.

"Yes, you may. I am here to see Doctor Lassoe. My name is Bishop John Everly," he said, smiling at her.

"Yes, Bishop, Doctor Lassoe has been expecting you. Let me call him on his extension," she said, returning his smile.

"Thank you," he said.

She picked up the phone and dialed Lassoe's extension.

"Doctor Lassoe?... Bishop Everly is here to see you... I'll tell him you'll be out in a minute."

She hung up the phone and turned back to Bishop Everly, who was looking around.

"Doctor Lassoe will be out in a minute, Bishop Everly."

"Thank you very much," he said.

"You're quite welcome."

A minute later, Ben Lassoe was walking down the hall. Bishop Everly studied him as he drew nearer, impressed by what he saw.

"Bishop Everly?"

"Yes. Doctor Lassoe?"

"At your service, sir."

The two men shook hands.

"Before you see Father Bennett, I'd like to talk to you in my office," Lassoe said.

"That will be fine."

"Please come with me."

The two men walked down the hall to Lassoe's office.

"How is Joseph?" Bishop Everly asked, concerned.

"He's doing much better today as you will see for yourself after we've talked," Lassoe said.

"He's like a son to me. Every father wants his son to follow in his footsteps."

Lassoe nodded.

At the open door to his office, he stepped aside to let Bishop Everly precede him then followed him in, closing the door behind them.

"Please, sit down. Would you like to sit on the sofa?"

Bishop Everly smiled.

"So that you can psychoanalyze me?"

Lassoe looked surprised then smiled.

"I have no intention of doing that to such an august personage as yourself, Bishop Everly. I thought that you might be more comfortable sitting on the couch."

"Just a little joke."Bishop Everly seated himself on one of the two chairs facing Lassoe's desk.

"Would you like some coffee? Tea?"

"No, thank you."

Lassoe moved around behind his desk and sat down facing Bishop Everly. For a moment, the two men studied each other in silence as if trying to read the other's mind. Finally, Lassoe broke the silence.

"When Father Bennett was first brought in here, he was in a state of severe catatonia. He didn't respond to anything. Gradually, he started to come around and finally, yesterday; he was able to tell his story. It is quite a story."

Bishop Everly leaned back in his chair.

"Are you able to tell me anything of his story?" he asked.

"Father Bennett wanted me to tell you everything. He considers you very highly as you consider him."

"That's very kind of Joseph," Bishop Everly murmured, looking pleased.

Lassoe reached into his desk drawer and brought out the tape recorder, setting it on the desk in front of him. Bishop Everly looked at the machine.

"When Father Bennett first began telling his story, I was taking notes, but as I sensed that he was about to get into what happened to drive him over the edge, I asked him if I could tape the rest of his story. He gave me permission. I'm going to play the recording so that you'll understand what happened to him."

"I would very much like to hear it."

"I must caution you that at times this is pretty intense."

"I seriously doubt, Doctor Lassoe, that anything on that tape will... cause me to go over the edge."

There was a faint smile on Bishop Everly's face.

Lassoe studied him for a minute.

"I believe that you're right."

He switched on the machine and the two men listened to Father Bennett's story. As the tape played, Lassoe studied Bishop Everly's reactions to various parts of Father Bennett's story. He saw the deepening concern on the man's face, especially in the final part of the story. When the tape had run out, Lassoe switched off the machine. There was a moment of silence as Bishop Everly digested what he had heard.

"Dear God!" he whispered." Poor Joseph. What he went through."

He shook his head sadly and looked at Lassoe.

"That was quiet an experience. I told him not to go, that there might be sorcery involved but he felt that he had a duty to discharge."

"It was an experience that not many people have," Lassoe agreed.

"What is his prognosis, Doctor Lassoe for a complete recovery?" Bishop Everly asked, leaning forward in his seat.

"Very good. There is no doubt that he was severely traumatized by the events in that house. Also, there is no doubt, at least in my mind, that his amnesia regarding the rape on the night of the Winter Solstice was caused by a powerful hallucinogen..."

"What makes you so sure?" Bishop Everly asked, interrupting.

Lassoe looked surprised at the interruption as well at the question.

"First off, Bishop Everly, according to what you heard and what you know of him, do you think that under normal, rational circumstances that he would be capable of performing such an act; especially being so erratic?" Lassoe asked, leaning forward.

"No," Bishop Everly said, shaking his head." Joseph is one of the most rational people that I know. But if you theory is correct, Doctor Lassoe, how did he ingest the hallucinogen?"

"Ask me something simple," Lassoe said with a rueful smile." He obviously can't recall. I don't think that he was aware of the drug. Maybe it was slipped into the wine before he began performing the mass. Or maybe he ingested it before. I don't know and I don't believe that he knows."

Bishop Everly nodded as if conceding Lassoe's point.

"So, accepting that, is he to blame for the rape of Sister Marcia?"

"Maybe legally. I don't know about morally."

"I don't either."

For a moment, Doctor Lassoe folded his hands under his chin in a contemplative mode.

"What was Father Bennett's experience with the Dogon tribe in Mali?"

Bishop Everly paused for a moment, looking down at the floor. He then looked at Lassoe squarely in the eyes.

"Why do you want to know what happened to him with the Dogon tribe in Mali?"

"You've heard the tape and I believe that a direct correlation can be drawn between his experience with the Dogon tribe and what just happened to him recently." replied Lassoe.

Abruptly, Bishop Everly rose from the couch and walked over to the window, looking out. Lassoe swiveled his chair to face the bishop's back. He could see the tension in the other man's posture. The silence lengthened, until it became almost unbearable.

Bishop Everly slowly turned from the window facing Lassoe. There was a silent plea in his eyes. Lassoe waited.

As if coming to a decision, Bishop Everly walked stiffly back to the couch and sank down on it.

"As far as I am concerned, I believe that his obsession with the amphibious Oannes was the central problem of his experience."

"Could you please explain?" asked Lassoe.

"According to legend, Oannes was credited for instructing the ancient Sumerians in art, science and letters. The Dogon tribe knew him as Nommo, who visited them over five thousand years ago from Sirius. He was known as Enki to the Babylonians and was purported to have warned Noah of the impending Deluge, according to the *Fragments of Berossus*, who lived during the time of Alexander the Great. In other words, the fish-god was credited for introducing the gifts of civilization to mankind. Legend has it that he was referred to as an abomination and would retreat into the amniotic depths of the ocean at night."

"Fascinating! Father Bennett really believed this?" asked Lassoe.

"He believed in the Second Coming of Oannes as did the Dogon tribe and I must admit that this really bothered me. I simply felt that he had confused mythology with history and taken it to its ultimate extreme."

"So, in other words, he believed that an extraterrestrial would again save mankind?"

"Yes and as strange as it may seem, I truly believe that his knowledge of this abomination is the reason why the witch was ever on to Joseph in the first place." remarked Bishop Everly.

Doctor Lassoe became introspective. He seemed to be lost in thought.

"Are you okay, Doctor?"

Lassoe looked up.

"Yes… Yes, I'm fine. What you have just confided in me is totally incredible… That's all I can say… There is something that I must tell you."

"What is it?" Bishop Everly asked, leaning forward.

"When Father Bennett was admitted, my nurse saw claw marks on his arms and fang marks on his neck. She turned away for a second and when she turned back around, the marks were gone."

Bishop Everly turned pale. He crossed himself.

"Dear God" , he whispered.

"What does that mean to you, Your Eminence? Is it like a stigmata?

"The stigmata, according to theological doctrine, is a sign of Divine favor. I won't bore you with all the nitpicking that theologians engage in, but suffice it to say, these people who bore the mark of the stigmata were chosen for some special mission. Like Saint Francis. What you just told me leaves me with no doubt. That infernal witch has got her claws on Father Bennett. I'm afraid for him," Bishop Everly said grimly.

"Sir, he can be salvaged," Lassoe said earnestly, consoling the older man with his right arm.

"Of course," Bishop Everly said brightening." Of course he can through the love of our Lord Jesus Christ."

Lassoe nodded. He felt that he had given the bishop something to hold on to.

" Well, let's just hope that he has made a complete recovery." said Bishop Everly.

"As far as I am concerned, he's fine and my prognosis for him is very optimistic."

"Then I think that we should both be very optimistic for Joseph." remarked Bishop Everly.

"I completely concur with you, Sir."

At this point, Lassoe changed the topic for conversation.

"Last night I went to Provincetown," Lassoe announced calmly.

"Why?"

"I listened to the tape after my session with Father Bennett. I'm something of a skeptic and I was curious. His story sounded a bit... fantastic, if you will. I suppose that I wanted to verify it. Also, I wanted to get the full impact of a night visit. I wanted to see for myself if there were any supernatural happenings going on."

"And did you?" Bishop Everly asked.

"Let's just say that my trip there made me a believer."

"What happened?"

"I had the eerie feeling that the wind spoke to me. I entered the bedroom that played such a big part in Father Bennett's story. I was getting spooked by the moaning of the wind, by the noises made by the tree branches scraping against the window. I saw the paintings that Father Bennett had seen and described in his story. I expected to see either Diana Clements or the old woman. What I saw was Father Bennett's clothes laid out neatly on the bed with his wallet on top and also the bloodstained nightgown that Diana Clements was wearing that night. The impression that I received from seeing that, was of a bride and groom on their wedding night."

Bishop Everly looked thoughtfully at Lassoe.

"Go on," he urged the younger man when he paused." What about the wind talking to you?"

Lassoe looked up at the ceiling as if searching for the proper words to continue his story.

"I admit, without shame, that by this time I was getting scared... so scared that the hairs on the back of my neck were trying to stand up. I was stunned by what lay before my eyes and then the wind picked up in intensity. And it seemed to me that it said: '*Would you like to come and play with me?*'

"How very odd," Bishop Everly said thoughtfully." Very odd. Then what happened?"

"I shone my flashlight all around the room and thought that I caught a glimpse of Diana Clements but it was just my overwrought imagination. Then, from outside, a loud clap came. It scared me so much that I scooped up Father Bennett's clothes and wallet and got the hell out of there... pardon my language," Lassoe said.Bishop Everly smiled.

"I think that accurately describes that house. And after you got the... hell out of there, what happened next or is that the end of the story?"

Lassoe shook his head.

"Not quite. Just a moment."

He got up from his desk and went to the closet in his office and from it brought out a paper bag and set it down in front of Bishop Everly on the desk. Bishop Everly looked inside.

"Those are Father Bennett's clothes and his wallet," Lassoe said.

Bishop Everly took the wallet out and then looked inside at the clothes. Satisfying himself, he folded them neatly and replaced them in the bag.

"What happened next?"

"I thought about Father Bennett's car so I went to the police station and there it was. All four wheels had been removed and it was up on blocks. If he wants the car back, he'll have to replace the wheels."

"And that's the end of your story?"

"I came home and had a couple of stiff drinks then went to bed. I was pretty worn out by that time as you might imagine."

"Yes, I can very well imagine that," Bishop Everly said.

He got up from his chair and walked to the window behind Lassoe's desk. Lassoe swiveled his chair and watched him, seeing only his profile.

"What do you think, Bishop Everly?" Lassoe asked.

Bishop Everly turned back to face the doctor.

"What amazes me is the fact that two very logical, rational men like yourself and Joseph should resort... or should I say fall back on... the urge to flee when scared. This primal intuitive mode of thinking caused by fear is very interesting," he said thoughtfully.

"How so?" Lassoe asked, curious as to what the bishop would say next.

"Both you and Joseph reverted to a fear of the dark. Have you ever heard the term *dues ex machina*?"

"It sounds familiar, but I can't quite place it."

"It's an ancient Greek term which means roughly 'ghost in the machine'. The ancient Greeks used that device in their tragedies in which a god was brought to the stage in a mechanical device to intervene in the action. About a month ago, I visited a kindergarten class at a parochial school in Marlborough. The teacher brought out a box--quite a good size one at that--and told the children that there was a ghost in there and asked them to come up to see the box closer. Well, none of those children wanted to get anywhere near that box. They were convinced that there was, indeed, a ghost in there. Children are more in tune with the primitive, the magical mode of thinking than most adults, simply due to the fact that children haven't quite been conditioned to reject these concepts out of hand. As we get older, Doctor Lassoe, the more conditioned we become, rejecting those things that scared us as children like a ghost in a box. We've taken the Cartesian view of nature, which is primarily mechanistic and have completely forgotten that the 'ghost in the machine' is the animating principle of nature. You do see where I'm going with this, don't you?"

"Yes, I believe that I do," Lassoe said thoughtfully." When an adult gets scared by experiencing something like I did last night, he's likely to revert to the primitive. It's instinctual."

"Exactly. It's instinctual," Bishop Everly agreed, smiling a little." I have no doubt that what you and Joseph experienced was--at least to both of you--very real. You were scared, so scared that you literally got the 'hell' out of there."

"And Father Bennett, who experienced more than I did, was driven by his experience over the edge into catatonia."

Bishop Everly nodded.

"Yes. He received the full impact. It sounds to me that he went on, what the ancient Greek's called, a katabasis or an interior journey into the underworld or the dark recesses of the soul. Homer used it in *The Odyssey*."

"I remember reading that in high school. What Father Bennett experienced was very powerful but as I said earlier, he's making a remarkable recovery."

"Let me ask you something, Doctor Lassoe."

"Ask me anything that you want," Lassoe said.

Bishop Everly moved back to his chair and sat down.

"In your professional opinion, is Joseph ready to resume his duties as priest and spiritual counselor?"

"I won't tell you how to run your diocese, but in my professional opinion, I would give him a little more time to acclimate. I don't hold with the theory that after a severe trauma that the best thing for the patient is to get right back to what he was doing. He's going to have doubts about himself as a priest, which is only natural. He's also going to wonder if he's worthy of being a spiritual counselor to others. These doubts are natural and normal. It's all part of the healing process. I wouldn't rush him into resuming his normal duties. But as I said, I don't presume to tell you how to run your diocese."

Bishop Everly laughed.

"Thank you. I won't tell you how to run your practice. I just wanted your professional opinion on when he could return to his normal duties."

"Would you like to see him now?"

"Very much. When did you say that he was going to be released?"

"Tomorrow. I want to keep him one more night to make sure that he won't be overwhelmed when he's back in the world again. This is a very cloistered environment."

"So is the church," Bishop Everly said, smiling at Lassoe gently as if in reproach.

Lassoe nodded.

"Yes, I suppose that it is. I'm not a Catholic so I don't really know just how cloistered a Catholic church can be for its priests."

Lassoe stood up.

"Let me take to you to see Father Bennett," Lassoe said.

"Thank you. I am most anxious to see and talk to him," Bishop Everly said.

"Don't forget his clothes," Lassoe said.

Bishop Everly, for a reply, picked up the bag containing Father Bennett's clothes and wallet and the two men left Lassoe's office walking down the hall past the nurses' station to Father Bennett's room. The door was closed.

Lassoe knocked on the door.

"Come in," Father Bennett said from the other side.

Lassoe opened the door and he and Bishop Everly stepped into the room. Father Bennett was sitting in a chair, his hair neatly combed, his face clean-shaven. He was wearing a robe and had slippers on his feet. He put down the book he had been reading and stood up as the two men entered the room, a smile on his face.

"Father Bennett, as you can see, you have a visitor," Lassoe said.

"So I see. It's good to see Your Eminence again," Father Bennett said, taking Bishop Everly's outstretched hand.

"It's so very good to see you, Joseph. I was quite worried about you," Bishop Everly said, looking Father Bennett over carefully.

"I'll leave the two of you alone," Lassoe said." I'm sure that you have a lot to talk about."

"Yes, we do," Father Bennett and Bishop Everly said in unison.

They looked at each other and laughed.

Lassoe laughed with them.

"I'm releasing you tomorrow, Father Bennett. I want you to stay one more night just to be on the safe side."

"That's fine. I understand."

"Have a nice visit. It was very nice meeting you, Bishop Everly," Lassoe said shaking the prelate's hand.

"And it was very nice meeting you, too, Doctor Lassoe. I hope to see you again but under better circumstances," Bishop Everly said, smiling at the doctor.

"You'll see me tomorrow when I release Father Bennett. Have a nice day."

"You have the same."

"I'll see you later, Father Bennett," Lassoe said.

"I'll look forward to it," Father Bennett said.

Lassoe left the room and closed the door behind him to give the two men their privacy. When he was gone, Bishop Everly looked carefully at Father Bennett.

"Well, Joseph, you're looking quite well. To be honest, I really didn't know what to expect when I came here to see you."

Father Bennett smiled at his superior and father confessor.

"I feel much better than when I was first brought in here," he said." But please, have a seat."

"Thank you, my son."

He noticed Father Bennett looking at the bag that he held.

"Last night, Doctor Lassoe went to Provincetown and brought your clothes and your wallet back," Bishop Everly said, handing the bag to Father Bennett.

"He did? Is he alright?" he asked with concern in his voice.

"Yes, he's fine, although never having met the man before today, I really have no way of knowing. How did he seem to you?"

"Normal."Father Bennett looked in the bag and took out first his wallet, looking in it to make sure that everything was there. Then he took out his clothes and looked at each item as if he hadn't seen them in a very, very long time. He placed them neatly on the bed then looked at Bishop Everly, who was observing him closely. Father Bennett seemed a little embarrassed.

"Doctor Lassoe appraised me of your stable condition. I am very pleased to hear that, Joseph."

Father Bennett nodded.

"He told you about the condition that I was in when I was brought in?"

"Yes, he did. He assured me that you have made a complete recovery."

"He said that I'll be discharged tomorrow. I'm looking forward to resuming my duties at the church. What I have been through does not jeopardize my being a spiritual counselor, does it Your Eminence?" Father Bennett asked anxiously.

"We'll discuss all that when you return, Joseph. Please don't agitate yourself."

"No, I won't. You say that Doctor Lassoe went to Provincetown last night and brought back my clothes. Where did he find them? And my wallet?"

"In the bedroom of that house that you went to. He said that they were laid out very neatly on the bed. Your wallet was on top of your clothes."

"Laid out how?"

Bishop Everly paused for a moment considering whether to tell the priest in front of him everything that Lassoe had told him about the discovery of the clothes.

"He said that they were laid out like someone lying there. Next to your clothes was a blood-stained nightgown."

Father Bennett looked startled.

"Who...?" he began.

Bishop Everly shook his head.

"Let's talk of something else," he said hastily.

"Did Doctor Lassoe tell you everything about what happened to me?"

"He played the tape that he made of your story. He is also to be credited with sharing with me your own katabasis. Sometimes, the Lord allows certain individuals such as the desert saints to see things that to the rational mind seem to border on the fantastic... the marvelous in other words," Bishop Everly said, choosing his words carefully while looking at Father Bennett, trying to gauge his reactions to his words and their implications.

Father Bennett frowned thoughtfully, looking at his superior.

"Well," he asked," what is your analysis of my experience?"

"There is no doubt that you had one very incredible vision and most importantly a very relevant one at that... the war to end all wars is actually a war of the opposites within the human soul. Actually, Saint John's 'Revelations' is basically the same phenomenon and even Jung re-evaluated the ancient concept of the *coincidentia oppositorum* and postulated the idea of God as an antinomy or a conjunction of the opposites. In my view, achieving a true psychological equilibrium is never a constant factor, as there seems to be a dynamic tension between the opposites. As active symbiosis with nature or an intimate rapport with the unconscious, while the privilege of an elite few, is the gift that modern man has lost sight of. The war of the opposites results from a violation of nature by the way man perceives her as an object. In your vision, you had lost the Crown of Kether and the holy wall elicited these sacrilegious feelings within you because your eroticism had become localized. We have no conception of how extended the mind is, but when one's eroticism has become localized, he is no longer in the sacred sphere. The dualistic rift between you and the wall became so intensified that a porno film was projected on the wall. What had become the last vestige of the sacred had become desacralized as did all of nature and the supreme psychological consequence was the war to end all wars. The basic problem here is that analytical or depth psychology, accepts the psyche as a basic component in empiricism, while eastern mysticism realizes the interrelatedness or the interrelationship of all consciousness. If one were to achieve a synthesis of phenomenology, in which the things of this world are seen as entities instead of objects and analytical psychology, in which the human psyche is accepted as the 'telos' of evolution then one would come to accept the higher faculty of the imagination as intrinsic to nature. In other words, just as we know the inner terrain of our own minds such as the idea of kinship libido in a dream, the same a priori understanding extends to the whole of nature... Unfortunately, civilization has erected a barrier to this understanding..."

" How did this barrier come about?" Father Bennett asked, seating himself on the bed.

"You could see the earliest indications of this barrier in the play *Antigone* by Sophocles. For the first time, the essence of being human came to be defined and delineated as the very strangeness caught in the mutual relation between 'Techne' or the violence of knowledge and 'Dike' or the overpowering character of being. This 'strangeness' originally meant a sense of wonder for to the ancient Greeks man was not at home with himself. In other words, when we stepped into history for the first time, there was a strangeness between the violence of knowledge, which modern technology represents and the overpowering character of being. To understand this 'strangeness', we must take technology into careful consideration and not allow it to master us. For technology is the guise of being in its state of withdrawal. It is the night of the Evening-Land before the New Dawn."

"I find it interesting that you speak in metaphors for there is no better way to describe our present predicament. However, if technology is indeed the artificial barrier between man and his relationship to the sacred, then what is religion?"

Bishop Everly looked at Father Bennett approvingly. He had been afraid that the ordeal the younger man had gone through might have dulled his intelligence. He was very pleased to find that this was not so. He enjoyed intellectual conversations like this, especially with the priest who sat across the room from him. He smiled broadly at Father Bennett who smiled back at him.

"It is the only structured way we have left of understanding and respecting our relationship to a higher power, but instead science has become a form of idolatry. It has launched an all out effort to define the marvels of creation, but in the process, we have lost our sense of wonder and awe... these precious first sensations of reality before the analytical mind takes over... Thus, these initial sensations of nature in her pristine state are somehow lost... But of course, the dream is a compensation for this loss because if we cannot see the entire forest for the trees then the dream or the nightmare is the way in which nature comes to life within us again and again and again..."

Bishop Everly got up and began pacing the floor.

"So the dream is one's own personal myth in a way... Because Christianity, as we know it, is the literalization of the mythic and maybe... just maybe our only structured way that we have of understanding our relationship to a higher power has been divested of the real truth because of dogma, which the Christian adheres to for he lacks an ontological foundation," Father Bennett said thoughtfully, a frown creasing his brow.

At Father Bennett's words, the bishop smiled and stopped pacing the floor for a moment. He stood before the priest still seated on the bed.

"As far as I am concerned, it all comes down to the human will and the 'game' of nature. Towards the end of your vision, the shekinah asked you to remember the child with the 'royal power'. Man has no say so in Nature's game of Hide and Seek. According to Martin Heidegger, the New Dawn will occur when Being shows a new 'face'. Thus, we will experience a prolonged epiphany or the myriad possibilities of the moment, in other words. However, we cannot will this to happen, instead the advent of the New Dawn will happen of its own volition."

"I... I remember something Sister Marcia tried to explain to me at the Confessional after her second dream. She said that to totally submit herself to this mystery is a high and dangerous game as the kingdom may indeed be in the hands of a child. It is rather ominous if there is any validity to this because it's as if we are literally at the mercy of the unconscious," Father Bennett said as he pondered not only his answer, but also what Bishop Everly had previously said.

Both men were silent for several minutes as the conversation seemed to have reached an impasse, then Bishop Everly smiled.

"I attended the original operatic rendition of *Faust* by the Boston Symphony several months ago and I know beyond a doubt, as sure as I'm sitting here, that I saw Sister Marcia playing the role of Helen in her apotheosis of light. Faust had prayed to Persephone and had her resurrected from Hades as a gestalt or an absolute form much as the bronze statues of Apollo that time alone could not destroy because of its inherent beauty. Anyway, Mephistopheles orchestrated the entire drama in which they both fell in love and retreated to a dark cave where Euphorion or the modern Hermes was born. His song and his poetry were more Dionysian than the original Hermes as there seemed to be a sense of contagion. However, his life was rather short-lived as he felt trapped in the subterranean chambers and suffered the same fate as Icarus who flew too near the sun. After his tragic death, Helen sadly returned to Hades, but left behind her dress and veil, which dissolved and were transformed into a luminous cloud, which transported Faust to Germany. As far as I'm concerned, the Hermetic poetry of Euphorion was superior to Apollo, who exercises his powers in a single aspect of poetic intelligence... absolute form... Hermetic poetry, on the other hand, has something of the impure... perhaps of the orgiastic... and even deeper seduction of absolute mystery. Thus, I feel that true poetry has the gift of 'flight', which is the impulse of true love. In modern times, the true poetic moment is a rarity and the epiphanies are of a rather short duration."

At this point, Father Bennett offered his own summation as he looked down at the floor.

"I'm interested, Your Eminence, did your version of *Faust* include the 'Walpurgis Night'?" he asked.

Bishop Everly considered the question.

"Why, I cannot remember... I don't think so..." he said hesitantly.

"Well, because you cannot remember, then what you saw was a bastardized version," Father Bennett replied seriously.

"What do you mean?" Bishop Everly asked, taken aback.

"The Walpurgis Night is another aspect of nature, which we Christians tend to ignore or maybe have even forgotten about. Sure, fairies and goblins are the stuff of fairy tales, however we would not dare even to consider pantheism as part of our belief system. Nonetheless, as you told me before I left for Provincetown the other day, 'the eternal struggle between Eros and Thanatos goes on within our souls' and I would add that the focal point is nature," Father Bennett replied seriously, looking at his friend and mentor.

Bishop Everly sat down again and he leaned forward, looking seriously at Father Bennett. His comment had made him think very seriously.

"It is the ongoing dialectic with nature that we attempt to transcend, however at a much deeper level we are psychically linked to nature and the return to paradise beyond good and evil can occur within the context of the moment. However, as historical beings, the return to paradise would be as difficult as learning how to play again with the supreme element of spontaneity," he said, his face creased into a frown.

Father Bennett got up from the bed and began pacing the floor. Bishop Everly watched him as he paced, looking for signs of agitation. But Father Bennett didn't seem agitated. He looked out the window and then walked back to where the bishop was sitting, watching him.

"During my sojourn in west Africa several years ago, I stayed with the Elgonyi tribe on Mount Elgon for several months. In many ways, they still experienced the 'participation-mystique' that Levy-Bruhl referred to. These people had an optimism, which defied rational understanding, as they believed that the Creator had made everything good and beautiful. When I asked them why their cattle were killed or why they suffered from numerous diseases, they replied with an 'everything is beautiful' philosophy. However, this naiveté soon disappeared when the night approached for this was the dark world of the Ayik, who was everything evil. They stayed in their huts and the shaman performed some type of exorcism for the entire village in order to 'ward off evil spirits'. Ironically enough, when it was sunshine the next day, this childish optimism would return as always and everything was beautiful once again. They were unlike the Dogon tribe, who lived for the night with a fascinating nostalgia for the Nommos or the Monitors, who came from beyond. Anyway, how do you explain the childish behavior of the Elgonyi tribe in light of what you said earlier?"

Bishop Everly sat back in his chair, considering how to answer Father Bennett's last question. He had never heard this story before and it had intrigued him. It was in line with what they were discussing.

"Despite the fact that twelve hours out of every day were spent in almost total bliss, the doubt never occurred about the Other. Here, we have primitive man in a state of animism for the world of the Father implies nature in her pristine state of original unity. This primitive animistic relationship is seen as the 'participation mystique' of Levy-Bruhl, but instead of the popular psychoanalytical theory of the projection of one's own unconscious contents upon the external world, the phenomenologist views this 'art of seeing' as pure objectivity in allowing the pre-logical mind to observe and even to participate in the phenomena of nature as a continuous state of primal becoming... from potentiality to actuality. I use the word 'primal' because primitive man is continually referring back to the beginning. However, it is inevitable that the question of good and evil be asked for it expresses doubt about God's perfection. Both Gnosticism and Christianity presented this as the principle problem of morality. Therefore, the need for a messiah came about as a direct correlation of man's relationship to nature being in a state of jeopardy. In other words, this longing for redemption and the nostalgia for paradise came about because of an irreversible increase in man's consciousness, which made him independent of creation. Thus, subjectivism is the bane or the ruin of western civilization," Bishop Everly explained.

"What do you mean by subjectivism?" Father Bennett asked as he sat back down on the edge of the bed.

"We must go back to Plato. Plato relegated being to the Idea and thus it became a transcendent factor. The external world in its 'thingness' became separated from being in proportion to its essence. His allegory of the cave became the disparagement of man's relationship to being as the shadows on the wall represented the aesthetic distance created by metaphysics. In other words, there was no ontological difference between being and thing. The archetypal realm of the Ideas as a transcendent phenomenon left nature de-sanctified and denuded of her essence as physis or dynamic being. The birth of the western philosophical tradition came out of this failure to make this vital distinction and is responsible for this forgetting of being, which in modern times has led to the misery of nihilism. It is a time of waiting... for the gods have fled and the god, who has yet to arrive..."

"During this time of waiting are we at the mercy of the behavioral sciences as well as technology? Is it a matter of who can manipulate the other by power?" Father Bennett asked, leaning forward.

"All I know is that during this time of waiting our very essence is at stake," Bishop Everly replied.

Father Bennett considered the bishop's reply.

"So, I guess that the ultimate question remains," Father Bennett said slowly." If modern man's notion of the infinite has fallen into disrepute, then how do we progress? Should one remain in a type of homeostasis with the satori as a type of mystical experience or should one evolve with endless psychic transformations as a way of overcoming the human predicament?"

"The latter way of western occultism has its genesis in the concept of the 'will to power' expounded upon by the philosopher, Fredrich Nietzsche. As far as I am concerned, the Promethean 'will to power' is unnatural because the philosopher believed that nature was 'extravagant and indifferent' and must therefore be overcome. Either we are as 'gods' or in the end, we must totally surrender our will to the higher orchestration of nature or to the true Logos," Bishop Everly said as he got up from his chair and walked over to the window. He looked out for a moment then turned and walked back to where Father Bennett sat.

"We must somehow renew our relationship to the world," he continued." Understanding the world is seeing for the first time the daylight for what it is as I saw the sunrise this morning. Understanding the world is allowing the darkness of the night to unfold as a mystery... seeing the shimmering ocean for the first time with an awe for its unknown depths... seeing the majestic grandeur of its mountains... bathing in its streams and digging your hands into the soil for the first time... In other words, this renewed relationship to the world that I speak of is a way of allowing the sacred phenomena of nature to speak to you. In a way, technology robs us of our self worth and perpetuates a sense of youthful vitality. It prevents us from knowing the true rhythms of nature and therefore we have no real ontological foundation. What I am saying, Joseph, is that we must persist in a type of primal thinking... persist in preparing a readiness for Being's coming... this guest over whom we have no authority. We must open ourselves up to the way nature presents herself without any preconceived notions or opinions, which logic presents. In the meantime, in the time of waiting, the darkness will persist and perhaps even spread..."

As Bishop Everly's voice trailed off, there was a period of silence as the two men realized in their hearts the ramifications of what they had said. Father Bennett looked over at Bishop Everly, who sat staring down at the floor.

They were startled by a knock on the door.

"Who can that be?" Bishop Everly asked.

Father Bennett shrugged.

The door opened and an orderly came in bearing two trays.

"Dinner time," he said.

"Dinner? Already?" Father Bennett asked.

Since he had regained his senses, in a matter of speaking, he had lost all conception of time. The concept of time seemed to belong to another world, another time. He saw Bishop Everly look at his watch.

"It's after five o'clock," he said, surprised." My how the time seems to have flown by, Joseph. I mustn't keep you."

The orderly set the two trays down on the table.

"It seems," Father Bennett observed," that he brought two trays. Would you care to join me for supper, Your Eminence?"

"Why, yes, Joseph, however I feel that we should emulate our Jewish brethren with their ancient tradition of setting aside a chair at the dinner table for the prophet, Elijah," Bishop Everly said, bemused.

"Could you bring another chair?" Father Bennett asked the orderly.

He looked at the two men as if they were in the right place.

"Sure," he said.

They watched him go.

"May I ask why?"

"The extra chair?"

"Yes."

The orderly chose that moment to return with another chair.

"Where do you want it?" he asked.

"By the table," Bishop Everly said.

The orderly placed the chair where Bishop Everly wanted it. He left with a backwards glance. He would sure have something to tell the other orderlies.

"In answer to your question, Joseph, think about what this whole conversation has led us to realize," he said as he positioned the chair.

Father Bennett pondered for a moment then with a look of comprehension on his face, he looked directly at the bishop.

"The chair is a metaphor for we are preparing a place for a guest over whom we have no authority," Father Bennett said triumphantly.

Smiling, Bishop Everly placed his hands on the priest's shoulders.

"You have seen the Light, my son...You have seen the Light..."

Chapter Nine

To Grandmother's House

Father Bennett lay in his hospital bed on the morning of his release from Boston General with his eyes wide open as the dawn light began to streak across the eastern sky. He had a hard time sleeping the night before due to the fact that he was going to be released and would be able to go home to Marlborough to take up the shattered threads of his life. It seemed like an eternity since he had seen Marlborough and the familiar faces that had made up his daily life and whom he had begun to take for granted. He was a little uneasy about Bishop Everly's skirting the issue of his resuming his duties as spiritual counselor, putting it off until the ride home. He also had residual flashbacks of the ordeal that he had gone through. But the one thing that really excited him that morning as he watched the sky grow lighter, was that he could return to the Old Village Park and the fountain. For some reason the very thought of the fountain drew him like a magnet drew iron filings. It was the magic fountain of his dreams. It was like a lodestar. It was almost as if the fountain contained a hidden message that he had to decipher.

It was almost, and here he smiled at the whimsy of his thoughts, like a lover that he couldn't wait to see and embrace.

He sat up in bed, frowning at that last thought and the image of Diana Clements flashed briefly in his mind as he had last seen her before she had run back to the house. Just the thought of that house sent shivers of dread through him.

"I never want to see that house again as long as I live!" he said to himself." I never want to see that old woman, either! Was it real or did I imagine it? I have to talk to Doctor Lassoe about his trip to Provincetown."

He got out of bed and turned on the light. His clothes had been hung up in the closet before Bishop Everly had left the night before. He went to the closet and took them out, examining each item carefully before putting them on. He was beginning to experience an anxiety attack; his hands shook as he fastened the white collar around his neck then put on his shirt. He walked to the mirror that hung over the sink in the corner of the room by the door to the bathroom. A stubble was on his cheeks. Yesterday, an orderly had shaved him. He looked in the medicine cabinet, trying to find a razor but there were none to be found. He turned his head first one way then the other trying to see if the stubble was all that noticeable. It was. He would have to ask the orderly when he brought breakfast to also bring him a razor so that he could shave. He brushed his teeth and washed his hands and face then walked to the window.

The sun was rising now in all its glory. For the first time in a long time, he felt at one with nature. He experienced with his senses what the sight of that golden orb rising meant to all of mankind since the beginning of time. The anxiety that he had felt was replaced, instead, by a feeling of serenity; a feeling that had been too long missing from his psyche. How long, he didn't know. All he knew was that a feeling of utter peace and tranquility had descended upon him like a curtain being lowered after the last act of a stage play. This feeling was a balm to his wounded spirit. He wondered, briefly as he turned from the spectacle, what Doctor Lassoe would think of his sentiment if he told him? He smiled, the first genuine smile since he had recovered his senses.

A rumbling noise in his stomach made his smile broader as it coincided with a sharp knock on the door. He was about to call out for the person to enter when the door opened and an orderly carrying a tray came in.If the orderly was surprised to see Father Bennett up and dressed, he gave no indication of it as he set the tray down on the table.

"Breakfast," he announced as if to an idiot child.

"Thank you," Father Bennett said, watching him remove the cover from the tray." Could you bring me a razor, please?"

"Sure. You want me to shave you?"

"No, I'll do it myself."

The orderly shrugged.

"Sure. No problem. I'll be back in a moment."

"Thank you."

He watched the orderly leave the room and then walked to where his breakfast was. He sat on the edge of the bed and began to eat the scrambled eggs, bacon, hash brown potatoes and the toast. He sweetened his coffee and felt the peaceful feeling stealing over him again like a blanket.

The orderly returned with a razor and shaving cream that he placed on the sink.

"Are you sure you don't want me to shave you?" he asked, watching Father Bennett as he ate with dubious eyes.

Father Bennett, his mouth full, shook his head.

"Okay," the orderly said, shrugging his shoulders as if absolved of all responsibility in case of an accident; although how anyone could have an accident with disposable razors baffled him.

"Thank you," Father Bennett said after he had swallowed his food.

"Hey, no problem."

"Is Doctor Lassoe in yet?"

"No. He won't be in until later. Want a nurse?"

"No, I just wanted to talk to Doctor Lassoe."

"He'll be making his rounds."

Father Bennett nodded.

"Then I'll just have to wait until he does."

Father Bennett finished eating.

"May I have another cup of coffee, please?"

"Sure."

The orderly took the tray and left the room. Father Bennett walked to the sink and turned on the hot water. He washed his face and then lathered it up with the shaving cream before wetting the razor. He shaved, his hands steady. He was wiping the remaining lather from his face with a towel when the orderly returned with his second cup of coffee.

"Here it is," the orderly announced as he placed it on the table.

"Thank you," Father Bennett said, turning to address him.

"Want me to take that razor for you or do you want to put it in the disposable bag?"

"I'll put it in the disposable bag."

"Okay. Anything else that you need?"

"Not right now, thank you."

"Just ring if you do."

"I'll do that."

The orderly, not knowing what else to say, shrugged his shoulders once more and left the room. Father Bennett fixed his coffee the way that he liked it and returned to looking out the window with the coffee cup in his hand.

He felt better now that he had eaten and had shaved. Dressed, he felt less like a patient in a mental ward of a hospital and more like his former self. He sipped his coffee reflecting on that change in his perspective; how being dressed normally instead of wearing a hospital gown changed a person's entire view of himself. He watched the traffic increase as full day broke upon the city. From his perspective, they looked almost ant-like hurrying on their way to their colony. He had never thought of such things before; how things looked from higher up then when you were down at a level with the object whether it was people or machines. He wondered if God saw his creations like that. He didn't feel that that was something he should bring up with Bishop Everly. He didn't know how the older man would feel about such a question or observation.

He drained the coffee in his cup and turned from his study of the teeming city below to return the cup to the table. He felt at loose ends, waiting. He began pacing as if time would pass faster if he were in motion. But the rational part of his mind told him that time moved at its own pace regardless of whether he was active or passive.

Tired of pacing, he sat down in the chair by the bed and looked up at the silent television set debating whether to turn it on or not. He wasn't much for watching television. He preferred reading the newspaper to get his news. He looked at the book on the nightstand by the bed. He had finished it and there was nothing to read. He wondered if he should take a walk and if that was allowed. He felt at odds. He was not a man of action. As a child he had never been interested in sports. He enjoyed contemplation; long walks that helped focus his thoughts. He didn't envy those who at times, seemed to him, to be perpetual motion machines. Unconsciously, his fingers began drumming on the arms of the chair.

He suddenly got up and went to the open door. He looked out at the corridor, hesitantly trying to make up his mind on whether to leave the room before Doctor Lassoe arrived or take a walk down the corridor to the recreation room. He didn't know when the doctor would arrive to begin his rounds and he was beginning to feel claustrophobic in the narrow confines of the hospital room. He made his mind up and stepped out into the corridor. A passing nurse gave him a cursory look as she passed him on her way to another room further down the corridor. He almost expected her to tell him to return to his room, but she didn't. She murmured a good morning and they passed each other going in opposite directions.

He walked slowly. There was no hurry. He neared the nurse's station. The head nurse looked up as he approached.

"Good morning," she said, smiling at him.

"Good morning," he said." Has Doctor Lassoe arrived yet?"

"No, he's running a little late this morning. But he'll be here. Going for a walk?"

"Yes, I am."

"Good. Exercise is good not only for the body but also for the mind. Do you get a lot of exercise, Father?"

"I like to take long walks."

She nodded.

"Walking is very good exercise. Well, enjoy your walk. I understand, from Doctor Lassoe, that you're being released today."

"Yes, I am."

"I'll bet you'll be glad to get out of here and to get back home."

"Yes, I will. I hope that doesn't offend you."

She looked at him in surprise.

"Gracious, no. If I was a patient, I'd be glad to leave here and go home. Waiting to be released is the hardest part, isn't it?"

"Yes, it is," he said, smiling.

"Be patient, Father. You'll soon be out of here and back home. Where is your home?"

"Marlborough. Have you ever been there, nurse?"

"No, I never have. Is it a nice town?"

"Very nice. Well, I won't keep you any longer."

"Enjoy your walk."

"Thank you."

He was about to leave when a thought suddenly struck him.

"Is it permissible to leave this floor and go to another floor or even outside?"

"No, I'm afraid not. Doctor Lassoe doesn't like his patients wandering off. I'm sorry."

"That's alright. I was just curious. I really didn't expect you to say that I could."

"Hospital rules," she said as if that explained everything.

"Of course."

He nodded to her then resumed his walk down the hall.

He stopped outside the doorway to the recreation room looking in, undecided whether to enter or turn back and go to his room. He entered the room and looked at the people already there. Some were alertly watching the television; others were staring vacuously into space as if seeing something that nobody else could see. They wore the standard hospital attire: robes over hospital gowns, slippers on their feet. There were nurses and orderlies circulating around the room as if they were looking for signs of trouble, but the patients were absorbed either in the real world around them or the world that, to some, was more real than the actual world. He walked purposefully over to where the books were and contemplated the titles. It was strange that there wasn't a single Bible among the books. He studied the titles as if trying to find one that interested him, but there were none that appealed to him.

"Help you find something?" a voice at his elbow asked.

He looked in that direction. It was his orderly. He thought of the man as his, simply because he seemed to be always waiting on him; bringing his meals, shaving him (except for that last morning), and generally being in his immediate vicinity whenever he was conscious of his presence. He was almost like a guardian angel.

"No, thank you. I'm just trying to see if there's anything here that I want to read."

"Newspapers are over there by the magazines," the orderly said, pointing in a direction a little further down from the bookshelves." They're today's papers, in case you're interested."

"Thank you," Father Bennett said politely." I'll take a look."

The orderly nodded and left to return to his vigil of the room. Father Bennett walked over to the table where the magazines and newspapers were. He picked up *The Boston Globe* and looked at the headlines noting the increasing violence in the Holy Land for that's how he viewed the Middle East, especially Israel. He shook his head and a brief flashback of the Wailing Wall in Jerusalem impinged upon his memory then like a specter was gone.

He found a seat and began reading the paper.

Ben Lassoe stepped off the elevator at the third floor.

"Good morning," he said to the head nurse as he stopped at the nurse's station.

"Good morning, Doctor," she said." If you're looking for one of your patient's, he's in the recreation room."

"What's he doing?" Lassoe asked curiously.

"Reading the morning paper."

"I'll go collect him," he said as he began to walk towards the recreation room.

"Oh, Doctor," she called after him.

He turned.

"Yes?"

"Bishop Everly called and left a message for you."

He came back to the nurse's station.

"What was the message?"

"That he's tied up this morning and won't be able to make it until this afternoon," she said, handing him the message.

He took it and looked at it, frowning.

"Well, he is a busy man. It looks like my patient will have to compose himself to wait until this afternoon to be discharged."

"Yes, sir."

"I'll go collect him from the recreation room, then. Have you told him?"

"No, Doctor. I thought I'd let you do that."

"Yes, it is my responsibility, isn't it?"

She looked at him, not saying a word. He smiled at her and walked to the recreation room. He stood in the doorway observing the activity or lack of it before entering. He found Father Bennett sitting in a chair with the newspaper in his hand, concentrating on what he was reading. Lassoe walked up to him and stood before him, observing him before he spoke.

"Good morning," he said softly not wishing to startle the priest.

Father Bennett looked up from the paper and smiled at Lassoe.

"Good morning, Doctor Lassoe," he said, folding the paper back into its original shape, placing it in his lap.

"How did you sleep last night?"

"I had a sort of restless night."

"Is there anything the matter?" Lassoe asked, concerned.

"No, I was just excited about being released this morning. I suppose that's natural?"

"Yes, it is natural. Why don't we talk in my office? I don't believe that you've ever been there. Have you?"

Father Bennett shook his head.

"Not that I can recall," he said, smiling.

He rose to his feet, still holding the paper. On his way to Lassoe's office, he put the newspaper back on the table.

"Does it feel good to be dressed again?" Lassoe asked as they left the recreation room.

"Yes, it does. I feel like a semblance of normality is returning to my life."

"Good."

They walked down the hall in silence until they reached Lassoe's office. He opened the door and turned on the overhead light, letting Father Bennett precede him into the room.

"Have a seat. Would you like some tea?"

"No, thank you. I had two cups of coffee this morning and that's enough for me."

Lassoe walked behind his desk and sat down, observing his patient as he looked around the room. He looked at his messages then up at Father Bennett.

"The head nurse received a call from Bishop Everly this morning that he's going to be tied up and won't be able to pick you up until this afternoon."

Father Bennett said nothing.

"Does that disturb you?" Lassoe asked, gently probing.

Father Bennett smiled and shook his head.

"The bishop is a busy man."

"I know that you're anxious to leave and return home," he began.

"Yes, I am," Father Bennett interrupted." I'm looking forward to picking up the threads of my interrupted life."

"That's natural," Lassoe said, then paused." However, you underwent a severe trauma and I feel that you need a little time to re-acclimate to the real world again."

Father Bennett frowned.

"Don't you think that resuming my duties in the church would be more beneficial to my re-acclimating, in your words, than doing nothing?" he asked, leaning forward tensely in his chair and staring at Lassoe as if trying to read his mind.

"If you had suffered a physical injury, that would be different. The mind is a tricky thing. For all the advances that we've made in understanding the unconscious, we're still not quite sure how each individual reacts after they suffered the extreme trauma that you have. I don't want you to rush into something that you or Bishop Everly feels may be safe. I might be erring on the side of caution, but doctors do that. We're conservative by nature; more concerned with our patient's total well being. So, please, do this my way. Okay?" Lassoe said earnestly.

The two men's eyes met in what seemed to be a silent battle of each other's wills. Father Bennett was the first to lower his gaze.

"Alright, Doctor Lassoe," he said softly." I'll do what you want me to do. What will I tell Bishop Everly though?"

"Let him tell you."

Father Bennett digested this piece of information.

"Did Bishop Everly say what time this afternoon he'll be able to pick me up?"

"No, the message didn't say, but I'm sure that before he comes over, he'll call."

"Yes, he's that type of person."

"Is there anything that you want to tell me?"

"This morning, before you came, I was reading the headlines in the paper and I noticed the continuing violence in the Middle-East. I had a flashback of the Wailing Wall."

"Interesting. What type of a flashback?" Lassoe asked, leaning forward.

"Very, very brief. It was like I was seeing that wall again. It probably lasted a couple of seconds and then faded into the mist."

Father Bennett stared pensively at his feet.

Lassoe leaned back in his chair.

"Did this... flashback alarm you?" he asked gently.

"A little," Father Bennett admitted, quickly looking up at Lassoe as if trying to determine whether this admission would cancel his release.

"That's natural. Association."

Father Bennett looked blankly at him.

"I'm afraid that I don't understand what you mean, Doctor," he said.

"One of the last things that you related in your story was visiting Jerusalem and being at the Wailing Wall. So when you saw the headlines, your unconscious mind made the connection between your... journey and what you saw before you with your own eyes. That's what I mean by association. You associated one event with another and the result was a flashback."

"Hmmm. So I'm not regressing? That's normal?" Father Bennett asked almost anxiously.

Lassoe smiled reassuringly.

"That's very normal," he said." Don't be alarmed."

"That's very reassuring," Father Bennett said.

"I hope so."

"Bishop Everly told me that you went to Provincetown the other night. Why?"

"Your story, especially that house intrigued me and I wanted to see it for myself. So after I left you, I drove there and looked around. I found your clothes, the clothes that you're wearing now."

"Thank you for that," Father Bennett said, feeling that there was something that Lassoe was keeping from him." What did you think of the house?"

Lassoe looked at him.

"It was quite spooky in my opinion. I don't think that I would want to return."

"I wouldn't either."

Lassoe looked at his watch.

"Time for my rounds," he said. Are you going back to the recreation room or back to your room?"

"The recreation room."

"I'll probably see you later before you're officially released."

"In case you get tied up with other patients, I want to thank you for everything that you've done for me," Father Bennett said, extending his hand.

"You're quite welcome," Lassoe said, taking the extended hand and shaking it." Don't overdo it at first. Just take things nice and easy. Okay?"

"Okay."

The two men left Lassoe's office. Father Bennett returned to the recreation room while Lassoe started his rounds.

It was mid-afternoon before Bishop Everly finally arrived at the hospital. He came into Father Bennett's room apologetic.

"I'm terribly sorry, Joseph for not being here sooner."

"It's quite alright, Your Eminence. I understand the demands on your time, especially when you're here in Boston," Father Bennett said.

"Yes, the archbishop likes to keep me occupied. I'm sure that you're ready to go home."

"More than ready."

Bishop Everly laughed.

There was a knock on the door.

"Come in," Father Bennett called out.

The door opened and a nurse came in pushing a wheelchair in front of her.

Father Bennett frowned when he saw it

"What's that for?" he asked.

"That's for you," the nurse said." Hospital rules state that all patients being released must be in a wheelchair even though they can walk."

"Looks like you have to bow to officialdom, Joseph," Bishop Everly said jovially.

"Looks that way," Father Bennett said good-naturedly." Is Doctor Lassoe coming?"

"No, unfortunately he had an emergency," the nurse said.

Making sure that he had everything, Father Bennett sat in the wheelchair.

"Ready?" the nurse asked.

"Yes, I am ready," Father Bennett said.

"Should I bring my car around? It's parked in the parking garage," Bishop Everly said to the nurse.

"Yes, that would be best," she said.

"I'll see you in a few minutes, Joseph," Bishop Everly told Father Bennett.

Father Bennett nodded and watched as the elderly prelate hurriedly left the room. A minute later, the nurse wheeled Father Bennett from the room and to the elevator. She pressed the button and a couple of minutes later, the elevator arrived. She pushed him on then pushed the button for the first floor. They rode down in silence. When the elevator reached the first floor, she pushed him off and headed for the front door. The automatic doors whooshed open at their approach and she wheeled him out to the front of the hospital just as Bishop Everly turned his car into the driveway. He pulled up under the portico and put the car in park. He hurriedly got out of the car and came around to the passenger side, opening the door.

At a nod from the nurse, Father Bennett got out of the wheelchair.

"Thank you," he said.

"You're quite welcome. Have a nice day."

"You have one, too."

"I'll try," she said, smiling.

Father Bennett got into the car and Bishop Everly closed the door and then got in on the driver's side.

"Are you ready to go, Joseph?" he asked.

"More than ready," Father Bennett said.

"Then let's go home."

As they left the hospital, they didn't talk until they were out of Boston and on the way back to Marlborough. As many times as he had been to Boston, Father Bennett had never really paid attention to his surroundings before. Now, he looked around as they threaded their way through traffic that even in mid-afternoon was beginning to get heavy. Finally, they left Boston behind.

"We should be home in about an hour," Bishop Everly said.

"That will be fine. I'm very anxious to return," Father Bennett said.

"Yes, I sure that you are, Joseph."

Father Bennett looked over at Bishop Everly. He studied his profile intently.

"Your Eminence, about my duties..." he began.

Bishop Everly spared him a quick look before returning his attention to the road in front of him.

"Yes, I've been meaning to talk to you about that, Joseph," he said." Before visiting you yesterday, I spoke with Doctor Lassoe."

He glanced over at Father Bennett again.

The priest waited in silence for his superior to continue.

"Doctor Lassoe is of the opinion, and I must say that I agree with him, that you need time to re-acclimate yourself. He feels that because of the trauma that you suffered, your mind needs time to heal."

"Yes, he told me that this morning," Father Bennett replied." So what will my duties be while I'm re-acclimating myself to the real world?"

"I've been thinking about that and also talked it over with the archbishop. We both feel that you should be a Witness for Christ. Go to hospitals and prisons, take their testimony. You can administer Last Rites."

"And performing the mass, conducting services, giving sermons?"

Bishop Everly shook his head.

"Not until you're fully back to being your old self again. I'm truly sorry, Joseph."

Father Bennett looked out the passenger window seeing the trees in their seasonal finery; the reds and golds of the leaves that gave all of New England a sort of festive air. In the past, this sight always made him feel alive even though the seasons were changing and soon the leaves would fall off the trees. Now, at the bishop's words, he felt a heaviness in his heart.

"Joseph?" Bishop Everly said with concern in his voice.

Father Bennett looked at him.

"If that's what you want me to do, Your Eminence, then I'll do it. Part of my vows includes the vow of obedience."

"I'm sure that it won't be for long, Joseph. The Mother Superior has been praying for you."

"How is she?"

"Concerned about you."

"She has a good heart and is a kind person."

"Yes, she is. When we get back to Marlborough, I'll take you straight to the rectory. I'm sure that you'd like to rest."

Father Bennett shook his head.

"I'd rather, if it's not too much trouble, be let out at the Old Village Park instead."

"Why there?" Bishop Everly asked curiously.

"We talked about the sacred before and to me that's sacred ground. I'd like to meditate. I'll probably walk back to the rectory afterwards. It's not all that far. By the way, whatever happened to my car?"

"Doctor Lassoe, after he visited that house, went to the police station to inquire about your car. He found that all the wheels had been taken off and it was sitting up on blocks. I don't know how you'll get it back."

"I don't either. I suppose that I have to buy four new wheels before I can get it back. I really don't want to return to Provincetown after all that's happened to me."

"I can't say that I blame you. So what will you do about your car?"

"Maybe I'll meditate on that while I'm at the park."

Bishop Everly nodded, started to say something, then fell silent.

Father Bennett turned his attention back to studying the passing landscape.

Forty-five minutes later, they approached the outskirts of Marlborough.

"The park is just up ahead," Father Bennett said.

Bishop Everly nodded.

"Are you sure that you want me to drop you off there, Joseph?" he asked, looking at his companion.

"Yes, if it's not too much trouble," Father Bennett said.

"No, it's no trouble at all."

Bishop Everly pulled up to the curb in front of the Old Village Park and stopped the car.

"If there's anything that you need, Joseph, please don't hesitate to call me," he said, placing his hand on Father Bennett's arm.

Father Bennett looked at him and covered the bishop's hand with his own. He smiled.

"I will," he promised.

"God be with you, Joseph. May He keep you in His hand and keep you safe from future harm."

"Thank you," Father Bennett said softly.

"I have never doubted your faith, Joseph. I don't doubt it now. I don't want you to doubt it. Promise me?"

"I promise."

"Good."

There was an awkwardness that both men felt. Silently, Father Bennett got out of the car closing the door. He waved to Bishop Everly who waved back then drove off towards town. Father Bennett stood on the curb and watched the car grow smaller and smaller until finally, turning a corner, it was gone. Bishop Everly had thrown him a curve that, after his conversation that morning with Doctor Lassoe, he should have expected. Still, the news of what his new assignment would be was like a blow to the solar plexus. On top of that, the news about his car didn't help matters any either.He didn't know how long he stood on the curb looking towards town. He felt a little adrift. There was a feeling that it might be a long time before he was fully re-acclimated and could resume his duties again. It was something that he had to bear in mind. He looked up at the sky as if seeking inspiration in this hour of need and finally turned from his contemplation of the sky and the empty roadway to the park itself. He turned slowly towards the park as if he wanted his first view of it to have the maximum effect on him; as if the impression that he received would be the determining factor that would chart the course for the rest of his life.

He turned slowly as if to prolong the ultimate moment and saw the fountain. Four jets of water were shooting skywards. He also noticed a little girl playing in the fountain as he began walking slowly towards the object that had remained in his memory. He could hardly believe his eyes as he drew nearer. He noticed that the swing set was upright and that the merry-go-round was on its hinges. As he passed it, he gave it a twirl.

He stopped short of his goal, staring at the fountain and the little girl. His first thought was that the park including the fountain had been restored. To him that was a logical assumption. He was very familiar with the fountain and looking at it closely, he detected that no work had been done to it. He turned his attention to the little girl. Her back was to him and she happily splashed her hands in the water, laughing with the pure abandon of a child. He noticed how her long dark hair fell over her shoulders.

"Well, you look like you're having fun," he said.

She seemed oblivious to the priest's presence and continued splashing her hands in the water and laughing.

He thought, at first, that she might be deaf.

He came to a point where he could move into her line of vision. He looked at her in profile. As if catching something out of the corner of her eye, she slowly turned towards him.

"What's your name, little girl?" he asked her gently, trying not to frighten her." Do you have a name?"

The little girl looked up at the priest with her puppy dog brown eyes. She smiled as she gently pulled back her shimmering black hair, which glistened in the late afternoon sun. She was wearing a knee-length gray dress with a white smocked lace collar.

"Are you a priest, mister?" she asked in her childish, piping voice.

"Yes, I am, little girl. I am Father Bennett from the Holy Rosary Church in Marlborough. What's your name?"

"I'm Lucia Marcia and I'm five years old today," she said proudly.

There was something hauntingly familiar about her face that eluded him like a fragment of a dream that slips away upon awakening. He was also a little confused about the coincidence of her last name. He shook his head and continued on with his conversation.

"So, today is your birthday. Happy birthday, Lucia. Why aren't you having a party? Where are your friends?" he asked, gently probing.

Lucia threw back her head emitting peals of silvery laughter as if she found his questions hilarious.

"I am playing with my friends, silly," she said, chortling." Only I can see them, 'cause this is the magic fountain! Do you believe in magic, mister?"

Her guileless eyes looked deep into his.

"No, Lucia, I can't say that I do, but I do know that this is a very special fountain," he said gently." To be honest with you, I only come here on certain occasions just to see the fountain and I'm glad that it's been fixed."

She stared at him puzzled.

"Was it broken?" she asked.

"What do you mean? This is the first time that the water has been sprouting from its jets. The last time I was here there was no water. The whole park seemed uncared for."

She shook her head as if to refute the priest's words. He was beginning to get a funny feeling in the pit of his stomach at her reaction. It was evident, to him, that she didn't believe him. Did she think that the fountain and the park were always the way it was now? Should he question her about it? He was trying to make up his mind when she began tugging on his sleeve.

"Mister, would you push me on the swing?" she asked, beginning to hop and down on first one foot then the other. Her eyes appealed silently to him to grant her this wish on her birthday.

"Of course, I'll give you a push on the swing, Lucia," he said smiling down into her face.

"Oh boy!" she cried happily.

She began running towards the swing set, looking back over her shoulder to see if he was following her.

"Hurry!" she cried with the impatience of youth.

"I'm coming," he said.

The distance from the fountain to the swing set wasn't all that far. When he got there, she had already seated herself on the seat; her hands clutched the metal links that held the seat up.

"Push me real high!" she commanded, almost imperiously like a queen to her subjects.

He came behind her and drew the swing seat back towards him. He gave it a gentle push, watching as the child and the swing that she was sitting on made a gentle arc.

"Push me harder!" she said.

"Okay," he said dubiously." I don't want you to get hurt."

He pushed with all his strength, not sure why he did so.

"Is that hard enough?" he asked.

"Ouch!" she cried reproachfully." That hurt! Have you forgotten how to play, mister?"

Her question caught him off guard.

"Uh... now you're getting a little personal. You see, Lucia, I forgot how to play a long time ago."

"Why?" she asked, looking back over her shoulder.

"I'm grown up now," he answered.

He remembered Kierkegaard, who never knew sheer spontaneity. The Danish philosopher literally had to fake jumping in the air.

"Could you swing with me?" she asked.

"Oh, I'm too overweight for that... I would probably break the swing set if I got on it."

She giggled. Her giggling turned into joyous shouts of laughter. She threw her head back as he drew the seat back and pushed her again. She leaned back with her feet straight out.

"Wheee!" she cried joyously." This is fun!"

He had to smile at her exuberance. She was very appealing, reminding him slightly of a street urchin out of a Charles Dickens novel. He was struck anew by the sheer joy of childhood; how a child could amuse itself endlessly with even the simplest of materials at hand. The one thing that they supplied in great abundance was their imagination.

"Can you slide?" she asked.

He shook his head.

"No, Lucia, I would have the same problems.""We could sit in the sandbox and make sand castles," she said hopefully.

"I'm afraid that I would get dirty because I have on my church clothes."

"Well, you can put on your bathing suit. Don't you know that you can put on your bathing suit and sit in the sandbox?" she asked, exasperated.

Her tone of voice amused him. It was almost as if their positions were reversed.

"No, I'm afraid it's too cold for that," he said.

"Well, I think that you need to go home and take a nap 'cause you're grouchy."

"I'm sorry if I appear grouchy, it's just that I'm getting older."

She said nothing in response.

"Are your parents at work?" he asked.

She shook her head.

"They're on a trip and I don't know when they'll be back."

"Who are you staying with then?"

"My grandma. Sometimes my sister comes. She looks like me, you know."

"No, I don't think I ever met your sister."

She said nothing to that either.

In the distance came the sound of music like the type ice-cream trucks made. The music was drawing nearer to the park. He tried to remember what the tune was that the truck was playing.

"How would you like an ice-cream cone to celebrate your birthday?" he asked, suddenly trying to get her to smile again.

She looked up at the priest with unsure eyes.

"My grandma says that I should never take anything from a stranger without asking her first."

"And she's absolutely right, Lucia."

Suddenly with excitement in her eyes, she exclaimed:

"I know! We can go and ask my grandma 'cause she just lives right up the road!"

"Okay. Let's go."

They left the park and walked quickly down the sidewalk with her tugging at his hand.

"Hurry! Hurry! Before the ice-cream man leaves!" she cried as if just the urgency in her voice would make him move faster.

Excitedly, the little girl skipped down the sidewalk with the priest trailing behind her. They came around a bend in the road and he saw a house nestled in a little grove of trees. As they approached the house, he noticed the familiarity of the octagonal shaped polished stepping stones leading up to the porch. He looked up at the wood frame house and above the porch was a segmental arch window with white Victorian lace curtains. Feeling overwhelmed, he slowed down his pace and took the entire house into perspective. He knew he had been there before, but exactly when remained a mystery. There was an aura about the house with the high gabled roof and the bushes growing around the house that made him stop and look.

Lucia, not noticing that her new companion wasn't with her, ran up the porch and flung the door open.

"Grandma! Hurry! Come here!" she cried.

"I'm coming, child," a voice said from inside.Lucia emerged from the house pulling her grandmother by the hand.

"Grandma! Father Bennett wants to buy me an ice cream for my birthday! Can he? Can he? Please?" she said imploringly with both her eyes and the tone of her voice.

The old woman looked at Father Bennett and their eyes met without acknowledging each other. Lucia was adamant.

"Hurry!" she said." Here he is! Can I have some, please?"

Tenderly, the old woman looked down into the upturned face that beseeched her and smiled, stroking the child's head.

"Yes, dear, that will be fine. But don't ruin your appetite."

"I won't," Lucia promised.

Father Bennett dug into his pocket and came up with a handful of coins.

"Here, Lucia," he said, handing the coins to her.

"Thanks," she said as her tiny hand closed over the coins clutching them tightly." Gotta go!"

She bounded off the porch like a gazelle. She ran towards the truck waving her hands. The truck stopped in front of the house. Father Bennett and the old woman watched her as she got her ice cream. Looking back at the porch, she smiled happily, waving. They waved back. They watched her as she skipped over to her tire swing that was suspended from a large oak tree. She began swinging, eating her ice-cream cone with the joyful abandon of a child.

Now that Lucia was out of hearing range, the priest turned to the old woman with a very serious look on his face.

"Lucia seems somehow familiar to me. It's like I've seen her before, but I don't know where I've seen her."

The old woman looked down at him from her vantage point on the porch. There was an inscrutable look on her face.

"You have," she said softly.

"Where?"

"In the convent."

He looked blankly at her.

"Do you remember Sister Marcia?" the old woman asked.

"Yes," he said." Do you mean...?"

The old woman nodded her head.

Father Bennett looked stunned by her silent acknowledgement to his question.

"How?" he asked, bewildered looking into her impassive face, the dark eyes seemed to burn into him.

The question hung on the air, unanswered. Suddenly, the answer dawned on him, stunning him in its implications.

"Even though I cannot conceive of such a thing as witchcraft, you did this to her, didn't you?" he asked, his question an accusation.

The old woman looked steadily at him before replying."Yes, I did this to erase from her memory the trauma... the scars that you inflicted upon her that tragic night... Today was to have been her thirtieth birthday and I sent her back twenty-five years. You might say that I restored her to her innocence once again because she always loved to play. There is such a thing as sheer spontaneity... absolute freedom that only a child can experience before society modifies their behavior."

Father Bennett shook his head in dismay trying to dispel the old woman's words.

"My God, woman!" he cried, shocked." Even though you believe that I was solely responsible for what happened that night, how could you have done this? The sad irony of the fact is that no one in their right mind would ever believe me if I told them about such a diabolical thing."

"Well, I guess you could say that people disguise their fear of what they do not understand and maybe it is better that way. Most people just simply laugh at the notion of witchcraft, but what I practice has been an ancient tradition since the beginning of time. In other words, the man outside of nature accepts dogma, while the man in nature knows magick."

The old witch scrutinized the priest for several moments.

"Something else is bothering you besides what I did to her, isn't it? Come on now, dear... You know better than to be scared of me... What's really bugging you?"

Father Bennett looked at his surroundings again, studying the stepping stones leading up to the porch where he was standing. He then looked back into the witch's eyes.

"I have the feeling that I've been here before... but that there is a missing link somewhere..."

"Why don't you come on in? I have a story to tell you and I think that the inside of my house will help to facilitate your memory. Besides, there is someone here whom you should meet."

The old witch and the priest went into the house. Lucia was still swinging in her tire swing.

As he walked into the living room, Father Bennett was baffled by all the strange paraphernalia. There were a variety of brass and silver bells, a large rope with peppers and garlic and four brass half moons all hanging on the walls surrounding the room. Sitting on the floor along the right wall were, what appeared to be, several Chinese wizards and in the far right-hand corner stood an old grandfather clock with signs of the zodiac on it's door. He followed the old witch down the hall to the kitchen where he discovered a large black cauldron. He studied it for several moments and then looked up with astonishment in his eyes.

"I can't help but remember this! I have been here before, but I have no idea as to why I was here...You said you had a story to tell me... What happened?"

The old witch smiled at the priest as she ran her hands along the rim of the cauldron.

"You ought to remember this... The witch's cauldron is the most ancient symbol of transformation and we both spent a lot of time here at this very spot."

Suddenly, Father Bennett grabbed the witch's hands as if in desperation.

"You said you had a story to tell me. What happened?"

"Hey... calm down, dear child... After all, you are the solar hero... Everything is going to be all right for the worst is over now... You have to realize that the night of the Winter Solstice is very significant to us pagans for when the sun goes into Capricorn; it is at its lowest ebb... the lowest region in the underworld, in which the eternal mysteries of death unravel like Satan's worst nightmare... But out of death comes regeneration and renewal... It was my intention to take you to the next level of the Sirian Mystery and even though you were unprepared and went off the deep end, you still remained the Beast that you are. The Great Old Ones are proud of you, especially Oannes."

"What do you mean?" asked Father Bennett frantically.

"On the night of the Winter Solstice, you were out wandering around where you shouldn't have been. You were wandering around the Old Village Park and you should have known better..."

There was a wicked glint in the witch's eyes as she looked at Father Bennett.

"What do you mean, I should have known better?" he demanded.

"Do you remember how Sister Marcia was dressed on Easter Sunday after she returned from Japan and after you had performed the mass? Something about her really disturbed you, didn't it?"

"Uh... Uh... I remember now... She was wearing a veil as if she were in a state of mourning... Everything she wore was black and when I asked her why, she said that she was mourning the death of her husband... I never recalled her being married and then she said that she was a bride of Christ... I remember that I was not at all amused by her statement... and then she added insult to injury by insinuating that I did not really understand the true significance of the mass."

He stopped and looked at the old witch.

"What does this all add up to?" he asked.

"Well, I have a little surprise for you," the old witch said, smiling." Lucinda?"

Suddenly, as if by magic, a woman wearing a long black robe appeared. She stood lounging outside her bedroom door.

"This is Lucia's identical twin sister who is well experienced in the Craft. She has powers that would exceed your imagination and I believe you know what I'm talking about."

There was a hint of malice in the old witch's tone of voice; a contempt that also showed in her eyes.

Father Bennett stared at Lucinda feeling overwhelmed.

"She... she is the woman who appeared in my dreams," he whispered hoarsely." My God! This is too much... I don't know what to say."

He felt as if his legs would no longer support him and that the room was beginning to whirl around. He continued staring at Lucinda as if she were an apparition. There was a touch of the surreal about this whole thing to him. He felt that he couldn't quite grasp what was happening.

The old witch smiled at him seeming to enjoy his discomfiture.

"You better not stare at her too long or she might make you fall in love with her," the witch said." She had given you a clue... then she sent you a dream after you confronted Lucia in the park that afternoon for they have always been telepathically linked. Let me ask you this... What exactly drew you into the park after you had that initial dream?"

Father Bennett began pacing back and forth nervously. The action seemed to settle his vertigo.

"I... I don't know for sure..." he stammered.

"Come now, dear... You know better than to play games with me," the old witch said chidingly.

"Okay," he admitted." It was the fountain... There was always something very special about the fountain... as if it's symbolic of something, but as to what exactly, I don't know."

"Listen," she said," you can kid yourself, but you can't kid me. You know what this is all about. My child, in the dream, the fountain is where you had your first realization of the deity within yourself... On several occasions, you kept going back for further realizations, until nature finally intervened."

"What do you mean, until nature intervened?" he asked, stopping before her.

"On the night of the Winter Solstice, you were bitten by a snake...

a very venomous snake and you came here for help. I took you into the kitchen here by the cauldron and I conjured up an herbal remedy, but it remained rather ambiguous as to whether it worked or not."

"You really have me in a quandary here... What do you mean?"

"Whatever infiltrated your neurological system that night had some very strong hallucinogenic properties... I know that for sure and the rest is history..."

Suddenly, the screen door slammed and the little girl entered the kitchen.

"Mister," she said," would you like to see my doll house and my pet, Noah?"

She was tugging on his sleeve to get his attention. He looked down at her.

"Come here, Lucia," the old witch said.

The child ran to her and hugged her. The old witch caressed the child's face with her gnarled hands that looked like claws to Father Bennett.

"Did you have fun, Lucia?"

"Yes, grandma... I really had a lot of fun! Can I show Father Bennett my room? I really think that he would like it!"

"Why sure... I think it's something he needs to see."

There seemed to be a message in the old witch's glance at him. Lucia took the priest by the hand and led him to her room. The room seemed to be a normal little girl's room, all pink and feminine. On the floor was a dollhouse with a kitchenette in one corner, but his attention was directed to a glass case. What seemed to be a piece of wood suddenly came to life and began to undulate.

"That's Noah," Lucia announced, pointing to the glass case and the occupant within." He's been in the family for a very long time. Sometimes, we let him out and he takes care of the mice. Would you like to see my dolls?"

In absolute horror, Father Bennett watched the well-camouflaged snake crawling along the bottom of the cage. The old witch approached from behind him.

"He doesn't even have a zoological name yet. My husband and I brought him here from Ecuador over fifty years ago," the old witch said softly.

"I... I don't know what to say..." Father Bennett said overwhelmed.

The old witch smiled enigmatically.

"Why don't we step back onto the porch and observe the sunset. We have fascinating sunsets," she suggested.

"Yes, I think that is a good idea," he said automatically.

Like an automaton, he followed her back out onto the porch. The sun was beginning to set. In the west, the clouds were tinted with mauve, pink, and purple. It seemed like soft shafts of light descended from the bottom of the clouds like an unspoken benediction. There seemed to be a stillness, a serenity that acted as a balm for troubled souls. Nature's perfume permeated the air around them. Father Bennett and the old witch stood there on the porch as in silent communion.

"It's so lovely; so peaceful," the old witch murmured softly.

How long they stood there watching the sun set, he would never know. Finally, he turned to her. Their eyes met and held for a long moment.

"I just have one last question," he said.

"And what is that my dear?" the old witch asked softly.

"Who or what is the hidden god?"

She paused to consider the full portent of his question. Her black obsidian eyes glittered in the fading light as she stared at him.

"There was the 'Wrong of the Beginning' and the Shadow took the form of a woman in the Garden of Eden as the dove of the Holy Ghost became the bird of Venus and brought pleasure even though the Sons of God had discovered the Logos of nature in her pristine state of original beauty. Eve introduced Adam to the nightside of Eden and as a result, there was a sundering of the earth from heaven and for the second time darkness reigned supreme even though Sirius or Set was the brightest star or Hadit under Nuit. The Hidden God is Set as the epitome of the True Will. Thus, the Hidden God is mankind's vital link with the Great Old Ones, who are the prototypes of alien intelligence. There was a time when man walked and talked with the Gods beginning with the Red Temple Mysteries of Atlantis, which was the exploration of the Tree of Life as sex magick and thought reification. The next school was the Mysteries of the Black Temple, which was an exploration of the Tree of Death involving the assumption of an atavistic power or animal form and the method of creating a Zombie on the astral plane. In other words, the original Initiates discovered the unique ability to travel on the astral plane as a form of self-empowerment. Then the Gods left, however the Initiates still had more to learn about magick and for the first time the descending 'Mercuries' caused mass confusion. Unfortunately, mankind lost access to the Tree. At this point in our evolution, Anthropoid Man had appeared on earth and only knew the cruelty of nature. Atlantis was destroyed, however after the Great Deluge of the Abyss, the totally polarized beings of Nu's ark re-discovered that they had the power of the Hidden God, who is the true origin of the Cosmic Libido. Again, they re-populated the planet through thought reification. After many aeons, mankind still experienced a symbiosis with nature and discovered the gift of the Holy Ghost. In his attempt to reach God, mankind built the Tower of Babel based on the 'neters' or primordial principles, however Divine Wrath ensued and brought about mass confusion and thus the multiplicity of languages. Organized religion was born and brought about extreme secular strife. As a result, civilization became a facsimile or a simulacrum of true culture or Atlantis. On the night of the meteor shower, you gave the right oracle even though you don't remember for the original Initiates of Atlantis are with us now and are preparing us for the next 'flooding of the Abyss' because the destructive Mercuries will succeed in creating mass confusion or extreme secular strife again to the point of the 'Nightmare of History' when the Great Old Ones will re-enter Malkuth or the terrestrial plane and act as giants, who bring about earthquakes because society has become too aberrated. Only those, who have successfully achieved the Crossing of the Abyss or the 'Crucified' will make it over to the Clear Light of the Void for they have achieved a reconciliation of the Holy Ghost with the Hidden God or a synthesis of the conscious mind with the unconscious, which will lead to a direct communion with one's Holy Guardian Angel."

At this point, she looked directly at the priest.

"I acknowledge that you have traversed the terra incognita or the unknown and have successfully made it back to the terra firma or the Earth Mother, however you are still the Holy Fool and will be faced with the Vagina Dentata again for the third time around in the underworld is a charm. In other words, you must experience the death of the ego and in doing so come to a deeper understanding of the soul of ISIS. If you should endure the Ordeal of the Abyss then you will become the next hotr priest or the ultimate priest, who will give the Word, which will usher in the Black Aeon. Without the Word, this will be a most frightful aeon, while Daleth is in course for Daleth is the Venusian Door beneath the Desert of Set and we remember that the dove of blood came before the dove of the air. You received the Satanic Stigmata as a token of divine favor. We have always known the great potential that you have, Joseph. We know that you won't let us down this time around the backside of the Tree. Should you fail in your attempt to give the Word then you will embark upon the Black Pilgrimage to Chorazin. "

For some strange reason, a paralysis suddenly overcame Father Bennett as he stood there on the porch feeling so far removed from anything resembling civilization. Could he remember the way back again? Should he beware too light that weighs?

THE END

GLOSSARY

Amenta- The Egyptian term for Hades or the underworld.

Anthropos- The psychic 'inner man' or the archetype of the Self externalized as the Christ figure.

Choronzon- An Enochian designation which Dr. John Dee (1527-1608) described as " that Mighty Devil" . Choronzon is one half of the Beast 666, the Guardian of the threshold of the unknown universe or universe 'B'.

Hadit under Nuit- Hadit is the sun that illumines the dark, as the son illumines or fulfills the hidden potential of the mother (Nuit), for without him She cannot be.

Hecate- The goddess of witchcraft associated with the dark side of the moon.

Hidden God-The primordial mystery of the Kundalini power or the Kacodamian (the dark serpent of the Abyss) as the origin of the libido.

Hierosgamos- The mystical wedding between the lunar queen and the solar king or salt and sulphur in alchemy.

Horaria- A schedule by which a monastic order adheres to.

Kether- The first Sephira or power-zone of the Tree of Life.

Kundalini- The magical power in man symbolized by a serpent having 3 ½ coils which lies dormant at the base of the spine in the region of the Muladhara chakra. It is known to initiates, in whom it can be activated, as the Goddess of the Fire Snake.

Lilith- The consort of Samael, who is a prince of the Qliphoth or the shadowy world of shells or reflections. According to legend, Lilith was Adam's first wife, who introduced into the human life-wave the alien seed. She is the mother of Succubi and a companion of Hecate.

Lingam- A Tantric term for the penis.

Malkuth- The tenth power-zone on the Tree of Life connected with the total manifestation of matter.

Mandala- The 'magic circle', which is a symbol of psychic wholeness often represented as a quaternity.

Mercurius- The alchemical personification of Mercury as a nature deity having a bisexual aspect. Thus, Mercurius was the ultimate alchemical paradox as both the Devil and the Holy Ghost.

Nous- The higher reason or emanation of the divine principle.

Physis- Dynamic Being or a symbiosis with nature as opposed to dualism.

Samsara- In Buddhism, the cause of mundane existence; the endless cycle of birth, death and rebirth; the wheel of causation.

Shadow- In Jungian psychology, the archaic, primitive and demonic aspect of the psyche, which resists the light of consciousness as the 'inferior function'. In Tantric terms, the Shadow is one's astral twin or double.

Shekinah- A protective feminine spirit. According to cabbalistic lore, the Shekinah is Malkuth the Widow estranged from her heavenly spouse.

Soteriology- The branch of theology that treats of salvation by Jesus Christ. In alchemical terms, the redemption of matter.

Sparagamos- In ancient times, an act of communion by which the dead king was cannibalized.

Telos- The ultimate aim or perfection of any evolutionary process.

Thanatos- The death instinct opposed to Eros, the life instinct.

Uroboros- The serpent eating its own tail; a magic circle of regeneration and rebirth.